Also by Shari Shattuck

Eye of the Beholder

SPEAK OF
THE DEVIL

Shari Shattuck

A SIGNET BOOK

SIGNET
Published by New American Library, a division of
Penguin Group (USA) Inc., 375 Hudson Street,
New York, New York 10014, USA
Penguin Group (Canada), 90 Eglinton Avenue East, Suite 700, Toronto,
Ontario M4P 2Y3, Canada (a division of Pearson Penguin Canada Inc.)
Penguin Books Ltd., 80 Strand, London WC2R 0RL, England
Penguin Ireland, 25 St. Stephen's Green, Dublin 2,
Ireland (a division of Penguin Books Ltd.)
Penguin Group (Australia), 250 Camberwell Road, Camberwell, Victoria 3124,
Australia (a division of Pearson Australia Group Pty. Ltd.)
Penguin Books India Pvt. Ltd., 11 Community Centre, Panchsheel Park,
New Delhi - 110 017, India
Penguin Group (NZ), 67 Apollo Drive, Rosedale, North Shore 0632,
New Zealand (a division of Pearson New Zealand Ltd.)
Penguin Books (South Africa) (Pty.) Ltd., 24 Sturdee Avenue,
Rosebank, Johannesburg 2196, South Africa

Penguin Books Ltd., Registered Offices:
80 Strand, London WC2R 0RL, England

First published by Signet, an imprint of New American Library,
a division of Penguin Group (USA) Inc.

First Printing, September 2008
10 9 8 7 6 5 4 3 2 1

Oh, my Calee, I wanted to give something to match your joyous spirit and your inimitable comedy, and I will, I promise, but for now, I give you this. I hope you enjoy the funnier bits. I love you, Mommy.

ACKNOWLEDGMENTS

A million thank-yous to:

Laura Cifelli, your kindness and intelligence amaze me, *and* you make me laugh.

Paul Fedorko, you are the rock of confidence: What would I stand on without you?

Creason Moss, wisdom and kindness seldom touched a teenager as much as they have you. Lucky, lucky me.

Joseph Stachura, you are my ever-present strength and joy.

All the smarter-than-me editors at NAL, you make me look like I passed tenth-grade English.

The many firefighters whose lunches I interrupted to pester with questions about arson for not having me arrested on suspicion.

Captain Anthony Williams, whom I accosted in line at See's Candies on Valentine's Day, and who provided me with so much crucial information. (I hope your wife enjoyed the orange creams.)

The friends I quizzed about banking, building, and business, *su* knowledge *es mi* knowledge.

Sure, I could have done it without all of you, but it wouldn't have been as much fun, the punctuation would have been horrible, and most of it would have been wrong.

SPEAK OF
THE DEVIL

Chapter 1

The fierce wind swept across the dusty, faded green sage, bending brittle branches and tugging roots from the parched earth. It pushed ruthlessly at the skeletal leaves of the sycamores in the dry riverbed as it threw its vicious weight against the arid hills of Angeles Crest.

Every year it came, sweeping the heat in from the desert to Los Angeles with punishing, dehydrating gusts. After almost six months without a drop of rain it came, turning the landscape into acres of kindling, vast swatches of dry brush leading to heartier fuel: drought-weakened trees and countless homes.

Greer Sands stood at the window, watching the wind blasting the distressed foliage. In the room behind her, friends were celebrating the expected birth of a new child, laughing and sharing their wisdom. Greer felt drawn away from them, pulled instead toward the unstable weather outside. It was impossible for anyone who lived in fear of fire to ignore the threat of those winds, but for Greer it was something more.

All her life, she had seen glimpses of the future. She had felt the undulations of the natural world playing through her body, and these winds strummed a melody both forlorn and ominous. She was filled with a feeling of vulnerability. Greer bowed her head in acknowledgment of the power and fury she perceived and then exhaled the shakiness that had possessed her.

"Greer," called her friend Whitney's voice behind her, "are you okay?"

Whitney and Greer had met nine months before when Greer moved into a home pocketed in the national forest above Los Angeles in the ranch community of Shadow Hills. Whitney was a full-bodied, dark-haired beauty of forty, who was half–Native American. As a Cree Indian she was given a name with each stage of life, and looking at her glowing smile now, Greer thought again that the Elder who had bestowed on Whitney the name Shiny Girl had captured her very essence with those two words.

When they'd met, Whitney had accepted Greer's sixth sense without question, and she could see that Greer was awash with something now. Greer smiled back at Whitney and hastened to reassure her. "I'm fine. It's just this wind—it's hard for me not to listen to it."

Whitney nodded, easily understanding the submerged meaning beneath her friend's surface explanation. She moved closer and asked in a quiet voice, "Everything copacetic?"

Focusing on the question brought a quiver to Greer's breastbone. She placed a palm flat against it and half closed her eyes, letting the quiver expand until she could read it, see it as a color or a shape. It glowed in her mind's eye, like a huge cloud of light, multicolored, with dark impenetrable sections. "I don't know," Greer said slowly. "I can feel something huge. . . ."

"Oh my God, how cute is that!" came a voice from the sofa behind them. It was accompanied by oohs and aahs, in a range of soprano notes.

Happily distracted, Greer and Whitney turned to admire the blue sleeper that their friend Jenny was holding up over her swelled stomach. Even seven months pregnant, Jenny looked sexy. Her Hispanic heritage was serving her well through her pregnancy, her golden skin glowed with a sunny flush, and her extra weight only served to flatter her natural curves.

"Oh," she beamed, "Lewis is going to love this. He so wants it to be a boy." She smiled a little sadly. "I wish he was here."

"When's he coming back?" asked Mindy, the party's

hostess. She was a small, energetic woman whose life-long association with horses had given her that happy, weathered look that comes to those who experience much of their life from the back of a horse under an open sky, laughing heartily all the while. The creases on her face were fixed in a smile.

"Three weeks, I hope," Jenny said wistfully. "The building should be finished by then, but they just keep having delays with the permits. Every time they finish a stage, they have to wait for the inspector to sign off, and he takes days to get out there." She sighed again. "He wouldn't be there at all, but he couldn't turn down this huge contract." After a few years of struggling, her husband, Lewis, had finally hit the big time with his contracting business, and though Jenny was enjoying the financial fruits of his labors, she wasn't too keen on the cost of his absences.

"Has Lewis built an apartment building before?" Mindy asked.

"No. Condos, yes, but this is the first multistory building he's contracted. He hated going away right now, but it's a three-complex deal and the next two are back in LA County."

"Score!" Mindy laughed. "Pretty soon I'll be lodging horses at *your* ranch!"

"Let me get used to having one horse first. I always promised myself I would get one when I could afford it, so I let you talk me into taking him, but King is a good bit more time-consuming than I expected. Especially with Lewis gone."

Greer rejoined the small group and sat down on an ottoman that had been pulled up to complete an informal circle. "Well, Bakersfield isn't that far. He can be back in, what, three hours if he needs to be."

"And he's made it back at least one day a week," Jenny said. "I know he worries about me, and I just wish he could feel every kick like I do."

Mindy's voice dropped to a sarcastic growl. "Wait 'til you go into labor. You'll wish you were the one kicking him, wearing steel-toed boots."

The group of women shared a laugh that cut off abruptly as the kitchen door swung open and a man entered the female population. He was large and burly under his cowboy hat, and he stopped when he saw the dozen women looking at him expectantly. His eyes scanned the room, and then turning his meaty palms up he asked, "What?"

The women burst into laughter again, and Mindy got up and crossed over to her husband.

"I'm sorry, honey. It's not you—it's just your timing. I think everyone's met my husband, Reading, except you two." Mindy pointed to Leah and Greer. "Reading, this is Whitney's new neighbor, Greer."

"You have a lovely home," Greer said, gesturing to the spacious vaulted ceiling of the ranch house before reaching out to shake hands. As her soft skin met his rough fingers, a distinctly unpleasant jolt went through her fingers. It didn't travel up her arm, as sometimes happened when she met a person intent on harm, but the jolt caused her to look more deeply at the man. His eyes were guarded, but she sensed nothing more.

"Nice to meet you too," Reading was saying. He released Greer's hand and she wondered if her reaction had been a residual effect of her overall unease.

"And this is Leah Falconer, Jenny's best friend and our local bank manager," Mindy was saying proudly, laying an affectionate hand on Leah's shoulder. The conservatively dressed, aristocratic brunette shrugged herself politely out from under it. Greetings were exchanged, and then Mindy asked Reading if he would like a glass of wine.

"No, thanks anyway. I've got to go out and hose off a couple of the horses, they get overheated in this infernal wind."

When Leah asked politely about how many horses they had at the ranch, Reading told them a total of twenty-one. Only five, he explained, belonged to him and Mindy; the rest were boarded.

"I told you about Mindy and Reading," Jenny told Leah with mock exasperation. "Remember? This is where I board King. I bought him from Mindy." Leah and Jenny's friendship had happened upon them quickly because of a shared harrowing experience that had pre-empted the usual years of trust building. The result was that they seemed as though they'd known each other for far longer than a few months, but details sometimes got lost.

Reading nodded. "She found you a real sweetheart too. You want me to give King a hose-down?"

"Yes, please." Jenny looked relieved. "I worry about him so much in this weather."

Leah squinted her intelligent eyes at Reading and asked, "Don't you worry about fire?"

"Don't even say it!" shrieked Mindy. "It's our worst fear. We have all kinds of evacuation plans, but it would not be easy. Basically we have friends with ranches down in the flats where we would relocate the horses if they were in danger."

Greer grimaced and said to Reading, "I don't know how *you* can stand to work outside in this dry heat."

Reading looked at her with a glint of devilish humor in his eyes as he surveyed the room full of women. "Well, today, it's either heatstroke or estrogen radiation."

With that, he waved a hand at the laughing women, kissed Mindy, and headed out. Greer watched him go, wondering what the pain in her hand when she touched him had meant. Once or twice before, a chilling sensation had traveled to her heart when she'd come across someone intent on harm, but she hadn't made the connection until later. She didn't read men very well, never had, and this sensation had been different, localized and quick, definitely not pleasant. But that wasn't consistent with a person who would willingly spend time in heat like a furnace blast to make sure that horses, some of which didn't even belong to him, were more comfortable.

Greer sat back and sipped at her soda, letting the soft feeling of female company hold her in its sway. A feeling not unlike weightlessness came over her as she watched Leah and Jenny together. They were so different, Jenny

with her street style and toughness, with her wavy hair
caught up in a casual ponytail, and Leah in her perfectly
pressed silk blouse and tailored gray skirt, her short,
dark hair stick straight and severely styled. Yet they
were so often together now. Only nine months ago,
things had been very different for Leah. She had been
lucky to survive that difficult time, and Greer often worried what lingering scars it would leave.

"I'm betting it's a girl," Whitney said. And with a
pleased smile, she pulled out a pink wrapped gift and
handed it over.

Jenny looked very touched when she removed the lid
of the small white box and gazed down on a child-sized
silver bracelet with a single turquoise stone banded in
silver.

"Oh"—there were tears in Jenny's eyes as she looked
up at her friend—"you made this, didn't you?"

"Yes, and I can make it bigger as she grows."

"What if it's a boy?" Leah asked Whitney.

Whitney waved a hand airily. "I'll turn it into a tie
tack."

Jenny put her hand over her stomach with a small
exclamation. "Oh my goodness, she didn't like that," she
said with a smile. "I'm sure it's a girl. See here." Much
to the other woman's surprise and consternation, Jenny
took Leah's hand and guided it along her stomach, pressing down. Greer and Whitney exchanged a look of
guarded amusement at Leah's scandalized face. Leah
was alarmed by familiarity in general, and her mouth
had gone tight with discomfiture at having her hand
pressed against another woman's abdomen. "See," Jenny
was saying as she guided Leah's hand along, "there's her
tiara, and over here, that *must* be a high heel."

"It's a pointy little thing," Leah agreed, smiling
fixedly. Greer wondered if, after the trauma Leah had
been through, she would ever be able to enjoy even the
most innocent physical contact without a repulsive knee-
jerk reaction. When her hand was released, Leah pulled
it back and straightened her blouse before entwining her
fingers tightly in her lap as though to keep anyone else

from snatching up one of her hands again. Greer was pleased to see Jenny note this, and she watched as Jenny placed a hand momentarily on Leah's knee for a casual pat—not too long, just a short firm pat and a distinct removal—to break the barrier once more, to keep the wall of separation from strengthening. Leah's grip on her own hands relaxed, as Greer had known it would.

"I think we should ask Greer if it's a boy or a girl," Whitney said with a sly smile.

"Oh, that's right—you're psychic!" Mindy gushed.

Greer squirmed. Her ability to sometimes perceive future events had never sat very comfortably on her, so she had always kept it to herself, but several months ago, when she'd first moved into Shadow Hills, premonitions had assailed her, and when Whitney's daughter, Joy, had disappeared, she'd made the choice to use her gift openly to try to find the teenager. Surprisingly, her son, Joshua, had begun to have visions at the same time, and it was his talent, and perhaps his special connection to Joy, that had located her in the end. But Joshua had been afraid of what was happening to him, and he and his mother had kept his abilities secret from all but a few of their closest friends, pretending that it had been Greer's skill alone that had saved Joy. After that harrowing and very public incident, Greer had been swamped with requests and offers, some of them quite lucrative, to do readings, but Greer had never taken money for her unbidden talent. It was something that she had grown up with, come to accept, but it was interpretive at best, and she was not comfortable with being paid to make predictions—even if the images were clear—when it was still only her best guess as to what they might mean.

"I told you before," Greer said, "I've never done that and, please, I don't want you painting the nursery pink or blue based on a feeling I might get. . . ."

"Oh, please," Jenny pleaded, cutting her off. She had asked before, but Greer had flatly refused. Now Jenny had a room full of enthusiastic women on her side.

"All right," Greer agreed reluctantly. "But only if

everyone in the room makes a guess. We can write them all down and see who was right later. You cannot take my impression as final." Greer had some feelings that were vague and some that were undeniably distinct. Then there were the visions, which were as clear as watching a moving picture, but once again open to interpretation. She had no idea what she might see today.

"You said you knew Joshua was going to be a boy," Whitney challenged.

"That was my own son! Every woman has a feeling about their own child."

"And fifty percent of the time," Mindy chimed in, "they're one hundred percent right!"

"Okay, Greer goes last. Everyone else make a line." Leah, always the efficient manager, stood up and took control. "Mindy, can you get me a pad of paper and a pencil? I'll keep the list. I'll start with me, because I already went, and I say, 'girl.'"

The ladies all lined up and took their time rubbing Jenny's surrendered belly like a crystal ball, doing different bad impressions of stereotypical fortune-tellers. Greer pursed her full lips into a puffy moue so her mouth resembled a round, overstuffed, pink satin cushion; this was exactly why she had never advertised her ability, though she knew this was all meant in fun.

As she waited her turn, Greer's grass green eyes floated around the handsome room. The rough pine beams of the ceiling and the comfortable mission-style furniture all pleased her aesthetically. Her gaze landed on a lovely landscape painting over the stone fireplace, a peaceful mountainous view; it looked vaguely familiar.

"Mindy," Greer asked the smaller woman, who had just proclaimed Jenny's child a bucking-bronco-riding cowboy and come to sit near her, "is that a painting of one of the canyons near here?"

Mindy's eyes followed Greer's gaze. "Oh yeah, that's one of R. J. River's paintings. I'm surprised you haven't met him. He's a friend of Whitney's, a local Native American artist. Very active in the conservation scene. It's beautiful, isn't it?"

"Very," Greer agreed. "Which canyon is it?"

"It's a view from up above the dam. I don't know the name of it, but I just love his work. I own three of his paintings." She smiled proudly.

Greer left the group to their fun and went to stand in front of the painting. She imagined that she did know the spot. The artist had captured that luminous quality of the light just before dusk that makes it so easy to fall into the feeling of the place. Greer relaxed her eyes and let her mind wander over the sensation of the picture rather than observe the paint and the artist's technique.

It happened before she could even sense it was coming. Without warning, the picture before her became real, the greens and golds leapt to life, and then, in a flash that Greer could actually feel on her face, they burst into flames. She stepped back suddenly from the painting, raising one hand protectively to block the heat, but the image had cooled to green again and only the canvas hung on the wall in front of her. Or, no, there was something else: Even with her eyes open, something lingered, an image, like a ring from a flashbulb.

Trying to steady her breathing, Greer leaned against the back of an armchair and closed her eyes. There was imprinted, as though burned on her retina, a distinct object, an old-fashioned key, blackened by fire.

Greer searched through her body for a feeling connected to that image to give her a clue what it meant. But before she could locate anything, Jenny's voice called out from behind her, "Greer, your turn!" and the image faded as suddenly as it had come.

Greer spun around; she had forgotten that she was in a room filled with women who saw only the objects struck by light in the field of their vision. She tried to smile, to recover quickly, but she saw Whitney's face tighten in concern at her own expression.

"You okay?" Jenny asked.

All the women were looking at her quizzically. Greer took a deep breath and smiled. "Oh sure. It's just the heat—I felt a little light-headed for a minute," she lied.

Whitney frowned. She had not bought it.

Throwing Whitney a glance that she hoped would read
as *I'll tell you later,* Greer crossed over to the sofa where
Jenny was lying with her tummy exposed like the back
of a baby whale cresting the sea. Greer sat down on the
coffee table facing her and took three deep, cleansing
breaths, willing the shock that she had felt at the vision
of fire to calm and leave her body so that she could get
a clear reading, if one came.

Greer rubbed her hands together to make sure they
were warm, placed them flat on Jenny's belly, and closed
her eyes.

Immediately an image came to mind. A girl, definitely
a girl, with dark hair and shining eyes, was walking
toward her with sunlight glinting off her thick, long hair.
The picture was so stunning and charming that Greer
laughed out loud. "She's going to be a beauty," said
Greer, and most of the women clapped their hands and
cheered. Only Mindy and another woman who had
guessed male booed. "It's funny," Greer went on when
they quieted. "I see her grown up, about fourteen. I
think . . ."

But Greer forgot entirely what she was about to say.
Over the image that she held in her mind, so beautiful
and blissful, had come another. It was Jenny's face that
leapt into Greer's mind, and her expression was as far
from happy and sunny as was possible. In Greer's vision
Jenny's face held a look of sheer terror, her eyes darted
everywhere as though looking for some way of escape,
and over her, blotting out all else, hovered crow black
wings.

Greer had seen those wings before, she was sure of
it. What did they mean to her? Where had she seen
them? She forced herself to focus on the feeling they
gave her and remember it. Yes! She had seen them before in another work of art, been struck by their perfection as a metaphor. They had been on an angel. Huge
black wings on an angel of terrible and final beauty.

The angel of death.

Chapter 2

The gusting wind on Joshua's face made him feel as if he were halfway through the cycle in a clothes dryer and it was set on high. As he pushed up the new trail, he thought, "Mental note to self: Only hike before the sun is up."

Greer's son, Joshua Sands, was a tall, strong eighteen-year-old with a love of nature he had inherited from both his parents, but mostly from his father. To hike willingly in this weather seemed like an act of insanity to most people, but for Joshua, a day without time alone in the outdoors was the crazy maker. He paused and finished off the first of two large water bottles that he carried in his small backpack. He supposed he was sweating as fast as he was drinking, but the air was so dry it left no evidence of perspiration on his skin.

The trail switchbacked and then passed mercifully under a large grove of shady oaks. Joshua took off his hat to let the wind into his hair. Hot as it was, it relieved him somewhat. As he walked, he watched the trail under his feet with interest. There were many dusty footprints in the few places where the ground was loose enough to show an imprint. Work boots, it looked like, various sizes; a group had passed by here not long ago.

He also looked for signs of wildlife. He knew that the animals would be driven lower this time of year, looking for any water they could find. He saw the dried scat of coyote, bobcat, and deer, but none of the animals showed themselves in this heat.

After fifteen minutes of gentle but steady incline, he emerged on the lip of the canyon into the glaring sunlight. From here he could see almost all the way back down into the valley. Pausing to get his bearings, he noted that the national forest area was behind him, and the populated Los Angeles suburbs of Shadow Hills and Sunland lay stretched out before him, just beyond the ridge that blocked his view of the Two-ten freeway a few miles away. To his right, the hills rose, steep and greenish brown, covered with the natural brush and scrubby oaks that made this place so beautiful. To his left was a sight that sobered him: The entire top of a gently sloping mountain ridge had been sheered off and was nothing but a dusty, lifeless swath of dirt. From this viewpoint Joshua could see the gigantic land movers mowing down more living earth, five of them spewing black smoke, moving in a line, remorselessly leveling out the peaks and curves of nature's hand. To the far right of this gaping wound stood the frames of a hundred houses, built with mere feet between them like huge boxes shelved in neat little rows; the space between the rows was barren and brown, ready to be paved with shiny black asphalt, leaving the ground nowhere to breathe.

Along that tight grid of streets, spaced maybe fifty feet apart, there stood the tall, naked arms of streetlights. There would be thousands of them by the time the gigantic development was finished, and each home— spurred by its owner's fear of the dark—would have its own exterior lighting. The overall effect, here on the edge of a national forest, would be an inverted bowl of light that never dimmed, shrouding the night sky from view. Joshua had seen it before, this side effect of civilization: They were stealing the stars.

A sadness that was all too familiar gripped Joshua. Trying to focus on the positive, on the people who would fill those houses with laughter, who would plant new trees and hopefully teach their children to love the natural world the way his father had taught him, Joshua turned away and went on.

According to his trail map, in about a half a mile this

path should meet the fire road, which would take him back down where he had parked his car on Osborne Avenue. He was a good bit west of his own neighborhood, but he'd been curious to explore this section of the county as it was all connected by high trails back into the canyon where his own home sat nestled in a copse of pines at the end of a short dirt road. That would be too far to hike on a day like today, so his goal was to reach the fire road near the top and get an overview of the lay of the land on the far side before doubling back.

Another twenty minutes and half a bottle of water brought him to that perch. He had expected to meet no one in this heat, one reason he had decided to risk it, so he was surprised to hear voices and the scrape of tools as he crested the trail onto the wide dirt road.

It was a work team clearing underbrush back from the edge of the firebreak, composed of a senior fireman and about ten young men, all in their teens from the look of them. They were a mix—Hispanic, black, white—but they all had a similar look, the expression that came from fear heavily disguised as indifference and spite. Joshua recognized the group immediately as detainees from the probation fire camp just down the road from his home, a juvenile detention center where young males convicted of everything from misdemeanors to felonies spent time working off part of their sentences. He'd run into them before, maintaining trails or clearing brush by the side of the roads, and he'd always received that same blank, soulless stare when he'd tried to look friendly.

Nonetheless, Joshua smiled at the closest boy in acknowledgment as he passed him. The young man leaned on his shovel and did not register any sign of response. It was as though Joshua were invisible.

As he drew level with the guard, Joshua nodded his head and paused. "Hello. Bitch of day to be working with a shovel."

"Could be worse." The fireman, who was lanky and weathered, smiled with movie-star white teeth at Joshua.

"Can't really see how." Joshua grimaced as a blast of air toasted his skin, making his lips feel like jerky.

The fireman laughed. "It could be this hot and the hills could be on fire."

"Good point." Joshua extended a hand. "I'm Joshua Sands. I live up the road from the camp, off Silver Line Creek."

"Bob Pariche. You've got one of those cabins tucked in that canyon? Nice," he commented after Joshua's nod. The hand that took Joshua's was calloused and rough with work. His eyes flicked back to his young laborers. He called out to the boy Joshua had passed, "Simon, good job with that section. You can take a five-minute break, rehydrate, and then, since you finished first, you can use the weed whacker on that section over there. Take the fire extinguisher and watch out for sparks. Okay?" As he addressed the boy, his voice was both firm and polite. There were assorted calls of "No way" and "That sucks" from the other boys. Apparently, using the gas-powered tool was a reward of some kind. Joshua ventured a guess that the supervisor was one of those rare people who—even faced with the reality of seemingly unbeatable odds—really try to make a difference. From the way Simon reacted, surly, but with his gratitude sneaking out in a suppressed twitch of a smile, it apparently pleased the boy that he had garnered a fractional recognition.

Joshua watched the boy named Simon settle down on the dirt and pull out his water bottle. He appeared to be looking out over the view, but Joshua could see Simon watching him from the corner of his eye.

And then, before Joshua looked away, the boy was no longer alone. At least, he was still sitting alone, but he had a visitor that only Joshua could see. Just over his left shoulder, the figure of a man had appeared, dark gray and hunched menacingly toward Simon. Joshua, who was getting used to the sudden appearance of images that were unseen to everyone else around him, was taken aback by the aggressiveness of the figure. He had seen, in the few months since his gift had begun to develop, many such visions. Sometimes they came when he looked for them, but mostly they appeared to him at random moments, over friends and strangers alike, but they had all seemed passive or protective. This was something altogether new. The male figure glared hatefully down at Simon.

"Damn it," Joshua muttered under his breath as he was overwhelmed by the sensation of being knocked down by a crashing wave. The instinct that he must somehow protect this boy was all-consuming and unwanted. It was bad enough that he saw these images, but it felt cruelly unfair when he sensed that he was expected to do something about them. He knew that he was the only one who could see the danger literally hovering over Simon, which left him trapped into making a decision. At eighteen and headed for college, Joshua felt he had more than enough to get on with just figuring out what to do with his life; adding on feeling responsible for helping people he didn't even know really sucked. "Damn it," he sighed again, but with resignation.

Joshua walked several yards in Simon's direction and came to a stop a few feet away from the teenager, who was sitting on the ground, his shoulders slumped forward in a petulant slouch. He said nothing to the boy, just scanned the hills, half looking for the trails that would lead over the next range into his own, more familiar extended backyard.

Joshua didn't look at Simon directly, but he could see the figure, fading now but still present over the boy's left shoulder. And then Joshua almost jumped as he saw something he had never visualized before.

Another figure had revealed itself to him, an animal. This was a first for Joshua, and he had to turn and look directly at it to make out what it was. When he did, he almost laughed. It was a small dog, of indeterminate heritage, which was barking with silent fury almost comically at the fading threatening figure.

Simon, of course, was oblivious to Joshua's visions, oblivious to the presences that were attracted—maybe even attached—to him. Joshua hadn't figured out yet what exactly his visions were. It had been only a few months since this second sight had interrupted his senior year at high school, and he was still struggling to interpret their meanings, but across the board the people had been blissfully ignorant of the otherworldly activity around them. Even his mother, Greer, who had very accurate visions of her own, did not share his particular ability. She saw colors and images—she called it energy—around people. Joshua saw human shapes. And they usually turned out to represent people whom either he or the subject had known and who had died.

Slightly unnerved and appropriately uncomfortable at addressing a juvenile delinquent with whom he had absolutely no previous connection, Joshua made a feeble attempt to open a conversation. "You think that's Little Tujunga Canyon over those hills?"

Simon looked equally unnerved to be spoken to, so much so that at first he merely stiffened as though bracing to ward off a blow, but then he shrugged, glanced uneasily up at Joshua, and mumbled, "Don't know."

"Yeah," Joshua pushed on as though he had received an interested reply, "I think it must be, because the Two-ten runs parallel to that ridge behind us, and the canyons connect down toward it." He nodded knowingly without looking at Simon for a few seconds, then squatted down to be more on the same level with the other boy, pulling a number of prickly hitchhikers off his socks as a pretense. Both the animated dog and the menacing male figure had disappeared. "You live around here?"

That brought a snort of unamused laughter from Simon. "Temporarily," he said bitterly.

Not knowing what else to do, Joshua ignored the attitude and went on as though having a friendly conversation. "Where do you usually live?"

Joshua thought that the boy would not answer, but then, "Sunland," came the disinterested reply.

"Oh, so in the general vicinity anyway," Joshua said, still floundering. What was he doing? What could he do? It seemed apparent to him that this kid had a very negative influence around him, but hell, you didn't have to be psychic to make that guess, seeing how Simon was wearing a work suit and digging up shrubbery after an hour's hike uphill on one of the most unpleasant days of the year while his detention officer looked on.

"I live just over that mountain there," Joshua told Simon, who glanced at the indicated landmark and then busied himself with the cap of his water bottle. A minute crawled past them. "Well," Joshua straightened up, not having any other bright ideas. "Try to stay cool."

Simon looked up at him briefly with a mixture of disdain and curiosity and then stared off again into the hazy distance.

"See ya." Joshua turned away, expecting no response, but he was surprised again.

"What's your name?" Simon asked flatly, as though he didn't care one way or the other whether Joshua answered.

"Joshua."

"I'm Simon." The younger boy's eyes met Joshua's for the briefest moment, but Joshua got the feeling that it had cost him an effort to do even that.

"Nice to meet you, Simon," Joshua said, and walked away.

Backtracking to the head of the trail he'd come up, he nodded at the fireman as he passed him, calling out, "See you down the hill!" before he increased his stride, aware of the resentful yet apathetic stares on his back as he went. He worked his way back down to the shade of the oaks, then found a log to rest on, and took from his backpack a small leather notebook and a pen.

Opening to a new page, he wrote, *Simon, age about sixteen, male over left shoulder.* He paused for a moment to think about it; then, smiling, he added, *Small mongrel dog, very animated, between the image and the subject.* Now came the hard part. He closed his eyes and tried to focus on the images he'd seen, and as he did, he tried to do what his mother had advised him to do, to see what kind of *feeling* he got from the images.

He started with the little dog. It made him laugh out loud at first, the way the dog had jumped and barked without sound, but there was something else, a sense of protection and warning. The dog was fairly easy to label, very pure in the impression it gave. Joshua wrote it down: *Protective*.

The next image was much more difficult; Joshua's instincts were telling him not to go there. The male figure exuded a dangerous murkiness. . . . No, *exuded* was the wrong word—it was the opposite, a kind of suction, like a tar pit in human form. Even as Joshua focused on it to try to "read" it, he felt it try to draw him in and he pulled away, opening his eyes to cut the connection.

"Wow," he breathed. "Okay, that's one scary apparition." He shook off the jittery feeling it gave him and wrote down his impression in the notebook: *Dangerous, malevolent, intent on evil, both toward subject and myself when attention is drawn to me.* Then he tried to remember what his mom had said about blocking negativity from "crossing boundaries," as she put it. It had to do with visualizing light around him. Feeling silly, Joshua closed his eyes again, imagined a white sphere around him like clear shining glass, and then pretended to be looking through it at the figure.

It helped. He was able to observe without taking on the energy. The figure seemed to ooze darkness, like thick smoke from a burning tire, yet at the same time it was magnetic—it had wanted something, and it had been trying to draw something out of Simon.

With a jolt, Joshua realized what it was. The figure wanted Simon, his life, his future.

It wanted his very soul.

Running his hands through his unkempt dark blond hair, Joshua muttered, "I've got to help him."

Even as a frisson of resentment that he would feel obliged passed through Joshua, he wondered how in the hell he was going to help a boy he didn't even know.

Chapter 3

He poured with sloppy carelessness into the clear plastic water bottle, letting the lethal brown liquid slosh onto the brittle, crispy stalks of last year's sage and watched it stain the loose earth as it soaked into the dirt. Then, setting the bottle on a bed of the dry stalks, he took out a small magnifying glass and a roll of tape from his sock. It took only a few seconds more to attach the magnifying glass to the side of the bottle and position it so that the sun struck directly through it onto the fuel inside.

He straightened up and looked around, but the ridge behind him hid him from any possible detection, and the steep, rocky slope facing him was inhabited only by hawks and foxes.

A snapping of branches made his head jerk to the side and he turned to see three deer, a doe and two yearlings, watching him from a few yards away down the slope. He made a clicking noise with his mouth and mentally took aim down gun sights.

Another sound was carried to him on the hot gusts of wind from over the ridge. Someone was calling his name.

He looked down quickly to check his creation; then, raising his hands, he shouted at the deer, "Arrg!" They scurried away, graceful even in their terror, all four feet springing them forward off the ground. He laughed at the power he felt. They *should* fear him. He climbed back up to the lip of the ridge, the loose, desperately dry earth giving way with each step as he climbed.

For a half hour the concentrated rays of the sun

through the convex glass beat down on the gasoline in
its plastic shell until a small wisp of smoke began to rise,
curling toward the open mouth of the bottle, where it
was snatched away by wind that fed the phenomenon in
the bottle, superheating until finally it combusted, melting a hole in the thin plastic and spilling the burning
gasoline onto the dry tinder beneath it. Fanned by the
extreme winds, the flames spread quickly, gulping up the
underbrush in huge hungry bites, eager to sate a craving
after a long, dry famine.

   The first serious smoke was dissipated by the searing
winds, but as the fire ate its way through the low brush
and began to make a meal of some larger scrub oaks,
an undeniable belching of blackness began to gather in
spite of the season's best efforts to sweep it away, until
soon an expanding stain on the sky gave evidence of the
orgy of destruction below.

Chapter 4

Joshua had driven halfway back down the narrow, deserted road that led from the trailhead when he saw the plume of smoke.

"Oh God, no," he muttered to himself. He pulled his car over and climbed onto the roof, ignoring the sting of hot metal on his hands. He stood up and tried to get the fire's bearings. Pulling out his cell phone, he cursed when he saw the hateful words *searching for service* on the display. It would have taken a miracle to get reception in these deep canyons.

He searched the hills around him for signs of habitation and quickly realized that no one would see the evidence of this brush fire until it crested the ridge. By that time, it would have scorched at least twenty acres and become a formidable foe. He knew that, from this point, it would take him a good fifteen to twenty minutes to get back down to the highway, and he had just passed a small driveway a minute back. It was more of a dirt track, but the presence of a lone mailbox had told him that someone lived there, someone who would probably have a phone, someone who—depending on the whim of the winds—might also be in the direct path of the flames that Joshua could now see jerking angrily below the black smoke.

He jumped to the ground, hitting it with a hard thump that stung his feet even in his heavy hiking boots. Inside the car, he made a U-turn and sped back up the road, turning left into the uneven driveway. He bumped along for a couple hundred feet until a small ranch house came into view. Inside a neatly kept split-rail fence, an old tractor, rusted beyond usefulness, and an old-model Toyota, which had also seen better days, sat baking in the relentless heat.

Honking his horn and praying that someone was home, Joshua jumped from his car and ran to the door. It was opened by an elderly man wearing a torn T-shirt, what looked like old gym shorts, socks, and sandals. From behind him a white-haired woman peered at Joshua through thick and smudgy spectacles.

"Can I help you?" the man asked Joshua in a querulous voice.

"Could I use your phone? It's an emergency. There's a fire just over the ridge behind your house."

Alarm registered instantly on the couple's faces.

"Please, if you could just show me where the phone is." Joshua stepped toward them as he spoke.

But these people were more resilient than they looked. The woman snapped into action first. "This way. The phone is right over here." She was already on the move into the small living room. The man stepped out into the yard and squinted up at the rising line of smoke being buffeted by the wind not more than a half mile from his home. "I'm gonna water down the roof, Emily. You shut down the gas," he called out as he reached just inside the door and grabbed an ancient brimmed hat off a hook.

Emily dialed 911 on the premillennium rotary phone and handed Joshua the receiver before disappearing out a back door. The emergency operator connected him with the national forest fire department, and Joshua gave them as precise details about the location of the flames as he could. Emily appeared again as he was speaking and added some details of her own for him to relate.

As he hung up the phone, Joshua looked up at the woman. "Thank you. Is there anything I can do to help you?" he asked, aware of the possibility that fate might very well take her home today.

"I'm Emily," she said first, putting out a hand crooked with age. "My husband is Larry. We're the Caseys."

"I'm Joshua Sands. I was driving back from a hike up Oak Springs and I saw the smoke."

"You were hiking *today*?" Emily asked with a strong vein of suspicion through the words.

Joshua nodded and hoped the fact that he was telling the truth would be enough to convince her that he was. "I hike every day."

To his relief, Emily smiled, her wrinkled face breaking easily into a wide grin in spite of the fear that persisted in her eyes. "Damn young fool. Larry used to be just like that." She turned and headed to a wall of books and photos. "If you want to help, you can put some of these in a box. We'll get them in the car, just in case."

Within ten minutes they had both their car and Joshua's loaded to the max, mostly with faded photos of family members, a few books, and what looked like legal papers and records. The smell of smoke grew tangy and strong in the air. As they debated whether or not they could tie a rocking chair made by Emily's father onto the roof of the tiny Toyota, they heard the first helicopter.

The smoke had begun to mushroom now, and though the wind seemed to be blowing mostly away from the house toward the fire, there were frequent unpredictable blasts back toward them. So far, the flames had not crested the ridge, but judging from the smoke, the area that was burning had mushroomed as well.

The helicopter circled the area once; then swooping like a hawk toward an unsuspecting prey, it shot toward the edge of the fire nearest the house, spraying a load of chemical flame retardant in a long neat row, extinguishing flames and creating a barrier between the fire and Larry and Emily's home. It was a temporary barrier at best, Joshua realized, as bits of burning ash were blown over the break and threatened to reignite on the near side.

The helicopter sped away, but a second one appeared

only moments later, repeating the action of the first with impressive accuracy, and moments after that, the sounds of the arriving ground support could be heard from back down the road.

It was an awe-inspiring display of efficiency. The smaller of the two pale green fire service vehicles pulled up the driveway and, after a hurried conference with Larry, hooked up to the huge tank that held the water from the Caseys' well. Using the fire hoses and a pump to increase the pressure, they soon had the Caseys' house and the area around it well soaked. At the same time, five firemen hiked up the hill with pickaxes and shovels and started to dig a firebreak, quickly clearing away the brush and creating a wide swath of brown dirt in the path of the fire.

Joshua wanted so much to help, to do something, but he and the Caseys were ordered to evacuate immediately.

"If the fire breaches the road, you'll have no exit route down, and this road up is over fifty rough miles until you come to Angeles Crest Highway," the supervisor told them. He glanced meaningfully at the Caseys' broken-down old Toyota and then up at Joshua. "And I don't like those odds," he said.

"I understand. Yes, sir." Joshua turned to the older couple, who—now that the cavalry had arrived—seemed to shrink back into fragile frames as they anxiously watched the activity around their home. "Listen, why don't you come to my house until it's safe to come back here? I'll give the fire chief my number and we can wait for news there." They both turned and looked at him as though they couldn't fathom the idea. Joshua could see defiance beginning to gather like storm clouds on Larry's face, but Emily short-circuited whatever refusal he might have been mustering by laying a gentle hand on her husband's arm and saying, "Of course. Thank you, Joshua. We can call our son from there and then he won't be so worried." She turned her eyes meaningfully up to Larry's as she spoke, and his expression tempered.

He dropped his head in acquiescence and allowed her to hustle him off to their packed car.

As they drove away, bits of gray ash, some still edged with glowing orange trim, fell on the hood of Joshua's car and lingered precariously until they were blown impatiently away.

Chapter 5

Simon dropped his gear on the foot of his bed and hurried to the showers. He didn't want to have to wait for a turn; Sunday was visiting day and he was expecting someone.

The water in the open bank of showers ran lukewarm at best, but today Simon didn't care. He turned the handle to cold and reveled in the few minutes of relief from the domineering heat. His respite was short-lived because he knew he must relinquish the shower quickly or suffer the certain backlash. His first night here, he'd unknowingly sat in someone else's place at dinner and been woken by a hand over his mouth in the middle of the night. What had followed still caused him pain when it flashed unwanted into his mind, but he shut the recall down quickly. He had grown proficient at selective memory.

The rec room was feebly air-conditioned; the merciless heat could barely be disguised by the complaining whines of the outdated window units, and in minutes his white T-shirt was moist with perspiration. Simon spotted his guest and crossed quickly over to where she sat, still and stern.

"Hey, Aunt Rosa." He nodded, trying to keep the relief and pleasure off his face. He would take a strong ribbing later if he showed anything that could even be mistaken for affection.

"Simon." She watched him severely but could not keep a small smile from breaking the stern lines of her face. Rosa was a formidable woman, both in size and personality. She was the sister of Simon's mother, and he always wondered if they hadn't really been related. His mother, who had taken off when Simon was five, he remembered as having the thinness that comes with debilitating drug abuse and the frightened look of a whipped dog. He supposed there wasn't much difference between a dog whipped by its master and a wife beaten by her husband. But the memory of his mother was another one that came to Simon only in the last moments before sleep, when his defenses crumbled.

"How you doing? You being good?" Rosa asked Simon in Spanish.

"*Sí*," he responded flatly. "How's Valeria?" Simon hoped that asking about his cousin would derail Rosa from focusing on him. Besides, though he tried to hide it, he really liked his eight-year-old cousin. She was the only person who looked at him with something like trust in her young face.

"She's good, but don't you try to distract me. Are you behaving?" Rosa asked unsmilingly.

"Yes, ma'am," Simon said.

"They feeding you enough?"

"Yes, ma'am. It's not very good, but there's a lot of it." He was relieved to see his aunt have to look away to cover her amusement.

"This isn't supposed to be a vacation."

Simon dropped his eyes to his lap. "I know."

"You got to turn yourself around, boy, or you won't make it to your seventeenth birthday." Simon nodded without looking up. He'd heard this many times, each year of his life in fact, and though he knew it was true, he had resented it more each time. Now the familiar refrain gnawed at him, making him feel raw and irritable.

Behind his aunt a group of young men had entered the room. They were all dressed in baggy jeans and white T-shirts. They spotted Simon with his aunt and then halted, looking surly and would-be tough, in the corner of the big room. Their bad-ass attitudes were laughable in a place that dealt with young gang members and felons on a daily basis, and the people in charge reacted with nothing more than a bored glance. Simon noted all of this, and felt a kind of shame, a crack forming in his rigidly created belief system.

Aunt Rosa followed his look and saw the boys hovering in the corner. Turning back to Simon, she fixed him with a hard, brown stare. "What are they doing here?" she demanded flatly.

"Visiting," Simon muttered, afraid to make eye contact.

"Simon, I know you think they're your friends, but they're nothing but poison." Rosa leaned in and grabbed Simon's face roughly, forcing him to look at her. Simon could only stand the gaze for a couple of seconds before he pulled away angrily. Rosa sighed and slumped back in the folding chair. "You've got to choose, boy; nobody can help you if you keep acting like a fool."

Feeling honestly frightened that she would give up on him, Simon looked up appealingly to his aunt. She was the only family he had. His friends had become his family, protected him, saved his life even; Rosa didn't understand that, but he was terrified of losing her.

"They're my friends," he said with a mixture of defiance and despair.

Rosa sighed deeply again, her huge chest rising and falling like a swell in the sea. "I know you think that, but they are *not* your friends."

Simon turned his face away from her and said, "Thanks for coming," as coldly as he could. But when he heard Rosa's chair scrape back as she stood to go, he spun back and peered up at her desperately. "I'm sorry," he muttered. He wondered whether she'd be too angry to come pick him up when he was released tomorrow. It wouldn't be the first time he'd been stranded miles from a bus stop.

"I know," Rosa said. She sounded tired beyond her forty years. "Just try to get through this." Then she fixed him with a searching stare. "But hear me, boy. *Friends* don't put you in danger. If you don't cut them loose, you can't come back to me. It's not good for Valeria, and it's not good for you." She must have seen the panic in Simon's eyes because she softened somewhat and added, "I know it's hard. I know they've been there for you when nobody else was. But we all got a choice, Simon, and you're grown up enough to know the right choice from the wrong one. I tried to teach you right, but if you haven't learned it by now"—her shoulders sloped forward—"then I'm gonna miss you."

Then, with a quick squeeze of Simon's hand, she turned without looking at him again and strode out of the room, ignoring the gang of boys in the corner.

For their part, the boys watched Rosa warily, as though hoping she wouldn't spot them. Simon actually saw them shrink against the wall as the large woman stalked past them. Then they crossed to Simon and tapped their fists against his.

"Yo, what's up, Sy?" asked the first to reach him.

"Yo, Loc, Tic, Juice." Simon nodded at each boy. "Wha's up?"

"Shit, Sy, your aunt is one scary bitch," said the tallest of the three as they sat down across from Simon. This was Loc, the natural leader of the group.

Simon smiled. "You fucking telling *me* that?" he asked. Then he settled back in his seat and, crossing his arms tightly over his chest, glanced around the room to make sure none of the keepers were within earshot. He looked to Loc. The other two sat slightly back from the tall boy and deferred to his every movement. "You got news for me?"

"We hear some shit," Loc said, his eyes roaming the room as well. His shaved head shone in the fluorescent overhead lights, and his forearms, toned from hours in the gym, rested with deceiving passivity on his thick thighs. "Don't sweat it. We'll take care of it." Next to him, the smallest of the three, Tic, moved constantly, fidgeting and tapping one black sneaker against the linoleum floor.

"I want the fucker who put me in here to—"

"Chill, fucker," Loc said with a warning note in his voice. "I told you, we'll take care of it. When you out?"

"Tomorrow, but listen to this shit. I can only go if I do community hours or get a job."

"That sucks," said Juice eloquently. He was a large young man, not fat, but big, and his lazy body language disguised a rippling strength that could be sparked into action by the smallest ember of anger.

"Can you pick me up?" Simon asked, trying to look like he didn't care, and half hoping they would say no in case his aunt showed up.

"Not tomorrow. Got some bin-niss," Loc said to him with a pointed look at the other two boys.

Simon nodded. "That's cool."

"We'll meet you at the joint," Loc said. "Tomorrow night."

Simon's heart fluttered, but he kept his face cool. The joint meant a night of tequila drinking and dope smoking in a junkyard. He hadn't had alcohol or drugs for over two months, and in that two months he'd had regular meals and more physical exercise than he'd thought he could survive, but his muscles felt strong, and his body felt clean. The thought of drinking till he puked made his stomach churn. A little bit of smoke sounded good, but with Loc and the others, there was no such thing as a little bit of anything.

The quiet lull of voices in the rec room was shattered by a jarring alarm bell. Everyone in the room jerked spasmodically at the harsh assault on their nervous systems and shot panicked looks around. Simon saw Loc reach fruitlessly toward the back of his baggy pants. Subject to search when he came to the camp, he would have left his piece in the car.

The only people who didn't react convulsively at the noise were the firemen. They calmly walked to the middle of the room and waited for the three long, harsh bell blasts to subside; then one of them spoke in a clear, calm voice that carried in the postalarm silence.

He addressed the visitors first. "I'm sorry, but that

means we have to cut visiting day short. We've been called out to work a fire." His attention and tone shifted as he addressed the inmates themselves. "Okay, guys, let's gear up and meet by the trucks in two minutes." He indicated the large industrial-looking clock on the wall. "That will be at two twenty-seven. Go."

The young men scattered with varying degrees of reluctance. Simon offered a roll of his eyes to Loc, Juice, and Tic as he passed them, but once he reached the bustle of efficient action in the open yard and his back was to his friends, a thin, self-satisfied smile twisted his lips, like a wisp of smoke gathering itself and then curling lazily upward.

Chapter 6

Al Wright's restaurant looked like a dive, but inside it was sumptuously done in deep red booths, a long oak bar, and the delicious smell of prime rib. Greer sipped at her soda water, set it on the counter, and gave her appearance an appraising once-over in the mirror behind the bar. She was satisfied with what she saw there, but she thought that must be mostly because she liked who she was. It would have surprised her in her modesty to know that the bartender and indeed every other man in the place had been admiring her since her arrival. At a glance, Greer saw a woman with a contented face: Her green eyes were striking, yes, and her mouth had the kind of fullness that she knew men thought attractive. Her wavy auburn hair and her plumper-than-magazine-fashionable curves were also traits that men found far more alluring than popular culture would admit. Then a quickening of her pulse told her to turn to the door, and a second later her date, Sterling, walked through it.

As always when she first saw him, Greer felt delight, and secretly surprised that such a handsome, manly man would have found her equally attractive. Sterling Fincher had skin the color of strong coffee that framed his incongruously green eyes to their best advantage. He was wearing a silver-gray dress shirt that did little to hide the impressive strength in his arms and shoulders. He zoned in on Greer as though drawn like a magnet and moving quickly to her, he kissed her luxuriously on the plush cushions of her lips as though enjoying a drink of cool water after a long thirst.

"You look beautiful," he murmured.

"Thank you," Greer responded as the fluttering of swallows stirred in her chest. "And you look very handsome, as usual."

Sterling laughed, showing his perfect white teeth, and Greer felt the rich, honest, rumbling laugh as a pleasant ripple through her body. "I don't know how handsome I can be after having my face pummeled half a dozen times." His voice was thickly accented, a testament to his upbringing in the south of London. It was true that he looked like a man who had never shied away from a fight, but his ruggedness added to his masculine attractiveness because he looked as if he'd won more fights than he'd lost.

"Thanks for putting up with a business dinner instead of a legitimate date. I'll make it up to you," he said, taking the bar stool next to her.

"I'll give you ample opportunity to try."

The barman approached them with a smile. How different from their first date at this same restaurant, Greer thought, which had been a setup by her business partner, Dario, when this same bartender had studiously ignored them. Now, of course, Greer and Sterling were "locals" and that's what they liked to see at good ol' Al's.

"Hello, Alan," Sterling greeted him with a firm handshake. "Having a good one?"

"Oh, I've got a good one," said the wiry septuagenarian. "What I need is a good place to put it." Both Greer and Sterling snorted with surprised laughter. Alan was famous for lines like these, but looking at his ornery, lined face, it was hard to get used to them coming from him.

"You want a drink here or at the table?" he asked Sterling with only the faintest glimmer in his eye to show that he had enjoyed their response.

"Here. We're waiting for another couple. Actually, the man responsible for that giant subdivision everyone resents so much," Sterling told him. "Don't blame me though, I already turned him down, but he still wants me to do the landscaping."

"What landscaping?" Alan asked dryly as he reached for the gin bottle, poured a shot and a half into a tall glass, and then sprayed tonic into it with the soda gun. "What's to landscape? They're leaving yards the size of my back doormat."

"I know," Sterling sighed and took the offered drink. "And what happens to those minibackyards is up to the home owners. He wants me to do the breaks and common areas, what little there is of those. I turned it down at first, but he's offered to make some concessions, so that's what I'm here to discuss. I was hoping I might be able to influence him to leave at least some open space."

Alan's snort as he turned away was an eloquent expression of a large portion of the local population's sentiment. He muttered something about greedy somethings and went on studiously ignoring a gesticulating newcomer at the other end of the bar.

The door opened again, letting in a blast of hot air along with an unlikely couple, who stood blinking around in the comparative dimness of the bar. The man was friendly looking. His Santa Claus figure was awkwardly covered by what was obviously an expensive but ill-fitting suit, making Greer think that here was a man who could afford the best but couldn't be bothered to show up for the fitting. His once-blond hair was mostly gray now, thin on top and combed over to one side in an oddly endearing attempt to disguise his diminishing hairline. He wore rectangular glasses that were a decade or so out of fashion, on a bemused face. As he surveyed the restaurant, he had the pleased, doughy expression of someone who has entered a place with no particular expectations and found it surprisingly quaint.

The woman next to him was in sharp contrast to her husband in almost every aspect. She was quite beautiful in a very well-preserved way, as though at about thirty-five she had dug in her heels, decided that's as far as she was willing to go, and refused to acknowledge the next fifteen or so years. She was definitely Asian in descent, very thin and svelte. Her shoulder-length black hair was meticulously styled, her fingernails were manicured, and her nose was in the air. Her crème silk suit fit her like the sleeve of an umbrella; you could almost hear the smooth swish of fabric as she moved toward them. Her exact age was hard to place, thought Greer, probably early fifties, but Greer didn't need any special abilities to instinctively know that inquiring about this woman's age would be a faux pas from which she might never recover.

Spotting Sterling, Rowland took his wife's arm and steered her toward the bar. As they came closer, her face arranged itself into a beaming smile, somehow without seeming to crease her face, and she extended a strong white hand first toward Sterling.

"Hello there. I'm Susan Hughs," she introduced herself, and then smiled politely at Greer as the gentlemen exchanged greetings and handshakes.

"Allow me to introduce Greer Sands," Sterling said. "She owns Eye of the Beholder beauty salon, right next to my office. Greer, this is Rowland and Susan Hughs."

"Pleasure to meet you," Rowland said, and his voice had the slide of the south in it. As he shook Greer's hand, she noticed that his palm felt slightly damp from the residual outside heat, but other than that, Greer sensed nothing unusual.

Susan cut in: "I've seen your salon, and I've heard very good things about it. You're next to that coffee shop, aren't you?" Susan was focused on her so intently that Greer felt as if she were answering a question of national importance.

"Yes. I'm pleased that you've heard good things."

"I was told you have the best hairstylist in the area. Is that true?"

Greer smiled warmly at the thought of her showy partner. "Absolutely. But don't take my word for it. Ask him—*he'll* tell you."

Susan extended her graceful white hand again. Greer

took it and instantly wished she hadn't. An image like a black mass appeared to her in the vicinity of Susan's chest. The alarm she felt must have shown on her face because, without releasing Greer's hand, Susan asked, "Are you feeling all right?"

Sterling's eyes cut quickly to Greer. He knew too much about her psychic impressions to think that this was anything other than a reading.

Greer recovered quickly. "I'm fine. I was going to ask you the same thing."

Susan's brows lifted and she released Greer's hand. "Why would you ask me that?"

Greer was trapped. How could she say, "Because it looks like you have a cancer in your chest"? So she just laughed it off by replying, "Because you've been out in that awful heat and we've been sitting in here enjoying a gin and tonic."

Susan seemed appeased, if not convinced, and with a classy grace she waved the hand sporting a six-carat marquis diamond—a yellow diamond no less, Greer noted—and said, "Well, now that you mention it, I'm am feeling a tiny bit stressed, but I'm sure it's nothing a good, cold drink won't fix."

Stressed, thought Greer, was the understatement of the year. She felt sure that this woman was so tightly wound that even the smallest of punctures in her outer membrane might cause her to pop spontaneously. Blackness meant danger, and most often Greer "saw" it outside the person, but this was definitely inside Susan, and all Greer could think was that she was either close to an emotional collapse or seriously—possibly terminally—ill.

Sterling took the situation in hand by saying, "Shall we go to our table?"

They were soon settled in one of the large booths, the ladies on the inside next to each other and the men facing across the table. They each ordered prime rib, except for Susan, who wanted the duck—but without the orange sauce—and vegetables—no, not the medley, just broccoli, lightly steamed, no butter, some lemon slices, please—instead of the offered potatoes or rice. It struck

Greer that Susan probably always required a special order. That settled, the talk turned quickly to the project.

Sterling had been working on a smaller project for the Hughses' company, eleven high-end homes built on four acres. The homes were huge, over four thousand square feet each, and packed tightly together in a community that already held small homes on lots of five acres or more. All of Shadow Hills had been baffled as to how the zoning had gotten through, but as Sterling and Greer listened to Susan, it became crystal clear.

"You have to stay on these local politicians," she was saying as they discussed her efforts to push through a zoning variance for what would be stage three of the proposed seven-hundred-home development that was under way. "There are loopholes in most of the local zoning laws, and if you expedite your proposals by handling things personally, which I do," she stressed as Rowland beamed proudly at her, "then you can usually push things through as long as you don't get caught up by some busybody environmental group."

"You don't care for them?" Sterling asked, and Greer had to suppress a smile at the almost undetectable sarcasm in the question.

"The bane of my existence." Susan poked the table-cloth with an acrylic nail as she spoke. "I mean, we are building beautiful homes, adding value to the existing properties, bringing in new life and resources to a floundering community. Local businesses will profit more than they can imagine, and yet people want to fight us." She turned both her palms up and registered mock shock on her face. "I mean, I just don't get it."

Greer kept her voice friendly but she offered, "Maybe the local people like things the way they are. I know that some people I've talked to don't want the additional traffic, and they are sorry to see the open land developed. They love the hills the way they are." She smiled at Susan. "I mean, that's just what I've overheard in the salon."

Rowland sat forward and put his elbows on the edge

of the table. "It is every American's dream to own a nice home. I think that people who already have homes might think twice before they criticize other people for wanting one of their own. And," his friendly face grinned in a boyish way, "they might forget that the land where *their* houses are built was 'open land' once too."

Sterling interjected before Greer could state the obvious fact that a three-bedroom home on five acres left quite a bit more open land. "True enough, but here we are, with an opportunity to ease up on both sides," he said. "I know you've already started construction on phase one, so those houses and their lot size are set in stone, or in asphalt and concrete as the case may be, but you have an opportunity to make some changes for phase two, and three if it's approved," he added with a nod toward Susan. "I'm proposing that if you cut your number of homes by even one-fifth, you could leave communal open space and create corridors between streets where indigenous trees and shrubbery could be left intact, or replanted if it's more cost-effective. That would serve to make the development less of a visual impact from below, and give the buyers more of what is so special about Shadow Hills to start out with—a little more space."

Sterling sat back and waited to see what effect his suggestion would have on Rowland and Susan. They were looking at each other with knowing, piteous expressions on their faces. Then Rowland turned back to Sterling and shook his head sadly.

"I wish I could. But the fact is, people don't want yards, they don't want outside space. They want the biggest, most impressive house they can get for their hard-earned dollar, and that's *all* they're willing to pay for. If I were to cut the number of homes and increase open space, I would have to charge a fifth again as much as I'm asking now for each home, and that"—his face looked pained and he put a hand against his heart—"I just can't expect people to pay. And before you suggest I take a little less profit, remember that I've got investors to answer to, and they have a right to see a certain return on their money. That's how capitalism and this great democracy works. I'm proud that I can provide the American dream to so many people *on so many levels*. It really means a lot to me and I'm committed to giving as many people their dream homes as I possibly can." He smiled around warmly at all of them, his eyes shining.

Greer was stunned to find that she actually believed he was sincere. She had to admit that judging from the number of gigantic housing developments in and around LA County, and the trend toward massive homes on little land, people really didn't seem to mind being packed in; otherwise, she reasoned, they wouldn't buy the homes, though it had always baffled her that anyone would choose to live that way, and she had always assumed that if they were given an option, they would take it. But maybe she was wrong.

Susan was smiling kindly at Sterling too, as though at a precocious two-year-old who had asked for a real motorcycle. "We've already made allowances, as much as we can," she explained patiently. "I made a deal for smaller lot sizes in exchange for leaving two open acres, which will be in the steeper runoff area leading to the wash."

Greer couldn't help herself. "I heard that the city made you leave that area open because of erosion."

Susan winked and said brightly, "See, with a little forethought, things can work out nicely for everyone. Wendy Sostein, the local councilwoman, has been so helpful. She understands that if a community doesn't grow, it stagnates and dies, just like any other living thing."

Rowland put his arm around his wife. "Isn't she amazing?" he asked, beaming as though he'd found a van Gogh at a yard sale.

"Amazing," agreed Sterling, though he declined to say in what way.

Rowland released Susan, who straightened her jacket and folded her hands on the table in front of her. "Now," he said to Sterling, "let's hear your thoughts on shrubbery. I'm thinking lots of quick-growing ficus trees and ice plant for ground cover."

As Sterling tried to patiently explain that ice plant was a type of vegetation that supported absolutely no animal or insect life, and ficus trees were also an invasive non-native, so they might not be suitable for the national forest adjacent, Susan turned her attention to Greer.

"So, are you a hairdresser as well?"

"No, I do massage, reflexology, facials, those sorts of treatments. I'm more focused on the body than the hair," Greer answered.

"I wish I had more time for massages. I could really use one. This push for phase three has become much more complicated than I had hoped." Her face tightened into a mask of tension and Greer's instinctive nurturing tendency took over.

"But you must have been through this many times. Aren't you used to it?"

Susan shook her head. "Actually, though I have done this before, this is the first time that it's been this size project and it's our first one in California."

"Where are you from?"

"Florida. I met Rowland when I was working for a law firm in Tampa and I was assigned to one of his projects there."

"How long have you been married?" Greer asked, hoping to turn the conversation to a more comfortable, female level.

"Almost a year," she said, "and no time for a honeymoon. Well, unless you count a weekend in Florida for his youngest daughter's college graduation. And I'm not exactly his ex's favorite person, so . . . I don't." Susan's mouth thinned to such a fine line that, for a moment, she lost her precarious hold on her late thirties and slipped into her fifth decade.

Laying a hand on Susan's arm, Greer said encouragingly, "Why don't you come into the salon and let me try some reflexology on you. I think it might be very good for you to let off some pressure." The darkness that she had sensed in Susan's chest came into her consciousness again as she touched the other woman. Greer tried to focus on it without losing her attention on the conversation.

The darkness had a definite outline, but it was without mass, more like the absence of light. In shape it was jagged, spiked outward. As Susan turned to comment on a suggestion that Sterling made about planting only native plants, Greer was able to focus on the impression it gave her. Whatever it was, it meant imminent danger for Susan, danger from within. Greer could feel a certain instability there. In spite of Susan's amazingly together front, Greer sensed strife and conflict, but before she could identify whether the danger was emotional, physical, or something else, she found herself drawn back into the conversation and the opportunity was lost.

As they ate and the evening wore on, Greer kept watching the other woman surreptitiously. What did the darkness mean? She had detected the tinge of death, but mostly danger, and every time she looked at the prettily practiced face, all she could think was *Something is killing you.*

Chapter 7

Greer stepped out of the restaurant into the too-hot night air, and the tinge of wood smoke filled her nostrils. Her first thought was *Who's built a fire on a night this warm?* but the disconcerting premise was quickly replaced by logical alarm. It was wood that was burning, but not in the safety of someone's fireplace.

Sterling had smelled it too, and they exchanged looks of concern before scanning the hills that rose, still and solid, beyond Foothill Boulevard, their shadowy presence beyond the scattered lights of the residential streets revealing no secrets.

"Oh no," Greer said softly as she and Sterling headed for the car, "I hope it's nothing bad."

"It won't take much in this weather," he said. "We'll check the news when we get home."

But they didn't need to. As they drove the seven miles up to Greer's house, the scent, even in the closed, air-conditioned car, didn't go away, though it didn't grow stronger either. Greer scanned the dark canyons as they drove, looking for signs of the source, but she saw nothing. Yet when they pulled into the parking area in front of Greer's lovely mission-style home, they saw Joshua's car, loaded to the max, and next to it, a car that neither of them recognized, so heavily packed that its back axle was almost touching the unpaved ground.

"Hi, Mom. Hi, Sterling," Joshua called out from the kitchen table, where he sat with the Caseys. He introduced everyone and quickly explained what had happened, ending on a cheerful note: "We got the call about five minutes ago that the fire is contained and nowhere near their house anymore, so it's safe for them to go back. We were just having a celebratory cup of tea, before we drive back up there."

Emily was just shaking hands with Greer as Joshua finished, and she held tight to Greer's hand as she said, "We're so grateful to your son. I don't know what would have happened if he hadn't come along when he did." Her eyes filled with tears and she turned to Joshua. "You know it was your warning that saved our home, and maybe us."

Greer felt a surging pride in Joshua; he was exceptional in so many ways. She beamed gratefully at her son. But it was Sterling who had crossed to him and, after shaking Joshua's hand, pulled him into a tight hug.

"Good job. I'm proud of you," he said, his eyes glowing with admiration.

Greer thought her heart would burst. She could see how much it meant to Joshua to have this strong, capable man think so highly of him. He had lost his father when he was eight, and though Greer's business partner had filled that place as best he could, it meant so much to her to have the man she had brought into her life and her son caring for each other. Filled with pride as thick and foamy as the crown of a double latte, she joined the Caseys at the table and asked, "Do they know how the fire started?"

Larry exchanged a tired look with his wife and then said, "No. We've had small fires nearby before, but they started near the road—some idiot tossing a cigarette out the window. They think this one started a long ways from the road, which means . . ." His voice trailed off and he sighed deeply.

"Arson," Sterling finished for him. His strong, dark hands had balled to fists on the table in front of him. "What would possess someone to do something like that?"

"It's hard to fathom," Larry said grimly.

Watching the faces of this elderly couple and knowing

what it would have meant for them to lose their home, their memories, their security, Greer went beyond unfathomable to wondering what kind of evil had to be in a person's heart for them to want to harm someone they didn't even know, to destroy at random. A tide of hot, bitter bile rose up in her.

Outside, a forest service helicopter passed only a couple hundred feet above them. The aircraft pounded the night with its thrumming and rattled the glass in the windows of the house, violently reminding them of the threat that, though dispelled for the moment, would remain until the first true, forgiving rainfall.

Chapter 8

"Ooph," Jenny stopped and placed a hand against her tummy as she used the other hand to agitate the metal pitcher up and down under the steamer, turning the cold milk into a sensual froth.

"Baby says, 'Hi'?" Leah asked as she leaned against the counter of Jenny's coffee shop waiting for her second double latte of the morning, and it wasn't even seven.

"More like *'Hey!'*" Jenny shouted so loudly that Leah jumped back slightly and all the other customers in the shop turned from their papers and computers to see why. Jenny just waved cheerfully and called out, "Sorry," to the assembled observers.

Leah laughed and broke off a tiny portion of the muffin waiting for her on the counter. She had just placed it neatly on her tongue, so as not to disturb the carefully applied lipstick, when the bells on the door chimed. She turned automatically at the sound, and what she saw made her catch her breath, resulting in sucking an errant crumb down her windpipe.

Walking through the door was the handsomest man she'd ever seen. He was tall and dark, and his chiseled jaw had a day's worth of stubble that lent him the romance of a cowboy back from rounding up stallions on the range. His eyes were blue, his stride long and confident. And if all that weren't enough, he was dressed in the unmistakable uniform of a fireman. Leah, choking on the pastry, was unable to swallow or look away as this young Sam Shepard walked right out of her personal fantasies and into her personal space, so that she found herself staring and incapable of answering when he reached the counter and said in a deep, sonorous, playful voice, "Good morning."

Suddenly aware that she was also in this movie, Leah struggled to clear her throat and find her voice simultaneously. The result was that she croaked out a "Good morning," swallowed more crumbs the wrong way, and went into a fit of coughing.

The apparition reached out and thumped her firmly on the back. "You all right?" he asked, holding her forearm firmly with his other hand, as though securing her in case she fainted.

Looking up into almost royal blue eyes through the mist of her own tears, Leah thought that she just might swoon. Maybe it would be a good move. *Rescue me,* she thought dreamily, imagining those strong arms lifting her up and holding her tight against that broad chest. The next thought she had was far more severe, a loud voice screaming in her head, *Don't let him touch you!*

"Uh, I'm fine. Thank you," she said as soon as she could speak. She pulled her arm away and stepped back, placing an invisible barrier between her and the devastatingly handsome fireman. Her face hot with embarrassment and discomfort, she turned to take her latte from Jenny only to find that Jenny was standing limply, a dreamy expression on her face, looking up at the fireman.

"Can I get you something?" Jenny asked. "Anything?"

Either the man was oblivious to the effect he had on women, or he was so used to it that it didn't affect him. Or maybe it was Leah's choking and Jenny's advanced pregnancy that disguised their overt admiration. He scanned the blackboard behind her. "Uh, let's see. How about a double latte, with a shot of vanilla, and cinnamon toast."

"Coming up." Jenny flashed a look at Leah that clearly said, "Hello! Talk to him!" before she turned to fill the order.

But Leah could think of nothing to say, so she just stood lamely by, wondering if she should chance another bite of her muffin as an excuse for her muteness.

Jenny shot her another impatient look and then filled in for her frozen friend. "I haven't seen you here before. Are you new in the neighborhood?"

"Kind of. I was called in on the brush fire yesterday afternoon. We've been working all night. I'm the relief pilot."

"Oh, you fly?" Jenny said in a singsong voice, as though it needed only this for him to achieve perfection. "Planes?"

"Yeah, but mostly helicopters. We spent last night doing drops on flare-ups."

"Flare-ups," Jenny repeated, and if she hadn't been so very pregnant, it would have sounded obscene. She set his coffee on the counter and extended a hand. "I'm Jenny Sanchez."

He shook it. "Weston Oakmont. Nice to meet you."

"And this is my friend," said Jenny pointedly, "Leah Falconer."

"Hi," said Leah, feeling stunted. She was furious at herself for allowing this irrational fear to get the best of her, but it had rendered her incapable of fluid movement or speech. It was as though she were disabled.

Weston turned his stunning face to her again, and Leah wondered if it was only her fevered imagination or if he really looked interested. "Leah." He nodded and kept his eyes on her for a fraction of a second longer than necessary. Leah's heart fluttered with irrational panic, and she looked to Jenny for backup, thinking, *What is wrong with me?*

Far from supportive, Jenny looked as though she would like to kill her. "So," Jenny said pointedly to Weston, "will you be around for long?"

"Oh yeah. Probably most of the fire season." His eyes flicked to Leah again. "They put us up at the ranger station. We do two-week shifts."

The sound of air brakes hissing loudly outside pulled all their attention to the windows. A big water truck had pulled up at the curb, and emerging from the cab was a tall, thin man in spotless, ironed jeans and a neatly pressed plaid shirt. He was older, his face creased and lined by upwards of sixty years. His angular jaw worked as he took a last deliberate draw on the butt of a cigarette; then he put it out carefully in the gutter before striding across the parking lot and into the coffee shop.

"Morning." He nodded to Weston and the ladies.

"Good morning." Jenny took his order—plain coffee, largest she had—and turned to fill it.

Weston seemed to recognize the newcomer. "They cut you loose?" he asked.

"Hell no." The older man's voice was gruff and hesitant, and his eyes darted around as he responded, as though uncomfortable with human connection. "I'm taking another load up Oak Springs. County had me sitting around all night before they used the first load."

"You don't have to tell me about waiting around for County to make a decision. If one of those administrators' hair caught on fire while they were standing next to a pool, they'd have to get three verbal approvals before they would jump in," commiserated Weston. "I'm Weston," he introduced himself.

The driver's eyes twitched around the room, flickering briefly over Weston's as he nodded curtly and said, "Sheldon Tucker."

"Maybe you'll be able catch some sleep later today."

The newcomer snorted. "Not likely in this weather. I got about ten houses with wells drying up. If I don't take 'em water, they'll be awful thirsty. No"—he smiled grimly and his eyes swept over Weston's face in passing again and landed on the safety of the bakery selection—"I might get some sleep late tonight, but not before then."

Weston smiled at the ladies as he took his change from Jenny. "And miles to go before I sleep," he quoted.

"That's my favorite Robert Frost," Leah managed to whisper barely audibly, showing her first sign of intelligent life, but Weston had already looked away.

"Here you are," said Jenny, handing the water-truck driver a large, steaming to-go cup and taking his money. "We sure are glad you're both out there." Her next comment was directed to both men as well, but she fixed her gaze on Weston. "Come in anytime you like," Jenny said warmly. She looked pointedly at Leah and stressed the next word. "*We* are always around."

"Thanks," mumbled Sheldon Tucker. He sloped over to the condiments, where he hoisted up the sugar dispenser and let it pour into his coffee as he picked up a discarded paper and started to read. Leah wondered if he would finish the article before he stopped adding sweetener.

Weston fixed Leah with a bemused smile and said, "See you around, I hope." Then without waiting for a response, which was good because Leah's jaw had locked again, he turned and left the shop, the bells jingling as the door closed behind what might possibly have been his better side.

Jenny and Leah watched him through the plate-glass windows until he had climbed into his truck and driven away, and then Jenny wheeled on Leah. "What the hell?" she said. "Why didn't you talk to him? He *obviously* thought you were . . ."

But Leah was wringing her hands, her face so twisted into a mass of self-hate and fear that Jenny's intended recrimination trailed off.

Leah stuttered, "I just can't. I mean, it's been a while, I know, but ever since . . . I just . . . Ahhr!" She let out a frustrated growl.

Jenny lifted the flap in the counter and came out to put an arm around her friend. After leading her to a small table near the back, Jenny waited until they were both seated and then patted Leah's hand. "I understand. It's okay. I know that what happened to you was horrible. I get that. But, girl"—Jenny's face had become fierce, even through the gentleness she was expressing—"you deserve to be happy. You deserve a good man. And I'm not saying you should rush it, but it is gonna mean taking a chance."

Feeling ambushed by the depth of her emotional paralysis, Leah vented a rush of anger at her friend, at life, at all the fucked-up men in the world. She snatched her hand away and flared, "I know that! Don't you think I fucking know that?" Yet even before the words were all out, she realized that her fury was not really directed at Jenny but at herself, and mortified, she apologized in the same breath. "I'm sorry. It's not your fault."

But Jenny hadn't even flinched. Too much violence had marred her own young life for her to think for a moment that she was the true target of her friend's animosity. It was that unique sympathy that had made them—so unlikely a pair—such close friends.

"Listen, girl. It would be stupid for me to say that I know how you feel, because I'm not you. But I've come back up from a long way down once or twice myself, as you know, and there's one thing I am absolutely sure of." Jenny put both her palms down on the table and leaned toward Leah. "*You chose not to be a victim,* but as long as what happened then controls your actions now, you are still the victim." Before Leah could summon an outraged denial or a defense, Jenny went on. "Don't let that son of a bitch own you. Make the choice not to be a victim now either. Do you understand?" There was a hardness in Jenny's voice that told Leah, more than any of Jenny's words, what she meant. "*You* own you," she ended emphatically.

Leah's indignant rage, which had swelled with the injustice of it all, subsided like the slap of a wave on rough rock and ebbed away, leaving her feeling as mushy as wet sand. The debilitating sponginess that had overtaken her chest and throat kept her from responding, but she nodded.

Jenny took a hit in her heart as she watched Leah's fingers brush unconsciously in a repetitive motion across a fine white scar that intersected the gentle bend of her upper lip.

The bells on the door rang again as more customers came into the shop. Jenny stood and her usual mischievous grin split her gorgeous face. "Now, if I were you, I'd bake some cookies and take them by the firehouse."

In spite of cradling a heart that felt battered and bruised, Leah couldn't suppress a barked laugh. Jenny winked and walked back to the counter, leaving Leah wondering desperately if she would ever be able to let a man touch her again.

Chapter 9

Midmorning Monday at Eye of the Beholder found the salon buzzing at about half speed. Greer was delighted to have Mindy, the hostess of Jenny's baby shower, as a new client. Mindy had an infectious cheerfulness and chatted animatedly with everyone within earshot of her pedicure. Whitney, who had been friends with Mindy for years, was there too, sitting in Dario's chair, getting her thick black tresses trimmed, and throwing the occasional comment across the floor, which would have been fine, except that she kept turning her head to do it.

"Woman," Dario said to her severely, "you do know that I'm working around your jugular vein with a very sharp instrument and you keep presenting a moving target." He was an intimidating man. Six foot four, dark haired and as handsome as midnight, with a personality just as daunting, he had a voice that could shake the mirrors in the salon, and it did now as he delivered his warning.

Whitney, however, knew Dario to be the large and cuddly bear that he was, and their repartee had always been quick and easy.

"Don't you sass me." She smiled up at him in the mirror through her wet, plastered-back bangs. "I'm sorry if I move my head when I speak. Most people do, you know. You should be used to it. What would you do if I wanted a whole new short style?"

"Give you four Valium and a neck brace," Dario retorted, but he smiled as he placed all ten huge, strong fingers on either side of her head and turned her face forward and down. "Now stay put."

"Yes, sahib," Whitney intoned obediently.

"Whitney!" called Mindy from across the room.

Whitney's head snapped up, and Dario snatched back the razor-sharp scissors just in time to prevent puncturing the base of her skull.

"That's it!" Dario crossed to face Mindy in two long strides. "I'm going to have to separate you two. Now, who wants to stand in the corner?"

Mindy looked up, way up, at the huge, famous hairdresser, dressed entirely in his signature black, towering above her. "I'm sorry," she squeaked.

Dario leaned down and pointed his comb at her face. "Listen up. She can't control herself, so I'm going to ask you to refrain from shouting her name for the next five minutes. Could you do that for me, you gorgeous, fabulous woman?" There was such an overtly flirty purr on the last line that Mindy actually blushed as she nodded, caught in his powerful, masculine spell.

Watching from the front, Greer laughed quietly. It was always the same. Dario charmed them all, and the fact that he was gay and overtly vocal about it never seemed to deter the fluttering devotion he inspired in his female clients.

The circular conversations, which rose and fell as people came in and out of the salon, were centered mostly on yesterday's fire. Greer found this interesting because the subject had seldom been mentioned, as though to speak of the devil would make him appear. But now that the first fire of season had broken out—and been suppressed—the taboo had somehow been lifted.

A huge pickup truck, fitted for off-roading, pulled up in the parking lot out front, causing Greer to frown as she watched it through the plate-glass windows. Ripping up the environment was never something she could define as a sport. She watched as Mindy's husband, Reading, emerged from the cab and paused just outside the glass door to finish his cigarette and toss it onto the sidewalk. Her frown deepened. When had cigarette butts ceased to be litter?

As Reading grabbed the handle of the door and pulled it open, the heat from the parking lot behind him bent the light. Greer saw him surrounded by a rusty brown aura. The color faded away as he entered the salon, but not before she identified it for what it was: an indicator of greed and imbalance. The aura was not black, which to her signified evil, but it showed her that this was a man who felt vaguely lost and unsure how to prove himself. She sensed confusion, and constant restlessness. This was so common with men in today's world that, instead of passing a judgment, Greer actually felt sorry for him.

So she greeted him warmly. "Reading, how nice to see you again. Have you come to pick up your wife?"

He looked a little taken aback to have his name recalled, and he seemed to fumble for a moment. Greer didn't let him squirm for long. "I'm Greer Sands. We met at the shower. I was one of a dozen women that day, but I remember you because you stood out somewhat." He still looked confused, so she added, "You being the only male within a ten-mile radius."

"Yes, I remember. How you doing?" He looked around, seeming unsure of himself in the sleek surroundings. "Is Mindy about done?"

"I think so. She's right over there." Greer pointed toward the back of the salon where his wife, bound by her vow of silence, was gesticulating wildly in his direction, indicating that she would be another five minutes. He waved hesitantly back and then crossed his arms and looked for something to do with himself.

"Did the fire come anywhere near your ranch?" Greer asked politely as a conversation opener.

"No, thank God. We've got a plan to evacuate all the horses if it ever does, but I sure as hell don't ever want to have to test it out." He seemed to relax into the topic. "I've seen some pretty hellacious wildfires, and let me tell you, they move fast and unpredictably."

"So I've heard." Greer nodded.

"I remember watching one, out in Malibu, from a friend's ranch. We were a good ten miles away, but it was awesome." His eyes had lit with a strange fire of their own, and it was clear that the memory stimulated him. "It was like a live thing, clawing its way down the hills, like some kind of huge cougar, crouching and then pouncing forward."

"How terrifying," said Greer, chilled by his enamored tone.

"But beautiful, and *awesome*." He used the word again, as though he could find none better. Looking into Greer's eyes, he leaned forward a little across the counter and almost whispered, "It was a powerful thing. You know what I mean?"

Greer felt a creeping tingling on her skin. "Yes, I think I do. An out-of-control fire is a very *terrifying* thing."

Reading straightened up and glanced around the salon, a bemused look on his face. "Same thing," he commented.

Before Greer could summon a response to that, Whitney had spotted Reading in the mirror and she called out from her bowed position. "Reading, come over here! I'm not allowed to move."

"You can move now," Dario said. "I'm through with the dangerous part."

Greer drifted with Reading over to stand between the two stations where Whitney and Mindy were receiving their respective treatments. Whitney introduced Dario and Reading, who did not shake hands since Dario's were otherwise employed, and the conversation about the fire continued.

"A lady who was in here before," Mindy was telling her husband, "said that the fire department suspects arson."

Reading grunted and shrugged. "Could be," he said. "But there're other things that can start a fire."

"Like what?" asked Whitney.

"Like stupidity. A beer bottle with a few drops of dew

in it. The glass can act like a magnifying glass when the sun passes through it, and in just the right conditions, create enough heat to turn this dry brush into tinder."

Dario sighed. "We've certainly had the right conditions. If it gets any hotter and drier, I won't have to bother with this." He motioned toward the blow-dryer in its holder. "I'll just send my clients outside for five minutes."

"Save on electricity," Whitney commented.

They talked about the number of people in the hills who had no access to city water and how the forest and fire services dealt with that. Reading seemed very well informed about all the procedures.

When Greer asked how he knew so much about it, it was Mindy who explained. "Reading used to be part of the volunteer fire department when we lived up in Oregon."

"Lumber town," Reading filled in.

"That's what he used to do," Mindy said with a grin. "I married a lumberjack."

Dario looked amused at the thought. He asked, "What do you do now?"

"Security systems," Reading said. "Started up my own company back in 'ninety-five."

"Going well?" Dario asked out of politeness.

"Very. I just got the contract for the new development. Seven hundred homes, all told, in one easy place."

"Sweet," said Dario, but there was a tinge of sour in the word. He didn't think much of paving the hills either. "But I thought there were *four* hundred homes."

"Planned so far, but there's a stage three that will add another three hundred on the back side," Reading told them.

"That's not for sure yet though, is it?" Greer asked, thinking of her conversation with Susan and Rowland Hughs the night before. "I thought the zoning wasn't passed through yet."

"Oh, it's a done deal." Reading looked smugly confident. "With Susan Hughs, I don't see it not happening. *That* is a woman who gets things done. She's the best thing to happen to this community in years."

Greer could see the muscles in Whitney's jaw working and knew her friend was biting back a sharp retort. When Whitney did speak, she kept the barb sheathed. "That depends on your point of view," she said.

"Really?" Reading's willingness to argue was less disguised; his tone was loaded for bear. "Do you have any idea how many people have been employed on this project and how much money it will bring into the community?"

Whitney let loose. "Do you have any idea how much traffic and noise and trash it will bring to the community? How much sensitive wildlife habitat it will destroy?"

"It's progress," Reading said coldly. "And if you're afraid of progress, then you're willing to let things stagnate and die."

"Oh, I'm not afraid of progress," Whitney fired back. "I just have a hard time distinguishing it from destruction in this case."

"Okay, okay," Mindy interjected. "Everybody gets to have a different opinion. Now, be nice, honey," she said soothingly to her husband. But she also quickly defended him. "Whitney, you know that Reading is a hunter and a camper, he has as much respect for the open space as anybody, but there has got to be a balance. I mean, people need a place to live, right?" She appealed to Greer and Dario, as though asking them to mediate.

"Well," Dario said in a low rumble, "I think there's a flip side to that too. I'm sorry, but the fact is it's the developers who are making out like bandits, putting up these communities with no regard for the effect they have on the environment, and then they ditch with a wad of cash. It's not like they live in these cardboard cutouts themselves, do they?"

Reading's stance had switched, Greer noticed, from casual to firmly planted. Like the fire he had described,

he looked a bit like a cougar ready to pounce. "The
Hughses are. They kept the four acres at the top to build
a house for themselves."

"Oh," said Whitney, "so their house will be on four
acres. I see."

"You know what?" Reading said bitterly, "I'm about
done having this same tired conversation. The fact is,
the homes are going in, so if you don't like it, too fucking bad." With that, he turned on his heel. "I'll be in
the truck," he threw over his shoulder at Mindy.

"Honey, please," she called after him as the others
looked uncomfortably away, but to no avail. "Shit," she
muttered as he left. "Now he'll be in a bad mood all
day. The truth is, I think he's sort of torn himself."

"I'm sorry," Greer said sincerely. "I hope he isn't too
upset. You know we didn't mean to offend him. It's a
touchy subject. That's not the first argument we've had
in here over those homes."

"It's funny though," said Whitney in her still-cheerful
tone, "how it seems that people's point of view is always
in direct proportion to how it will effect *them*. There's
very little principle involved. I mean, you guys are for
the development," she said to Mindy, "because he's
going to get a lot of work from it. The developers are
for it because they're going to get richer. The people
who are buying the homes are for it, I guess. Those whose
views are ruined don't want it, the people defending the
environment don't want it, and the naturalists don't even
want to consider whether it's reasonable or not. You
know what I mean?"

Dario's assistant, Jonathan, had come around the corner from the shampoo area. Blond, tan, twenty-four and
as sassy as they come, he had listened to the tail end of
this argument. Now he piped up with his own words
of wisdom.

"It's like *Us* magazine," he said sagely.

"What?" Dario narrowed his eyes at his assistant,
wary of what might be coming next.

"Well, if you're a star and you want publicity, you're

glad to be all over that cover, every damn week. 'Look at her new baby, look at her new boyfriend, look at her new dress. Isn't she glamorous!' But when that same celebrity wants to get away with something, the last thing they want to see is their own ugly, pimpled, makeupless mug, wearing a startled expression staring down at the masses waiting in line at the grocery store, with the caption, 'Star caught on naked cocaine binge! See disgusting cellulite photos on page three!' It's all a question of how it serves you." He pulled the wet towel from Whitney's shoulders and gave her a dry one as Dario picked up the blow-dryer. "It's a selfish world."

Dario frowned at the young man. "Bit cynical, don't you think?"

"Depends." Jonathan grinned.

"On what?" asked Greer.

"On what's in it for me." Jonathan flashed a brilliant smile and sashayed away.

Greer turned to Mindy, who was watching the young man's back retreat and looking utterly lost. "Never mind Jonathan," she said. "He's obsessed with being famous."

"No," sighed Mindy. "He's absolutely right. If it weren't for Reading making so much money on this project, I'd probably be down there with the Sierra Club gathering signatures on a petition to try to stop it. I am just as selfish as anybody." She looked absolutely disgusted with herself.

"Congratulations," Dario said, and smiled kindly down at Mindy.

"For what?" Mindy asked.

"You just realized that you're human. You're selfish *and* kind, and now you have the freedom to choose what you are going to do about it." He didn't speak the question, but it hung in the room.

Mindy looked stunned, then relieved, then deeply torn in turns as she studied her freshly painted toes. Everyone else watched her surreptitiously.

After a long, introspective moment, an impish smile creased her outdoorsy face. She looked at each of the people gathered around her in succession. Finally she offered sheepishly, "I didn't know there was going to be a test."

Dario ran his fingers through Whitney's rapidly smoothing hair. "Every day," he said. "Every waking day."

Chapter 10

It was ironic, Joshua thought, how the heat on the asphalt gave the illusion of water. As he drove down the long, slow curves nestled in the canyon that made this road so popular with motorcyclists and day-trippers alike, he leaned forward over the steering wheel of his car and looked up into the hills. The opalescent haze of blue in the sky above them was uninterrupted by cloud or smoke. Far to the east, the jet stream of a plane was hanging lazily like the discarded thread of a spider drifting through the remarkably thin air.

"At least it's not as windy," he thought to himself. Which was a good thing, since he'd be working outside today on one of Sterling's projects. Overall, the landscaping projects gave him a sense of satisfaction, leaving him pleasantly exhausted from the physical exertion and pleased to look around at the new plants and trees taking root at the end of the day. But when it was brutally hot like this, the labor often became more about beating the elements before they beat you. Joshua glanced over at the small cooler next to him. It was loaded with ice and sports drinks. He checked his pocket for the bandanna he would fill with ice and wrap around his neck—got it. Hat—got it.

As he passed the dry riverbed, he saw a lone figure walking on the shoulder of the road up ahead distorted by the waves of heat shimmering between them. "Bummer of a day to not have a car," Joshua thought, as it was a good four miles down to Foothill Boulevard and any kind of bus service. The figure must have heard his car approaching because he turned quickly and stuck out his thumb. Joshua braked and as he drew closer and recognized the figure. A thrill of expectation made his scalp prickle.

It was Simon. Joshua pulled the car up on the shoulder of the road just in front of him and rolled down the passenger window as Simon approached warily.

"Hi," Joshua said pleasantly. "Remember me?"

"Yeah." Simon's eyes were narrowed against the glare of the sun. Joshua could see the sweat on his upper lip, yet the young man gave no other signs of discomfort or weakness. "You want a ride?" Joshua asked after a long, silent beat.

"Yeah, thanks," mumbled Simon, and he opened the door and got in, arranging himself in a sprawling slouch. Joshua thought that everything about this guy shouted he was afraid, though he took such pains to portray the opposite.

"You get out?" Joshua asked, and hoped that it sounded conversational.

"Yeah."

Restraining himself from asking if that was the only syllable Simon knew, Joshua asked casually, "So, where do you want to go?"

"The bus stop. You can drop me anywhere on Foothill."

"Okay. I'm actually going to work, there." Joshua pointed at the new houses about a half mile up ahead on the corner of the only road intersecting the one they were on. "So I'll drop you wherever you want and then come back."

"I can walk from there," Simon said, but his flushed face looked stricken.

"No biggie," Joshua said. "It's, like, a mile out of my way."

They sat in silence until they had made the turn and were entering the residential flats; then Simon spoke suddenly. "What do you work at?"

Taken by surprise, Joshua stuttered a little. "Oh, uh,

I work for a landscaper, my mom's boyfriend, actually. I'm not starting college until winter semester, and I like working with my hands and things that grow, so he asked me to help him." The whole time he was rambling Joshua was thinking he must sound like a idiot to this kid who would probably never go to college and to whom "working with his hands" would mean demeaning—and inevitable—manual labor.

"He need somebody else?" Simon had kept his voice flat, but Joshua could hear the want in it.

"I don't know. I know I could use some help on this job right now. He has a couple other guys he usually uses, but I think they're busy on another site. I could ask him." Joshua hoped he didn't sound too hopeful; he wasn't sure how Sterling would feel about hiring a convicted juvenile felon, but he thought it was the best chance he was likely to get to find out more about Simon.

"Whatever," Simon said dismissively.

"I'll ask. You got a phone number?" Joshua fumbled in the storage space in the armrest, coming up with a pen and an old envelope, but before handing it over to Simon, he got a better idea. "You know, he's meeting me at work. If you have a few minutes, I could introduce you and you could ask him yourself."

Simon's body went, if possible, even more tense than it was already. "Yeah, I can spare a few," he said.

"Great." Joshua slowed the car and readied to make a U-turn at a four-way stop. As he glanced to his right to check for cars, he saw the unmistakable figure of the little dog just over Simon's shoulder, and it was yapping silently, furiously at him.

Joshua searched for a way to open the subject. Just to one side of them, a large golden retriever lay sprawled out in the iffy shade of an aluminum carport.

"I like those dogs," Joshua offered lamely. Simon did not comment, so he went on. "Do you have a dog?"

The entire right side of Simon's body seemed to twitch; his shoulder and his knee both jerked forward before Simon was able to repress the movement. He turned to look out the window, away from Joshua, but he said, "Used to."

"Oh, what kind?" asked Joshua, well aware that he'd hit a sensitive spot and trying to act as if he were completely unaware of it.

"Just a mutt."

"What happened to him?" Joshua asked, hating himself for pressing right now but unable to stop himself.

"Died." The slight jerk happened again, but not as dramatically, as though Simon had been ready for it and reined it in.

"Oh, I'm sorry," Joshua said sincerely. Though, of course, he had already known that it must be dead, or he wouldn't be seeing it.

"It was just a fucking dog," Simon said.

Thinking it was time to change the subject, Joshua tried another topic. "So, do you mind my asking what you were in the camp for? I mean, partly I'm curious, and partly I think Sterling, that's my boss, might want to know."

Simon was nodding resignedly, as though he knew that would be the first question. "I was in because some fucker ran their mouth." His own mouth had thinned into a hard line, and his hands, Joshua noticed, had curled into tightly balled fists.

"Really?" exclaimed Joshua with genuine surprise. "So, you didn't do anything?"

The idea seemed to take Simon aback, as though it had never occurred to him that he might have been punished because of something he did. Joshua came to the slow realization that, in Simon's world, breaking the law might be the norm rather than the exception, and punishment was expected only if you got *caught*. It was an interesting concept.

Slowly, Simon turned and looked Joshua in the face for the first time. "I wouldn't have been in that shithole if somebody hadn't snitched," he said as though struggling to make his point clear to himself as well as to Joshua.

Joshua turned his attention back to the road and said,

with as little emotion as he could, "But for somebody to snitch on you, you've got to do something to snitch about." He glanced at Simon and shrugged. "I'm just saying."

Simon said nothing for a couple of blocks, and then, his voice dripping with acid, he said, "You don't know shit."

"I'm just saying," Joshua said again quickly, "that maybe sometimes we are responsible for what happens to us. I mean, a little bit. Right?" He fell silent, thinking of the images that came to him unbidden—that were changing his life, altering every plan he had made. Then he thought of how presumptuous it was of him to judge Simon, and he felt a flash of shame. Finally, Joshua laughed out loud and Simon's head snapped around to look at him as though he were about to be attacked. "Then again," Joshua said, still laughing, "maybe not." He grinned at Simon's alarmed face. "You're right, what do I know? I don't fucking know."

Then it happened, a sneaky, unbidden smile crept across Simon's high-security face. "I don't fucking know either," he said.

They had reached the new homes, and Joshua was pleased to see that Sterling's truck was already there, the back of it loaded solid with plants in one-gallon containers. Joshua recognized coyote bush, white sage, and California sunflower, all low-water natives.

He pulled the car into the driveway of one of the nearly finished houses and got out. Simon followed him hesitantly.

Sterling was marking the brief hillside that sloped sharply down from the retaining wall—which had been built to create enough additional space to squeeze in one more five-bedroom home—with small, flagged sticks. Each stick bore a different colored tape to signify which plant went where.

"Reporting for duty, sir," Joshua called out.

Sterling straightened up and gave Simon an appraising look. "Who's your friend?" he asked.

"Oh, this is Simon. He's looking for work, so I said I'd introduce him."

Sterling climbed the burlap-covered hillside and stood looking down on the smaller Simon, his mocha skin glowing with perspiration in the unforgiving sun. "So you want to work?" he asked him.

Simon seemed to find it difficult to look the commanding black man in the eye. "Yeah," he muttered. It seemed to confuse him that Simon spoke with a sharp British accent; Joshua would have been amused if he hadn't felt so anxious for Simon.

"You ever done yard work or landscaping before?" Sterling asked the teenager.

"No."

Joshua thought, *At least he's honest.* He knew that would count for something with Sterling.

"When do you go back to school?"

Simon snorted slightly. "I don't."

"Yes, you do, if you want a job with me. You get in trouble? Is that why you need a job?"

Simon hesitated and then nodded without looking up.

Joshua stared in open amazement, but Sterling's seeming clairvoyance was explained in his next statement. "Yeah, you're not the first kid from the fire camp I've hired. And I've developed a few rules over the years. You show up on time, you do what I or Joshua here asks you to do, and if I catch you stealing or destroying anything, I will not only prosecute you, I will personally kick your butt." Sterling paused and leaned closer, waiting until Simon, out of sheer curiosity, looked him in the eye. Then he said softly, "And you do not want to test me on that."

It was clear to Joshua that Sterling had experience dealing with what might be considered the rougher element, and he could see from the grudging respect on Simon's face that Sterling's tactics had been effective.

Sterling straightened up. "So, as long as you work hard and earn it, I'll sign off on your hours and give you a paycheck for it. Fair enough?"

His face lighting into a grin in spite of himself, Simon spoke up: "That's cool." Though he tried to hide it, there was a sense of satisfaction around Simon that made him seem taller.

"You want to start now, or tomorrow?" Sterling asked.

"I got nothing else to do today."

"All right. Grab some work gloves out of the truck and start unloading those plants. Let's line them up along here, and then we'll dig the holes and I'll show you how to prepare the soil mixture." Sterling waited until the boy had walked away before asking Joshua, "What's the deal?"

By way of explanation, Joshua just said, "I ran into him working on a crew when I was hiking, and then I saw him walking down from the camp by himself. Nobody even to pick him up?" Joshua shrugged. "I figured he could use a little help."

Sterling looked over to the truck where the young man was enthusiastically pulling the black plastic containers and their contents out of the bed and said, "That's for damn sure." Then he narrowed his eyes at Joshua. "There's more to it than that, isn't there?" When Joshua nodded but said nothing, he sighed. "Just be careful. Some of these kids are bad news, and I know you want to help him, but they don't always thank you for it." He watched Simon again before adding, "I should know." The last statement was spoken so softly that Joshua felt he had eavesdropped on a private thought and, pretending he hadn't heard, turned quickly away.

Chapter II

The air in the upstairs room of Greer's house was tinted with sweet-smelling smoke that rose in animated paisley curls from a small brazier before dispersing into the atmosphere. It was the smoke of lotus oil and althea leaves, dropped and crushed onto the small circular charcoal that burned, sparking and graying, on the tiny brass grill.

On a purple cloth in front of the brazier, Greer had placed two items. She now picked up the first of these, a small leaf from a live oak, and turned it slowly in the smoke, making sure every surface was touched by the energy she saw imbued in the pearl gray tendrils.

When Greer was satisfied with that step, she placed the leaf carefully into a small bowl, the bottom of which was filled with oil she had made herself, steeping it with sage and rosemary until the mixture was a thick, pungent green. She held the leaf submerged until it was completely saturated, then laid it on the purple cloth and took up the second item, an acorn, repeating the ritual with first the smoke and then the oil.

And as she worked, she kept intoning the same words over and over under her breath: "Safe from harm. Safe from harm. Safe from harm." The words merged together until they were almost indistinguishable from each other and became more of a chant than a phrase.

Moving slowly, her eyes fixed, almost trancelike, on the slow dance of white smoke, Greer finished the first part of her task. Next she opened a blue silk bag, about two inches square, and after placing both objects inside of it, she tied it closed with a long, blue ribbon knotted at its ends, creating something like a necklace with a charm. Then she held the silken bag between her palms in a prayer position, the ribbon swaying gently beneath, and closed her eyes.

> *"As the mother, so the child,*
> *Turn all fear and harm aside.*
> *Circle them in golden light,*
> *Protecting them both day and night."*

Three times Greer repeated the verse; then she remained motionless for a long time as the late-afternoon sun infiltrated the room and dropped behind the high canyon walls, lending the partial relief of shadow from October's constant heat.

Finally, with a deep, filling breath, Greer opened her eyes and looked at the small talisman that she held in her hand. There was one thing left to do. Standing, she went to an old wooden box in which she kept her most treasured objects and took out a small knife with a blade that glinted gold as she held it up in the dusky light. Placing its sharp point against the pad of her middle finger, she pressed down, hard and fast. A drop of blood rose from the tiny puncture, and Greer pressed it into the fabric, where it was quickly absorbed into a circular stain with tiny, fluted edges.

Greer felt the energy pass from her body like an electric shock. With a strong exhalation, she dropped to her knees and leaned limply forward onto her hands to steady herself. A few deep breaths later, she was able to stand again, though she felt slightly light-headed.

The sensation would pass, she knew, and it was with the sense of having done all she could that she pocketed the charm and went cautiously down the stairs.

Joshua was at the refrigerator, filling a huge cup with ice and water. He gulped it down eagerly and then started to refill. "Hi, Mom," he said.

"Hi, sweetie. Did you have a hard day?" She sank

down onto one of the wooden chairs at the large oak
table and rested her head on her hands.

"Actually," answered Joshua, "it turned out to be a
pretty decent one." He was thinking of how Simon had
shown up again and wondering if that was actually good
or bad, but then he frowned, noticing his mother's unusual lethargy. "It was hot."

Greer blinked heavily and she smiled at her son a bit
wanly. "Yes, it was. Still is, actually."

"Are you okay?" Joshua asked. "You look really
tired."

"I'll be fine in a little while. I just borrowed a little
energy to lend to a friend. By the time I go to bed, I'll
be my old, peppy self."

"Good timing."

"I thought so." Greer smiled at him, mustering enough
verve to dispel some of his concern.

"Tell you what," he offered, "why don't I make dinner?" He opened the refrigerator door and started to
rummage around. "What've we got in here?"

"I bought fresh pasta and there're veggies. I was planning on making primavera."

"That sounds great. I think I can handle that. You,
uh, fry the pasta, right?" Joshua, who had always loved
to cook, tossed a grin over his shoulder at his mom and
started pulling peppers and onions from the crisper.

"I'm sure you could." Greer mustered a little laugh.
"So, what made the day a good one?"

Placing his fresh finds on the butcher block, Joshua
glanced at his mother and reached again into the fridge.
He came up with a pitcher of iced tea, which he mixed
with some peach nectar in a tall glass, and put it in her
hand before he answered.

"Well, you know I've been trying to learn to control
what I see," he began hesitantly. Even though his mother
understood his sensitivities perfectly, Joshua still felt
self-conscious talking about it at all. "I ran into this kid
when I was hiking. He was working with one of the fire-
camp crews, and I saw something near him, and . . ."

Joshua fumbled a little, feeling color come to his face. This all sounded so ridiculous now. "Well, you know how you tell me that I should see what kind of feeling I get from the images, and I got a really bad feeling from this one." He glanced up at his mom to see if she was skeptical.

But he should have known better. She was watching him thoughtfully, her brow creased in focused attention. "Really?" she asked. "Did you block it?"

Her matter-of-fact tone made it so much easier for Joshua. It was as though they were discussing buying a new car. "Yeah. I mean, I did the white-light-circle thing you told me about. It seemed to work," he said, though it still felt strange to him that he was actually having this conversation. Then, as his mother's eyes blinked sleepily again, a thought hit him. "Hey," he said suspiciously, "how come it's all right for you to tire yourself out 'lending energy' and I'm supposed to block anything negative?"

Greer sighed and sat up a little straighter. "It's not the same thing," she explained. "When I make a talisman for someone, I sometimes, though very rarely, put some of my own energy into it. The reason I do it so rarely is because it does cost me. Also, I'm putting positive energy in. That's not the same as taking on negative energy. The gifts we have are different. Mine is all future, and yours is, well, so far it seems to be all in the present."

Joshua picked up a sharp knife and started chopping the vegetables. He muttered, "If dead people *can* be present."

"They can, and they are, to you," Greer said firmly. "Now, what they really are—if it's some energy people have left behind, or just another way that the infinite universe communicates with you—you might never know."

"I'll never understand it, that's for damn sure," Joshua said in an exasperated voice, and raising the knife in the air, he brought it down with a *thwack* that split an onion

cleanly in half. "And I don't want it either. All I want
is to learn how to control it so I can pick a major and
not be a freak at college."

"But exactly *what* it is doesn't matter," Greer said
reassuringly, nudging forward the argument that he'd
been given this gift for reason. "What's important is
that you can use it to help people, if—and when—you
choose to."

Joshua continued chopping with slightly more force
than necessary. "But that's the thing, isn't it? I don't
really seem to have a choice." The chunks of onion were
becoming increasingly smaller and the gases that the action released were rising to sting his eyes, until tears
began to blur his vision. Joshua wiped at them furiously
and then resumed his attack on the hapless root vegetable.

Greer stood up and moved slowly across the kitchen
to Joshua. She took the knife from his hand and scraped
the now-minced onions into a frying pan she pulled
down from an overhead rack, then set it aside. Then she
lit a candle and stood it on the chopping block; the flame
quickly burned away the irritating vapors. "I know it
seems that way, and I understand you feel compelled to
help. But I don't believe that's always the reason the
images appear. Sometimes, maybe an energy just wants
to say hello."

"Not this one." Joshua snorted. "I never felt anything
like this before. Usually, no, almost always, the human
figures that I see are . . . Oh, what's the word?" Joshua
racked his mental dictionary to find the right definition.
"Benevolent," he said, finding it. "They want to help or
hang around, or they just sort of stand there beaming at
me or the person I see them over. Sometimes they show
me something, and I get the feeling that whatever it is
has meaning for the person they are with. But this was
very different. It was *evil*."

Greer was watching her son, concerned. "In what
way?" she asked softly.

"Well, he was kind of glaring at this kid, as though

he wanted to hurt him, to get at him. I felt like it was a really strong influence."

His mother was nodding. "There's another difference between us. I believe that I see an image of the evil intention itself. I see it as a color or a shape, like a jagged piece of glass. But energy can't come from nowhere. It has to be generated. Maybe you are seeing the source of some kind of evil that is affecting this kid." She cocked her head to one side and asked, "Does that feel like it could be right?"

Joshua stood in the kitchen and thought about it. "Ye-es, I guess so."

Greer took her son's hand and led him to the table, where they sat down next to each other. "Listen to me. You have to be very careful. You are not responsible for the things you see—"

"But that's why I hate this! I feel like I have to try to help him!" Joshua said, frustrated. "Like I have no choice!"

"I know," Greer soothed, "but listen to me. *Altering energy by using your own is very dangerous.*" She gazed intently into his eyes.

"You do it!" he said accusingly.

"I know, but like I said, not very often, and I'm very aware of the cost, and I'm very careful not to give too much. You don't know what too much is yet."

Joshua dropped his eyes and nodded. They sat for a moment in silence and then he spoke: "I met him again today. I picked him up on the road and Sterling gave him a job. I think that was a pretty big coincidence, don't you?"

Greer leaned forward and kissed her son on the top of his blond head. "No. I don't believe in coincidences." She took a deep breath and let it out with an exasperated sound. Joshua looked up at her, surprised. "Okay, maybe you are supposed to help this kid. What's his name?"

"Simon."

"Simon. Right. But you have to go slow; you're just learning. Actually we both are."

"I know. I've got some help anyway." Joshua grinned at his mom. "There's a little dog that's doing its damnedest to keep the bad guy back."

Greer smiled warmly for a moment, and then her face tightened with worry again. "What do you think the spirit—" Joshua winced at the word *spirit,* so she added, "If that's what it is, wants from Simon?"

"I don't know," Joshua said, shaking his head thoughtfully. "I'm probably crazy, but I know what I *think* it is." He looked up at his mom, and the concern in her eyes gave him the confidence to speak his fear. "I think it wants him dead."

Chapter 12

Even at dawn the temperature was uncomfortable, but Greer had promised Jenny she'd go riding with her, and this was the only part of the day when that would be possible. Jenny had picked her up in the pitch dark, and they had made the drive up the canyon under a sky of dimming stars. Now Greer brushed down the horse that Mindy had lent her, a sweet-natured mare named Buttermilk, with a fond hand. It had been years since she'd ridden. She and her husband, Geoffrey, had gone often when they'd been married; she had loved the sensation of riding the forested trails near their home, and the warm smell of hay and horses was sending a flood of sweet memories back to her.

She finished brushing out Buttermilk's mane and then went to lift the heavy western saddle from its rack for Jenny.

"Sorry to have to ask you to do that," Jenny said, watching Greer heave the saddle onto King's back jealously. Her normal pride in her self-sufficiency was suffering a major hit.

"No problem, and remember you promised: an easy ride, nothing too strenuous."

Jenny laughed and massaged her compact, circular tummy. "I know, I know. The doctor said I *was* only allowed to walk the horse, and I *wasn't* allowed to fall off the horse. I told him I could just walk beside the horse, but he told me to ride him. In this heat, he'd rather King do the work than me. People who don't know King seem to think I'm taking some awful risk, but Dr. Blackwood just pooh-poohs all that. He said, 'As long as you're fine, the baby's fine.' "

"I know. Everyone wants to give you advice, like they all know better than you about how to take care of yourself when you're pregnant. 'Don't walk, don't bike-ride, don't take a hot bath, don't eat purple food.' Most of it is just old wives' tales. I hiked though Joshua's whole gestation, including four miles the day he was born!"

"It's only the people who never exercise before they get pregnant who are afraid to, and probably shouldn't. Dr. Blackwood says I have as much chance hurting the baby tripping up a stair as I do sitting on a walking horse. And when I told him I get anxious and feel terrible when I don't go, he said, 'Go! The baby probably enjoys the rocking sensation.' He did say that I should probably sit it out for the last month. So I've got two weeks left." She smiled down and patted her stomach.

"What if he were to spook and you fell off?" Greer asked, trying to disguise the unease that her premonition had given her.

Jenny walked around behind King. She stood there for a moment and then, without warning, she let out a bloodcurdling scream. Greer jumped six inches in the air and her hair stood on end. King's ears went back, but nothing else so much as twitched. Then, very slowly, his head swiveled on his powerful neck to see what in hell this crazy human was up to.

"But I guess that's not likely to happen," Greer observed.

"No," Jenny said. "This horse has come face-to-hoof with a six-foot rattlesnake stretched out in the sun and stepped politely over it. I didn't even see it until it was behind us. He was a working roper. He's stood still while bulls—big ones with horns—stampeded toward him. The guy who owned him before me did six-gun shooting events from his back. It would take a bomb to spook this guy. I think we're good." She looked seriously at Greer. "You know that if I thought there was any chance I would hurt this baby, I wouldn't be here. I'd be home in bed with the door locked."

"Can't live like that," Greer said. She tried to keep the shadow she felt in her heart from crossing her face. Instead, she felt in her pocket for the charm she had made and pulled it out. "Speaking of which," she said, holding up the small silk sack, "I made you and the baby something."

Once before Greer had made a talisman for Jenny. That one had been to ease the strain between her and her husband. Because of the strong, existing love between the two, it had not required any of Greer's personal strength, only a reawakening of the bonds between the couple. This was different.

But Jenny didn't know that, only that her relationship with Lewis had flourished after she received the charm. When she saw the tiny pouch suspended from Greer's hand, she looked absolutely delighted. "Oh, thank you. What's it for?"

"Protection, mostly," Greer said, trying to sound light. "Happiness, harmony, the usual."

As she took it and cradled it like a pearl in her hands, Jenny asked, "What's in it?" in a whisper, as though the contents were a secret.

"A few different things," Greer said evasively. "You can either wear it around your neck, or keep it in your pocket. But it will work best if you have it near you, for now anyway. Later you can throw it in a drawer and the energy will still stay with you."

Jenny had raised it to her face. "It smells good," she complimented, and then pulled the cord over her head and let the pouch fall down under her T-shirt. "If it works as well as the last one you gave me, I'm not ever taking it off. Thank you."

"You're welcome," Greer told her sincerely as she said a silent prayer that her small act of sheltering would be enough, would hold against whatever force she had detected over her friend.

"Okay, let's get going before it's too damn toasty to

go at all!" Jenny said, and turned to put the bridle on King, her huge black gelding. The horse stood almost seventeen hands high, and, gentle though he was, a sense of sheer power radiated from his powerful flanks and alert black eyes.

Soon, both horses were saddled and ready to go. Greer unhooked the docile Buttermilk from the cross ties and led her out of the barn. The first rays of the sun fell into the canyon where Mindy and Reading's ranch sat nestled in a prime area of softer rolling land between rugged hills.

"Oh," Greer said, "I left my helmet. Here, hold Buttermilk." She handed the reins to Jenny and hurried back into the barn. She strode down the long corridor, open at both ends, to where she'd left the riding helmet Mindy had lent her on a hook near the tack room. Even as she walked, the slanting morning sun entered the far end and illuminated the wood of the first stall. It glowed with a red-orange haze. Something about it made Greer pause in her step. As she reached for the helmet, she caught the toe of her boot on the slanted concrete of the floor and lost her balance. She stumbled forward, put up her hands to brace herself against the wood walls, and gasped.

The wood against her palms was so hot that she pulled them away in alarm. "What the . . . ?" In confusion, she reached out gingerly again and touched a finger to the wood. It felt normal, only as warm as the sultry air around it. Yet she had felt a searing heat, she was sure; her palms were still stinging from it. Greer stood for a moment, looking up and down the barn, wondering what had just happened.

Before she had time to think about it, Jenny called out from outside, "Are you coming? It's getting hot already!"

"I'm coming," Greer called back. She gave the corridor one more appraising look. Everything seemed fine, normal, still. Once more, Greer laid a tentative hand on the wall next to the helmet. Tepid. With a shake of her head, she removed the helmet from its hook and buckled it on as she went to rejoin Jenny, who mounted with care from a step.

"You look good on that horse. When did you start riding?" Greer asked her.

Jenny sighed and a bittersweet look came to her face. "When I was about eleven, things at home weren't so good. I read all the time, as an escape, and I fell in love with horse stories. So, anyway, I started going to the stables at Griffith Park—it was only two bus rides away—and hanging out, asking people if I could help with their horses, that kind of thing. There was this one nice lady—her name was Maudine. She told me that if I shoveled out her horse's stall every day, she'd give me a lesson for a half hour once a week." Jenny paused and smiled. "His name was Texas." She twisted up her face thoughtfully and said, "You know, it's funny: I never thought of it this way before, but maybe that's why I was able to fight someone bigger and stronger than me, because I had learned how to handle an unruly horse." Greer remained silent. Jenny had never told her about her abusive past, and she would wait until she was ready to share it. Jenny went on. "That barn was my escape from hell. I spent all my time there. Even tried sleeping there once, but they caught me. Anyway, things changed. I grew up and got interested in boys and got married, but I always promised myself that one day I'd have a horse of my own, just like Texas. And it still amazes me that I remembered and that I can." She patted King's muscular neck and turned away from Greer, who thoughtfully said nothing about her friend's tears.

"Well, you're a natural-born cowgirl," Greer offered softly.

They were headed down toward the now-dry riverbed when they passed a large storage shed. Along the back of it, mounted on the wall facing the increasingly brutal morning sun, were dozens of sets of antlers, some of larger game, possibly elk, but most were the smaller, more graceful remains of deer. There were also several hides nailed to the wooden exterior. Greer felt a shiver go through her.

"I call it the wall of death," Jenny said grimly. "Just don't look at it." They rode on past all that now remained of the once magnificent, peaceful creatures, sobered by the sight.

"Can't say I understand that," Greer said, though she tried to. "I mean, I think it's a good thing in some ways. I'm assuming that Reading and Mindy actually eat what they kill?"

"I think so," Jenny told her with a sour face. "I shouldn't be critical. I eat venison, and if I'm willing to eat it, I suppose I should realize that somebody's got to kill it."

"True enough," Greer agreed. "With today's buying everything sanitized and cellophane wrapped at the grocery store, we've lost touch with where our food comes from, and there's something to be said for doing it consciously." She glanced back at the large number of racks jutting like dead branches from the side of the building. "But it seems like you'd have to enjoy the killing to have that many."

"I suppose it's the primitive hunter part of them. The joy of stalking and the thrill of the kill. Some people like it," Jenny offered.

Yes, thought Greer soberly, *some people do.*

Chapter 13

Leah Falconer looked across her desk at Susan Hughs. The woman's style was expensive without any apparent ostentation.

"So the loan will be received in two installments," Susan was saying, "the first fourteen million on execution of the agreement, the second on the first day of construction." Susan Hughs always spoke, Leah noticed, as though it was a done deal.

Leah leaned back in her chair and pretended to review the papers in the file on her lap. The small office that she had taken over since her promotion to branch manager seven months ago suited her, and she liked being able to shut the door. She had taken some time to review the paperwork before Susan came in, and she was very familiar with the terms of the existing loan, having written it herself, and she knew that the Hughses' company, Golden Door, had made all its payments on a timely basis and the deal had been a profitable one for the bank. "You'll be using the project and the land itself as collateral?"

"Of course," Susan said with a smooth smile.

"How's the first phase selling?" Leah asked, unable to keep a twinge from twisting her chest. Though she had structured the loan deal, and been proud of it, the irony had not been lost on her that from her own home, far above Foothill Boulevard, she had been forced to oversee the harsh reality of its manifestation from attractive deal on paper to actual physical effect. The green, undulating hillsides across the valley from her, once so beautiful in their natural state, had been scraped of vegetation and flattened by land movers until they resembled nothing so much as a postapocalyptic wasteland. Each day she had felt the further scarring of the earth like a wound that wouldn't heal. She had watched, unable to avoid the view from her living room window, as week by week her once-beautiful view had been leveled, paved, and covered with the frames of over two hundred homes, while next to them phase two had begun, with the inevitable evisceration of the landscape. It had been like watching a bunch of thugs work over a victim, leaving her for dead.

The deal had helped her professional career, there was no doubt about that, and career advancement had been the sole focus of Leah's life in the past couple of years since her divorce. She knew that her clout in the banking community had risen considerably with the Golden Door deal and several others, and she was utterly amazed at the absolute lack of satisfaction she had received from it. She had achieved one of her many goals, branch manager, and was well on her way to rising again in the corporate ranks, yet the victories felt hollow. She wondered, as she sat across from the accomplished Susan Hughs, if it was different for her. After all, Susan had a husband, a partner, someone to share her triumphs and her life with.

Leah shook herself out of it and tried to focus on the deal. She was vaguely aware that Susan had been telling her that phase one was almost sold out and they had begun presales on phase two, which offered even better views because of its superior location.

"Of course," Susan was saying, "only the homes on the south-facing streets will have that view, but we've graded the hillsides so that each street has a seventeen-foot-altitude increase, and the homes are placed the minimum required feet apart, maximizing the number of homes that can take advantage of the view."

"And your profit," Leah said, trying to make it sound like a compliment.

Susan took it as one. "Naturally." She winked. "We're not in this just for the fun of it." Leaning forward, she placed one hand on the table and said conspiratorially, "Are we?"

Distinctly uncomfortable, Leah looked down again at the proposal in her hand; a request for twenty-eight million dollars and change, on a ten-year loan. "I take it you've got the zoning approval in place?"

"I will," Susan said with iron in her voice. "There's one detail I have to sort out, but it won't be a problem."

"My understanding," said Leah, fully aware that she was voicing more of a personal concern than a business one, "is that the city council was concerned about traffic and emergency vehicle access. Since there will be only one route in and out of the entire development."

"Oh, I've got that worked out," Susan said dismissively, standing and closing her slim Prada briefcase. "You deal with the bank's board of trustees, and I'll take care of the city council." She reached across the desk and shook Leah's hand with so much confidence that Leah had to exert considerable pressure to equal the force of the squeeze. "We're a good team," Susan was saying. "I really enjoy working with you." She paused and took a moment to give Leah an approving look. "You're going to go far," she said. "I can see that." Then, with a last nod, she turned and left the office.

Leah, who had risen with her client, stood watching the door after it had closed behind Susan with the distinct knowledge that she'd just been worked. While she felt the compliment of being told she would be successful by a woman who clearly knew what that meant, Leah wasn't stupid or naïve enough to think that Susan Hughs was a woman who handed out compliments just to be nice. There was no doubt in Leah's mind that the woman who had just left her office did absolutely nothing without knowing the cause and effect back to herself.

With a sigh Leah realized that Susan was exactly the kind of woman she had always envisioned herself becoming. Susan Hughs was beautifully presented, sharp as a rapier, and uncompromisingly aggressive, and she made it all seem effortless, a trick Leah had yet to pull off. Leah had made progress, but it had always felt like a muddy, uphill struggle in heavy rain. This woman was a doer and a leader. There was absolutely no question that Susan Hughs was—and would continue to be—a success. She was everything that Leah had always wanted to be.

So why did she find the woman so distasteful?

As if to escape the uncomfortable thought, Leah left the office with the pretense of checking the floor. She went out into the tellers' area, sectioned off by thick bulletproof glass and a buzzer door to the main floor. Three tellers were at their stations, and as she watched their performances with an appraising eye, the street doors opened and someone new entered.

Something about the new arrival's shape and walk arrested Leah's attention. Her head shot up to stare at him, and her mouth fell open in amazement as she watched Weston Oakmont look around the floor, then walk to the desk where Leah's friend Towler, recently promoted to new accounts, sat across from an elderly couple.

She couldn't hear the following exchange across the room and through the glass, but she saw Weston address Towler, who then looked around and spotted her. He gestured Weston to one of the couches on the side of the room, then seemed to excuse himself from the couple seated with their backs to her. With his eyes fixed on Leah, he pointedly picked up his phone. She heard the buzzer on the phone go off in the office behind her.

Back behind the desk with her door firmly shut, Leah fumbled to pick it up and tried to sound casual. "Yes?"

"Hi, it's me," Towler said. "There's someone asking for you." He made the statement sound like a playground tease.

"Oh? Who?" Leah struggled to maintain her calm.

"He gave his name as a Mr. Oakmont, but personally I think he must be some kind of minor deity once removed. Don't you dare pretend you didn't see him." Towler, who was gay and never missed a chance to com-

ment on the physical attributes of the bank's more attractive customers, had been trying to entice Leah to get
out and improve her social life for the two years he had
known her. Since Leah hadn't dated since her divorce,
he'd had scant opportunity to exercise his prowess with
licentious jibes, a skill he'd been perfecting since his
early teens. She could hear his pleasure in the rare occasion now.

"Towler, are you being professional?" She tried to
sound stern, but she couldn't help but forgive him. He'd
always been a splash of colorful fun on an otherwise
spanking-white environment.

"Certainly not!" he snorted. "I consider that I have
maintained my amateur status. But I'd go pro for this
one."

"Please ask him to wait. I'll be right out." Leah hung
up the phone and took a few deep breaths. Why was
Weston here? Could he have come in for business reasons? Maybe he wanted to open a local account while
he was here, or cash a large check and was hoping for
her to approve it. But that didn't make any sense; his
check would be government issued and therefore cash-
able at any bank. Could he have come in to see her
personally? Leah found she was hyperventilating, and
she had to put her head down between her legs for a
few moments. She hoped that no one would come in
and see her in this undignified position before she could
pull herself together.

But the door remained mercifully closed as she sucked
air into her lungs until she was able to slow her breathing and regain at least a semblance of control. A debilitating panic had risen unreasonably in her. It wasn't him,
of course; she didn't know Weston personally, but her
last experience with a man had been so bad, so abusive
and violent, that . . .

"Okay," she told herself out loud. "Get it together.
It's just a guy, albeit a very cute guy. You manage a
bank, you own a home, you can prorate annuities at a
variety of interests. You can do this."

She didn't really believe it, but having no choice, she

checked her lipstick in a small vanity mirror that she kept in her desk, paused for a deep calming breath, and then threw open her office door, asked a teller to buzz her out, and strode onto the floor with all the bravado she could muster.

But as she went, she couldn't stop comparing the walk to a quick trip down the plank. She was painfully regretting the fact that she had chosen a rather bland outfit today: a gray suit with a white silk shirt. Weston stood as she approached and Towler swiveled in his chair to watch her as she passed, like a sunflower tracks the sun across the sky. She shot Towler what she hoped was a stern look of reproach, and then extended a hand. "Mr. Oakmont. How nice to see you again." She was chagrined to find that his hand felt very warm and dry, which must have meant that hers was cold and clammy; she tried to ignore her subsequent mortification. "How can I help you?"

Weston looked around at Towler and the older couple, who were clearly listening from two yards away, and dropped his voice when he spoke. "Actually, I, uh . . . It isn't bank business." He smiled and shrugged apologetically, and Leah thought she would melt from the charm of his obvious, and very disarming, discomfort. Was he nervous about coming to see her? "I was wondering, if it's not too presumptuous," he continued in something just above a whisper, causing her to lean in until she felt a blush of heat rising from her skin, "if you might like to have lunch, or just coffee, whatever, with me sometime?" He looked endearingly uncertain of her response.

"Excuse me," came a voice from behind Leah. Thrown, she turned to see the elderly couple rising from their seats. "Are you one of the firemen who worked on the fire up at Oak Springs?"

Weston turned his attention and professional face to them. "Yes, ma'am, I am." He addressed the woman, who had asked the question.

It was the elderly man who stepped forward now, extending a hand and a warm smile from a beaming, grate-

ful face. "We just want to thank you. It was our home
that you saved, and we can't tell you how much it means
to us. You gentlemen were just amazing."

"Wonderful," chimed in his wife, and while Weston
thanked them and shook their hands, Leah watched with
a growing feeling of exclusion. Something was being
shared that she didn't even understand, and it left her
feeling dull witted, as though her head were full of sand.

"We didn't mean to interrupt you," the woman said
to Weston, patting his arm. "You go right ahead with
your business"—she cut a sly, knowing look at Leah—
"but if you're ever up Oak Springs, you drop in for some
iced tea and cake."

"Thank you. I'd really like that," Weston told her,
and he sounded sincere. "I'm very happy that we were
able to help. It's always good to win one."

Unable to restrain himself, Towler had come to join
the small group, hovering just outside the circle. Now he
stepped in and gestured to the elderly pair. "Leah, these
are the Caseys. Emily and Larry, this is Leah Falconer,
our branch manager." Leah shook hands all around, putting off her response to Weston's invitation and feeling
his eyes on her as she went through the more familiar
motions that until a moment ago had made her feel
important. She asked what had brought in the Caseys
today.

"We were interested in finding out about the loan
rates, and how much we could afford to pay."

"The Caseys don't have a mortgage. Their home is
paid off," Towler explained.

"And you want to move?" Leah asked perfunctorily.
"I think you'll find our rates are very competitive
and—"

"No, we don't want to move," Larry said quickly.
"We want to stay right in the house where we raised
our kids, but after that fire . . ." He shook his head.
"Emily wants to find out if we could afford to, and I
can't say I blame her."

Leah felt a spark of something snap her professional
crust like a dry twig. Instead of her usual tendency to

file customers in categories of size of loan and potential profit, she looked at the faces of these simple people and was moved to think of them as, well, people, with lives and feelings. The thought took her off guard. It was apparent from their rough hands and unassuming faces that this man and this woman had worked hard their whole lives. They had built a home, paid off the mortgage, and should be able to enjoy their remaining years; that was how it was supposed to work. She felt outrage that someone could thoughtlessly, or even deliberately, rob them of their peace of mind.

She reached out impulsively and did something she hadn't done in a long time: She took Emily's hand in hers. "If you decide that's what you want to do, I promise you that we will help you find the very best rates." She smiled at the look of relief, and surprise, on Emily's face. With an inner shudder, Leah realized that these kind people hadn't expected anyone at a bank to take a personal interest—and yesterday, they would have been right.

"Oh, thank you," the elderly woman told her, squeezing Leah's hand gratefully. "We were starting to think that we should have taken that offer from the real estate agent when someone wanted to buy the place a year ago but we told her we'd never sell. Maybe we should have jumped at the chance. I don't think many people these days want a place that doesn't even have city water. Especially with all those fancy new homes going up nearby, I don't know who'd buy it."

Weston spoke up now: "That's a very beautiful spot you've got there, Emily. And I believe there're still people who value peace and quiet. You might have to look for the right buyer, but I bet you'd do okay. If that's what you decide." He smiled reassuringly. Then his voice dropped and Leah watched him make eye contact with Larry. "But it sure would be a shame to give it up."

For a second, Leah thought that the old man was going to cry. Then with a sniff and a jut of his chin he thanked everyone, accepted Towler's card, and led his wife toward the glass doors.

Leah watched them for as long as she could before she had to turn back to the two men. Her first look was a warning to Towler. She smiled thinly and asked, "Don't you have some papers to file?"

"No," he said with a bright smile. "Nothing pressing." He looked from her to Weston and back again, openly wearing a look of enthusiastic voyeurism. The only thing he didn't do, Leah thought, was rub his hands together or twirl his mustache.

"Find something," she suggested flatly.

"Aw, man!" Towler protested comically, but he went.

"I'm sorry for the distraction," Leah said, and was uncertain whether to wait for Weston to repeat his request or pretend that he hadn't made it.

"So?" Weston asked with a small self-conscious smile. *Damn, he's handsome,* Leah couldn't help thinking. For the few seconds while she admired him physically, she was perfectly all right, but when she realized that a response was required and a positive one would mean spending time with a man she didn't know, with whom she didn't have the safety net of professional boundaries, she was seized once again by an irrational shortness of breath and nervous tremors in her chest. "Well, I, uh, I don't really date," she said lamely.

"I see. I'm sorry, but your friend at the coffee shop, Jenny?" Leah nodded. "She seemed to think you might. I'm sorry if I interrupted your day." He truly looked it.

Leah felt as though she were standing at the edge of a bottomless crevasse and Weston, though only a few feet away, were on the other side of it. The only way across would be to launch herself out over a terrifying depth, in which lay dangers and fears—some half-imagined, some only half-hidden in the darkness below—and stepping off the edge would mean facing those things. But as he began to turn away, Leah suddenly felt that standing safely on her side would be the scariest, most terrible fate of all.

"Wait," she called out before he'd gone two steps. "I mean, I haven't dated in a long time, and I'm sure I'm not very good at it, obviously. . . ." she fumbled again, feeling her face redden with the hated sensation of being out of control.

But Weston had turned back and was waiting patiently. He said softly, "It's okay if you don't date."

I've blown it, Leah thought, and the disappointment was so surprisingly heavy that she bowed her head under its weight.

"Do you eat?" Weston asked. "I mean, we don't have to date. We could just eat a meal together. Talk a little. I'm new around here, and you probably know just about everybody and every business; maybe you could fill me in on what's what in the neighborhood."

He had offered her a safe alternative. Leah looked into those late-afternoon blue eyes and said, "I could do *that*." And for the first time since her horrible marriage, she believed that she could.

Chapter 14

"This one's magnificent," Sterling said to Joshua and Simon. The three of them had driven out to the phase-two site of the Golden Door development to take a look at it. The naked earth, stripped of any living thing, was jarring enough in small patches, but this, almost fifty acres, was disturbing to both Sterling and Joshua. Simon's reaction was much harder to read. He hung back from the other two, following behind them as they paced along the dry, broken bits of earth, from one terraced swath to the next, and kicking at clods of dirt with a slight scowl on his face. The wind had come up again, and the dust, churned up from the defenseless ground, clogged their noses and stung their eyes.

Below them, a Range Rover pulled up the graded but unpaved road and parked next to Sterling's pickup. Susan Hughs got out and, shading her eyes to look up at them, gave them a wave, and then she opened the back of her car and changed her obviously expensive heels for more practical footwear. Clad in the unlikely combination of a well-tailored suit skirt and work boots, she started up the slope. "Hi! I'm glad you could meet me. What do you think of the site?" she asked Sterling when she got to the top. "Great view, huh?"

"Yes, it's a lovely view," Sterling answered, sidestepping telling her what he thought of the site as a whole. "I was just commenting on this gorgeous tree. I'm glad you saved the oaks."

Susan looked around at the sparse spattering of trees

that still stood on the crumbled, parched earth. Her pretty face soured. "So ridiculous," she mumbled. "The county came and tagged the trees we had to leave. Now we have to work around them. I can't tell you what that costs us." She shook her head as though the idiocy was beyond her understanding. "I mean, we're planning on planting lots of fast-growing saplings, maybe some pepper trees, and within five years, they'll be as big as this one!"

Joshua could see a vein on Sterling's brow begin to throb, and he knew the self-possession it took for him to respond so calmly. "I don't think so," Sterling said to Susan. "This tree trunk is huge. My best guess is it's been here more than seven hundred years. That's before Columbus came to America. Think about that for a minute. This tree has been standing here looking at this view for centuries before any Europeans glimpsed it." He was speaking clearly, but Susan did not seem to be absorbing any of it. He added quietly, "Not to mention long before they decided they could parcel it off and own it."

"It is a great view, and that's what's going to sell, sell, sell these houses." She looked at the tree again and frowned. "This one is right in a prime spot. Typical. So, anyway"—she seemed to brighten—"we thought we should sort of feature it, light it up from underneath and make the walls for the two yards on either side sort of angled to leave it in the middle. You would see it from the approach. If we have to keep it, we can at least use it as a selling point."

"Let me think about it." Sterling turned away at her callous apathy and walked under the tree. As Joshua watched, Sterling laid a hand on the trunk. Above his head, the branches arched gracefully from the huge trunk and almost brushed the ground, forming an open yet protected space, a natural cathedral.

Joshua joined him and they shared a pained look before Sterling walked back to continue his discussion with Susan. Motioning to Simon with a jerk of his head to come out of the sun and leave the two grown-ups to their debating, Joshua walked under the shade of the oak and leaned one hand against the trunk of the tree. As he did so, a vision came suddenly into his mind. It was a shape really, of a web in simple, fragile black lines. He pulled his hand away and the image disappeared.

Almost simultaneously, the sound of shots rang out across the canyon. Though they were clearly distant, Joshua noticed how Simon instinctively jerked his arms above his head, as though this was a long-learned reflex.

"What the hell was that?" Simon asked before he was able to recover his practiced indifference.

Joshua shrugged and his face tightened. "Hunters probably. It's the start of the season. Or it could just be some idiots firing off their guns. I find shells all the time when I'm hiking." He was remembering his father telling him how dangerous that kind of trash was for the animals, when a look at the ravaged landscape brought that trail of thought to a screeching halt. Compared with a couple of weeks of bulldozers and gigantic land-moving machines, littering the landscape with toxic lead remnants seemed relatively innocuous.

Simon didn't appear to be listening to him. He was peering down into the shrubbery several hundred yards distant, where it was still thick in a ravine, the area from which the gun retorts seemed to have come. Joshua followed his look, but he could make out nothing.

"Little jumpy, aren't you?" Joshua said, trying to make light of Simon's reaction.

"Shit," was Simon's only response, but he grinned a little sheepishly at Joshua.

Sterling and Susan had walked back to the cars and Sterling was rolling up a blueprint as he called out to them, "Joshua, Simon! Let's go."

As they made their way down the hill, Joshua noticed that Simon fell behind, as though he was keeping Joshua between him and the line of fire, and he reflected that if he'd grown up in a world where people routinely got shot before they were eighteen, he'd probably be gun-shy himself. That must suck, he thought.

Susan was already driving away, spewing clouds of dust and clumps of earth as she sped off.

"So, are you going to take the job?" Joshua asked Sterling, sure that someone with Sterling's interest in both aesthetics and the environment would never allow him to deal with citified developers.

"Yes. Because if I don't," he continued over Joshua's disbelieving expression, "they'll get somebody in here who'll do exactly what they've done at every other site. They'll plant a whole bunch of the cheapest, nonindigenous, water-thirsty, quick-fix shrubbery, and every other plant and animal in at least a ten-mile radius will suffer. At least I can steer them toward blending into the environment, and avoid too many invasive species on the edge of a national forest."

He paused and looked past the huge man-made steppes of dirt that had been gouged into the hillside and then let his eyes rest on the natural folds and creases formed over thousands of years in the remaining undeveloped terrain; then he turned and fixed his disarmingly green eyes on first Joshua, and then Simon. "Sometimes," he said quietly, "we have to do what we *can,* even if it doesn't seem like enough."

They all climbed into the pickup truck and followed in the trail of Susan's dust. They hit the temporary paved road of phase one and drove past seemingly endless frame-ups of houses. For now, Joshua could still see across the valley through their skeletons, but soon, he knew, there would be walls and fences, and anyone passing here would see nothing but garage doors and curtained windows.

To try to ease the claustrophobic feeling, he sat back and adjusted the air-conditioning vent a little more toward his face. They came to the main road, and Sterling stopped to wait for a passing car, looking hard over his left shoulder to see around the curve of the highway. Out of habit, Joshua followed his look and then checked in the other direction.

To his right, in a turn off the road, sat another truck. This one was a large white pickup, and on the side were painted the words FORTRESS SECURITY: THE KEY TO YOUR PEACE OF MIND, in black and gold lettering. But it wasn't the whiteness of the truck or the precision of the lettering that arrested Joshua's stare. It was the blood that dripped down over both. Laid across the hood was a large buck, his swollen tongue lolling out of a mouth opened at an unnatural angle. Standing around the hood looking at the deer were four men in combat fatigues with high-powered rifles sporting long-range sights balanced carelessly over their shoulders.

Joshua felt a strange fluttering in his chest, and an image appeared over the deer. A large gray owl was looking down at the dead animal with round, sad eyes.

"Fuck," breathed Simon, next to him, dispelling the snapshot vision.

"Welcome to fall," Sterling said dryly. "When any good ol' boy with a couple hundred bucks can go to Wal-Mart and get himself a rifle and a hunting permit."

It was legal, Joshua knew. In fact, it was a popular pastime. Yet the scene brought bile to Joshua's mouth. It wasn't the dead deer that moved Joshua particularly. In the end death, he thought, comes to us all. It wasn't the hunting—that too had gone on since the origins of time, and he felt that in a way it was part of the natural order of things. It was the expressions on the faces of these particular men: looks of salacious pleasure and self-congratulation. Even as Joshua watched, two of the men shouldered their lethal weapons and high-fived each other over the body of the dead animal.

In spite of the heat, Joshua shuddered and looked away.

Chapter 15

By midmorning on Wednesday, the temperature had already reached the high nineties, and the continued dry wind added a brown haze to the sky that gave it the hue of coffee-stained gauze. Still, no clouds broke the monotony of the sun's glare.

Even inside the salon, Greer could feel the air conditioners struggling to keep up. She was actually grateful for her small, windowless treatment room and the cool it afforded as she finished up a reflexology treatment by resting her hands lightly on the soles of her client's feet. She remained in that position for a long moment and felt her hands heat up without moving as she focused on clearing any dark energy. Her client was a regular of about fifty named Valerie. She was a happy, relaxed woman, a career mother with a loving husband, and it was a pleasure for Greer to work on someone without hidden recesses of stress and what Greer liked to call city smut. Visualizing for one last time golden light passing up the left side of Valerie's body and down the right, Greer took a deep breath and stood up from her stool near Valerie's feet.

In a soft voice she said, "Take your time getting dressed. I'll be up front."

The trace of a smile on the unlined face and a murmured "Thank you" let Greer know that Valerie wasn't sleeping and would be out before it was time for her next appointment in ten minutes. Greer always left enough breathing room between appointments to allow her clients to ease gently back into the world.

She went out as quietly as possible and walked the short hallway to the main floor of the salon. Dario was so focused on a style that he didn't even glance at her, but Jonathan blew her a kiss hello and she winked at him.

Up front, her receptionist, Celia, was on the phone. Greer felt a sense of accomplishment as she watched Celia confidently juggling appointments in the large book that broke up their days in vertical columns labeled by employee and horizontal lines for each ten minutes. The pages were heavily penciled with names and phone numbers with neat diagonal slashes to indicate the times blocked out, most of them in Celia's tightly grouped writing. The nineteen-year-old had flourished since she began work there, and with Greer's encouragement and willingness to offer a flexible schedule, she had enrolled in a community college where she was now studying for a business degree.

Celia's dark hair was styled by Dario into chunky sections, and it created a flattering frame around her narrow face. The thin, smartly dressed girl hung up the phone and said, "Your one o'clock called and was running late, so I switched her with your four fifteen, who had wanted to add a facial, so I made time by slipping it into the five-thirty slot. Do you want to approve it?"

"No, I'm sure it's fine," Greer told the girl, and reflected happily for a moment that it was wonderful to be able to make that simple statement to Celia without adding on a profusion of reassurances. It felt good, giving someone responsibility that had grown in a few short months into confidence, and it was interesting, Greer thought warmly, to realize that most people really only needed the chance and someone—anyone—to believe in them.

On the sidewalk in front of the salon, a stocky man with a cell phone to his ear paced slowly, passing the window once, then turning and wandering in a preoccu-

pied way back the other direction, before seeming to
lose his momentum and coming to a full stop. He had
his back to the glass doors, but Greer had gotten enough
of a look at him to know that it was Rowland Hughs.
She thought of the darkness she had sensed from Susan
at dinner and suddenly felt compelled to enlist Rowland's help in figuring it out. Greer was quite certain
that Rowland Hughs would be incapable of listening to
any metaphysical explanation of Greer's, but she also
felt certain that he was a loving husband who would
welcome · some stress relief for his obviously over-
worked wife.

So straightening her blouse and donning a pleasant
smile, Greer went to the door and opened it. Rowland
was scowling as he snapped his phone closed, but when
he spotted Greer, his amiable face regained its pleasant,
boyish expression. "Hi there!" He came forward quickly
and shook Greer's hand.

"Nice to see you again," she said sincerely. The man
had an enthusiasm about him that made him impossible
to dislike. "What are you doing over here?"

Rowland looked up at the painted words on the door
that she was still holding open, half in the cool of the
air-conditioned salon, and half in the shake-and-bake
heat. They read: EYE OF THE BEHOLDER BEAUTY SALON
AND DAY SPA. He smiled at her. "Oh, that's right—your
'curl up and dye' is right next to Mr. Fincher's office. I
remember now."

"My . . . what?" Greer asked, confused.

"Curl up and dye, d-y-e, not d-i-e." He grinned like
an eleven-year-old who just told a good joke. "That's
what my girls used to call beauty shops when they were
growing up in Florida."

Greer laughed. "That's funny. I'll have to tell Dario
that. Would you like to come in out of the heat?"

"Sure." He looked relieved as he followed her into
the chilled environment. "I was actually looking for your
husband."

"Boyfriend," Greer corrected quickly, almost too
quickly. "We just met a few months ago."

Rowland looked genuinely surprised. "I just assumed. You seem so comfortable together."

She wasn't sure why, but Greer felt a wash of pleasure. It was nice to be recognized as a couple again. It had been a long time. "I take it Sterling isn't in his office?"

"No, and I can't get him on his cell phone; it keeps going to his voice mail. I guess he's on it."

"More likely he's at one of his jobs where there is no service. You must have noticed that cell phone service is splotchy up here."

"Yeah, I noticed. At the new site, there isn't any yet." A shadow crossed his face as though he'd been reminded of something distasteful. "That'll be another improvement for this area: With so many new customers, I'm already talking to the server about putting up a new tower."

Great, thought Greer, *yet another ugly metal interruption in the already fractured sky.* But what she said was, "I think he actually said that he was going out to meet your wife at the, uh, phase two?" she asked uncertainly. She and Sterling didn't share too many mundane details of their work, preferring to focus on shared ideals and interests.

Rowland shook his head. "I wish she would let me do more of that kind of work. That woman just drives herself too hard."

Perfect, an opening, Greer thought. "And speaking of which, I would love to offer her a massage, or a treatment, on me, just as a little introduction to the neighborhood." She laid her hand on Rowland's thick forearm. The smooth fabric of his suit sleeve was still hot from his pause in the sun. "Between you and me, I think it would do her a world of good. I've been in this business a long time, and I think I know when someone is really in need of a little R and R." Greer hoped that she sounded like a coconspirator.

But she needn't have worried. Rowland was already nodding with concerned enthusiasm. "I keep telling her," he said in his quick but distinct southern drawl. "Frankly, I'm worried about her. She's been driving herself so hard on this deal. I know it's important to her—it's the first time she's been above the line on the deal—but you've got to have some balance between work and down time." He pronounced the word *down* with two distinct syllables. Greer thought that it would be easy to misjudge this man as not very bright. She also noted that his eyes were worried. "I know she really thrives on it, but sometimes I just wish she would *relax*."

Greer was a good businesswoman—though it wasn't the aspect of what she did that she enjoyed most—and she knew that *above the line* meant that Susan was in for a portion of the profits, not just a salary. She also knew what that meant to many women who had struggled to break into what were still predominantly male professions; she had many clients who shared their frustrations with her on a daily basis.

"Listen, why don't you insist that she take some time to come in and treat herself. I can do it on a Saturday when there might not be so many other pressing things to do."

Rowland was smiling sadly. "You don't know Susan. She doesn't differentiate between a weekend and a weekday and a holiday. I have to remind her that not everyone who works for or with us is on the same schedule. It bugs the hell out of her." Though he seemed genuinely frustrated, there was an unmistakable note of admiration in his voice.

"Well, I'm sure she loves you very much. Maybe she'll do it if you ask her. I'm here, and I'd like to help if I can."

She could see before she finished the sentence that he had mentally moved to a different subject. "There is something you could maybe help with," he said, and reaching into his coat pocket, he pulled out a single sheet of newsprint, folded several times until only a selected article was exposed. He handed it over to Greer and asked grimly, "Have you seen this?"

It was an editorial in the local paper. Greer had not seen this particular one, but she recognized it as one of a series on a theme, and that theme was being particularly virulent about the Golden Door development project in general and the Hughses in particular. Greer glanced down at the body of the article and spotted the words *disgusting, corporate land-grabbers,* and *disease.*

"No," she said honestly, "I haven't seen this one, but there have been quite a few articles in the local paper. Not everyone is happy about the development; you must know that. I mean, the city council rejected the deal for over two years." Greer watched his face, thinking that this must be par for the course for his business.

"But why?" Rowland asked, looking down at the paper. "I mean, I know there's always some people who object to just about any change, but this guy is demanding a hearing, after we've gotten the approval." He looked up with round, almost childlike eyes at Greer, and she wondered if his naïveté could be sincere.

"What do you want me to do?" Greer asked hesitantly.

"Well, I wondered if you know the guy who wrote this. He's the head of some community action group, and he's gotten the councilwoman to agree to a hearing about the impact of the next phase. I think that if people understood how nice these homes are going to be, if they really stopped and thought about how many jobs we're creating and the business we're bringing in, then maybe they would feel differently. I just thought . . . I mean, I know that people come in beauty parlors and talk, and maybe you could explain a little bit about that."

When Greer had suppressed her amusement at having her business referred to as a beauty parlor, she looked into Rowland's eyes and said with gentle frankness, "I don't happen to know Mr., uh"—Greer glanced at the name on the article and struggled with the pronunciation— "Farrad? But I don't disagree with all his points. I'm sorry, Rowland. You seem to be sincere about being happy to give people nice homes, and that's important. But lots of people live out here because it feels more rural, and when it turns into a sea of homes, we lose that."

"But that's why people want to live here, it's a beautiful place, and that's why I want to build houses here." Rowland's voice was a pained plea, as though he really wanted her to be on his side, to cheer for his team.

"I know," Greer said as understandingly as she would to a child being told he couldn't have an overly expensive toy. "But when you build the kind of neighborhoods that you are constructing here, then it isn't the same place anymore. You must understand that some people, many people, don't want to turn the hills into packed suburbs, they don't want their quiet streets to be clogged through ways, they don't want their stars to be replaced by streetlights."

She was thinking that this was it, she was probably blowing it for Sterling as well as herself, but to her complete surprise, Rowland sighed deeply and nodded. "I understand that. I guess I just wish people would let other people share what they have."

Greer could have laughed, if it hadn't been so frustrating. "I don't think it's the sharing so much as the *taking.*" She watched him think about that and then said, "Tell you what, I'll do what I can to let people know that you're a nice guy and you're willing to talk with them about their concerns. Is that fair?"

She saw the glint of intelligence in his eye and recognized for the first time the man who was capable of building a gigantic company from nothing. "Fair," he said. Then he leaned in and said mischievously, "But I'm gonna win you over, 'cause I like you, and me and Susan want to stay in this neighborhood for a good long time." Then with a glance around he whispered, "And we plan to build a home for ourselves up on the top of that hill, and we hope you and your boyfriend will come and spend some time with us there."

Greer didn't tell him that Reading had already given her that information. And she was now openly amazed at his charisma when it was turned on her. "I'm sure we'll be delighted. And here, if I'm not mistaken, is the man you wanted to see."

Beyond the glass, Sterling had just pulled his pickup

truck into a space in front of his office. Spotting Greer waving at him, he got out of the cab and came toward the salon.

Rowland gave Greer a last wink and then went out to meet Sterling, who let his eyes linger on Greer's through the huge windows before he turned his attention to Rowland Hughs, and she felt a thrill go through her.

As she watched the two men walk out of her view, she wondered again about Rowland. Was he authentic in his protestations of handing out the American dream, or were there undetectable machinations going on behind that schoolboy facade?

She sighed. Sometimes, she thought, even being psychic couldn't help her fathom the myriad of thoughts, experiences, and motivations that added up to create even one single human being.

Chapter 16

The afternoon heat was almost unendurable. Both Joshua and Simon paused frequently to gulp greedily from their water bottles or refill the quickly melting ice that they had wrapped in bandannas and fastened around their necks. Digging the holes twice the size of the gallon containers took far more effort than they had expected. The ground was loose and crumbly on the steep abbreviated hillside, but it was also filled with large rocks that seemed to always be in the exact spot where Sterling had placed a marker.

They labored on without comment or discourse. For Joshua's part, it was both too hot and he couldn't think of anything to say. Simon seemed to be naturally reticent when it came to communication, and this morning when Joshua had picked him up on Foothill Boulevard, he had looked the worse for wear. Joshua suspected that he had spent the previous evening celebrating his release with an excess of mind-altering substances and an absence of sleep.

Nonetheless, Simon had shown up and he had worked steadily throughout the day. Both Sterling and Joshua had posed tentative questions about Simon's family and living arrangements during the drive to the new housing site, but they had been detoured with noncommittal answers. The most they had gotten out of him was that he lived with an aunt.

Balancing himself precariously on the steeply banked ground, Joshua raised a pointed shovel and thrust downward. He heard the metal connect with stone and felt the contact shudder up his arms into his shoulders. "Damn," he grunted, and began to use the shovel to explore the extent and size of the obstruction. In about five minutes he had it uncovered, but it was too big to move on his own. He put the shovel down and picked up a crowbar that he used to break up the harder ground, wedging it under the uphill side of the stone, which was roughly as big as a rolled-up sleeping bag.

"Simon!" Joshua called out after a couple of fruitless efforts with the bar. "Can you help me? I think we can roll this baby down out of the way."

Simon looked up from his own section of the planting, dropped his shovel, and made his way slowly across to Joshua, sending miniature avalanches down the slope with each step. He stood across from Joshua without speaking and looked down at the metal bar, which had left an impression in the earth. "Not gonna work," he said. "You need leverage." A naughty smile flickered across his face. "Trust me, I know how to use a crowbar." Joshua didn't ask. Simon turned and looked around. Just up the hill there was a stone the size of a loaf of bread that Joshua had removed from his last hole. Simon clambered up to it, heaved it into his arms like a football, and came back. After digging out a space for the rock, he placed it under the pry bar, and then he and Joshua threw their combined weight on the bar. The small boulder rocked once and then flipped and slid several feet down the hill, coming to rest just above another flag.

"Good spot for it. I think we'll work it into the landscape," Joshua said with a wry smile to Simon. "I mean, unless you think we should carry it back up to the top."

Simon stared blankly at the two-hundred-pound mass for a moment, and just when Joshua thought that the sarcasm had been lost on him, he said, "I think it looks *sweet* right there."

Joshua's smile deepened. "That spot needed a focal point."

Simon was nodding knowingly. "It's been bugging me all day. *Now* it looks cool."

Pleased, the two young men both took a moment to straighten their aching spines, first stretching and then resting a moment as they stared out at the view.

Although he didn't understand squeezing fifteen gigantic houses onto such a small amount of land, Joshua had to admit that the spot was a nice one. Across the street was state-owned open land. Rocks and shrubs sloped quickly down to a seasonal riverbed, completely dry now and punctuated with cottonwood trees and the occasional sycamore. On the far side, the hills rose suddenly, creating a dramatic view of exposed rock and silver greens.

Faded signs, some covered with graffiti, proclaimed the area a sensitive wildlife habitat. There were restrictions on entry: no motorized vehicles, no dumping, and so forth. Directly across the street, an abandoned sofa sat next to a pile of yard cuttings and discarded planting trays. From their slightly higher vantage point, Joshua could see the tracks of motocross bikes and all-terrain vehicles intersecting each other in a patchwork pattern of loops and crisscrosses.

As he studied the landscape, his experienced eye caught a movement in the shrubbery at the edge of the riverbed. At first he thought it was a small deer, maybe a doe; it was the right color, but it didn't move like a deer. It moved in a jerky, almost clumsy way. The animal came out of the shade of the shrubbery and headed straight across the rocky ground toward the street. It was a dog, a light brown dog with no collar. Even from fifty feet away, Joshua could see the animal's ribs and the way it carried its head in a low, furtive manner, kept its tail tucked between its legs.

"Ah, man," Joshua moaned. "Not another one. Shit." Simon followed his look and spotted the emaciated dog. His face remained expressionless as Joshua went on to explain. "People ditch their pets up here. I've already picked up four and taken them to the Humane Society."

Simon said nothing, just watched the dog's progress toward the road. It didn't seem to have noticed them. From the road above, beyond a long, arching curve,

Joshua could hear an approaching car. At first, the sound of the engine washed over him like so much background noise, but as it grew more prominent, fear crept into him. He watched the dog's gangly trot toward the road and computed it with the approaching noise of hot, heavy steel. The car appeared around the curve; the dog was fifteen feet from the road. Under his breath, Joshua said, "Stop."

But neither the car nor the dog even slowed down or indeed seemed to have noticed the other. The car was going fast, way too fast, but nine out of ten cars did on this open road.

"Stop! Go back!" Joshua shouted at the dog, hoping to frighten it, to get its attention and arrest its forward motion, which was a beeline for death. But the dog didn't seem to hear—perhaps it couldn't. Turning toward the car, Joshua began to wave his arms furiously. The driver only accelerated when he hit the straightaway. Joshua started forward, well aware that he was too far from the road to stop the impending collision. Unable to look away, he saw the dog hop the curb, the distance closing. He screamed out at the car, "Slow down, you stupid bastard!"

Another figure streaked into the road, this one from his side of the street. Simon, waving his arms and shouting wildly, ran right into the path of the oncoming automobile. The dog spotted Simon, cringed away, and ran back the other direction. The car's wheels squealed in protest as the driver finally registered his surroundings and locked up the brakes. All of the breath in Joshua's chest was sucked out as though by a vacuum, and he was incapable of crying out as he hurled himself down the hill.

As though the seconds were slowed to a tenth of actual time, Joshua watched the car, a big sedan, go into a slide, the rear end fishtailing first one way and then the other as the driver tried to correct the skid. Simon stood frozen, directly in its path. It seemed to Joshua that the last few feet took an eternity. The bumper was maybe four feet away when Simon's body moved, launching laterally as though it been hit by an invisible force that propelled him toward the side of the road, where he landed and was blocked from Joshua's view by the car as it passed by, or possibly over, Simon. Then the car careened another few yards down the road and came to a stop, the wheels smoking, and Joshua could see Simon lying motionless, his body in the street and his head on the concrete curb.

"Jesus Christ," Joshua breathed and forced his feet to move faster, to escape the paralysis that was overwhelming him. He hit the street with a jump that covered the last few feet of hillside and rushed across to where Simon lay perfectly still on the hot asphalt. The driver, a large, stocky man in a wife-beater T-shirt and a cowboy hat, was emerging from his car, cursing angrily.

Joshua ignored him, couldn't make out what the man was shouting over the pounding in his own ears. He fell to his knees beside Simon. At a glance, he couldn't see any blood and it didn't look as though Simon had been crushed anywhere, but his eyes were closed and Joshua saw no signs of breathing.

"Simon!" he shouted at the inert boy. "Simon, are you okay?" As gently as he could, Joshua reached down and put his hand on Simon's shoulder. "Simon?" he called more softly.

Simon's eyes fluttered open and he sat up fast, looking startled and terrified. He shook off Joshua's hand and scuttled away from him, like a crab.

"It's okay, Simon. It's me, Joshua. Are you okay?" Joshua asked. Coming to his feet but staying in a crouch, he moved forward cautiously. "Are you hurt?"

Simon's face seemed to clear. There was a bruise on his forehead, where he'd hit the curb, and he touched it gingerly with one hand.

"What the fuck were you doing?" a loud, abrasively aggressive voice said from behind Joshua. "You jumped right in front of my fucking car. You could have killed me!"

Rage seemed to inflate Joshua into something bigger than his thin, six-foot frame as he rose and turned to face the accuser. Struggling to control himself, Joshua said in a choked voice, "Keep your voice down."

"Yeah? And who the fuck are you?" demanded the hefty man. He took a step forward and got right in Joshua's face, his jaw jutting out. He had the look of a man who had once had a formidable physique that had atrophied and overripened into a mushy version of his former self.

Joshua felt no fear; his anger was holding him rooted to the spot. "I'm the one who saw you doing close to eighty in a forty-five-mile-an-hour zone. I'd keep my mouth shut if I were you."

The man blinked puffy lids over small, mean eyes. Joshua was forcibly reminded of every playground bully he'd ever dealt with. This one leaned in even farther, and Joshua could smell liquor on his rancid breath. "You keep out of this, you little piece of shit."

It happened before Joshua was even aware that Simon had gotten up. The bully's ugly face was six inches from his own, and then it was gone, swept sideways with a loud thump and an exhalation of air, but not before it had registered a look of utter surprise. Simon had hit the man hard from the side, running his shoulder into the man's midsection and knocking him clean to the pavement. Simon was on top of him now, pummeling him with his fists as the bully cringed and tried to cover his face and stomach.

Regaining his wits, Joshua got behind Simon and grabbed him around the waist, pulling him off. "Cut it out, cut it out," he kept repeating with growing hysteria. But Simon fought him off, throwing his head back, and Joshua felt a hard whack as Simon's rock-hard skull made contact with his mouth. The taste of blood and the shock of pain made Joshua stumble backward in surprise.

Simon went after the man on the ground again with renewed frenzy, striking and kicking. His rage—clearly beyond his control—was far more frightening than the minimal damage he was inflicting.

His eyes watering with pain and his head spinning

from the blow, Joshua was barely aware of the sound of another car pulling up and stopping abruptly in the middle of the road, but within seconds, Sterling had appeared, taken hold of Simon, and was effectively restraining him. Though Sterling had pinioned Simon's arms to his sides, the boy was still trying to kick at the man on the ground while Sterling spoke low and steadily into Simon's ear.

After a moment, Sterling had calmed Simon down enough to release him. Wary of being on the receiving end of Simon's anger again, Joshua moved toward them cautiously and answered Sterling's queries about what had happened. The man on the ground, realizing that his attacker had been restrained, scrambled up and started shouting again. "I'll sue you, you little fucker! You'll go to jail! You can't assault me and get away with it."

Sterling released Simon and stepped directly in front of him. He wasn't any taller than the sunburned white man before him, but unlike the bully, who was sporting a paunch and flaccid arms, Sterling's strength emanated from him. His dark-skinned, muscular arms hung loosely but ready by his side, and his gaze was remorseless.

"Let me get this straight," he said, his deep voice as strong and steady as steel. "You were speeding, you almost ran over a pedestrian, you've obviously been drinking, you verbally assaulted and threatened a minor, who came to the defense of his friend whom you were threatening, and you want to sue somebody? You want to wait around and fill out a police report with liquor on your breath and *that* story?" Sterling looked pointedly at the expensive car that was still idling in the road, the door open. The bell alerting the driver to the fact that the key had been left in the ignition was chiming out a hollow, pointless note. "I don't think that even a lawyer with his picture on the back of a bus would take that case. But I've got a friend who would love to make mincemeat out of your ass in a court of law. So unless you want to hand over your vehicle-slash-weapon, as well as any cash or property you might have, to this boy, whom you injured with your reckless, drunken driving, I suggest you get back in that car, go home, and take a cold shower, because you need to cool off, sober up, *and* you stink."

The bully was breathing heavily through his nose, his beady eyes narrowed against the brightness and Sterling's considerable power. He seemed, like a confused, cornered animal, incapable of deciding what to do. He also looked perplexed to be hearing a British accent coming from a black man. Joshua could almost hear the thought process: *Them English are white, ain't they?*

Sterling turned to Simon and said, "How's the head?"

Simon was still glaring at the bully with so much hate that Joshua could almost taste it in the air. A bitter, rancid hate.

"Any permanent damage?" Sterling asked, his voice taking on a note of fun now. "Do you think it might have affected your ability to reproduce or to work?" He waited while Simon glared. "Simon," Sterling said pointedly and waited for him to break his malignant stare. "Do you feel that this pointless accident will scar you emotionally? How many fingers do you see?" Sterling waved his hand four inches from Simon's face, rapidly changing the number of fingers on one hand from two to four to three and back to two. "Speak to me, Simon." Sterling grabbed Simon's shoulders dramatically.

Simon smiled now, finally catching on. "Yeah, all those," he said venomously, turning a twisted grin back on the bully. "Get the fuck out of here before I find you again." There was a chill in his words that finished the scenario.

Trying for the last shot, the bully raised a fist and snarled, "I'll find you, you little shit. You won't get away with this!"

His last line was directed at Sterling, who shrugged and said, "Whatever," before crossing his meaty arms in a casually unconcerned stance and stood waiting while the man hightailed it back to his car, slammed the door, and lost a good bit more rubber from his tires as he peeled away.

Now Sterling turned to Simon again. "Are you really

okay?" he asked, concerned. Two more cars, these moving at a more conservative speed, came up the road and stopped, the drivers looking confused at the stranded pickup in their path. "Come on," Sterling ordered. "We're done working today. Let's go."

They all climbed into the truck, and Sterling cranked up the air-conditioning. He made a wide U-turn, pulled into the entrance of the housing project, and waited while Joshua collected their cooler and tools. Then he started out along the neighborhood toward the main drag. As he drove, Joshua made makeshift ice packs for Simon's bump and his own swollen lip from the ice left in the cooler and two plastic bags he found in the glove compartment. He assembled the packs with hands shaking from an overdose of adrenaline; his stomach felt as though someone had put acetone in a cocktail shaker with crushed ice and agitated it vigorously.

"I don't know about you two," Sterling said musingly as both young men sat back, nursing their wounds, "but back on Tooting High Street, where I began my professional career as a bouncer in one of south London's less sophisticated pubs, I always liked to have some meat and some sugar after a good fight. How about a double chili-cheese and a chocolate shake from Tommy's?"

"I'm in," Simon said enthusiastically without looking up, and Joshua was surprised to find not only that he was hungry, but that sinking his teeth into something chewy and following it with something sickeningly sweet sounded perfect. He nodded his agreement.

"Okay, my treat." Sterling grinned at both boys. "Simon?"

Slowly, as though afraid of what he might be about to receive, Simon turned and looked up at Sterling. "Yeah?"

"You all right?" Sterling's voice was gentle, but very firm; there was no trace of pity in it.

Joshua held his breath as he waited to see how Simon would respond.

"My head hurts a little, but . . ." He paused, and then, so suddenly that it blurted out, Simon laughed loudly and said, "Shit! You told that motherfucker! That was the bounce!"

Sterling chuckled and nodded, "Yes, sir, that was the bounce."

"You should have kicked his snow-white ass."

"I think you'll find," Sterling said as he pulled away from a stop sign, "that most bullies don't actually want to fight; they just want to scare you. Once they know they can't, they've shot their wad. Plus"—he glanced over at both boys with a impish grin on his handsome mug—"you'll stay much prettier if you use your brain instead of your face to end an argument."

Joshua touched his tender lip, and found it numb from the ice. "I didn't intentionally get my face in the way of the back of your head," he said to Simon with some bitterness.

"Sorry," Simon muttered. "I go a little loco when I get pissed off."

"Always stay in control. That's how you win," Sterling told him in a voice that was both educational and cautioning.

Joshua watched both of them in amazement. He was still vibrating from the exposure to physical danger and rerunning the incident over and over in his mind, feeling the panic and the tension, but they seemed to be *enjoying* the sensation.

As much as it confused him, he found himself feeling slightly envious.

Chapter 17

To facilitate the date that was masquerading as a guided tour, Leah had arranged to meet Weston at a small, family-run Mexican restaurant that only the locals knew about. The choice assisted the illusion in several ways: the ambiance was distinctly not romantic, no alcohol was served, and the music was teeth-grinding brassy, annoying enough to easily bully out any stray amorous sensation, but the food was excellent and the place was clean and friendly. She carefully chose an outfit of jeans and an expensive T-shirt to match the non-come-hither theme, deliberately ignoring the fact that, although her outfit was casual and revealed little skin, it fit snugly and showed off her trim curves to their best advantage.

She was prompt as usual and only mildly surprised to find him already there, waiting for her by the door. She tensed as she walked toward him, wondering if he would expect a hug or even a kiss of greeting, but he dispelled her qualms by shaking her hand and thanking her for coming.

"This looks great," he commented as he held the door open for her. "I've been craving good Mexican for the last week, and I don't mean Green Burrito. What's good here?"

She told him that the seafood dishes were their specialty and was gratified that he looked pleased. Many men she knew were strictly beef and bean; it had always bored her.

They went to the counter and ordered two seafood

burritos, a ceviche, and a pair of cactus sodas, then retreated to a booth in the corner. Weston thoughtfully
took the side facing the wall. Her ex-husband, Vince,
had always given himself the better seat facing out
toward the restaurant, but Leah had been taught by her
father that a gentleman should always face the wall. He
should be content to look at his date, and no one else.
Leah wondered, for the six-millionth time, why she had
ever fallen for Vince. And for the six-millionth time she
came to the same conclusion she always did, that it must
have been some great deficiency in her.

"So, authentic Mexican. Check. How about coffee
shops? In my business, a good twenty-four-hour joint is
worth more than any five-star restaurant."

"Well, let's see. There's Sweet Cheri's—that's always
good," Leah offered. "I've never been there in the middle of the night, but the breakfast is really good."

"Omelets fluffy or thin?"

"Thin," Leah said with a grimace. She liked them that
way but she knew most people didn't.

"Perfect. I can't stand when they're three inches thick
and you can't get a bite with enough filling."

Leah concurred, then said, "They make a great Spanish omelet."

"I like Spanish omelets with avocado and cheddar."

"That sounds great," Leah said. She seldom requested
special orders at restaurants and always admired people
who came up with their own unique selections. Though
she had a few friends she suspected of confusing discrim-
inating with demanding, trying to make themselves seem
more important by taxing the restaurant staff.

"Anything else I should know about?"

"Well, the best thing about the area is really the hiking. There are some lovely little parks, a terrific branch
library, small but good, and quite a few nice shops. The
people around here have resisted having all the same ol'
big retail outlets, so there are still some great neighborhood grocery stores and actually one really good sushi
bar."

"In Shadow Hills?"

Leah laughed. "In Tujunga, actually. Even more shocking."

"Tujunga sushi. Hmm." Weston looked dubious. "You'll have to convince me of that one. Maybe if I don't scare you away today, you could introduce me to the Tujunga roll."

Shifting uncomfortably, Leah ventured a question that surprised her. "Why would you think you'd scare me away?"

Weston arranged his plasticware on his napkin in front of him before he answered. When he did, he looked up at her with frank, open eyes. "You said you don't date. When a woman is as beautiful and successful as you and she's made that choice, it seems like it could only mean two things. But you tell me."

"What two things?" Leah pressed, though her voice shook slightly. She was half-afraid he would get it wrong, and half-terrified he would hit the nail on the head.

"Well, either you've dated a succession of losers who were inept at relationships and unsatisfying, probably had a lot of their own baggage, and you came to the conclusion that *relationships* in general were more trouble than they were worth."

There was something in his rote recital of this theory that snapped a light on in Leah's head. *That's why he's available,* she thought. *He's doesn't know any women who are worth it.* Her second thought was that if he was looking for a woman without baggage, she might as well pay the check, stack up her steamer trunks, and call a porter.

"Or," he continued, unaware of her revelations, "you were with someone who was such a bastard that it put you off *men* as opposed to relationships." He did not phrase it as a question, but neither did he look away.

With a deep intake of breath, Leah said softly, "The second one."

Weston nodded, and then shook his head with a gesture of disgust. "I'm sorry," he said, and gracefully left it at that. "So, what's it like working in a bank?"

Expecting him to want her to elaborate on her miserable experiences, and startled by his tactfulness, Leah laughed. "It's, uh, fine. I always liked numbers and finance; it's something I'm good at, and you can rely on them," she said; then hearing how revealing that sounded, she quickly added, "But being the manager means that I have to deal with human resources a great deal, so it's not just all balance sheets."

"Does human resources mean *people*?" Weston asked as he took a drink from a long-necked glass bottle of cactus soda. He looked amused.

"Well, yes. But more than that, it means finding out their strengths and their talents and putting them to best use."

"You have a lot of friends from the bank?"

"Yes," Leah answered quickly, and then paused. For some reason, giving stock responses to this man felt like cheating. She sensed he wouldn't be content with polite banter. After all, she thought, this was a man who ran toward the fire, not away from it. "Actually, I would say that I have a few friendly acquaintances at the bank," she confessed, surprising herself. "I don't socialize with my coworkers much outside work hours. Every once in a while I go to lunch with my friend Towler, whom I believe you met," she said dryly, "or have drinks with a group, but, well, the fact is that most of the people I count as my friends are either left over from college—and most of them are lost in their own careers or married with children and obsessed with preschools and nannies. I do have a couple of newer friends. Jenny from the coffee shop is one of them. It's somehow, I don't know, safer for me not to have relationships with people from work." As she made the simple statement, it hit Leah hard, and for the first time, that perhaps this was because of her debacle with Vince, whom she had met at work.

"And you're divorced?" he asked, and when she nodded, he said, "That can end quite a few friendships too, I noticed. Friends find it uncomfortable, and they don't have the strength to lend you any, so they fade out."

"Are you divorced?" Leah asked, reluctant to share the observation that she and her ex hadn't really had many friends since he was such an asshole.

His clear blue eyes clouded. "Yes, I'm divorced," he confessed. "And I can't say I blame her. I wasn't home much, and the life of a fireman doesn't offer a huge scope of material wealth."

"She wanted jewelry?" Leah said, hoping to lighten his mood and sound sympathetic at the same time.

"She wanted jewelry," he confirmed, his rugged jaw creasing with lines from his wry smile. "But mostly she wanted more attention." He sighed and said wisely, "And that was fair. She was very beautiful and very full of life, and she wanted—and deserved—to be admired. I wanted to do it; I just wasn't home often enough."

"Do you travel that much?"

"I did then. I was training as a flyer and working as a fire jumper. You know, those idiots that parachute into wildfires? You get assigned to some pretty remote places, sometimes for months at a time. I think I must have been in Alaska when she got together with John."

"Her new husband?" Leah asked.

"Oh no, that would be Eric. No, John was just this friend of mine. You know." He smiled at her sadly, and she felt as though the subject would be better shelved for now.

The fact that he had shared something obviously painful encouraged her somewhat. Leah had always been competitive, and somehow, she felt challenged, in a good way, to meet him evenly on the playing field. But she had absolutely no idea what to say. *My ex beat the crap out of me* just sounded like a little too much for show-and-tell at this kindergarten stage, and lurking behind the naked truth of it was the heavily hooded suspicion that it was all her fault anyway. That she had chosen it, that she had failed.

So she tried a different tack. "Where is she now?"

"Um, Pittsburgh, I think. How about yours?"

"Prison." Leah mimicked his cadence and hoped that would lighten the impact.

"Equally picturesque. I hope they're both very happy," he said without even blinking, and Leah had to laugh.

The woman behind the counter called out their names at this moment, thankfully relieving Leah from any further explanation. Weston rose to fetch the plates, and they made mutual noises of contentment as they ate the fat, snugly wrapped burritos and experimented with the variety of salsas, red and green, that ranged from saucily mild to eyeball-sweating hot.

"Whew." Leah tried to cool her mouth with air and then a drink from her soda after she had eaten all she could hold. "That was good. Spicy, but good."

"Very," agreed Weston, who seemed less affected by the burn of crushed jalapeños laced into the salsa. "Now what? I'm thinking ice cream."

"Actually, there's a carnival in the park on the corner." Leah surprised herself again with the suggestion. "I haven't been to one of those since I was a kid, but I saw a sign for soft ice cream."

"Let's go." Weston was already rising, pulling some bills out of his pocket and leaving them on the table.

Leah stood and gathered her purse. "But I have to tell you, I'm no good on any of those rides. Especially not after a seafood burrito."

Weston looked serious. "As a public safety professional, I have to advise against them, *especially* after seafood burritos. But I think maybe once or twice around in the Ferris wheel might not be too risky."

"Ooh . . . high," Leah said as they started for the door.

Weston's eyes twinkled. "Wait until I get you up in a helicopter."

Leah wasn't sure if it was the thought of flying or the fact that Weston wanted to take her that made her stomach dip and swirl.

Chapter 18

The garish, constantly flickering and winking lights of the carnival gave the open park the dizzying feel of liquid, translucent color caught in a swirling, unpredictable eddy. The warm night was heavily laden with the smells of sugar and fried foods.

Joshua and his friend Joy had arrived just before dark and spent the last hour testing out all the rides they could stomach. She was his neighbor Whitney's stepdaughter, a year and a half younger than Joshua, with very pretty almond eyes in a delicate face, a full mouth, and straight brown hair cut in flattering layers that continued to move after she did. It reminded Joshua of a grass skirt on a hula girl, but he didn't tell her that. He thought that this style was a vast improvement over the purple streaks and Gothic makeup she had worn to aggressively disguise her prettiness when he had first met her. In fact, in the months that he'd known her, she'd changed in many ways. They had become good friends who often sat and talked for hours about the crucial nothings upon which a tentative teenager builds a stable adulthood.

Joshua stole a glance at her now. Her body had filled out with her healthier outlook on life, her figure had gone from adolescent to enticing, and she was so much prettier without the war paint she had donned to angrily repel a disapproving world. She lived with her father and Whitney full-time now, and without the negative influence of a dysfunctional, destructive mother, she had—

he searched for the word—blossomed. Even as the verb occurred to him, he felt slightly embarrassed by the poetic reference, but it suited. He had always been attracted to Joy, but the combination of her youth and emotional instability had inspired in him a protective, big-brother impulse. Without really understanding it fully, he had begun to feel a sense of entitlement to her affection, as though he were waiting for her to be ready for a boyfriend, and then, of course, he would be there.

For her part, Joy's recalcitrant adolescence combined with a recent scarring experience had left her with a kind of paranoia, a distrust of even the most innocent sexual attention. Her phobia was one that she could not yet acknowledge or understand, and she was simply grateful and content with Joshua's presence and protectiveness—though she never doubted the strength of the bond between them, she didn't think of him romantically. It hadn't occurred to her to question why it always stung when pretty girls flirted with him, which they often did. She had given only sparse consideration to how she would feel when he went away to college in a couple of months, because when she did, it gave her a feeling that was hated but not totally unfamiliar. After some effort, she had identified it as the same feeling she'd had when she'd been coerced into trying a long, steep, spiral tunnel at Raging Waters. She'd been whirled, frighteningly out of control, struggling to keep her head above the cold water as she'd been rocketed helplessly along until she shot out the bottom into an icy pool, where she had fought, panicked, to sort out which way was up. So, for the most part, she just didn't think about Joshua's impending departure, not if she could help it.

They bought ice creams, found a relatively open spot of grass to sit down on and eat them, and had just decided to head over to the game arcade next when Joshua spotted Simon with a group of like-looking teenagers.

"That's the kid I was telling you about," Joshua said. "The one Sterling hired, who saved the dog."

Joy's eyes trailed in the direction Joshua had indicated with his ice cream. "Which one?"

Here Joshua found it difficult to say. There were four
young men, all Hispanic, all with hair so short that it
looked as though their heads had been recently shaved,
and all dressed in identical white T-shirts and baggy
jeans. "The smallest one," Joshua finally said.

Joy turned her poker face to Joshua. "Great," she
intoned dryly. "You talked Sterling into hiring a gang
member."

"Come on," Joshua said defensively, though he knew
she was most likely right. "You can't go by how people
are dressed. I mean, look at you."

Joy smacked him hard on the shoulder with the hand
that wasn't holding her cone, but she was laughing.
"What the fuck does that mean?"

"Ow! I don't mean now. I mean when you were all
Goth, before . . ." He faltered a little as the smile died
from her eyes. "You know, when you were a punk kid."

She nodded and returned her attention to her ice
cream, and it was only because Joshua knew her so well
that he spotted the slight, involuntary shudder. "At least
I didn't look like a long-haired hippy geek," she teased.

"I liked my hair longer," Joshua said, relieved that
she had been able to let the moment pass. He was proud
of her.

"Right." She snorted a laugh and only prevented
spraying chocolate mint ice cream all over both of them
by clasping her hand to her mouth. Then she sang out
mockingly, "You were *so* cool."

"Shut up." Joshua could feel his face redden slightly.

"You look okay now," she said in a voice that had
dropped to a deeper, more natural place. For a split
second, Joshua saw Joy's expression open up as though
she'd drawn aside a heavy shade, and he got a glimpse
of the complete person that was growing inside of her.
Then they both felt the prickle of a blush and cast
around for a distraction.

It happened as Joshua turned his gaze back to Simon
and his friends. The figure of the little dog was hovering
again, just over Simon's right shoulder, and then the

dark male figure appeared over his left, and this time, the man was looking straight at Joshua.

The malevolence in the direct look made Joshua feel as though he'd been plunged into arctic water. "Holy shit," he said in a breath that was forced from his lungs.

"What?" Joy had tracked his gaze, but of course, she saw only the colored lights streaking across the people in the crowd.

Both images had faded as quickly as they had appeared, but Joshua was shaken. "Damn it, I wish that wouldn't happen when I wasn't expecting it."

Joy laid a hand on Joshua's arm. "Are you okay?"

"Yeah." He tried to laugh. "It was the two figures I told you about, the dog and the man who looks so evil. But this time the man wasn't looking at Simon. He was looking at me."

She nodded slowly. "Tell that fucker he's breaking the rules."

"What rules?"

Looking slightly embarrassed, Joy shrugged and said, "I've been reading up on this seeing-dead-people thing a little." She licked her ice cream and avoided eye contact. "I mean, more interesting than what they make you read at school, that *For Whom the Bell Rings*."

"Tolls," Joshua corrected automatically.

"Whatever. So, supposedly there's rules. They're not supposed to scare you."

"Really?" Joshua was watching her, feeling pleased. She was taking an interest in his unusual ability. "Who makes up these rules?"

"I don't fucking know. Who am I, John fucking Edward?"

Whenever Joy felt threatened or insecure, she reverted to her old favorite word. He let the subject pass, but he knew that she was right. One way or another, negative energy from such a powerful source must be blocked, and he assumed he would have to learn to do it.

The four boys were walking toward them through the crush of people near the food stalls, their eyes shifty, constantly glancing, moving with a jerky self-consciousness that seems to permeate the youth of their particular culture and social class. Joshua rose to his feet and called out casually, "Yo, Simon." At the same time he steeled himself to block any vision, to place a barrier between his mind and what he had come to think of as the other side.

Simon's eyes cut quickly to see who had addressed him, and while Joshua thought it would be exaggerating to say that Simon relaxed when he saw the two of them, he at least looked less afraid and more simply uncomfortable.

"Yo, Joshua. Wha's up?" The younger boy sauntered over with practiced nonchalance and pressed his fist against Joshua's. Joshua responded in kind, following the unfamiliar protocol.

"Not much. Meet my friend Joy."

Simon's eyes only flickered over Joy as his gaze passed by her in sweeping looks, like an oscillating fan. "Wha's up?" he repeated.

Not to be out-cooled, Joy responded with a "Jus' hanging."

"That's cool," Simon said. His eyes roved past again, on their ceaseless surveillance of his surroundings.

"Who're your friends?" Joshua asked, and hoped he didn't sound as intimidated as he felt by the cold, unfamiliar, staring trio.

"Oh." Simon turned and gestured to them. "This here is Tic, Juice, and Loc."

"But not necessarily in that order," said the tallest and meanest-looking of the group. The other two snickered sycophantically.

Forcing himself to remember his own words to Joy, Joshua stepped toward them and offered his hand. They each shook it politely, and on closer inspection, Joshua realized that their outwardly tough presentation was as thin a veneer over deep insecurity as was Simon's, and probably his own—to a lesser degree.

"You guys rode the Figure Eight yet?" he asked, choosing a neutral, comfortable subject.

"Not yet," the stocky boy, Juice, answered. "I think I might puke."

"Yeah," Joshua said, crossing his arms and looking up at the spinning cage. "It's not so much the puking as having it hit you in the face when you spin back around."

They liked that. Smiles of amusement broke out all over. Joy contributed. "I like the Sizzler best. It's spinny but without having to revisit your lunch."

"Yeah, Sizzler's cool," Loc said, and Joshua saw him give Joy an appraising look. She seemed to meet with his approval.

"Well, we're going over to the arcade," Joshua said. "Catch you guys later."

A quartet of variations on "Cool. See you around."

Simon added to Joshua, "See you Monday."

As they strolled toward the crazily lit bank of arcade trailers, Joshua jostled Joy's shoulder and said, "See? They're not so bad."

Joy just narrowed her eyes at him, but she said, "No, you're right. They seem okay. You can't always judge people by first impressions. I mean, fuck"—she smiled sheepishly—"I should know that better than anybody."

"Yeah." Joshua screwed up his face and pretended to be trying hard to remember. "As I recall, the first time I saw you, you were pretty damn scary."

The fist that caught him in the upper arm was so fast and forceful that only the powerful editing force of his teenage embarrassment could keep him from crying out, much less from smacking her back.

As he was massaging his injured limb, a voice called his name. "Joshua, Joy, over here!" Looking up, he saw his mother's friend Leah and waved back. The use of his arm caused him to wince and cast a resentful glance at Joy.

They met just in front of the balloon dart game, and Leah introduced the man she was with as a fireman named Weston. He was tall, obviously in peak condition, and Joshua immediately felt lacking, a sensation that was multiplied as he noted Joy's surreptitious glances up at Weston's chiseled jaw and his striking blue-eyed, black-haired combo as niceties were exchanged. Weston's physique was so impressive that Joshua found himself rolling his shoulders back and tensing his muscles in a competitive effort.

"Where's your mom?" Leah asked.

"She was going to a party later on with Luke and Whitney."

"And you guys weren't invited?"

"Nope. Thank God," Joy piped in.

"Besides, I got the distinct feeling that Mom and Sterling might like to get me out of the house," Joshua confessed, feeling a flush of embarrassment heat his cheeks. As much as he liked Sterling, it was still damn awkward to think of his mother being sexually active.

"Good for them," Weston said lightly, and Joshua watched the same flush he had felt—though he imagined for quite a different reason—appear on Leah's cheeks.

"You guys want to spend twenty bucks to see if you can win a one-dollar prize?" Joshua hurriedly changed the subject, gesturing to the cheap stuffed animals suspended by their necks from the roof of the game trailer like some bizarre, gang cartoon hanging.

"No. Thank you though," Leah said.

"We were just on our way over to the Ferris wheel."

"Oh, that sounds like fun," Joshua said. He turned to Joy. "We haven't done that."

Joy punched his tender upper arm again. "We'll pass," she said brightly. "I'm kind of in the mood to rescue one of those purple giraffes from imminent asphyxiation."

Weston glanced up at the blank-eyed grins of the assorted, oddly colored menagerie and commented, "They seem to be enjoying it."

"Nonetheless . . ." As Joy reached for Joshua's arm, he flinched slightly and she gave him a sad shake of the head. "C'mon. See you guys later!" she called as she led Joshua over to the cashier.

"What do you have against the Ferris wheel?" he demanded.

"I swear, sometimes you are about as dense as a rock," Joy admonished. She reached up and knocked lightly on his skull with her knuckles. "Hello? The Ferris wheel is where people go on a date to make out. And they are definitely on a date."

"Oh," said Joshua, feeling distinctly rocklike and wondering if he were igneous or sedimentary. "So that's why you didn't want to go on it," he said, unthinkingly offering yet another display of his denseness.

Joy released his arm as though it had burned her and fumbled in her pocket for money. "Um, how many tries do you want, two or five?" She didn't look at him, but there was no hiding the panic on her face.

"I didn't mean—" Joshua broke off. "I mean, I just wanted to ride on it. I didn't want to . . . Not that I wouldn't." He snapped his mouth closed and held his lips pressed together before he could use it to dig an even deeper hole in which to stick his stupid head.

"Relax," she said, his obvious distress seeming to defuse her alarm somewhat. "It's not like you're my boyfriend or anything like that."

"No," said Joshua, hoping that his disappointment didn't sound too pronounced. "Nothing like that."

Across the baseball field Weston and Leah waited for their turn on the rickety ride. Leah was eyeing it with double apprehension. On top of the fact that the bolts on which their lives might depend looked none too tight or new, there was the other danger: At the wheel's high point, where it stopped for regular intervals as riders disembarked or boarded directly below, the sloppily swaying seats were swathed in darkness—and uninterrupted privacy.

As though sensing her trepidation, Weston said, "It's not that high, but we should get a good view of the surrounding neighborhood." When she said nothing, he affected an overly proper demeanor and added priggishly, "But I'll only do this if you promise not to get fresh with me."

She tried to look mature as she asked, "Am I that pathetic?"

He looked genuinely startled for a moment and then

as though he was considering the question quite seriously. "Pathetic? No, that is *not* the adjective that leaps to mind."

She knew it was adolescent, but she couldn't stop herself from asking, "What is?"

The line moved, and they took a few steps forward before pausing again. He seemed to find the question important. Finally he said, "Can I have more than one?"

"Sure," she consented, and steeled herself to listen without commenting.

"Captivating, certainly. Beautiful, smart, very smart, opaque . . ."

In spite of her intentions, Leah burst out, "Opaque! What does that mean?"

"It means that I can't see through you. You're very hard to read, and I find that intriguing. Maybe that's the best overall word to describe you, intriguing."

They had reached the front of the line and it was their turn to clamber on. They stepped up onto the corrugated iron platform and then gingerly into the rickety basket. The grizzled attendant pulled the bar across their laps and grunted a monosyllable in response to their thanks.

The huge machinery ground its many wheels, and the chair moved abruptly up in a backward motion. They must have been the last of the new group to load, because it continued without stopping until it reached the top, making Leah catch her breath at the sudden height. The view of the carnival swirling below them and the dark hills rising in the distance was surreally beautiful and gave the sensation that they were floating on a sea of light.

As they hit the peak and started down again, Leah let out a small exclamation and held on tighter to the bar in front of her. "The ground just kind of went away, didn't it?" she said, looking over at Weston's face, dimly lit by the opalescent glow from below.

Weston was looking at her with amiable amusement. "That's what I thought the first time I went up in a helicopter. I was sitting there and all of a sudden the ground went away. It was the most amazing feeling. I knew right then I had to learn to fly one."

She rested her back against the side of the car so that she could face him better—and keep a safe distance. "What made you want to do what you do? I mean, it's very dangerous, and like you said, it's not exactly the most lucrative of careers."

He twisted his body to face her more comfortably as well, crossing one long leg over the other to facilitate the angle; the move put his leg very close to hers, and though she was acutely aware of its proximity, she willed herself not to retreat. She was surprised to find, a few seconds later, that she had almost—but not quite—acclimated to its being there.

"I suppose it was my parents," Weston said thoughtfully. "Both my mom and dad are very socially conscious people. We were a foster family; my mom taught kindergarten in a tough school to kids who didn't even speak English; my dad was a cop. They're retired now. We never had a ton of money, but that didn't seem very important. Making a heap of money just wasn't a value that I was given, if you can call acquiring wealth a value. What *was* impressed on me, from a very early age, was being of service to others, and being a decent person. *That* was being a success. Without those things, life didn't seem worth much." He shrugged as though she already knew this. "I like excitement and being physical, and community is really important to me—that was drilled into my brain early too—so when I went looking for careers, fire jumper seemed to sort of leap out at me, if you'll forgive the lame pun."

Leah was watching him, her feelings whirling faster than the Ferris wheel. His words had brought up a deep sense of inadequacy that felt like a lump of toxic sludge that had become lodged in her chest. *Being of service to others?* Finding a job that would help the community? She was stunned that she had never even considered that. Had she ever even thought of helping others as part of her *everyday* goals? She was horrified to find that the immediate answer was no. For some reason, it had always seemed like something that would come later, once she'd amassed all the career *success* and financial success that she craved so desperately. Yet she had to admit that, in spite of her elevating salary and position, she still felt lacking, incomplete, as though she wasn't there yet. She had thought that when she made more, owned more, hit some as yet unidentified goal, she would eventually feel fulfilled. She would be *successful*.

"So there's the basis of my operating systems," Weston was saying even as they passed the terminally bored attendant on the ground and started the upsweep again. "Why did you become a banker?"

Leah didn't respond for a moment. She was trying desperately to get ahold of her whiplash reaction, to justify, rationalize, to validate, not just this answer but her entire life. Finally, as they crested the night once again, she looked at him and gave her answer. "I became a mercenary career professional because my parents are divorced, spent their entire lives competing with each other and everyone else by acquiring as much money and as many material things as they could, and I grew up thinking that's what you were supposed to do." Her voice sounded flat and stunned, even to her. "I thought that's what made you happy."

"Were they happy?" Weston asked.

"No." Leah shook her head vehemently. "They were miserable. Still are."

Weston threw his head back and laughed from his gut. It was a fabulous, full-bodied laugh, the kind that Leah couldn't remember having since she was a child, and maybe she had only imagined it then. When he had recovered, he looked at her with tears of mirth in his eyes and said, "And *honest*. I would like to add that to my list of adjectives about you, brutally, ruthlessly, *fearlessly* honest."

Leah had seldom in her life ever felt two things so diametrically opposed and so strongly at the same time. She was elatedly pleased with Weston and absolutely mortified with herself. "I've just been so caught up with all my problems and, uh, tribulations," she offered, knowing it sounded trite, "that I never even thought about making an effort to help other people as a part of my overall plan, if you know what I mean."

Weston reached out and very quickly brushed a hair from Leah's face that had caught on the edge of her mouth, retracting his hand before she had time to react to the touch. "I always found," he said simply, "that the more you focus on good, the less bad there will be in your life. I don't know if it really changes anything, or just the way I look at it, but it sure does feel true."

"Can you give me an example?" Leah asked, feeling lost.

"Well, okay." He wrinkled his brow and then said, "I came to stop a brush fire in this neighborhood, which could be considered bad, but I met you, which I think is good." He said this so matter-of-factly and without expectation that Leah didn't squirm at all.

"But, I've had so many bad things happen to me," Leah protested weakly.

"We all have, some worse than others," Weston said sadly. He turned away from her and faced the dark hills. "But there comes a point when you have to get over your own problems and be of service to someone else."

"Who?" She looked at him with a dawning horror that he must think she was one of the most selfish people he had ever met. As for what she thought of him, he mystified her. He was so different from the men she'd been attracted to before, whose identities were displayed entirely in their showy vehicles and expensive homes. He actually seemed to care more about the usefulness of what he did than whether or not it impressed others. It struck her like a bomb that this might just be the difference between feeling happy or perpetually inadequate.

"You're a local bank manager," he offered. "You know the community. What does the community need?" He gave another dismissive shrug, as if to say, *Surely you've thought of this.*

Leah stared out at the hills. She had no idea what the

community needed; she supposed she'd always kidded herself into thinking she was doing good by lending people money and helping them build savings, but she knew that was bogus. Now she was going to make it a point to find out what she could do to help, because one thing was certain: The choices on which she'd based her life up until now damn sure weren't making her happy.

The Ferris wheel hit its peak again, and this time Leah felt a sense of elation and soaring joy. As she swept through the sultry night, she felt as though maybe, just maybe, she too could learn to fly.

Chapter 19

Greer was relieved to find that the party was a quiet, intimate affair. About twenty people milled around the small, tasteful home and backyard, where ropes of white lights had been strung in a crisscross pattern over the garden. Being naturally attracted to landscaping, Sterling stood with a glass of white wine in one hand surveying the neat, creative space with an approving admiration.

"Nice work," he said to Greer. "You see how well he's used the curves of the rock-lined path and miniature fruit trees to create an illusion of more space and intimate areas? And the corner fountain with the mirror behind it is really a lovely touch." He breathed deeply and sighed. "And the night-blooming jasmine . . . So many people forget scent when they create their garden. Big mistake."

"It's beautiful. I wonder which one is our host," Greer mused, peering around at the gathered guests.

Whitney and her husband, Luke, a tall, formidable-looking Native American man with a long, graying ponytail and a sharp wit, had joined them. "R.J. is . . ." Whitney looked around and pointed to a very handsome, dark-skinned man in his fifties. His still-black hair hung long, straight, and loose to the middle of his back over a starched, deep purple cotton shirt. His face was less angular than Luke's, its curves gentler and more disposed to look cheerful without trying, but he shared his taller friend's noble bearing and artistic presence.

"Wow," Greer said. "What a striking man."

"Isn't he though?" Whitney asked. "He's full-blooded Cherokee. You don't find that much anymore."

Luke smiled, showing his perfect, strong white teeth. "He's full-blooded all right, and as hot-blooded as a Pawnee on the warpath. R.J. is very active in Native American rights."

"R.J.," Greer said, reminded of something. "Was that his painting at Mindy's house?"

"Yes, the one you liked," Whitney said. She had not discussed Greer's reaction to the painting as her premonition about Jenny had superseded it. Though Greer had shared the alarming vision of the black wings hovering over Jenny's face with Whitney and they had discussed it between themselves, they had also made a pact not to tell Jenny about it. Both Whitney and Greer had grown up with a keen awareness of what others called the supernatural. Whitney's father had been a Cree medicine man, and both she and Greer understood all too well the damage that suggestion itself could do. So, they had both pledged to do what they could to protect and watch over Jenny without planting the seed of fear in her.

But now the memory of Greer's reaction to the painting in Mindy's living room the day of the shower came back to Whitney and she asked, "You did like the painting, yes?"

"Very much," Greer said. "And I'm extremely curious to know where he painted it."

"His work is amazing, isn't it?" Luke commented. "Looking at his paintings compared to mine makes me feel like he's a master craftsman and I'm some geek with a hammer who's constructed a pigsty out of some sticks I've found out in the yard."

"Oh, honey," Whitney said with a laugh, "your work is completely different."

"I love your art!" Sterling interjected. "That piece you gave Greer is amazing. I mean, it's a continuation of the style of the Native American art during the internment periods, right down to using actual documents of the time, and it's clever as hell. I mean, *When Poodles Ran*

Free in Beverly Hills. That's just brilliant." He was smiling brightly at the very thought of it.

"And," Greer pitched in, "I'll bet he doesn't make fabulous jewelry like you do."

At this comment both Luke and Whitney looked wryly at each other. "Yeah, he does," Whitney said, and pulled her lace cuff back to reveal a magnificent bracelet, an intricate masterpiece of brightly colored stones inlaid in an oval gold base strung on five strands of garnet crystals.

"Bastard," Luke muttered with so much admiration in the word that it was the highest of compliments. "I hate him so much," he said flatly, and then the twinkle in his eye caught each of them in turn. "Not that I'm bitter."

They all laughed.

"What, or maybe I should ask, who is so amusing?" asked their host, who had appeared next to Whitney and was shooting a knowing look at his friend Luke.

Introductions were made, and Greer was charmed to find that R.J. not only looked elegant, he acted it as well, stooping over her hand in an imitation of a kiss. Sterling's hand he shook strongly with eye contact and a welcoming smile.

"I really like what you've done with this space," Sterling told him. "In fact, I hope you don't mind, I've been taking some mental notes."

"Sterling is a landscape architect," Whitney explained.

"Oh, would I know any of your work?" R.J. asked with sincere enthusiasm.

Sterling mentioned several of the more striking homes in the area that he had done, and then with a shake of his head and a sigh he added, "And soon, I'll be the proud designer of one of the saddest landscape jobs in Shadow Hills, the Golden Door subdivision." He took a sip of his wine. "I tried to get out of it, but I knew if I did, we'd all be treated to a sterile view of ice plant and ficus. At least I can subtly force them to plant natives and try to hide some of the cancerous growths—I mean, houses."

R.J.'s face had gone hard, and lines that had been absent in his beaming smile appeared on his brow and around his mouth. "That thing should never have gone through. It was against every zoning law we have. Part of it is actually in a wash area; the first good rain will probably reroute most of the floodwaters right through a few of those McMansions' living rooms." He scowled. "Serve them right. I'll be out there cheering."

Luke said, "R.J. was one of the organizers of the petitions against it."

"It's not over yet," R.J. said grimly. "We've organized a hearing to try to stop phase three. For the *second* time." He shook his head, and his smooth hair swung like a solid sheet. "It's just unbelievable. If somebody comes in with enough money, they can basically talk the city council—who are supposed to be protecting the people who elected them—into anything."

"You think they bribed them?" Sterling asked, looking concerned.

"I don't know. I wish I could prove that they did, but it isn't that simple. You'd be amazed at the number of people who either wanted it or, worse, are just plain apathetic." He turned to the back door of the house as a new couple, whom Greer recognized as Mindy and Reading, emerged from it. "Speak of the devil," he said quietly.

Greer was nodding. "Yeah, he's pretty pro-development. We had a little, uh, heated discussion about it in the shop the other day."

Mindy had spotted the quintet and was heading over, dragging a reluctant Reading in her wake. Sterling was thinking that he looked vaguely familiar.

"Hi, everyone. The place looks beautiful, R.J.," she gushed as she kissed him on both cheeks.

"Thank you," R.J. said graciously, and then extended a hand to Reading. "Nice to see you, Reading. How's the hunting season going?"

The mention of hunting brought about a visual change in Reading's countenance. "Great. Me and Jojo brought down a six-point buck."

"Already?" R.J. looked surprised. "The season just opened Tuesday."

Sterling spoke up. "That's where I've seen you. Out by the Golden Door development with a recently dead hood ornament."

"Bagged it by noon," Reading said. Whitney made a disparaging sound, and Greer remembered the many pairs of antlers nailed to the wall of his storage shed.

"That's impressive," R.J. said.

"Well"—Reading dropped some of his self-congratulatory attitude—"to be honest, the fire up at Oak Springs helped somewhat. That's where we spotted him, out in the open. His usual cover was all burned away."

"I'm so upset," Mindy said, and there were tears in her eyes. Greer wondered if she cried every time her husband killed something. But it wasn't the dead deer that had affected Mindy. "Remember that painting in my living room?"

Greer and Whitney exchanged looks, and Greer felt an icy heat travel up both sides of her body.

"Well, it was a painting of almost exactly that area where the fire was, on the way up to Oak Springs, and now it's all black and sad."

"That fire was so frightening," Greer said, trying to cover her own shock at her premonition of the fire and wondering feverishly what possible meaning the image of the key could hold. "My son was the one who saw it and called it in. There was a really nice older couple, the Caseys, who almost lost their home."

There was a general clucking and sympathetic shaking of heads; then Reading spoke up, crossing his arms defensively across his wide chest. "I know it's hard, but fire is normal—even necessary—in these areas. The ecosystem depends on it; otherwise the shrubbery gets too dense. Look at the oaks: They are designed to survive brush fires. Most of the big ones have seen quite a few in the last couple of centuries."

Sterling nodded grudgingly. "That's basically true," he agreed. "But, as usual, we humans have changed things. We've added nonindigenous plants and we water out of season. Not to mention the fact that we've built our homes in this ecosystem that's *designed* to burn off every few years."

"It's amazing, when you see it," Reading said, almost as though Sterling hadn't spoken. His eyes had taken on that distant, hungry quality that Greer had seen when he spoke of the fire before. "When it's done right, everything is black for the first few days, and then, within just a couple of weeks, the seeds sprout and things grow back out of it. Hell, grow back *because* of it."

Mindy laid a hand on her husband's powerful arm. "Reading is an expert at controlled burn-offs. He says if everybody would do it, the risk of fire would be almost eliminated."

"True," agreed R.J. "Except for in the more remote and forested areas. The fire isn't as positive a thing there. And what we're dealing with now is once again human intervention: people making bonfires and throwing trash and lit cigarettes out, or worse—arson. It's not the same thing as the old lightning-strike burn-offs every few years. And now you've got this big subdivision right on the edge of the national forest land."

As Greer watched R.J. speak, she saw a glow around his darkened face, a crimson and orange light, a color that signified extreme anger, though he kept his voice controlled, conversational.

Perhaps also sensing potential discord, Mindy spoke up. "Let's not get into the pros and cons of the development tonight, gentlemen. It's a party."

The impending storm averted, the conversation turned to other things, including the upcoming Columbus Day parade, another subject on which R.J. had very distinct views.

"Columbus Day," he scoffed with a disgusted shake of his handsome head. "Columbus was a slave trader who was directly responsible for the deaths of over eight million native people. He wiped out an entire race of West Indians, and we have actually created a *national holiday* for this bastard who didn't even actually discover anything."

Luke cleared his throat and muttered, "Here we go." Then he waved his wineglass at R.J. and added, "Not that you're not absolutely right, of course."

"That can't be true! Where did you hear that?" Mindy asked, shocked.

"There are firsthand accounts written by a missionary who was in the West Indies at the time. And the facts were backed up by Columbus's own son in his personal journal when he took over his father's 'noble' work," Sterling told her. "We're talking about public records. It was all business transactions to them at the time. They didn't see any reason to suppress it."

"Why isn't this public knowledge?" Mindy's expression clearly told the tale that this was the first she had heard any of this.

R.J.'s voice softened. He laid a hand on Mindy's shoulder and said, "It is. Or rather, the information is out there, but it's mostly ignored because people want to be proud of their heritage. So, they are understandably reluctant to teach their children that not all their ancestors came here in pursuit of happiness and freedom, that quite a few of them came for gold and slaves. And who wants to tell eight-year-olds that the so-called discoverer of their country committed genocide on a scale that made Hitler look like a school-yard bully? Would you?"

Mindy's face had the same confused expression that Greer had seen on it in the salon, and then, in an instant, it solidified into something tougher and she said with conviction, "I would tell them the truth. You can't teach them lies."

Greer could see R.J.'s fingers tighten on Mindy's shoulder in an affectionate squeeze. "That's what I love about you. That, and the fact that you have such good taste in art," he added, leaning in with a mischievous smile. "Speaking of which"—he straightened up again—"I see a few newcomers who need to have their walls redecorated." With a wink and grin, he left them.

A small garage in the back corner of the garden had been refitted into a cozy painting studio. The French doors into the yard stood open, and several paintings rested on easels or were hung on the walls. The lights were on, and Greer and Sterling took it as an invitation to peruse the art. Excusing themselves, they drifted toward it.

The first canvas, lit by a small spot from overhead, was so beautiful that both Greer and Sterling took a deep, sighing breath in unison as they stopped in front of it. A creek bubbling over stones looked so full of motion and depth that Greer would have sworn the water was actually running. Over the stream, cottonwood trees in the first young green of spring dappled the sunlight on the water's surface, and where the sun struck the water, it lit up the depth beneath, showing the many colors of last year's fallen leaves.

"Oh my," Sterling sighed. "I like this guy!"

"I have to have that," Greer said. "Oh, I hope he hasn't sold it. I just feel like I have to have that in my home."

"We'll corner him in a minute," Sterling told her. "Don't you have a birthday coming up?"

Greer looked him in the face very solemnly. "You cannot buy me that painting," she told him severely.

"You're not the boss of me," Sterling said, a mischievous smile playing at the corners of his full mouth.

Greer's eyes caught the glint of his, and she whispered, "That's not what you said earlier tonight."

Sterling's strong hands reached out and encircled her waist. He pulled her up against him and pressed the small of her back with his palm, holding her firmly there. "I can give you anything I want," he said.

His voice had gone soft and deep; Greer didn't know how to respond, but she liked it. They stayed motionless for a moment, two pairs of green eyes, one set in crème satin and the other in polished mahogany, gazing into each other, caught up. Finally, sensing the presence of others, they broke away and moved on to the next painting.

This one was similar to the canyon view that Mindy owned. It was not the same canyon—this one was darker; only the very tops of the mountains were haloed in gold, as though touched by the first light of sunrise. It was beautiful but somehow harsher too, far more sparse and foreboding. Greer thought it looked vaguely familiar, as though she had seen the place from a different point of view, or in a different season.

Next to her, Sterling sighed again, but this sigh was filled with sorrow. "It sure doesn't look like that anymore," he said quietly.

"What do you mean?" Greer asked him.

"That's the hillside site of the development, before they sliced off the top, cut steps into it, and covered it in man-made materials."

"Oh," Greer said. The grading of the mountainside had begun before she had moved into the area; she had never seen it in its raw beauty. She stepped closer to the painting with the feeling of approaching a memorial.

As Greer studied the painting, she felt the internal sway of an approaching premonition, as if her very skeleton had softened and undulated in a wave, though outwardly she remained still.

Stepping forward once again and releasing Sterling's hand, she let go of the precise image and focused on the feeling welling up inside of her, willing herself to see.

There it was, just between the two main peaks of the hills in the foreground—an old-fashioned key, blackened by fire.

And then she stepped back as, with sudden violence, the entire hillside was engulfed in flame.

Chapter 20

Weston walked Leah to her car. It was a long walk for Leah, and as they went, she was forcibly reminded of an old print she had once seen in a psychiatrist's office.

The black-and-white lithograph was a cartoon for a periodical in the eighteen hundreds, showing a stylized image of a mentally disturbed man. In the picture, the man, his face twisted in a grotesque grimace of tortured agony, fought against a dozen tiny demons, each drawn with evil intent on their dwarfed, malignant faces. One stabbed at the man with a hot brazier, another pulled ruthlessly at a rope fastened tight around his neck, others pinched or worked away with miniscule pickaxes and pitchforks. The print was an exaggerated impression of misunderstood mental anguish, but right now, as Weston walked beside Leah to where they had left her car, she felt she could relate. If only she could have spotted one of the miniature devils that seemed to be laboring so diligently to cause her distress, she would have snatched it up by the back of its scrawny little neck and drop-kicked it into the middle of traffic on Foothill Boulevard.

But her personal demons remained invisible and impossible to contain. By the time they had reached the car, she had worked herself into a cold sweat of expectant fear. Would Weston want to kiss her good night? Would he never want to see her again? If he tried to touch her, would she recoil? Scream? Retch? Did she want him to touch her? She had a taste in her mouth like bad Gorgonzola, and her head was starting to pound.

She tried for casual friendliness. "Hop in and I'll take you back to your truck," she offered, but it was impossible to keep the trembling in her throat from making her voice warble.

"That's okay," Weston said easily, either not noticing or politely ignoring her visible discomfort. "It's only a few blocks back to the restaurant. I'll walk." After she had unlocked the car door with her remote, he moved next to her and opened it. "I had a great time. You've got my number; give me a call sometime if you'd like," he said. Keeping the door between them, he waited as she climbed into the BMW and then swung the door closed. Feeling churlish to let the evening end so abruptly, Leah rolled down her window.

Looking up at him from the relative safety of her leather seat, she said, "I had a great time too. Thank you."

The light in the parking lot was dim. The large fir trees that studded the ground around the play structure shadowed Weston so that she couldn't see his expression, giving him an ominous presence. As though sensing that the angle was too foreboding, he bent down until he was level with her window.

Then, without speaking, he leaned in, kissed her lightly on the forehead, and then straightened up and headed under the trees toward the street. Leah could make out his excellent form, striding confidently away from her, leaving her safe and alone.

It was a sensation she didn't care for.

Joy and Joshua climbed out of his car noisily in the parking area shared by both their houses.

"You want me to walk you home?" Joshua asked mockingly, as her front steps were less than ten feet from where he had parked.

"I don't know—it's really far." Joy was holding the purple giraffe she had won under her arm as though it were a purse. She put her hands on her stomach and grimaced. "Man, I don't think I should have had that second chili dog."

Joshua tried to keep a straight face. "I don't think it was the chili dog so much as the cotton candy, the ice cream, the churros, and the funnel cake."

"Ugh, please." Joy threw up a hand to silence him. "I will hurl all over you if you don't shut up."

"You guys got any Alka-Seltzer?"

"I think I have a few packs left over from the good ol' days," she confirmed.

"Well, go take one and lie down. Or hurl, not on me, of course, but you might feel better if you do."

Joy laughed and clutched her stomach. "Shut up! Don't make me laugh; it hurts."

"Well," said Joshua, raising a hand in farewell, "Good night. Thanks for going with me. I had a really good time."

"Me too," Joy said. "It was fun, thanks." Then, as though it was a casual motion that they were both used to, she swooped up and kissed his cheek. "Good night!" she exclaimed as she made her escape up the steps onto her porch and let herself in with her key.

Joshua stood, his feet rooted to the gravel parking area, one hand on his cheek, his mind exploding with far too many explanations of just what that tiny, moist, warm spot could possibly, maybe, perhaps mean.

Simon rode in the back of Loc's car next to Tic. They cruised slowly down an alleyway that ran behind a group of stores on Foothill Boulevard. In the front passenger seat, Juice's shiny pate glowed as he turned from side to side, his dark eyes shining in the striped lights of the streetlamps, watching left and then right. Tic frequently jerked around to look behind them. Loc pulled up in a dark spot between the two exterior lights of different stores and left the motor running. "Go, man, go," he told Juice.

In response to the order, Juice jumped out of the car and, taking a spray can from the deep pocket of his jacket, quickly and expertly tagged the white back door of a tobacco shop. Then he walked, slumped, eyes shifting rapidly and watchfully from side to side, but feigning innocence, back to the car. Loc pulled away, moving farther down the alley.

"Teach that motherfucker to not sell me smokes," Loc muttered with malice in his voice. He looked pleased with himself. Then, without turning to look at him, he said, "Yo, Sy."

"Yo," Simon answered from his seat behind Loc.

Nothing else was spoken between them, but Simon knew what was coming. He'd been expecting it.

Loc drove two more blocks down the alley, crossing the quiet side streets to access it. Finally he pulled the car into the darkness under overhanging branches, away from the streetlights. They all four sat in the car.

Simon's eyes were fixed on the back of the building. He knew it. He knew the reason he was there. A churning fear and hatred turned his stomach.

The other boys were waiting. "What you gonna do?" Loc finally said.

"This is where I get out," Simon said, a deadness in his voice that he had deliberately put there. He could not let them taste his fear; they would make him pay for it. He knew that they would not tolerate weakness.

"Shit, fucker. You gonna walk on us?" Loc said. He did not look or sound happy.

"I got shit to do." Simon let his eyes rest on Loc's, knowing that the older boy would understand this.

A tight, twisted, mean smile crept across Loc's thin mouth. "Do what you gotta do. Later, Sy." Juice and Tic both swore softly and refused to look at Simon.

Simon said nothing as the car sped away, its old gears protesting with a whine. And for a long time after the red taillights of the car had faded, he stood in the gloomy shadows, looking at the empty blackness where the tiny crimson glow had disappeared.

He waited for a full sweep of an hour hand, standing perfectly still in the shadows on the far side of the alley, watching and listening. When he was convinced that the alley, the store, and the neighborhood were asleep, that no eyes were observing him, he moved out of the cover of darkness and crossed the alley.

Chapter 21

He lay in the hot, still air and stared at the crosshatches of light on the brick wall. He had lain down a half hour ago and no sleep had come. His body and his brain were saturated with the temperature. The arid heat was bringing his restless spirit to a boiling point. He threw off the sheets and lay sweating, rocking rhythmically from side to side.

The seductive image of fire dominated his thoughts. Undulating and alive, lapping at the earth like a thirsty dog. Powerful, insatiable, unleashed by him. The very thought of it excited him and sent a thrill of pleasure surging through him, causing his penis to stiffen, his breath to quicken. The erotic sensation was followed quickly by agitation, need, and a driving hunger.

The edginess made him rise from the bed and pace back and forth in front of his window. His fingers itched, and his lust for flames lured him like a siren call. Careful to be as silent as possible, he dressed himself, left the bedroom and went down the stairs, and exited through the back door, keeping a hand on the screen door to restrain the squeak that he had learned to silence long ago, when he began his nightly outings.

Free of the constraints of walls and doors, he stood in the open air and breathed deeply. The air was dry, almost painfully so, and it smelled clean; there was no trace of smoke or ash in it tonight.

He smiled and fingered the lighter in his pocket. Soon

enough, he would change that. He would change everything.

Clyde had worked as a security guard for the last fifteen of his sixty-seven years. He enjoyed the privacy it
usually afforded him, working at night, left alone with
his books or TV and his bottle of Seagram's.

The bottle and its effects he was careful to conceal
from his employers. The TV and books they never
minded as long as he made his rounds; in fact, most of
his bosses seemed sorry for him and glad that he had
the distractions. If their pity allowed him his pleasures,
that was fine by Clyde. He didn't much care for human
company. He had one fishing buddy who wasn't dead
yet, and they saw each other a few times a year. His
daughter lived with her fancy-shmancy husband in Tuc-
son and seldom, if ever, acknowledged his existence.
Bitch. He'd never thought she'd amount to much, so it
didn't surprise him now that she was a crap daughter.
He'd expected it. He'd told her she would be.

He'd finished his last check about twenty minutes ago,
and now he sat in the work-site trailer with his mini-
DVD player—a gift from Shaina, who had been too lazy
to visit him for Christmas—playing a Steven Seagal
movie. He loved the fight scenes, loved the way the big
man cut through dozens of bodies with minimal effort
and movement. Sure, he'd gotten fatter over the years,
but he was still a badass. The only thing Clyde didn't
like was when they tried to fit in too much moral. Fuck
that. Action pictures were for one thing, action. And the
more bodies that flew apart and necks that broke, the
better.

He reached for his bottle and poured another inch
into the dirty mug he was using tonight. It still smelled
of stale coffee as he raised it to his mouth, but the bite
of the liquor soon erased the odor.

The movie was passing through one of its long-winded
bits when he checked his watch. Time for a walk-
through. Pressing PAUSE on the little device, he rose

from his chair with a number of complaining creaks from his joints. But a series of rolling movements cracked most of the bits back into place, though his knees still objected strongly to the three steep steps down out of the mobile office. Pulling his heavy, black metal flashlight from his belt, he switched it on and started trudging along the broken earth away from the looming hills behind him. After a couple hundred yards he came to the end of the cleared ground and stood just in front of a framed-out home. His feet finding the more secure footing of asphalt, he increased his pace and walked to where he'd left the golf cart. He turned the key and pressed the accelerator. The vibrant hum of the little car gave him satisfaction as it surged forward, moving his face against the still air in a feeble imitation of a lukewarm breeze.

Sixty seconds brought him to the end of the cul-de-sac, and Clyde was making the wide circle when something from beyond the skeletal frames of the houses, below the edge of the man-made steppe, caught his attention.

It was the sound of a motor running. A sound that should not have been there. After parking the cart, Clyde ambled along the bare earth down the narrow corridor between two of the gigantic house frames. When he came out into what would eventually be the backyards, he walked the length of them in less than twenty paces and peered down over the incline to the back of the framed houses on the next planned street below.

On the far side of them, moving along very slowly with its lights off, was a barely visible car. Clyde shone his flashlight through the impossibly thin wood of the house frames, but just as the light was about to reveal the vehicle, the driver must have spotted the beam, because the car shot away down the street, around a curve that blocked it from Clyde's view. Cursing, he stood listening to the retreating engine.

"Fucking kids," he muttered. The only problems he had had on this development were teenagers trying to find an isolated spot for their amorous adventures. Clyde enjoyed sneaking up on them and either startling them, or, if the moon was right, watching them surreptitiously from a distance. He especially enjoyed the convertibles. One particularly obliging young man had used a flashlight in the darkness on his partner's body as she danced for him on the hood of the car. Clyde smiled, heated from the memory. That had been a good night. He'd waited until they were hot and heavy, and then he'd pulled up next to them in the golf cart and sounded his air horn. He cackled out loud now at the memory of how they jumped and the girl had started to sob. He'd enjoyed that.

Returning to the cart, he finished his rounds and then retreated to his trailer. He fast-forwarded through the expositional part of the film until he got to the next action sequence, poured himself a couple more inches of whiskey, and settled back to wait out the next half hour.

By the time the end credits were running, Clyde's head had dropped back to one side and a thin trail of drool snailing its way from his mouth was interrupted only by his raucous snoring.

He stood and listened. It had been a hike up here, and he was sure that the rasping of his breath could be heard in this absolutely still night. But though he waited long after his breathing had steadied, he heard absolutely nothing.

Picking up the heavy can he had brought with him, he proceeded cautiously into the open, making his way toward the darker mass that stood out in the night. A hundred yards away, he could see a flickering light in the office trailer, but this did not concern him. He was familiar with the lax work ethic of nocturnal security guards. And even if the man did come out, it was a hundred to one that he would see the single form among the piles of building materials, scrap wood, and large open spaces.

He made it to his destination, and paused. Pulling a short hunting knife from his pocket, he went to work, scratching away busily, occasionally flicking his lighter to admire his work and check on its progress. After fifteen minutes, he was content that it was deep enough, and he put the blade away.

Then he emptied the contents of the can all around, careful to let the liquid soak the places that he felt needed it most. This was the second such operation to-night. With the first he had scattered the accelerant more sparingly just below the mobile home, where the shrub-bery still grew unimpeded by bulldozers and land-moving monsters. He needed fuel for that job, the dry shrubbery supplied it, and all that was required was a little encouragement from the contents of the can. He liked the smell of the gasoline, always had. It reminded him of something that he couldn't place. A time when he had not always felt the gnawing of ravenous hunger.

The next part was a bit tricky—it necessitated no wind—and thankfully the night had obliged. Taking a small stump of candle from his pocket, he propped it up carefully in the loose earth and then piled some shred-ded paper around it, almost to the wick but not quite. Within ten minutes, he estimated, the flame would reach the paper, the paper would ignite, the fire would spread to the gasoline-soaked ground, and his work here would be done.

Time enough to separate himself from the scene and gain a view on the spectacular results of his efforts. This would be worth watching—from a comfortable distance.

The lighter flared in the shadow; the candle flickered to life. Straightening, he checked the trailer for signs of life—there were none—then he hurried through the open darkness, over the crest of the hill, back into the cover of the shrubbery, and within minutes was safely away, feeling the high, the elation, the power. The cour-age and nerve to do this made him invincible, a dark force to be reckoned with. This was his triumph, his legacy.

As he raced away, two small fires leapt to life behind him, spreading quickly as they seemed to strive to reach each other. The first, released in a field of dry tinder, crackled noisily as it ate, crunching and snapping the spines of its meat. The second fire flushed silently across the ground and then began to crawl upward, licking and lapping as it went, until it too settled into its meal.

Without warning, the wind began to move across the space between earth and sky, gusting lightly at first, but growing steadily more constant. It fanned the flames, already alive and happy with their work, and eased them in new directions, pushing gently, nudging. With a crack, a burning leaf fell from its broken branch and, encouraged by the wind beneath it, fluttered like some incendiary butterfly a few yards across open ground and landed on a pile of scrap lumber, choosing as its resting place a particularly narrow and brittle piece of wood that a workman had soaked in turpentine while thinning paint earlier that day.

The combustion was instantaneous, and the flames leapt merrily up from a new and willing source. Within minutes, a bonfire worthy of Guy Fawkes was scrabbling with greedy fingers toward the sky. Delighted with its newfound freedom, and cheered on by the strengthening wind, the fire skipped along from source to source until it reached the mobile home, where it stretched out its exploring hands and seemed to seek an entry along one side of the fake-panel exterior.

Halfway between deep sleep and a drunken stupor, Clyde snored loudly. He crossed his arms over his chest and shifted in the reclining chair, his head lolling from one side to the other, and into his addled dreams came sounds that created images he did not understand: the crackling sounds of paper rustling in the wind, of branches scratching at the window. He grimaced, flinching from some nameless threat; then he sank deeper into his nightmares.

Chapter 22

Joshua shot up in bed, his whole body soaked with sweat. The image of a burning tree was seared into his brain. He had seen it, as clearly as though he had been standing in front of it. A massive tree in full flame, he could almost feel its pain as the fire consumed its ancient life.

It had not been a dream, he was sure. One thing he had learned since his uncanny visions had begun, anything he saw was happening now. His mother saw images of the future, or glimpses and premonitions of what was to come, but *his* sixth sense was present.

Jumping to his feet in his loose cotton pajama pants, he pulled on a T-shirt and flung open his door. He went down the hallway and hesitated in front of the door to his mother's room. He knew that Sterling was in there, but he heard nothing except the sound of even breathing.

He knocked. "Mom?" he called out.

When he heard the urgency in his own voice, he was not surprised that she responded with "Joshua, what's wrong?"

"I think there's another fire."

"Come on in," Sterling said, and Joshua pushed open the door but stayed where he was. In the dim light coming from the moon outside, Joshua could see Sterling was already out of bed and pulling on a shirt. "Where? Can you see it?" Though there was concern in his voice, he sounded completely in control.

"No. I mean, yes, but it was a . . ." Joshua hesitated. Would he ever get used to talking about this, even with those who understood? "I *saw* it. It's a tree, a big one, and it's burning in an open place."

His mother was beside him in an instant, and they both squinted as Sterling switched on the bedside light.

"Where?" Not so much as a speck of doubt dulled her face or her eyes.

"I don't know!" Joshua moaned. "I just saw the tree and I know that it's happening now. Do you understand?"

"Of course I do." Greer guided Joshua over to the bed and sat him down, lowering herself next to him. "Okay, let's take a minute and you try to remember any other details, anything that would tell us where—" She cut off suddenly, and on her face was a look of startled realization.

"What? Mom? What is it?" Joshua felt two surges of emotion piston up and down forcefully inside of him, anxiety for his mom and relief that she might be able to relieve him of this responsibility.

"I think I know where," she whispered. Then she turned a stricken face to Sterling, who had come around to stand in front of them. "I think it's the development. Tonight, when I was looking at that painting, I saw the image of a blackened key over the painting R.J. had done of the area. I saw the same image over his painting of Oak Springs Canyon the day before the fire."

Sterling ran his hands over his close-cropped hair and then scratched furiously at his scalp as though this would loosen his brain and clarify the situation. "Do you think we should call the fire department? I mean, if it's a false alarm, they will not be happy, and if it isn't, they sure as hell are going be suspicious of how you knew about a fire you couldn't see, smell, or hear."

"I know," Greer stressed.

"I'm not even sure that they'll respond if you call from here and tell them you dreamed it," he said gently. "And as far as I know, there isn't anyone living up there. Wait!" His face lit up. "I have the site number in my folder. I'll call the mobile office, and if the security guard is in there, he can tell us. If he hasn't seen it already."

"That's right," Greer said, relieved. "There's a security guard on. He'll have seen it."

Sterling scowled. "If he's awake."

"Why do you think he'd be asleep?" Joshua asked, his sudden elation deflating at the possibility.

"Wouldn't you be?" Sterling said sourly. He left the room quickly, and Joshua and Greer followed. In the kitchen he opened his briefcase, found the folder and the number, and dialed it. As he waited for a response, he said, "The cell phone service is sporadic up there, so Rowland gave me this number to reach him." He waited again, his brow creased with concern. "Damn it," he cursed. "The machine." He waited briefly again and then spoke. "Hello? Is anyone there? I'm trying to reach the night security guard. Can you please pick up if you can hear me? Anyone? This is an emergency." He waited again, and then with a frustrated shrug, he hung up the phone. "Any other bright ideas?"

"We could drive up there." Joshua said.

But Sterling was already shaking his head. "That's at least fifteen miles from here. If there really is a fire in this dry heat, we need to do something now."

Greer was staring at the floor, her lovely mouth puckered in tense concentration. Suddenly she looked up at them both, her face clear and her eyes bright. Then she spoke one word, and it sounded like a hurray.

"Leah."

Next to the sleeping Clyde, the phone rang, its ringer muted by the music from the DVD, which had reverted to the title menu twenty minutes ago and had been repeating its thrilling but partial theme for as long. The top two feet of the mobile home were thick with smoke, an upside-down sea that was rising toward the motionless man below it.

The phone stopped ringing and the machine clicked on; a man's voice spoke urgently but fell on deaf ears. Then it cut off, and for a few moments the only sound was the crackling flames against the outside far wall of the of structure.

Then, with a crashing boom, there came furious banging on the locked door, and the sound of a woman's screaming voice cut through the night. But still Clyde did not wake.

A scarf tied over her mouth, Susan Hughs stood on the ground beside the trailer steps, reaching up to slam the locked, hot door with her fist again and again. "Wake up! Wake up!" she shouted as loudly as her lungs, painful from the smoke around her, would allow. But there was no response. In her other hand she held her cell phone, desperately punching in 911 and then SEND. Three tries produced a shaky connection, a scratchy operator's voice that cut in and out, and Susan shouted over it. "There's a fire and a man is trapped in a trailer at the Golden Door development site off of Viewpoint. Please, can you hear me?" As she shouted into the elegant little piece of technology, she thought she heard a fraction of a response, but when she backed away from the door and pressed the phone hard to her ear, she heard nothing more, and when she peered at it, it read, *Lost call.*

"Damn it!" Susan yelled to the night that was angry with flame and smoke. "Goddamn it!" A kind of fury rose up in her and possessed her with a superhuman determination. She would not let this happen, not on her property, not while she was here to do anything about it. She looked desperately around, her brain kicking into overdrive to find a solution, refusing to accept that there was no answer, no option.

Then she had it. The walls of the mobile home were thin and seconds away from succumbing to the flames that licked at the far side. She ran for her weapon of choice.

"Leah!" Greer said eagerly when her friend's groggy voice came on the line. "Are you awake?"

"Uh, who is this?" Leah asked, her head foggy and her mouth thick with the depth of sleep.

"It's Greer. I'm sorry to wake you but it's an emergency. Listen, I know you can see across the valley from your house to the new development. I need you to go look at it."

Leah looked instead at the receiver in her hand. She shook it slightly as though that might help to straighten out the words inside of it; then she put it back to her ear. "What? What time is it?"

"It's almost one o'clock. Please, I know it sounds crazy, but please do it!"

"Okay, okay," Leah muttered, climbing out of bed. She got to the living room and walked to the back windows that led to her patio. "Okay, I'm looking," she said in a tired voice.

"Do you see anything?"

"What am I supposed to see? It's the middle of the night, everything is dark and . . . Wait." Leah peered off into the distance. They were small, and hard to distinguish, but what struck her about the two bright lights was that they should *not* be there. Suddenly every fiber in her body snapped to attention. "Christ!" she exclaimed. "I think there's a fire—two fires, actually."

"Okay." Greer's exhale and single word sounded strangely relieved instead of surprised to Leah. "Can you call the fire department and report it?"

"I'm hanging up right now," Leah said. She disconnected and then dialed 911. The emergency operator connected her to the Shadow Hills Fire Department, and she gave them the information about the fire and her own name and location as succinctly as she possibly could, then hung up, sat down on the sofa, and stared across the lights of the valley to the two strangely beautiful golden glows on the black hills beyond.

It was a long time before it occurred to her to wonder at the fact that a friend of hers who lived deep in a valley miles away had called to waken her at one in morning about a fire she could not have known was burning.

*   *   *

The fire broke through the wall with a sucking *swoosh* of air. Clyde coughed once and then rolled unconscious out of the chair onto the floor. The orange light from the flames colored his otherwise deathly pale face.

Then, with a crash that literally turned the corner of the trailer inside out, a Range Rover smashed through the wall. The headlights pierced the smoke like lasers, their beams tracked and interrupted by the gray haze. There was a moment of confused noise, and then the wheels spun, caught, and the car jerked backward, taking part of the wall that was hooked onto the high bumper. A door slammed, and then Susan Hughs climbed up onto the floor of the room and crawled forward on her hands and knees, feeling in front of her, her eyes streaming with stinging tears. The trailer was fairly small, and in seconds she had located the inert security guard. Grasping him under his arms and staying low, she dragged him to the door, unlocked it, then heaved him halfway up, and, unable to carry him down the three steps, just fell backward onto the ground with him on top of her.

The hard ground and Clyde's weight knocked the air out of her. She lay there, winded for a few seconds, trying to draw in enough comparatively smoke-free air to enable herself to move again. In half a minute, she had rolled Clyde to one side and repeated her pull, dragging the dead weight of the guard away from the trailer, which, with the inrush of air, was rapidly engulfed in flames. Her back strained and aching, she stood up and looked around. Her car was wrecked, the front end seemed to be leaking gasoline, and she suspected it would explode any minute—that was not an escape option. She could not carry this man the two miles back to the main road, and her cell phone, on inspection, was still showing no service. Fighting off a growing panic, she set herself instead to care for the victim in front of her. He seemed to be breathing, but unconscious.

All around her the fire seemed to be moving, groping its way toward her, the smoke spreading its disorienting spell and choking poison in every direction, until she started to think that her only chance might be to leave him and try to get away on foot.

But still she doggedly willed herself to think of a way to save them both, determined that he would not die—she would not allow it. She got behind him and tried to find a way to lift him: If only she could get him up on her shoulder, maybe she could move them both to safety. The flames from the mobile home were so intense that she could feel the sting of the heat on her face, and a new, more lethal smell had joined the tang of burning sagebrush, chemicals and plastics releasing their toxic soup into the air that she was breathing.

She was still struggling a full minute later, when she heard the helicopters as they swooped in from overhead.

"Oh, thank God," she exclaimed, and collapsed onto her knees with her face in her hands, her body shaking with sobs that she needed to exorcise, and then wanted desperately to hide away, locked back down out of sight with any other chinks in her painstakingly constructed armor. She would bury this loss of control deep inside, next to any other discernible weakness that might reveal to a predatory world that she was not quite as invincible as she so fervently pretended to be.

Chapter 23

It wasn't as bad as it could have been, Joshua thought as he surveyed the shell of the trailer and the acre or so of burned underbrush at the Golden Door site the next morning. What would have happened if he hadn't awoken, he didn't want to think. He told himself that someone else would have seen the fires from across the valley. After all, it had been Friday night, only about one o'clock in the morning.

"Oh no," he heard Sterling moan next to him, and turning he saw what had elicited this emotion. The magnificent oak tree, spared from destruction once by an act of law, was now a charred, grotesque skeleton. All its branches remained, but they were blackened and bare. Instead of offering shade for the body and relief to the eye, the ravaged, jagged form offended and alarmed. Joshua found he couldn't look at it. The thought that it had stood sentinel in this valley, surviving the fires, droughts, and storms of nature for centuries only to be destroyed by a deliberate act of human vandalism in a single night, filled him with shame.

Sterling, however, was already walking toward it. Not knowing what else to do, Joshua followed him with the feeling that he was visiting the fresh grave of an old friend. They stopped near the charcoal black of the trunk and Sterling laid his hand on it in sorrow and apology, as he had done before in respect and admiration. "I'm sorry," he said out loud. "I'm so sorry that we've forgotten."

Joshua asked softly, "What have we forgotten?"

"That we are the stewards of the earth. That we were given brains to take care of it, not to exploit and abuse it."

He had never heard it put that way, but the words eloquently expressed a feeling that Joshua had had all his life. He began to circle the tree, letting his fingers trail along the trunk. On the far side, something brought him to a stop.

Into the trunk of the tree something had been carved. He didn't remember seeing that before, and it was carved deeply, deeply enough that the fire had exaggerated the shape rather than obliterating it.

It was a spider, roughly drawn, with an hourglass body and eight spindly legs. They had been hacked into the trunk with rough skill. The fire had dried up any sap that would have told Joshua if the wound was a new marking, but he felt sure he would have noticed such a blatant act of vandalism.

"Look at this," he said to Sterling, swiping his hands against each other, trying to loosen the inky dust that had stuck to them.

Sterling came around and peered intently at the form. "That wasn't there yesterday," he said sternly. He looked back at the fire chief, who was standing next to Susan and Rowland Hughs near their cars. "Hello," he called out. When the fireman looked up, he shouted, "You might want to see this."

Gray-haired and with the rounded belly of a once-active man who had retreated to a supervising job, the man strode across the open space and up the incline to where they were standing. He introduced himself as Captain Williams. Sterling showed him the spider and told him it hadn't been there before.

"It's a shame this tree got caught in this fire," Captain Williams said.

"It didn't 'get caught,'" Sterling said, giving the man a sideways glance. "You know as well as I do that these trees . . ."

But Sterling was interrupted by a shout from one of

the firemen who was still at work down below. The man beckoned to Captain Williams with a grim, exaggerated movement.

"Excuse me," Captain Williams said, and hurried off down the hillside, his large bulk slipping in the loose earth as he went.

Curious, Sterling and Joshua started to follow, but then stopped next to Susan and Rowland. Her left arm was bandaged and she held herself rigidly at a slight angle, as though it pained her to stand upright.

"What is it?" she asked Sterling anxiously. "What have they found? Do you think it's some kind of clue to who did *this*?" Her last word was spoken with such venom and disgust that Joshua thought for a moment that she might be sick.

Sterling answered her calmly. "I don't know yet."

Rowland's eyes were misty as he looked around at the burned trailer and land. "Why would someone want to do this? What on earth would possess them to attack us this way? And poor Clyde." He rubbed his eyes furiously for a moment. "If Susan hadn't come to get those papers last night—which I tried to talk her out of; thank God I didn't—he'd be dead now."

"Oh, how is he?" Joshua asked.

"Not real good," Susan said sarcastically. "I mean, he's closer to seventy than sixty, and he inhaled enough smoke to cure a ham."

Though her words were curt, Joshua saw her repress a wave of emotion. He said, "That was very brave what you did, getting him out."

"I don't know about brave," she said dismissively. "I was really angry, I'll tell you that. Can you imagine what that kind of publicity would do to the sales? Mostly, though, the thought that someone was going to die working for me was just plain unacceptable. I wasn't going to let it happen." Her voice had risen in pitch, and she took two deliberately deep breaths. The effort seemed to hurt her, because she let out a small exclamation and put both hands against the small of her back. "Damn it. I threw my back out pulling Clyde. It's harder than it looks on TV." She paused again and her eyes swept the ruined trailer. "Bastards," she said quietly.

"Do you come up here in the middle of the night very often?" Sterling asked.

Rowland was the first to respond. "The woman sleeps four hours a night. She's always working at some ungodly hour."

"It's quieter. I get more done. And in answer to your question, no, not very often, but last night I was getting ready for the citizens' committee meeting this evening, and I couldn't locate copies of some zoning papers that we have to keep on file at the site. So I decided to drive up here." She scowled furiously. "They're dust. Now I'll have to go back to the county records to get copies. Damn waste of time and energy."

"Could someone have wanted to destroy them?" Sterling asked, as though it were a casual question.

Rowland looked from Sterling to Susan. "You mean, you think somebody might have set this fire to destroy documents?" he asked incredulously. "I don't see why. We can get copies. I just thought it was kids vandalizing and it got a little out of control. But . . ." His voice trailed off and his usually carefree face creased with worry. "I just don't know," he said at last with a shake of his head. "I just don't understand why anyone would want to do this." He looked up at the charred oak. "And it even burned up that tree. I loved that tree." His voice actually broke as he said it.

Captain Williams was making his way slowly back toward them. Several of the firemen clustered around one small area behind him; they stood, picks and shovels forgotten in their hands, talking quietly among themselves or gazing at the ground.

"What is it?" Susan asked with authority. "What have you found?"

The man did not respond until he had come right up into their circle, and then he paused to look at each of them before saying, "I'm afraid it's a body."

There was a shocked silence, during which they stared at the chief as though he must be mistaken. Then, next to him, Joshua heard a choking sound. Turning, he saw Susan, one hand to her mouth, her face white and her eyes wide with horror. "No," she whispered. "No, that can't be. Someone died? Here? Who?" She began to take deep, shallow breaths.

"We can't know that right now," the fireman said. "I've already called the police, and when they arrive, we'll determine if this was an accident or a homicide. In either case, it seems apparent that whoever it was, they were a victim of arson. I have to ask you if you know of anyone who might have been here last night."

Over the shock and horror of realizing that someone lay dead a few yards away, Joshua felt an immense wave of relief that they had had Leah report the fire. He turned to look at the Hughses. Rowland's mouth was hanging open; Susan was shaking her head and looking nauseated. Both of them said they had no idea.

Joshua had a thought. "You know, I hike in this area quite a bit, and I often see places where homeless people have set up a camp. I mean, this is kind of far from the main road, but, what if it was one of them?"

Susan had both hands over her mouth. "Oh, how horrible," she said, barely audibly.

"That's a distinct possibility," the fireman agreed.

"Could it be"—Susan seemed afraid to speak—"the person who set the fire?"

"That was my first thought." The fireman looked back to the spot where the group of firemen stood, just near the edge of the burned-out area. "If it was somebody vandalizing, and they were drunk, which is a reasonable assumption, then they could have gotten disoriented and accidentally done themselves in." He turned back to the four civilians. "We'll have to wait and see. I'm afraid you'll have to answer some questions when the police come."

"Of course, anything we can do," Rowland said immediately.

Susan leaned toward her husband and winced again.

"Do you need to sit down?" the fire chief asked.

"No, I need to lie down, flat, with ice and painkillers,

but I don't have time for that," she said impatiently. She seemed to have regained control of herself.

Sterling was watching her with concern. "You know, Greer offered to give you a treatment. Maybe a massage and whatever magic she performs in that little room would be just the thing," he suggested.

Susan looked impatient, but Rowland cut in. "Honey, I'm going to insist on it. You need to relax. You've been through a horrible ordeal, and as usual, you've acted like a champ, but I will not let you run yourself into the ground. You call her and make an appointment."

"Rowland, I don't have ti—"

"Promise me," Rowland said with more power in his voice than Sterling had heard before, and it came to him that this was a man who, while appearing to be uniformly innocuous, could bear the scepter or the sword when necessary. He and his tough-as-nails wife now seemed more evenly matched, and sure enough, she succumbed to his insistence.

"All right. You're right. I'll do it." Once she agreed, it seemed a relief to her. "I could really use a break; this has all been very—" She broke off as her face twisted, and then she seemed to make a valiant effort to get her emotions under control. When she appeared to have won the battle, she said to her husband, "After the community meeting, okay? I've just got too much to do today and tonight to lie down."

Rowland did not look altogether happy, but a good leader knows when to compromise. "Not all right. You are going to call right now, and afterward you are going home to work in bed and on the phone until the meeting. Got it?"

He put a hand firmly around her waist and led her to his car.

The three men watched them go, and then, without looking at the other two, the fire captain said, "That's one tough lady."

Sterling peered at the man, his keen eyes squinting in the sun. "You should try doing business with her," he said dryly.

A small, mirthless laugh came from Captain Williams. "No, thank you" was all he said.

On the low road of packed dirt cut into the hillside just below them, a water truck had been standing since Joshua and Sterling arrived, no doubt on hand for the cleanup. Now, as Joshua watched, the door to the cab creaked open and a tall, thin man, as gangly and tough-looking as jerky, emerged. He was dangling a cigarette from his thin mouth, and he put it out carefully before coming to join the fire captain.

"Hey, George. What's going on?" he asked, flicking his baseball-capped head in the direction of the small group of blue uniforms.

"Hey, Sheldon," Captain Williams replied. "Found a victim."

Sheldon's skin looked so dry that Joshua wondered if it would be crunchy if he touched it. "Shit," he said, shaking his head.

At that point the truck's cab door opened again, and a small boy, his hair mussed to one side as though he had just woken up, stuck his head out and looked around.

"Tyler," Sheldon called out, "stay in the truck."

"I'm hot!" the boy called out.

Sheldon looked around. "All right, come on up here, and you can sit in the shade by the fire truck. Is that all right, George?" he asked the fire captain.

The captain smiled. "Sure. Hey, Tyler!" he called out. "You working with your grampa today?"

"Poor thing had to sleep in the truck last night. His mom ran away from the rehab, and I finally had to take custody." Sheldon, though apparently not loquacious, summed up what was probably a long story with that single sentence.

The boy, who looked to be about eight, was struggling up the hill. His jeans were clean and dark blue like his grandfather's; his T-shirt was not quite as clean, however, and looked as though a large portion of some fast food had touched down on it on the way to, or from, his mouth.

"You remember Captain Williams, Tyler?" Sheldon asked, and his voice gave the warning that a proper greeting was required.

"Yes, sir. How are you, sir?" Tyler reached out a slight hand, and the captain, looking amused, leaned down to shake it.

"I'm fine, thank you, Tyler. How are you?"

"I'm real good, thank you, sir." Tyler glanced up at Sterling and Joshua. Sheldon had not mentioned or acknowledged them past a nod of anonymous greeting.

"Hi there. I'm Joshua," Joshua said with a smile, deliberately not offering to shake to let the kid know that he was a kid too. "And this is Sterling."

"Nice to meet you, Mr. Sterling," Tyler said formally, offering the hand a bit more hesitantly.

In spite of the sobering situation at hand, Sterling couldn't repress a small laugh. "I'm Mr. Fincher, but you can call me Sterling; that's my first name."

Joshua was watching the boy, whose eyes had gone wide when he heard Sterling's accent. His small mouth tightened, and some sort of struggle seemed to be going on inside him. He looked up at his grandfather and the grin of pride on his stern, weathered face, but the boy received no warning from that quarter. Seemingly bolstered by that fact, he apparently came to a decision. Tyler looked back up at Sterling and asked, "Are you a foreigner?"

This time Sterling laughed outright. "Well, I was. I'm an American now."

Tyler nodded, looking pleased with his own astuteness. "I thought so."

Coming up the road was a car that Joshua recognized from past experience as an unmarked cop car, so he was not at all surprised when a man with a hard face topping a body that somewhat resembled a Peterbilt truck got out of the passenger side. "Detective Sheridan," Joshua said quietly to no one in particular. The senior detective took his time looking around the location. Spotting Captain Williams, he made his way toward the small group of men and a boy.

A younger man, dressed in jeans and a black polo shirt that gave a clear view of the badge and gun holster affixed to his belt, got out of the driver's side. He was sporting one of the most obvious hairpieces Joshua had ever seen.

When Detective Sheridan got to them, he shook hands with the fire captain and then looked long and hard at Joshua. Joshua tried to hold the officer's somewhat rheumy gaze but found himself squirming.

"Detective Sheridan," he said again, this time by way of greeting.

"Joshua Sands." The bulky man let the name hang for a few seconds as though considering it from all angles. "Fancy running into you in the middle of a murder." There was enough irony in the statement to defuse the innuendo somewhat.

Sterling interjected, "I'm not sure I should say it's nice to see you, given the circumstances, but let me reassure you, detective; Joshua is here only because he works for me and I'm the landscape architect working on the development."

"I see." The detective transferred his deceivingly indifferent gaze to Sterling. "Mr. Fincher, isn't it?"

"Yes, sir." The two men shook hands.

"This is my partner, Detective Wright," Sheridan said. The forty-something man standing beside him was red faced, well built, not more than five foot ten but with the muscular arms and thick legs of a man who considered a day wasted when he didn't bench-press the weight of a small pony several hundred times. Joshua tried hard not to stare at the place where the black of his hairpiece met the fading brown of his actual hair. He wondered how the man, a detective no less, could possibly have thought that no one would notice.

Introductions were made all around, and then the fire captain's walkie-talkie sputtered. After a quick consultation he turned to Sheldon.

"They're ready to spray the load," he told him.

Tyler started out after his grandfather, but Sheldon held him back. "You stay up here, young man. I've got to go turn the truck on so they can pump this water out where they need it."

"He can hang out with me for a few minutes," Joshua said.

Sheldon looked from the eight-year-old to Joshua and then back again. "You okay with that?"

"Yes, sir," Tyler answered. Sheldon looked up at Joshua, who nodded, before heading back to his truck.

Casting around for something to say, Joshua asked Tyler, "You been up here all night?"

"No, sir, we had to go up to Big Bear yesterday afternoon."

"Wow," said Joshua. "You drove that truck all the way up to Big Bear?"

Tyler looked seriously up at Joshua and shook his head. "No, sir. My grandfather drove it. I just rode along."

Joshua put a hand on the boy's shoulder as he suppressed a laugh. Another vehicle was making its way up the packed dirt road, the coroner's van.

"Come on," Joshua said, wanting to distract Tyler, and himself. "Let's go take a walk up here and see if we can find a fox hole or a wood rat home."

But Tyler was not so unaware as all that. He peered down to the spot around which the detectives were gathered and watched as the coroner's team climbed out of the van.

"What did they find?" he asked suspiciously.

"Let's go and let these people do their work, okay?"

"What did they find?" Tyler asked, more insistently.

Joshua looked down at the boy and knew he couldn't lie, but it wasn't his place to tell the whole truth.

Gently, he said, "You'll have to ask your grandfather, but it's something very bad."

Tyler seemed willing to accept this answer, and with the same trusting heart, he took Joshua's hand, and they both turned away from the direction of the charred, once-human remains.

Chapter 24

Even though it was not yet eight thirty in the morning, Jenny could see the sweat under King's saddle frothing with the repetitious motion of his walk. She'd decided this should be her last ride until after the baby, so she'd kept the ride short, easy, and early. Even so, she was grateful that they were almost back to the barn. The last part of the trail passed under a grove of live oaks, and Jenny sighed audibly as they passed into the relief of the shade.

Removing her cowboy hat, she anticipated with relish a cool-down from the hose for King and herself. Then, giving King his rein and leaning back, she closed her eyes and lost herself in the rhythm of his step.

"Morning." The voice came, deep and sudden from just a few feet to her right, startling her.

Sitting upright with a jerk and opening her eyes, Jenny tightened the reins and clucked soothingly to her horse, but King didn't so much as break his easy stride. Most likely he'd seen the man long before they got there.

A few feet off the trail, Reading leaned against the trunk of one of the largest oaks, a lit cigarette in one hand and smoke streaming from both nostrils like inverted twin chimneys.

"Oh, Reading." Jenny put a hand on her chest and brought King to a complete stop; he stamped impatiently and tossed his head, eager to get back to the barn. "You scared me. I wasn't paying any attention."

"Hard to when your eyes are closed," he noted.

"What are you doing up here?" Jenny asked, eyeing the lit cigarette like it was a Molotov cocktail.

He shrugged. "Took a little walk, having a smoke."

"Isn't that kind of dangerous? I mean, smoking up here when the fire hazard level is beyond extreme?" She asked, trying to make the question sound casual.

"Isn't it a little dangerous horseback riding eight months pregnant?" he retorted, raising his eyebrows knowingly.

"Seven months. And, touché," she said begrudgingly.

"How does your husband feel about you coming out here by yourself?"

"He's fine with it," Jenny lied. Something about Reading, the way he watched her without blinking, the stillness in his body as though waiting for something, gave her the creeps. She wondered how she could get such a different sense from Mindy, who was so kind and open. Well, it wasn't the first time she'd liked only one half of a couple; that happened. She was sure that her husband, Lewis, probably struck some people as unfriendly as well; he wasn't exactly the most gregarious person.

With an economy of movement, perhaps in defense against the heat, Reading lifted the cigarette to his mouth in a kind of slow-motion arc. "He's out of town on a job, right?"

"How did you know?" Jenny couldn't stop herself from asking.

He exhaled a luxurious stream of smoke. "Mindy. She loves talking."

"Oh, of course," Jenny laughed. But for some reason, she didn't feel comfortable discussing it with Reading.

"When's he coming back?" Reading asked.

Instead of telling him that it would be another three weeks, Jenny offered a chirpy "Soon, real soon." Then she gave King the smallest of nudges to urge him forward. "See you back at the barn!" she called over her shoulder.

If he made a response, she did not hear it. A minute later, she emerged from the grove and the sun hit her like a shovel on the back of the head. She could see the back of the barn at the far end of an open field, through which the path ran in a sultry curve. The air was suddenly so still that it felt like an expanding solid mass pressing in all around her.

As she neared the barn, she was struck by the silence of her surroundings. No breath of wind moved the dry scrub brush, no birds called, there were not even the chirrups of insects in this desert heat. Only King's footfalls, muffled by the deep layer of soft dust on the trail, sounded distantly, as though they were so heavy they couldn't lift themselves to her ears. Then one other noise floated through the thick stillness to her ears—one that she could not identify.

It was a repetitive *whoosh*, almost as though someone were blowing bellows at a fire: *whoo, whoo, whoo*. It was strange and solitary in the pressing stillness of the air. She looked around for the source, her mind searching for an image of something that she could attach to the airy wave. And then she saw it.

As she watched in amazement, a black crow, its feathers glowing with an indigo sheen in the unfiltered sun, passed above her, and with every beat of its dark wings she could hear the perfect rush of forced air, *whoo, whoo, whoo*.

Jenny rode on, feeling as though she alone had witnessed a moment in which the season had revealed itself to her in animal form: awesome, relentless, menacing, and very much alive. She had heard it breathing.

Chapter 25

"I can see a man with white hair, over your left shoulder," Joshua said in a hushed voice, as though if he spoke too loudly, the image would run away.

He was seated at Whitney's dining room table. They were spending the hot afternoon inside, and she had volunteered to let Joshua practice on her. Now that it had become apparent to Joshua that spirits, or whatever they were, were going to be popping into his field of vision whether he had asked for that particular talent or not, his primary goal had become to control and understand the phenomena.

With that objective in mind, he sat next to Whitney, their chairs turned toward each other, his notebook open on the table in front of him. Two large glasses of iced tea sweated rings onto the tablecloth in front of them.

"What's he doing?" Whitney asked.

"Looking happy, but I think that where the figures appear is important," Joshua tried to explain. "Over the left shoulder seems to be a man who knew you, like a father or a grandfather, or maybe a father figure."

"My father passed away two years ago," Whitney told him. "Is his hair long?"

"Longish." Joshua tried to focus on the figure. He was standing with his arms open, as though showing off how radiantly happy he was, and he kept pointing to his feet. But there was something else. As though the body of the figure were transparent, Joshua could see inside of him, and as he focused more closely, he could see movement. At first he thought it was blood pumping through veins, but then he realized it was a serpent, snaking its way through the man's body. Up, down, and around in a figure eight.

"Did your father have something to do with snakes?" Joshua asked, grasping for some way to interpret the meaning of the image.

"No-o," Whitney said slowly.

The snake was dark, reddish black. "Was he ever bitten by one? I think this has something to do with his death."

"No, he died of toxemia."

The image of the snake glowed and then disappeared. "You mean, poison?" Joshua asked.

"Yes, he was poisoned, and . . . Oh!" Whiney exclaimed. "Hey, that's pretty good."

Joshua felt a little swell of pride; he'd followed his instinct and guessed right. Of course, without Whitney to make the connection, he would have thought the man died of a snakebite. He looked down and wrote in his notebook, *Serpent in body=poison.*

"What else? Does he have a message for me?" Whitney asked, and for the first time, Joshua heard the need in her voice. He'd been so caught up in interpreting that he had forgotten he was seeing an image of someone she had loved and lost.

"He's definitely very happy. If I'm right, then he wants you to know that he's not just okay, but ecstatic. Does that sound right?"

"It sounds good," Whitney said, and there was a slight quiver in her usually cheerful, steady voice.

The figure of Whitney's father kept on beaming and gesturing to his feet. Joshua tried to see why. They seemed normal feet, very white, nice and clean.

"He keeps showing me his feet," Joshua said, confused. "I think he wants to show me how clean they are?" He finished as a question, wondering what that could mean.

Whitney looked at him with a befuddled expression. "His feet? He used to like to go barefoot a lot, especially in the summer, but I don't know."

Outside, the sound of a car on the gravel made them both look out the window, and the white-robed figure vanished. The plain, dark blue sedan driven by Detective Sheridan pulled up into the parking area.

"I wonder what he wants," Whitney said. Though Joshua knew she too had a history with the detective that had ended happily, he could also well imagine she would prefer not to be reminded of that dark time.

"I'll go see. He's working on the arson cases, and he might have some questions for me or Sterling about something at the site."

"Where's Joy?" Whitney asked, almost instinctively.

"I'm in the kitchen!" Joy called out. "You told me to make bread. I'm kneading my knuckles off."

Joshua put a hand on Whitney's and felt her sigh out her fear by association. "You okay?" he asked.

"I'm fine." Whitney smiled at him, her buoyant spirit and dynamic personality returning in full strength. "I think I'll go call my mom and ask her about that foot thing. You go see what the good detective wants. What time do you think your mom will be home?"

Joshua frowned. "Saturday is kind of a late day at the salon. I'd say we'd be ready for dinner by seven thirty."

"See you then." With one more glance out the window at the two detectives, who were now headed for Joshua's front door, she passed into the kitchen, boisterously egging on Joy to beat that bread.

Taking up his notebook, Joshua went out and intercepted Detective Sheridan and Detective Wright. "Hi there!" he called out. "Are you looking for me?"

Sheridan turned to him. "We were looking for Mr. Fincher, but I'd like to talk to you too."

"Sterling is in the house, marinating some steaks, I think. C'mon in. You want something to drink?" Joshua asked politely as he passed the two men on his wide porch and opened the screen door.

"Water would be great," said Detective Wright. "With

ice, please." Joshua could see the sweat trickling down his neck. He wondered how hot it was to wear that hairpiece, and why he didn't just switch it for a baseball cap, preferably the vented kind.

Sterling was working at the center island. He had obviously seen them coming, and he was finishing up quickly. He greeted them as they came in and moved next to the kitchen table. "Sit down, sit down," he offered.

"We won't keep you long," Sheridan said. "We've been doing a little research today, and we understand that you've recently employed a young man by the name of Simon Gomez. Is that correct?"

Sterling had joined the men at the table while Joshua got two big glasses and filled them with ice water. "That's right," Sterling said, nodding. "He needed a job to be on a work-release program. Is there a problem?"

Sheridan took the glass from Joshua when he offered it, and Detective Wright responded. "Not necessarily. We've been assigned to these arson cases now that there's been a suspected homicide. There was what may or may not be a connected matter on Friday night. An arson fire at a small convenience store on Foothill."

"How is that connected to Simon?" Joshua asked. Almost before the question was out, he caught a glance from Sterling that told him he should have kept his mouth shut.

"Do you think it is?" Wright asked him.

"No. I saw Simon with some friends at the carnival Friday night. They were still there when I left."

"What time was that?" Sheridan asked, pulling the same kind of small notebook that Joshua remembered so well from his breast pocket. It was the kind you buy at Rite Aid in a pack of three; spiral top, lined paper.

"I don't know. At least eleven. Joy and I went; she can tell you too."

At the mention of Joy's name, Sheridan glanced up sharply. Joshua thought his voice was falsely casual as he asked, "How's she doing?"

"Okay, I guess." Joshua felt flummoxed by the question.

Sterling intervened. "She's proved remarkably resilient. I'd say she's doing as well as anyone could expect. We're all really very proud of her."

For a split second, Joshua saw something flash over Detective Sheridan's usually granite face, something that looked distinctly relieved and victorious, but it was gone before it registered fully, and when the detective spoke, there was no trace of either sentiment. "That's good to hear," he said blandly.

"I'm sorry," Sterling said, "but I don't understand what my hiring Simon has to do with your arson investigation."

Sheridan and Wright exchanged an almost unnoticeable look. "The store that was vandalized by fire was also robbed a few months ago. Simon Gomez was ID'd by the shop owner, leading to his arrest. We went to the fire camp to talk to him, found out he'd been released, and that led us to you." Sheridan inclined his head in Sterling's direction.

"That doesn't mean it was him." Sterling looked grave.

"No, and we probably would have dropped it, except that it turns out that Simon Gomez was also on a work crew very near the Oak Springs fire the day it broke out."

Joshua was opening his mouth to object when he realized that this was true: He had first seen Simon there. So he snapped his mouth shut again, his mind swirling. Did this have something to do with the image of the malicious man he had seen lurking around Simon? Yet he felt sure that Simon was not responsible. He couldn't have said why exactly. He thought of how Simon had risked his own life to save that dog. Was that the action of someone who would deliberately and randomly set fires that could kill any number of living things?

"I'm afraid I can't tell you much," Sterling said. "He's shown up on time, worked hard, and thrown himself in front of a speeding car to save a dog. He seems like an okay kid who might have taken a wrong turn. But then"—Sterling paused and shrugged—"lots of people seem okay who aren't." He looked very pointedly at the detectives in turn and then added, "As well as the other way around."

Detective Sheridan looked like no one had ever spoken a truer word. "If the people who were criminals looked like criminals, and the ones who weren't didn't, my job would be a whole lot easier." Sighing, he flipped the notebook closed. "Well, we'll need to talk to him. That's our next stop." Both detectives came to their feet with a scraping of wood on wood as the chairs moved across the plank floor. "Thanks for the water."

They exited into the feverish autumn day, and Joshua watched them walk to the car with an undulating sensation in his chest that felt not unlike the heat waves coming off the hood of the car. Before the two men got to the car, Whitney came out of her house and intercepted them. Joshua watched them shake hands and exchange a few words, Whitney bestowing her thousand-watt smile on Sheridan. Then they left and she came over, climbing the stairs to the porch and sticking her head in the kitchen door.

"I called my mom," she said, and Joshua could see that she'd been crying. Her eyes, always bright, were especially luminous, and slightly red. "When I told her what you said, she burst into tears. She said that my father always used to go barefoot and it drove her crazy that his feet were always dirty. She was always after him to keep them clean."

Joshua smiled gently at her and said, "Well, he wants her to know that they're clean now, and he's really happy."

Whitney's eyes brightened with a shiny new wetness. "Thank you," she whispered, and then, as though eager to treasure her melancholy wonder in private, she was gone.

Chapter 26

Even at the salon, wrapped in a thick terry bathrobe after a quick shower, Susan Hughs looked professionally preoccupied and distracted. It couldn't have been any more apparent that she felt she was wasting her time.

"Thank you for fitting me in at the last minute on a Saturday. I can see how busy you are," Susan said to Greer as she came into the treatment room.

"No problem." Greer smiled as though it had been no big deal to move three other appointments, one of which had been scheduled over a month ago. "I've been wanting to work on you since I met you. I sensed a certain amount of what I call city smut on you that needs to be cleansed off."

Susan's left eyebrow had lifted a fraction of an inch. "You *sensed*?" she asked.

"Yes. I get these little feelings about things sometimes," Greer said, careful to keep it light. "I suppose it comes from dealing with people's bodies and energies on a daily basis. Quite a bit of my practice has to do with energy flow, or the interruption of it. Anyway, it's nothing you'd even really notice. I don't sacrifice goats or read chicken innards or anything like that."

"I see. How interesting." Susan looked as though she thought it was anything but and was eager to get the hell out of there.

Greer understood completely and decided to say no more. When a person was resistant to her sensibilities, she found it was best to leave it alone. "I'll just step

into the hallway while you take off your robe and get
under the sheet." She indicated the massage table. "Do
you like citrus smells?" Greer was positive she knew the
answer, but she asked it anyway out of politeness.

Susan looked surprised. "Yes, I like the stimulating
effect."

"Me too," Greer agreed as she opened the door. "I
think though, that for you and your intense stress level,
we'll add in some rosemary and lavender." She went out
and closed the door, ignoring Susan's slight eye roll,
which could not have been more easily interpreted if she
had said, "New age hippie," out loud. In the hallway,
Greer closed her eyes and summoned Susan's energy
into her mind's eye to have a look at it.

As she suspected, it was covered in a gray, mucuslike
mass, city smut. That would need clearing. There was
some fear there, appearing to Greer as a dark red glow,
and while that seemed incongruous in someone as confident as Susan, Greer had seen it too many times on
successful women to be surprised. The fear was so often
what motivated them.

Something else hovered around the center of her energy, something rusty colored and dense: greed, an un-
healthy, unbalanced set of values and needs. No big
revelation there either.

Turning, Greer knocked on the door before stepping
quietly into the room and dimming the lights. She selected three small bottles of oil and put a few drops of
each into an infuser, lighting the candle beneath it. Almost instantly a fresh, calming scent filled the room.

Greer walked to stand near the table, and after rubbing her hands together and taking a cleansing breath,
she placed both of her hands on Susan, one on the small
of her back and the other between her shoulder blades.

The jolt that came through them was so strong that
Greer had to force herself not to pull away. Instantly,
she could see the tight, inky mass in the vicinity of Susan's chest.

Exhaling hard to expel the negativity and block it
from coming into her own body, Greer threw up a wall

of white light and then began to gently prod and knead
the knots of tension.

It was apparent to Greer's expert touch that this was
a woman who seldom endured or even received physical
contact. At first Susan tensed and fought every attempt
to ease her muscular tightness, but then, almost inaudibly, Greer began to hum, just enough to create a vibration that traveled from her chest, down her arms, into
her hands, and to Susan. Greer continued to repeat and
send a few interchanging tones. Susan began to respond,
relaxing and releasing. Focusing primarily on the dark,
injurious energies that she could hardly contain, Greer
began to slide the tones, to change the notes, to extend
the healing sound, and as she did, the gray and the rust
and the dark red lessened, lightened, eased.

But the black would not budge. Again and again
Greer focused on it, tried to find its note, its vibration,
but it eluded her. She tried to sense what it was,
danger—certainly—but it was very difficult to read. She
wasn't very good at diagnosing illness, but Greer
couldn't help fearing that Susan's body was harboring
some kind of cancer or heart disease that would attack
in the near future. With a growing sense of desperation,
Greer realized she didn't know what to do to help Susan
if it were a serious physical illness. It would be completely inappropriate for her to suggest that a massage
client might have a malignant tumor.

After a full hour, Susan had relaxed enough to have
fallen asleep and was actually snoring lightly. Greer felt
that she could safely try something more extreme.

Stepping to the side of the room, she lifted the votive
candle and carried it over to the sleeping figure, holding
it in her right hand. Her left hand she placed against the
center of Susan's back, and after drawing a line of light
through her wrist, she focused hard on drawing the darkness into her hand. She could sense it moving, budging.
Small beads of sweat formed on Greer's lip as she tried
to lift the image of the dark mass from Susan's body
and spirit. Holding the candle ready, Greer began to lift
her left hand, as though pulling up on a great weight.

When it was only inches away from Susan's body, she moved the flame of the candle down toward the space between the two. She would burn away the energy; she would force it to leave Susan.

Slowly, she began to bring the candle into the space that felt as dense and tight as though she were pulling up on a thick rubber band. Greer slid the candle into place and mouthed the words, "Burn away this darkness, free this woman from this danger."

The candle sputtered and went out.

Shaken, Greer left Susan to sleep for a few minutes and retreated to the reassuring buzz of activity on the salon floor. She found Leah in Dario's chair. He was busy chopping her severely blunt haircut into a softer, layered look.

"So, something, or should I say, someone, inspire you to get a new look?" Greer asked, crossing her arms and leaning against Dario's station while secretly drawing comfort from the presence of her two friends.

"What?" Leah tried to feign ignorance, but the attempt was betrayed by a blush.

"Oh ho," said Dario. "So, we've got a boyfriend, then?" Well aware of Leah's past, he knew this was promising news, and he was determined to treat it as ruthlessly as he would any other gossip, to make her feel more like one of the gang.

"No. I had a sort of a date, yes, but it's not anything serious."

Dario's assistant, Jonathan, seemed to appear from nowhere, much like a greedy ant at a sloppy picnic. "Do tell," he said. "What does he do? No wait, let me guess. He's an investment banker . . . no, a mass tort lawyer."

Leah laughed, delighted at the fact that Weston was so very different from what they would all presume she would be attracted to.

"He's a fireman," Greer said before Leah could object.

"No way." Jonathan actually closed his eyes and licked his lips. "I've always wanted a fireman. How was it?"

Leah blushed again. "Couldn't tell you that, we've only had one date, but if I can work up the courage, I'm going to call him and see if he wants to have a drink tonight." She twisted her dark green smock in her fingers as she spoke.

Immediately picking up on Leah's residual fear of being alone with a man, any man, Greer said, "Hey, we're having a little barbecue at Whitney's, just us and them. Why don't you bring him by and have a beer with us? Just a casual drink."

Leah's pitiable look turned radiant at the safe suggestion.

"A fireman," Dario said approvingly. "Is he going to be in the Columbus Day parade? The firemen are always in the parade, on those big, shiny red trucks. Everybody likes that."

"It's the crossover fantasy." Jonathan was nodding. "Men want to ride on those big, red trucks, and women want to ride on those—"

"Okay, that's enough," Dario warned.

"When is Columbus Day?" Greer asked.

Since the bank was closed for the holiday, that was an easy one for Leah. "Monday. You're not open, are you?"

"We're not closed." Dario frowned. "What are we, a library? No, national holidays are like weekends for us, extra busy."

That reminded Greer that she had promised to re-schedule one of the appointments she had sloughed off to make room for Susan's.

"Excuse me," she said, and then added to Leah, "Don't you dare leave without letting me see Dario's work of art."

"We'll frame it," Dario muttered with a smile.

Greer walked to the front and was introduced to her next client by Celia. "I'll be right with you," she said to the timid woman who appeared to have a chronically apologetic look on her face.

She leafed through the appointment book until she found the upcoming Monday. As promised by Dario, the page was full of penciled-in appointments. Greer sighed and started looking for a place to fit in a full hour with the obliging client, making a mental note to give her a nice gift bag of beauty products and an aromatherapy candle for being so flexible, a rare quality in today's selfish world.

Even as she leaned down to focus on Celia's small writing and the times next to the names, her vision seemed to float out of focus. Greer had never needed reading glasses, and she blinked to clear her eyes, but the words did not congeal. Instead another image revealed itself to her, floating over the page.

A blackened key showed itself as clear as though it were hovering a few inches above the page. A key, clearly indicated over Monday, October tenth, Columbus Day.

A veneer of sweat seemed to glaze Greer's face as she stared at the key. Then, to break the alarming image, she looked up and into the mirror behind the counter.

And there she saw something else: two black wings, darker than a raven's, motionless and looming. Between them was strung a web in dark, tangled lines. Caught in the center of the web was the reflection of her own suddenly bloodless and horrified face.

Chapter 27

The steaks were settling nicely into their marinade of pineapple juice, Worcestershire sauce, and Guinness Stout when the unusual sound of a large truck navigating the rough dirt road came barging through Joshua's window. He laid down the book he was reading and went to see what it was.

Immediately recognizing Sheldon Tucker's profile and a small head bouncing just over the windowsill on the passenger side of the large cab, Joshua went down to see what they might be doing here.

Sheldon pulled the truck past the parking area shared by Greer's and Whitney's homes and up in front of the locked gate that was access for the forest service, the hiking trail, and the few cabins situated farther up the road.

As Joshua crossed the open area, Sheldon got out of the truck and started to sort through a huge ring of keys, no doubt looking for the unique match to one of the many locks on the chain that secured the yellow swinging gate.

"Hello again!" Joshua called out. A little concerned to see the water truck there, though he could smell no smoke, he asked, "What's going on?"

Sheldon looked up at him from under the brim of his spotless green John Deere hat. "One of your neighbors is having trouble with their well, so they ordered a load of water for their tank."

"Oh," Joshua said, relieved. Their house too was on a well-tank system, and he understood that when there was trouble with the pump, a depleted water table, or no electricity, there was no water. "Have you been working all night and all day?"

"I got a few hours' sleep last night."

"That sounds pretty tough," Joshua commiserated, but he was thinking more about Tyler. As though he'd been called out, the other door of the cab opened and the boy himself climbed cautiously down, jumping the last two feet from the metal grid stair to the ground. With a look of excited recognition on his face, he ran to where Joshua was standing.

"Hey Joshua!" he called out.

Joshua was pleased that the boy was so glad to see him. "Hey, Tyler, what's up?"

After trying a couple of keys unsuccessfully, Sheldon located the right fit and the heavy chain swung with a loud clink against the post. He started to push the gate's heavy arm around.

"Here, I'll get that for you," Joshua offered.

"Thanks," Sheldon muttered. He seemed unaccustomed to assistance. "Come on, Tyler. Let's go," he growled.

"Can I stay with Joshua?" the boy chirruped.

"Tyler, you can't just ask somebody . . ."

"No," Joshua cut in, "it's fine. I wasn't doing anything anyway. I was bored."

In spite of his overall gruff-and-skinny-bear demeanor, Sheldon looked pleased. "I'll be about an hour. They've got a small intake pipe, and it takes quite a while to pump thirty-eight hundred gallons."

"No problem," Joshua said.

"Okay, then." Sheldon fixed his grandson with a meaningful stare. "You behave."

"Yes, sir!" Tyler's little body almost snapped to attention with the promise.

As the big truck rumbled away up the rutted road, Joshua turned to Tyler. "You want to come meet my friend Joy?"

"A girl?"

"Yeah."

"Mmm." Tyler looked undecided.

"But she's cool, not real girly or anything dumb like that," Joshua told him, using boy code.

"Okay," Tyler agreed somewhat warily.

They marched up the steps to Luke and Whitney's and knocked on the door. It was Joy who answered it. "What are you knocking for? Just come in. I'm busy." Then she spotted Tyler. "Oh, hello."

"Joy, this is my buddy Tyler. He's working today with his grandfather, who owns the big water truck. We're gonna hang for an hour or so. You wanna do something?"

Joy smiled at the kid vernacular and slowly nodded as though that were the most fabulous idea she'd heard in a long, long time. "Great. Come on in. I'm making bread. Do you have strong arms, Tyler?" she asked as they went through the hall into the kitchen. There was a pile of dough on a floured board.

Tyler lifted a scrawny fist into the air and tensed his tiny bicep, Popeye style.

"Impressive," Joy said, her eyes sharing a charmed laugh with Joshua. "Okay, get that footstool and wash your hands. We've got work to do."

Five minutes later, Tyler's entire upper body was covered with edible white dust, and he was having the time of his life karate chopping the yielding mound of softness. Joy would turn the dough a quarter turn, fold it in, yell, "Now!" He would chop down with appropriate sound effects, and then she would complete the rolling knead, pushing and flattening with the palms of both hands. Then they would do it again.

"Okay, I think that looks perfect," Joy said. "Now we make it into a loaf and let it rise again." She glanced over to where she had three other loaves lined up on the counter with dish towels draped over them. "Look." Lifting one of the towels, she let Tyler peep underneath it. "See how nice and puffy it is? This one's going to get that big too."

Joshua was content to watch the whole ritual. His

mother made bread and he had often helped her. He wondered now if it had been like this, with him much more of a detriment than a help. Probably, he thought. Mostly though, he was amazed at Joy's ease with Tyler, and he wondered if nurturing came more naturally to women, if it was instinctive, or if it was learned by an individual, male or female. He thought briefly about Joy's real mother, Pam, quickly eliminated the first two options, and concluded it was definitely the last.

Tyler was instructed on how to set the oven to the right temperature and then watched, fascinated, as two of the earlier loaves were slid into it and the timer set.

"Now we wash our hands again and do the best part."

"What's that?" Tyler didn't seem to think there could be a better part than actively beating up the dough.

"Smell it while it's cooking," Joy said with a gleam in her eye. "You want a snack?" she asked the boy, but her eyes cut up to Joshua to include him.

"I'll wait for dinner," Joshua said. For steaks and fresh bread, he wanted a good appetite, but Tyler nodded.

"What do you like?" Joy asked him, leaning down to address him closer to his own level.

"I like Jack's. My grampa likes KFC, and that's okay too. But today we had McDonald's."

"I see." Joy tried not to look too judgmental. "Well, let me make you something and see if you like it." She set to work rummaging through the refrigerator and soon had a plate of sliced apples, grapes, some cheese, and whole-grain crackers. She set a cold glass of milk next to it. Tyler looked dubious, but once he started, he went through the whole thing with a ravenous appetite.

"So you live with your grampa?" Joy asked as she watched him devour the last cracker.

"Yeah. Grampa says that my mom needs to stop doing drugs, and then I can maybe live with her again." Tyler did not look at her as he said this.

"I had a mom like that too. It's not easy, is it?" Joy asked softly.

Tyler picked up his milk and took a small sip; then, still without looking up, he shook his head almost imperceptibly.

"But you've got your grampa," Joshua said, trying to be cheerful. "And that must be pretty neat riding around in the truck."

"Yeah, it's okay. But sometimes I get kinda bored, you know?"

"Do you have a grandma?"

"Yeah, she lives in Riverside. I don't really remember her."

"Have you got any brothers or sisters?" Joshua asked.

The little head started to nod, hesitated, and then shook no.

Wondering what that had meant, Joshua said, "Do you have stepbrothers and sisters?"

The no shake again, a small breath, and Tyler spoke in a hesitant voice that sounded as though the little boy had been rehearsed in—or perhaps had distanced himself from—the text. "I had a little sister, but she got sick and my mommy couldn't take care of her, so some people came and took her away."

Joshua could hear the tightness in Joy's voice as she asked, "Where is she now? Do you ever get to see her?"

This time the head shake was almost imperceptible and accompanied by a slight, almost apologetic shrug. "She died."

There was a quiet moment while Tyler scraped a dirty fingernail along the tabletop, seeming fascinated by something visible only to him.

"I'm sorry," Joy said empathetically.

The shrug again. Tyler's eyes squinted harder at the imaginary spot. "It's okay. I mean, she was a baby. I don't really remember her much, except that she used to cry a lot and my mom would get really mad."

Joy looked at Joshua and they sighed together silently. "Tell you what," Joy said. "Why don't I give your grampa my phone number, and if he's working in the neighborhood, he can drop you off here sometime, and we can hang out. Cool?"

"Cool!" Tyler said, and his eyes finally came up to meet hers.

When the rumble of Sheldon's truck announced his reappearance, they went out to meet him. He was fumbling through the huge ring of keys to unlock the gate again.

"Good grief," Joshua commented. "You must have keys to every locked gate in Shadow Hills."

"Just the ones that need water," Sheldon grumbled, then added with an amused snort, "And sooner or later that's most all of 'em."

Joy introduced herself and repeated her offer to watch Tyler on occasion. Sheldon asked her how much she would want to be paid, and she answered, "Nothing. I relate to the little guy, you know?" Much like Tyler had, she looked away when she spoke about her mother. "I spent some pretty hard years with a mom who couldn't get her shit together, and people helped me, so . . ." She let the statement drop off, but not without a glance at Joshua that told him the reference had meant him.

Sheldon's wrinkled face took on a rough smile. "That's real nice of you. I might just take you up on it." He shook his head. "This time of year, between the fires and the wells drying up, I don't get much time off. Ever. And now, with that Golden Door development ripping the skin off miles of dirt, they constantly need watering down to keep the dust from blinding everybody up there so bad they can't work."

Joshua thought of the sheer size of the exposed earth. "That must be a huge job for you."

Sheldon's face looked sour. "I don't care much for working for that outfit. That Rowland Hughs guy—" He seemed to check himself, and then he muttered, "It pays the bills." He turned to ruffle Tyler's hair. "Were you a good boy?"

"Yes, sir," Tyler said, beaming up at Joy. "I made bread!"

"You did?" Sheldon looked surprised but pleased.

"Oh yeah," Joy said, with only the slightest hint of sarcasm in her voice. "He was a *big* help."

For the first time ever, Joshua recognized the sensation of a vision coming to him well before it happened. There was a warming, prickling pulsing in his chest, and he actually turned from one person to another to see where the image would appear. As he watched, a figure materialized over Tyler's right shoulder.

It took most of Joshua's self-control to hide the tears he felt come into his eyes.

A small girl, less than two years old, with the thin, almost malnourished look of a neglected child, was looking straight at him with large eyes. Though her physical appearance should have been one reflecting her weak, depleted body, the glow of energy, peace, and joy coming from her incongruously wise face filled Joshua with a sense of wonder.

Seeming to be content that he had sensed her, the small figure turned her eyes down to the boy who Joshua knew must be her brother. She pointed a thin, childish finger at Tyler and then moved it slowly up to Sheldon; then she turned back to Joshua and shook her head, holding one hand up to signify that something must be stopped.

Unable to speak in present company, Joshua thought hard the words *I don't understand.*

The small, wise girl smiled kindly at him from forever and then faded.

Exhaling hard but forcing himself to remain inaudible, he turned away and pretended to be absorbed in the view as he thought about the feeling he had gotten from what he could only think of as a sound bite from eternity.

Something was wrong; he could sense that she had meant that. She hadn't just come to give him the message that she was all right, something he often felt when he saw images unbidden over people he didn't know. He'd even had a visit like that from his own father once, but this was different. She had wanted him to do something, to stop something.

He didn't know what, but he was damn sure it wasn't anything good.

"Well, we've got to get going. Thanks for watching Tyler," Sheldon was saying, and his gruffness had returned. He and Tyler climbed up into the big cab, and with a *whoosh* of air brakes and an easy grinding of gears, they drove their home away from home laboriously back up toward the highway.

Joy came up to stand beside Joshua and they watched the truck maneuver the rough road. "Poor little guy," Joy said. "He's really lucky he's got his grandfather. Not many single men that age would take on an eight-year-old."

Joshua said nothing. He was still thinking about the waiflike little girl and her warning. He wasn't so sure if her surviving brother was lucky or not.

Chapter 28

As Leah slid into her seat up front in the crowded community center, she was struck by how many people had turned out. The hall had been set up with folding chairs in rows with an aisle down the middle and an eight-foot folding table at the front, behind which six chairs faced the rest of the room.

As the primary bank officer on the Golden Door development site, she had been obliged to come. She could think of quite a few things she would rather be doing. Walking on hot coals toward hungry wolves came to mind.

Susan turned her head and smiled at Leah tightly. Leah noticed she was sitting oddly, as though the lower half of her body wanted to face the room and the upper part was more inclined to face the right wall; she appeared locked in that position.

Next to Susan sat an aging fire chief. He looked primarily bored. Leah knew that he was there to field any questions about public safety requirements. She also knew that, per the zoning agreement, all the statutes had been satisfied for stages one and two and they were attached to the loan deal, otherwise her bank would not have been able to approve the loan.

The meeting hadn't started yet. The councilwoman, Wendy Sostein, nodded hello to Leah and then checked her watch pointedly. There was one open chair at the table, and Leah assumed that they were waiting for its intended occupant. The other people in the room passed the time by talking among themselves and shooting murderous looks at Susan and, Leah noted with some alarm, herself. It was difficult to keep from mouthing, "I'm not with them; I'm with you," to the assorted members of the crowd. *Truth be told, I've sold out. I've learned to hate this development that I have to look at every day and that I'm here defending, I hate sacrificing anything and everything for profit, and I hate myself.*

It was a very strange setting for such a big self-confession. The fact was that Leah had never given much thought to how or where the money was made at her bank; she had just wanted to control it, to make a big chunk of it for herself, to *have*. Now, here in this ugly, sterile room filled with cold metal chairs and a mass of people, most of whom she didn't even know, Leah felt as though she'd been scratching and laboring and climbing all her life, so intent on reaching the summit that she had never bothered to notice that she had picked the wrong mountain.

But almost simultaneously the thought of all the people who came in and trusted her with their money, who expected dividends, who received loans for homes and schools and bills, rushed up on her. The services she provided for them didn't go very far toward making her feel like a philanthropist, but it was the system she'd come into and—when used ethically—worked better than most other financial systems.

Before she could begin to consider whether or not she'd be able to find a balance between her greed and her newfound sense of fair play, Wendy Sostein cleared her throat and spoke loudly.

"It appears that Mr. Farrad is either quite late or not coming, so I need to call the meeting to order without him."

This announcement was met with many angry shouts from the assembly.

Wendy spoke over them. "I'm sorry, but I see no alternative. Now, we are going to do this in an orderly and respectful way. One speaker at a time, please come to the podium at the front and speak into the microphone. You will have five minutes maximum, and you may ask questions of any of us seated at this table."

The councilwoman then introduced the people at the table; she started with herself and was met with a polite silence, then Susan Hughs, who received hisses. Leah's name elicited no outward signs of aggression—she could only assume most people didn't hold her personally responsible—and the fire chief received waves and nods from many of the assembled. Next the councilwoman gestured to the empty chair and said, "Mr. Farrad is the head of the neighborhood council. Please make a note in the minutes that he is absent." She nodded in the direction of a young man sitting at the end of the table with a laptop open in front of him, who seemed to be a kind of secretary taking notes. "At this time that means I need to ask if anyone else from the council is present and would like to take his place heading up the objections to the zoning ordinance being reviewed."

An elderly man, who looked as though he might not even make it to the table much less hold his own once he got there, stood and raised a shaky hand. "I'm John Selzin, I'm on the committee, but Mr. Farrad had all the notes and the petition."

"That's all right," Wendy Sostein said. "I've got a copy of the petition. If you'll join us, we can begin."

They're fucked, Leah thought as she watched the painful progression of the ancient Mr. Selzin toward the front.

The meeting opened peacefully enough; the councilwoman read the proposed plans for stage three of the Golden Door development and then opened the floor for comments. One by one, some shyly, some nervously, some furiously, people came forward to voice their objections or, far less often, their support. Leah had heard all the arguments against before, and she did not disagree with a single one of them. The development was an eyesore; it had received zoning variances on laws and restrictions in spite of the fact that they had been voted in and imposed on private home owners. Many of the people present had actually been denied those same reductions in lot size or building permits that would have increased the square footage of their homes beyond the amount allowed in proportion to their lots. Both restrictions were being flagrantly flaunted by the Golden Door development. One of the biggest objections was the proposed increase of children in the already crowded schools and traffic that would be funneled through the existing small neighborhoods.

One woman who spoke particularly well said, "You already have five hundred homes going in; each of those homes will have a minimum of two cars. That's one thousand cars driving past my front door once every morning and once every evening at the very least. Now you want to add another six hundred cars. Just getting through the stop signs is going to be a major problem. And as I understand it"—she shifted her reading glasses and referred to a single sheet—"you have only one route out of the development at this time for eight hundred homes. As I read the law, that's not legal for even one additional home, and I'd like to ask the councilwoman and Fire Captain Lopez what they expect will happen if there is a fire, or some other emergency?"

Wendy opened her mouth to speak, but Susan cut in. "If I may, councilwoman." Wendy nodded and sat back, looking slightly relieved for the support. "We are well aware of the zoning requirement for a second road access into the neighborhood for phase three to be safely built." She paused and rubbed her bandaged arm. "Believe me, I understand the need for fire safety in this and every neighborhood."

Leah noticed how Susan always used words like *neighborhood* or *homes* instead of *development* or *housing project*.

"The plans for the new homes," Susan continued, "already include a second road that will allow easy access for emergency vehicles and lessen the flow of traffic onto any one route."

At this point the fire captain seemed to come to life and take an interest long enough to lean forward and say, "The laws on this are very clear. There must be maintainable roads, standard turnaround clearance, correctly positioned hydrants, evenly spaced, and multiple accesses."

No one seemed to know what that meant, but the very fact that someone wearing a dark blue uniform was stating the mandatory requirements, and presumably overseeing them, seemed to muffle the objection.

Leah thought about the plans, a copy of which was in her office, and she could think of no such provision as a second access road. She would check that again tomorrow. She seemed to recall a gray area that had been in the initial buyout plans, an additional road, but even with the zoning variances they had been granted by the councilwoman and her office, that route, which ran through national forest, had been denied.

"I'd like to reassure all of you," Wendy Sostein was saying, "that the utmost care has been taken to balance the very important economic growth of this fine community with the ecological and practical considerations that you have all mentioned here tonight."

During the muttering and outright snorts of derision that followed this political sappiness, a man had walked forward and was standing at the podium. Leah recognized him from Jenny's shower. It was Mindy's husband, Reading.

The councilwoman nodded at him to take his turn.

Instead of speaking immediately, he turned and looked around at the room. "I know quite a few of you here this afternoon," Reading began. "Miles, you own the hardware store, and Sherry and Darrel, you guys have the café. Most of you have businesses in the area and all of you have homes, or you wouldn't be here." He paused and then leaned farther into the small microphone and spoke very clearly. "*You all have homes here.* That means somebody built them, on ground that used to not have homes. You all drive cars, on streets, I assume, that didn't have as much traffic before you came. You use electricity and have lights and play music and *work* here. Those of you who know me know that I'm working on this development. I live here, and I work here. This is my livelihood. I employ quite a few people too. I see Max Smith back there in the back. I employed your son for two years before he went away to college."

A kind of shameful hush had fallen over the room. Reading had presence, and he was using it to turn the tide. "This development provides work, income, and profit for many, many people. This is progress, people; this is the healthy growth of our economy. This is how it works in America, the greatest country in the world. Every one of you can sit there and complain about it, or you can benefit and profit from it. It's gonna happen; you can't stop it. It's not illegal to want to give people homes or make money, and if you want to sit there and act like someone else, who wants to work hard and make a better life for their family, is being corrupt or greedy in some way, then you go right ahead. But every single one of you has benefited from being an American, from the freedom that gives us the right to build a better life." He took a long moment to let his eyes sweep the crowd—Leah noticed that most of them did not meet his gaze—and then he said, "This is *America*. It's a free country; I fought to keep it free. And as an American I have a right to do the work I want to do and to make money doing it."

The sound of a clap pierced the air. A single pair of hands smacking together, slowly at first and then faster and faster, broke Reading's spell and caused everyone to turn and see who was making the sound.

Near the back Leah could see a arresting-looking man with long, black hair, obviously Native American, who had stood and was clapping alone, but the look on his face could not have been more disgusted.

"Very touching," he said. "Very moving, and very *American*, yes, I agree." He worked his way past the people on his row aisle and walked to the front. Leah found herself breathing in sharply as he passed Reading, almost expecting an act of physical violence, but both men turned their shoulders to allow for the other to move past respectfully and without overt confrontation.

The eye-catchingly dressed man reached the front.

Leah noted a bracelet of silver and turquoise on his wrist that she would have been very proud to own but probably afraid to wear.

"My name is R. J. River. I have lived here, in this valley, all my life. My family, I would venture to say—and I don't think I'm out of line—has lived here longer than anyone else's in this room. In fact"—he smiled and winked back at Wendy—"my family lived here long before any of your European, Asian, or African ancestors even knew this continent existed, much less became Americans." This got a few titters. "So, forgive me if I have a strong opinion about change and what it means to be an *American*."

R.J. shifted his weight, cleared his throat, and proceeded. "Now, while I might be descended from one of the first Americans, I'm also one who happens to believe in progress and change that benefits the whole." He gestured widely with a graceful hand. "I mean, I don't want to be living in a teepee, scraping deer hide to make moccasins. I like having Payless down the street." More laughs, slightly louder and braver, came from the crowd. "I bought a little house over on Apperson, fixed it up, sold it, bought a bigger one, fixed that up. I've profited from what we like to call the American way." Here he paused again, and his expression sobered. "But that is not what we are discussing here. We're talking about capitalism gone seriously wrong. I'm all for progress as it benefits the community, but, though this project benefits many in a smaller way, as my friend Reading pointed out, it primarily benefits only one person in this room." R.J. raised a finger and pointed it at Susan Hughs. "So, I have a question for our guest developer." He came to a full stop and looked directly at her. "How much does it cost you to build these atrocities per square foot, and what do you sell them for a square foot?"

Susan smiled smoothly. "I'm sorry, Mr. River, but our private financial records are not at issue here."

"No"—R.J. cut her off, his voice angry now—"but the fact that it costs you ninety dollars a square foot to build these houses and you sell them for over four hundred a square foot seems to clearly indicate that *profit*, rather than providing quality housing and healthy communities, is your primary, in fact your *sole* objective."

"As far as I know, it's not illegal to make a profit." Susan laughed innocently. "I don't think that's what's at issue."

"No," R.J. said again. "What *is* at issue is whether or not it's immoral and unethical, and yes, even illegal, to effect zoning changes, to build substandard housing that masquerades as luxury, to destroy an ecosystem in order for you to make not just a profit but an obscene fortune. What *is* at issue is whether or not it is acceptable to rape and pillage and disguise your abuse by calling yourself an *American*."

The crowd was on its feet, shouting its approval and support now. Susan Hughs was speaking in a loud, clear, would-be calm voice that no one could hear. Wendy Sostein was shouting for the meeting to come to order and that R.J.'s five minutes were up.

When things did finally calm down, R.J. was still at the podium.

"Thank you for your views, Mr. River. Your time is up," Wendy Sostein said again, clearly shaken.

"No," he said in a voice as low and rumbling as thunder, "*your* time is up. You cannot keep abusing the land and expect that it will continue to support you. Everything is connected, even your corruption."

"Are you accusing me of criminal action?" The councilwoman was on her feet, clearly outraged. "Are you slandering me?" Leah watched as Susan, still calm and controlled, placed a hand on the other woman's arm and pressed her back into her seat.

"You were elected to protect the interests of the citizens in this room," R.J. said very clearly, as though explaining this to a confused child. He looked around at the angry citizens again and then back to her. "They don't seem to feel very well protected." And with that he turned, his straight black hair moving gracefully as he stalked purposefully from the room.

There was an uncomfortable silence as Wendy, her

face red and tense, shuffled her papers as though trying to get control of herself. In the quiet a clear, even voice spoke. It was Susan Hughs.

"I'd like to address a few of those accusations, if I could. Councilwoman?" She looked to Wendy, who nodded curtly.

"First of all, I want you all to know that my husband and I have spent many years developing communities, quality communities, and we understand that these are places where people will live, make friends, patronize businesses; where their children will go to school, play sports, and grow up. Yes, we make a profit, we are not a charity, but we also do an amazing amount of work. We take a chance, we have investors who count on us to show a profit, and we feel indebted to make one. That is the financial system that this country's economy is based on."

She twisted a little in her seat and Leah saw a spasm of pain cross her face, but she doubted if anyone who was not sitting next to her would have noticed it, Susan had covered it so quickly. "Also, I would like to say that this neighborhood will soon become my own. My husband and I are building a house for ourselves in this community, and we have every interest in keeping it healthy, beautiful, and one of the nicest places to live in the Los Angeles area, not only as good businessmen, but as *residents*." She paused, taking advantage of the surprised looks her logic had spawned on many faces. "You all live here, so I know I'm preaching to the choir when I tell you how special Shadow Hills is, but I want you to know how much we care. I want you to feel reassured. This is our future home, and we would never do anything to jeopardize the integrity or the safety of our very own neighborhood."

Leah watched the effective use of what appeared to be sincerity as Susan's gaze swept the room, moving from one pair of eyes to the next, looking directly at as many of the attendees as possible. Leah was thinking, *This woman is a master. Watch and learn, Leah, watch and learn.*

"I understand that each of you wants to fight for the place where you live, that is commendable and I support your right to do it—and I *join* you in it." Susan glanced over to Wendy, who was looking back at her with her lips slightly parted, as though she were a student of political persuasion watching a seasoned professor. "I see that the meeting is just about over, and I'm sorry to say that I can't stay and field questions. There was a terrible arson fire last night at the work site, and in my effort to pull the night watchman from a burning trailer, I injured my back and my arm was burned, and though there was no way I was going to miss the opportunity to meet you all and hear your concerns tonight, I'm afraid I must leave you right now. But I want you to know that I'll be happy to discuss any of your concerns at a later date. I'm going to leave a stack of my cards here; please feel free to e-mail me with any questions you might have. Better yet, come up and see the site, get to know my husband and myself. After all, we're going to be neighbors."

After a quick, sweeping smile of the room, too short to invite further comment, Susan glanced at Wendy, who banged a small wooden gavel, officially closing the meeting. Then she stood and began to gather her things before anyone else could react, much less take the floor.

She was out the door in less than twenty seconds. Leah sat, observing the befuddled faces and behaviors of the citizens, who might or might not have realized yet that they had just been blindsided.

Leah had only one coherent thought.

Damn, she's good.

Chapter 29

Leaving Celia to close up for the day, Greer went out into the still-bright and hot early evening and got into her car. It was the first chance she'd had to be alone since seeing the midnight-colored wings hovering above her, and she'd had no time to stop the whirl of emotion and thought that had tossed and pulled her in so many directions, leaving her feeling seasick and off balance.

She turned on the air-conditioning and collapsed back against the seat, letting out an exasperated, strained sigh. What should she do? What *could* she do? Of one thing she felt certain: There would be another fire set the day after tomorrow, Columbus Day. But where? She had no starting place, no one to tell or warn. What would she say anyway? *Hello, Fire Department? Yes, you don't know me from Adam, but someone's going to set a fire on Monday. No, of course not me. Whatever would make you think that?*

She'd be suspect number one for absolutely no positive advantage.

Think, she told herself. *Put it together. There's a reason you've been shown all this. What is it?*

She could only think of one person who might be able to help her at all, and she didn't know why, but he was the only common denominator.

R.J. His paintings had illustrated both the scenes that had fallen prey so far. He would probably think she was insane, or worse, accusing him of inside information on arson, but she had to try. Fishing her phone from her purse, Greer called Whitney and got his number, making it sound like she was interested in one of his paintings.

"When'll you be home?" Whitney asked.

"Pretty soon. I may have something to do on the way, but I won't be long. I'll be there for dinner at seven thirty."

"Great. I've been smelling this bread baking all day, and if I can't slap some butter on it soon, I might lose it and run amock with a pair of pinking shears. So if you are late, you'll probably read about it in tomorrow's paper and it'll be on your head that Luke has a zigzag scar on one of his butt cheeks."

Greer laughed. "As long as you get a few women on the jury, I'm certain you'd get off. Especially if Luke shows them his scar."

"That's very reassuring," Whitney said, and hung up.

After a deep breath and a quick mental rehearsal, Greer dialed R.J.'s number. After three rings she was sure she'd get a machine, so she was almost taken aback when he answered curtly.

"Yes?"

"Hi, uh, R.J. It's Greer Sands, Whitney's friend. We met at your party last night."

His tone slid easily into confident amicability. She suspected that he'd been expecting an unpleasant call and was delighted that she wasn't it. She wondered how long the pleasure would last.

"Listen, I know that it's last-minute, but I was wondering if I could come by and talk to you about your paintings."

There was a moment's hesitation, but when he answered, R.J. seemed to have made up his mind. "Sure. I'd love some pleasant company. It's been kind of a tough afternoon."

"That's very nice of you to say. I could be there in about ten minutes. Is that too soon?"

"White or red?"

"Excuse me?" Greer asked, confused.

"Wine. Do you feel like white or red?"

"Oh, on a day this hot, definitely white, and if it's not sacrilegious, over ice."

"Fortunately," R.J. said with serious humor in his voice, "I'm a naturalist. My religion includes ice."

Greer pulled up outside R.J.'s and got her first look at his home in the daylight. The thing that struck her most was not that the house was stylish, or that the yard was beautifully landscaped—both pleasing to the eye—but that it was all so very harmonious, not just one with the other, but with the very area, with the mountains behind it. Nothing stood out, but everything was exceptional.

She already knew that R.J. was a man of great style, talent, and taste, but now she was beginning to sense a personality that understood the flow of living with the world around him. It was a consummation that she strived for in her own surroundings, and it was not without a twinge of jealousy that she realized she didn't pull it off nearly so well.

She opened the glove box and took out a neatly folded hiking map of the area that she knew Joshua had left there. She slipped it into her purse.

He met her at the door before she knocked and handed her a large crystal goblet filled with ice and what he mockingly announced was "an amusing little pinot grigio." They went through to the back garden and sat down in comfortably upholstered chairs with thick armrests near the studio doors, which were standing wide-open. The yard, probably a quarter acre, looked much bigger without all the guests and caterers from the night of the party.

After they'd chatted for a few moments, Greer felt that she would only be dishonest if she didn't come to the point of her visit.

"I was wondering," Greer said, "how you choose the locations that you paint."

The brows above the stunning black eyes went up in amusement. "That's an unusual question. Most people just assume it's because I think they are pretty."

Greer took a breath and plunged in. "I have a reason for asking you." She paused to try and read his reaction, to guess his level of skepticism. He said nothing, just regarded her with something that was almost, but not quite, wariness. She explained, as succinctly as she could, about her visions and the fact that both of the fires had taken place in areas painted by him.

His expression did not change, nor did he interrupt her as she spoke. When she finished, he leaned forward very slowly, setting his own glass down on the stone table between them, and looked intently at her.

"Now, isn't that interesting," he said, as though he honestly thought so but was not committing to anything. "Although," he continued, "not too terribly coincidental since I've been painting the area, almost all of it, for over twenty years."

"And beautifully," Greer said, noting that he hadn't commented at all on the fact that she had basically just told him she was psychic.

"I suppose the next question is, why have you come to me about it?" He was still leaning toward her, both elbows on his knees now, back straight, elegant and poised as ever.

"Because," Greer spoke softly, "I have reason to think it may happen again. What I didn't tell you was that both of the fires happened *after* I saw them in your paintings. My sight is pretty much always future."

"I see. And you've seen another fire in a different painting?"

"No, not exactly." Greer felt suddenly very uncomfortable with R.J.'s intense scrutiny of her face, and she turned away with the pretense of noticing some flowers. "Tell me, does the image of a key, the old-fashioned kind, mean anything to you?"

He did not answer immediately, and when Greer turned to see if there was a reason, he seemed to be considering the question. Finally he shook his head slightly and said, "No. Why?"

"Because I've seen the image of one, and it seems to be connected to the fires somehow, but maybe not. I don't know." Greer felt dense and frustrated. She realized how insane this must all sound. So the next time R.J. spoke, his words surprised her.

"It represents something, I suppose," he murmured. "It's symbolic. But it's not Native American. An old-fashioned key is more European, or at least has to do with something that can be kept locked up, like a secret." He smiled at Greer wryly. "We redskins didn't have much use for keys, or ownership for that matter, which, of course, turned out to be a big problem." He sighed and then stood as though to shake off whatever thought process that had started.

"Come on," he said, extending a hand to Greer. "I suppose we'd better go have a look at some other canvases."

"So you believe me?" Greer asked hesitantly.

He looked honestly taken aback. "Of course," he said. And then at Greer's incredulous look, he added as though divulging a sworn secret, "Whitney. She hinted, and I tortured her until she talked."

"Ah," breathed Greer.

For a moment R.J. looked at her with an infinite wonder in his eyes; then he said softly, "We will always be grateful."

Greer had forgotten that as Whitney's friend, Joy would have been a part of R.J.'s life too. But before she could think of any appropriate response, tell him that it had been more Joshua's doing that had saved Joy's life, R.J. was pulling her into his studio.

When they came to the painting on which Greer had seen the flames the night before, she pulled out the hiking map, and they found and marked the spot where it had happened, the site of the development. The new roads that had been, or were being, cut into that previously untouched land were not marked on the map. They did the same thing for the site of the Oak Springs fire. Then Greer took her time examining canvas after canvas that R.J. produced. She saw several more of them with fires, but only two with the key image, and they marked the map at those locations as well.

All the while R.J. watched Greer with fascinated interest, and never a hint of doubt or skepticism, for which she was grateful. Whitney, who had grown up with a medicine man for a father, had reacted the same way. Greer found herself thinking that their Native American background had prepared them to believe because they had grown up with a healthy awareness of the interconnectedness of everything, especially in nature, and that was exactly what Greer thought her talent was: just the unusual ability to see a connection, a dotted line invisible to others, between two things, between then and now, between energy and human.

There was one group of canvases stacked against the wall that R.J. did not take out. Greer asked him why and he pulled one out and showed it to her. "My First American symbolism period." He smiled. "Fun to do, but didn't sell real well."

The painting was beautiful. It was not a landscape but a conglomeration of animals, all of them seemingly embraced in the wings of an owl, but the head of the owl was that of an old, gray-haired woman who smiled lovingly down at all the creatures she seemed to protect.

"Grandmother owl," R.J. said, "protector of the forest creatures and considered to be one of the wisest of all medicine energies. It's interesting, because the owl image appears in Greek and Roman mythology as well. It's the companion of Athena, goddess of wisdom."

"It's lovely," Greer told him. Suddenly she remembered Joshua telling her about seeing the figure of the owl over the deer; she smiled slightly. Perhaps the owl was there as their protector, just as people could have others from their past to watch over them. She would have to tell him about this.

"Well, thank you, R.J. I don't know if any of this will help very much. I mean, there isn't really anything I can do unless I have some kind of clear idea about who's starting these fires and why. Which I do not." She laughed a little, just to ease the frustration.

He walked her to the door and they said good-bye. As he closed it behind her, she heard a soft clinking and turned automatically toward the noise.

Next to the wooden door, hanging from one of the rafters, was a wind chime. The air from the motion of the door had sent it gently swaying. Lost in her worries about the premonitions, she noted only in an absent-minded way that it was the kind of thing that R.J. would have, an artistic piece that looked as though it had been made from found items—an ornate spoon, an old metal bell, and various handmade metal items. Having identified the source of the noise without thinking more about it, she turned away.

Then something snagged her interest. She'd missed something, yet it had been there.

Turning back to scrutinize the mobile, she saw the very center piece of the wind chime, the one hanging lower than the rest so that it would set the others in motion when inspired by the wind. There, rotating slowly in midair, blackened by rust and age, was a heavy, metal, old-fashioned key.

Chapter 30

Greer walked through the door and went straight into Sterling's strong, comforting embrace. She wrapped her arms around his waist and felt the protective strength of his presence, taking in long, deep breaths of his scent.

He held her firmly and rocked slightly from side to side. "You okay?" he whispered into her auburn hair.

"I will be. I'll explain it all later. Right now I'm starving—I haven't eaten all day. What's the plan?" She looked up at him, reassured by his substantial solidity; she felt better already. He kissed her first, meeting her full mouth with his own, and enjoying the eagerness he found there.

After a moment or two, they parted just enough for him to smile contentedly and say, "Rib eyes have been marinating all day, Joy's been baking bread, and the smell has been delectably torturous."

"So I heard. Whitney threatened to go on a scissoring spree if she couldn't start spreading butter by seven thirty."

Sterling laughed his rich, molasses laugh, and Greer could feel the timbre of it in her own chest, which was still pressed against his. It excited her physically and calmed her emotionally. *Which,* she thought, *is exactly what a good man should do.*

"And I think that Whitney has veggies ready to go on the grill as well," he said.

"Let's get 'em and fire up," Greer said as the phone rang. Releasing Sterling reluctantly, she crossed to the counter and read the number of the incoming call. It was Leah.

"Hi. Are you bringing him over?" Greer said into the receiver.

There was a moment's clicking quiet, and then Leah asked, "How did you know it was me?"

Greer laughed. "That neat piece of psychic detection was assisted by caller ID and you telling me earlier you were going to ask him."

"Oh." Leah sounded like she didn't really believe it was all that simple. "Yes, if it's okay. We're actually on our way up toward you right now."

She sounds delighted, Greer thought happily. "Come on by. We'll probably be on the porch. You'll be able to recognize me by the large glass of white wine over ice I'll be holding in my right hand."

"What will your left hand be holding?" Leah asked, and Greer could hear the smile in her voice.

"Depends how long it takes you to get here," Greer said suggestively, making eye contact with Sterling as he crossed the kitchen. "But I'm pretty sure it will be something meaty."

Sterling paused at the doorway through which he was about to exit with a bag of charcoal and raised his eyebrows.

Greer hung up the phone and said, "Yes, I was talking about you."

Weston was introduced around to Luke, Whitney, Greer, and Sterling, each of them offering Leah different variations on an approving glance. Joshua was busy watching Joy for signs of infatuation, but he could detect nothing other than a slight increase of self-consciousness when she nodded her hello. Leah's new haircut was a big hit, especially with her friends who understood that it represented so much more than a new style; it was an outward illustration of a loosening up much more important going on inside.

"How did the meeting go?" Whitney asked Leah. "I

wanted to come, and then again, I didn't, if you know what I mean. It's just so friggin' frustrating."

"Very intuitive of you. The citizens were slaughtered. The head of the grievance committee didn't even show, a Mr. Farrad, and without him, they were flying without a pilot."

"I know him," Joshua said. "Armenian guy, owns a little store near the high school. He's always got a petition for something going on the counter, and lots of political posters in the window. You know, 'Keep Home Depot out of Shadow Hills!' 'Save our Schools,' that kind of thing."

"Nice guy," threw in Luke. "R.J. and he are cronies. They're always having some heated discussion or another, but they're usually on the same side. Come to think of it, I'm kind of surprised he wasn't at R.J.'s last night."

"He's a friend of R.J.'s?" Greer asked quickly.

"More like cohorts in political disruption," Luke told her. "Those two are always up to something. I can't say I disagree with them, but after a while, it seems like you'd get tired of ramming your head against a wall. Was there a handsome Indian there? About fifty, long, shiny hair?"

"Yes," said Leah, sitting up straighter. "He was one of the most outspoken. He pretty much accused Wendy Sostein of taking bribes."

Luke was shaking his head. "I'll bet she loved that."

Greer was following all this with intense interest. She turned to Luke. "Is R.J. pretty radical?" she asked, and took a sip to cover her reaction.

"On the edge," Luke said. "On the edge, but I've never known him to cross it. He must have been pissed that Armen didn't show."

"That's a shame," Whitney said. "It wasn't fair to have the meeting without him."

"You can say that again. It was like Henry the Fifth on St. Crispin's Day. Forty thousand French-slash-local citizens versus fifteen thousand English-slash-developers.

Should have been a bloodbath with the French-citizens victorious; instead the British-developer minority crushed the overwhelming opposition. It was surreal. That Susan Hughs is chillingly good."

Greer had been only half listening, lost deep in her own reflections of what the new information about R.J. might mean, but at the mention of Susan's name, she jumped in. "I gave her a treatment today. Do you know her?"

"Well, yes. I put the loan deal together. That's why I was there."

"Can I get you two something to drink?" Greer asked.

"White wine looks really good," Leah said.

"Weston?"

"Anything carbonated and nonalcoholic. I'm flying tomorrow." He smiled at Leah, revealing his deeply set dimples, and beside her, Greer could hear Whitney's soft swooning sigh.

"Leah, could you help me?" Greer asked, eager to get her alone for a minute.

Inside, Greer poured the drinks and then leaned against the counter, swirling the ice in her own wineglass. "You know, Susan has something going on. I don't know what, but something really dangerous is in store for her. I saw it the first time I met her."

Leah's eyes narrowed. Of Greer's new friends, she was the most linear and the least comfortable with Greer's premonitions. "Like what?" she asked.

"Don't know," Greer confessed. "I saw it like a dark, jagged mass. In the past that has meant danger, but I usually see it *outside* a person, trying to get at them. This is already inside her. That's why I think either it's a pending illness or maybe she's headed for an emotional meltdown, something like that. I sense that she's desperately unfulfilled. . . ." She trailed off, completely unsure of what it could be.

"Well," Leah said dryly, sipping her glass and picking up Weston's soda, "if she's unfulfilled, she's either the best actress I've ever met or completely oblivious to it. I've never seen anyone who is so focused on getting what she wants and so certain of what that is. If Susan Hughs is unhappy, she's convinced herself, and everybody else, that she's happy being unhappy."

In spite of her efforts not to, Greer smiled at her friend and said gently, "Remind you of anyone?"

Leah's hazel eyes went suddenly soft and wide. "Yes," she whispered, "and that scares the shit out of me. I was in the meeting today and I found myself thinking, 'Susan Hughs is everything I ever aspired to be,' and then I realized suddenly that she is also everything I'm afraid I'll become." Leah looked pleadingly up at Greer, as though she was silently begging for some kind of contradiction.

But Greer was nodding. And then she said slowly, "And the fact that you realize that changes everything."

"Even me?" Leah asked uncertainly.

"Especially you." Greer nodded. "And Susan Hughs could use a little of your newfound awareness, and she could really use a friend."

Leah's eyes glazed over for a moment. Then she spoke softly. "If it's true that she's like me, or like I was, then I don't think she'll be able to hear what anyone else has to say, in spite of their best intentions. Something will have to happen to open her eyes."

Greer knew that this was not only a truth for Susan but also a truth for Leah, which her friend was realizing even as she spoke. Leah looked through the kitchen window at Weston, who was facing them and conversing easily with the others. Greer followed her look.

"What do you think of him?" Leah asked, and tried to look as if it were a girlfriend question, but Greer could see from the intensity of her expression that it was much more, and it didn't surprise her at all that Leah would be soliciting her opinion. When they had first met, Greer had had an instant negative reaction to Leah's ex.

Watching him through the glass, Greer could see nothing around him but clear energy with a slight golden tint, which might even have been a trick of the early evening light. But she sighed and shook her head at her friend.

"You cannot base any relationship on my shaky-at-best first impressions of someone. I don't see anything evil or dangerous, but, girl"—Greer fixed a serious look on Leah, whose face had lit up—"not all doors are open to me. Just because I don't see any garbage doesn't mean that there isn't some piled up in the basement. Especially with men. I don't read men very well."

"But he seems okay?"

Greer shook her head but couldn't keep from laughing. "Speaking as your friend, not your psychic, he seems really nice. And more importantly, you like him, and you've grown a lot and you have to start to trust yourself."

They went back outside together and took their places on the comfortable porch furniture. Greer couldn't stop herself from watching Leah, who kept glancing surreptitiously over to Weston as though she couldn't quite believe he was still there.

Chapter 31

Sunday morning, Joshua got up early in a race against the heat. It was barely light when he started out on his hike. He was eager to connect the canyon above his house with the Oak Springs trail, and he knew it might take several hours. His mom had offered to come pick him up when he found out where he emerged. His best guess was that that would be about eight miles away.

He took some power bars, an apple, two honey sticks, and a gallon of water. The pack was heavy, but he knew it would be light soon enough.

After two hours he hit the fire road at the top of the trail from behind his house, and instead of turning back, he kept on. As he suspected, after he crested the highest ridge, he could see the twisting road up to Oak Springs, and it wasn't long until he found the connecting trail.

After almost three hours, his water was all but gone, and he guessed that the heat had risen into the nineties, but he came out on the paved road and started down. He checked his cell phone—no reception; he'd call when he got closer to the highway. Flipping it closed, he noticed that he was nearing the Caseys' driveway and decided to stop in and check on them.

Emily opened the door and looked delighted to see him.

"I hope I didn't startle you," Joshua said. "I just hiked over from my house and thought I'd drop by and say hi."

"Good heavens!" Emily exclaimed. "You're worse

than Larry! Come in, come in, and let me get you a big glass of ice water. Are you hungry?"

Joshua smiled. Emily reminded him of a Norman Rockwell grandmother. "No, thanks. My mom's going to pick me up, and we'll have lunch at that little café at the bottom of the hill, but water sounds fantastic."

"You can call your mom from here if you want. I know those cell phones don't work up here."

"True enough. Thanks." Joshua walked to the phone, set down his backpack, and made arrangements with his mom to start the drive up while he walked down. They'd meet wherever they met.

Emily came back in with a big plastic cup filled with ice and water. She had one for herself as well. They sat at the little table and Emily raised her glass to him. "To the craziest hiker since my husband." She smiled and started to move the glass to her mouth.

At first, Joshua thought that he was seeing a shadow of something inside the translucent orange plastic, or a trick of the light through the ice, but the serpent was so clear, and its meaning had been revealed to him so recently that he recognized it in the next instant.

"Don't drink that!" he shouted, and reached out to pull the cup forcibly away from her mouth.

Emily was so startled that she dropped the cup; the water spilled on the hem of her dress and all over the rag rug. She looked so fearful of Joshua's action that he started to apologize before the water had even begun to soak in.

"Oh, Emily, I'm so sorry, I didn't mean to scare you, but I'm afraid that there's something poisonous in the water. I don't know how to explain it, but please, you have to trust me. I'm almost positive it isn't safe. Did this come from the well?"

Shaking slightly, Emily broke her frightened eyes away from Joshua and leaned down to pick up the cup. "Yes, but why would you think that?"

"Where's Larry?" Joshua asked instead of answering her question. He was pretty sure she would think he was insane, and as much as he wanted to convince her otherwise, he knew the odds were against it.

"Our son picked him up and took him to Kaiser, to the urgent care. He hasn't felt very well. . . ." Her brow furrowed deeply and she looked suspiciously up at Joshua. "He's been nauseous for the last few days, and this morning, I made him go. I would have gone with him, but he wanted me to stay here and rest."

"Listen, Emily, I know it sounds crazy, but please, could I take a sample of the water to be tested? And could you not use it until you hear from me? It should only take a day or so, maybe less if I can round up anyone today." She was watching him with narrowed eyes, but there was a return of trust in them. "Please?" he begged.

"All right," she agreed. "If you say so, Joshua. I know you wouldn't lie to me."

"No, ma'am," he asserted. "I might be wrong, I hope I am, but I would *never* lie to you."

She fixed him with her clear blue eyes and leaned toward him. "Why do you think there's poison in our water, Joshua?"

He sighed. He hoped this didn't keep happening to him. It was one thing when people asked to be helped, another entirely when the warnings or the messages came unbidden. "The truth is, I see things. Mostly spirits, or whatever you want to call them." Afraid to see the doubt that was sure to be on Emily's face, he stared at the stain of water on the rug. "But I also sometimes see images that mean something, and recently I saw an image that meant poison. When you were about to drink, I saw that image again." He looked up. She was watching him skeptically, but it seemed to him that she was making an effort to believe him, because she smiled slightly and nodded as though he should go on. Heartened, he continued. "My mother has always had these, uh, visions, and she's been able to help people with what she sees. About nine or ten months ago, it started to happen to me." A sliver of his old reluctance and resent-

ment worked its way into his chest and pried open his
sense of unfairness. "I didn't ask for this," he blurted
out, suddenly angry and frustrated. "I'm sorry if you
think I'm a freak. I know it seems that way, but it's not
like I asked for it!"

He felt the pressure of Emily's hand on his arm and
he looked again into that transparent blue. "I don't
think you're a freak," she said gently. "I think you are
very brave, even to tell me what you did, much less to
put yourself on the line that way." She rubbed his arm
lightly, and the pressure and her words were very reassuring. "Now, I'm going to call my son's cell phone and
tell him that I think the water might be contaminated.
Maybe the doctors at Kaiser can tell us something before
the water test."

And that was it. His anxiety vanished with a poof.
With her simple act of trust, Joshua's warning had been
heeded, his bizarre talent considered a possibility instead
of a ridiculous farce, and his equanimity restored.

"Emily," said Joshua, taking her hand in his, "I think
maybe you just saved my life."

Her eyes twinkled at him. "About time I returned the
favor," she said as she rose and started for the phone.

Joshua sank back in his chair, exhausted by the hike
in the heat and the emotional stress. He fixed his eyes
on his cup, still filled with water and ice to the brim,
and watched as a tiny serpent, black as coal, twisted and
snaked along the icy droplets of condensation.

Chapter 32

Weston had been right, Leah thought. When they first took off in the helicopter, it wasn't so much as though they were going up as the ground was going down.

Leah gripped the straps of the door and closed her eyes.

"Well, that's no good." She heard Weston's voice, slightly tinny on the headset she was wearing. "There's no point in going up if you can't enjoy the view."

Steeling herself, she opened first one eye and then the other. As she did, the helicopter began to swoop gently forward and she gasped; it was an amazing sensation.

"What's with the papers?" Weston asked, gesturing with the hand that wasn't on the stick to the large roll of white paper in Leah's lap.

"It's the plans for the Golden Door development," Leah shouted, and immediately realized that she probably didn't need to. "I was hoping we could fly over it. I wanted to check something."

He looked at her for what she thought was entirely too long, though she had to admit there wasn't really anything to run into up this high. "Your wish . . ." he said, pushing the stick hard to the right, and suddenly Leah found herself looking almost straight down at the ground through the glass of her door as the helicopter leaned right and sped off in that direction. Leah's stomach dropped, but almost immediately she felt the exhilaration and had to contain herself from whooping like a teenager on a roller coaster.

What amazed her almost as much as the freedom of movement was how quickly you could move from one place to another in a straight line. It took only about two and a half minutes to make the trip from the fire station helicopter pad to the site; in a car on streets that were forced to follow the contours of a rippled landscape, it would have taken more than twenty.

Once she relaxed and got used to the sensation of having nothing under her but several thousand feet of open air, or was able to not think about it anyway, Leah started to enjoy the rare freedom of such an exalted point of view. The heat and the haze kept the more distant mountains to the east and north from being little more than a suggestion on the skyline, but she could make them out, waiting there for millennia, the elders of the hills below her, which, from her perch above them, seemed by comparison youthful and childlike.

"See any smoke?" Weston's voice came over the headset. Leah gazed around.

"No," she answered.

"Me neither. And that makes it a good day. Okay, can you see that big, ugly swath of earth and house frames?" He inclined his head toward what Leah knew must be the Golden Door development.

It was even more jarring from this perspective, a tear ripped into the hillside. The entire top of a small mountain had been sheared off and large chunks of its shoulders had been leveled into steppes. The far left side was completely covered in framed-out homes, two hundred and forty-three to be exact, Leah knew. That would be phase one. Next to it, a second rent was still a gaping scar without the patchwork bandaging of the houses on their tiny lots. She could see the darkened swatches across it, and on the adjacent land, where the fires had struck. "Yeah, I see it." Leah's voice felt as hollow and cold as her guilt.

As Weston circled it, Leah opened her maps and got her bearings with a little help from Weston and the compass on the dash of the helicopter. What she was interested in was the yet unbroken ground of phase three.

She pointed a finger at the proposed acreage on the map and then at the area below that it represented. "Can we take a closer look at this?" she asked him.

"Sure thing."

Twenty seconds later they were skimming the brown and dusty green scrub. Leah checked her map again and then asked, "Can you fly southwest?"

Weston changed course. Below them the land sloped gently down, crested over a ridge, and then fell away into a different valley, in the depths of which was a single, two-lane road.

Leah searched around and finally found what she was looking for—a few houses which were built off that road, one of which belonged to the Caseys. She checked her map a few more times before coming to the conclusion that the Caseys' house was not on, or even close to, the proposed phase three. She sighed, rolled up the map, and then gave Weston the thumbs-up. They rose quickly into the air, the ground falling away below them, taking all its confusion, secrets, and ownership with it.

When the ground was nothing but a carpet of khaki stretched out below them, Leah looked over at Weston, who met her eyes and didn't look away. For a long moment there was a link between them so raw that it left Leah feeling as though her skin had been peeled away.

When he turned his attention back to flying, breaking the spell, Leah felt as though he'd just surprised her naked, and she liked it.

Turning away to hide the smile that had crept across her face and taking a deep, calming breath, she muttered very quietly to herself, "I'm in big trouble."

She had forgotten the headset and the microphone hovering just in front of her mouth.

Into her earphones, Weston's amused, rich voice rumbled, "I'm so glad to hear that."

Pretending that she hadn't heard him, she focused hard on a specific spot below her that was absolutely identical to any other spot and wondered whether she should just throw herself out of the helicopter now, or die a slow and painful death of mortification.

Chapter 33

They knew just after Larry got home that the tank had been poisoned. Emily and Joshua had found an emergency number in the phone book for contaminated water supplies, and the county had dispatched a technician immediately. While they waited, Larry and his son, Adam, had returned, and Joshua had called Greer to ask her to hold off for a little while.

The woman from the county had shown up with a large yellow toolbox that turned out to be filled with various vials and test tubes. After only ten minutes of mixing and shaking, she had declared the water from the Caseys' metal holding tank undrinkable.

Further testing of the sealed well, however, showed no traces of the toxins that had been found in the tank, leading the expert to conclude that either the tank interior was compromised by rust and some kind of rat poison, or someone had deliberately added the dangerous combination of iron oxide and strychnine.

"We don't use rat poison," Emily said, shaking her head firmly. "We don't believe in it. Not up here. If we were to give it to the mice that live here, they would be eaten by the hawks and the coyotes and the snakes, and the poison would kill them too. Once it's in the food chain, it keeps on killing."

This didn't seem to be any revelation to the county poison expert. "That is correct," she said with the bland, studied disinterest that is only achieved after many years of government work comprised of one part egregious human apathy and three parts bureaucratic paperwork.

"And that tank is new," Larry said defiantly. "Well, anyway, we haven't had it more than three years now, and it's got a fifty-year warranty."

"What should we do?" Emily asked, wringing her hands.

"You'll have to flush the tank, and then we'll test it again."

Larry was shaking his head. "It'll take a week to fill that tank from the well right now. The water tables are low. We need rain, and we need it bad."

The county employee shrugged. "Not likely to get that until November at the earliest."

"Well, that's only three weeks away," Emily said hopefully, but they all knew that counting on rain this time of year, or even a month from now, was a crapshoot.

"I'll call Sheldon," Larry said. "Hell, it's worth a couple hundred dollars to get this done and sorted out."

Joshua had been listening quietly, but now he asked the question that so far had been left unsaid. "Who would poison your water?"

"Don't know," Larry said, looking disgusted. "I'd say kids, but it's a little sophisticated for a prank."

The county woman tilted her head farther over her clipboard as if to say, *That's not my department.*

"Have you had any arguments with anyone lately?" Joshua asked, grasping at straws.

"No."

Emily had a half-frightened look on her face, as though she was reluctant to say something that might not be polite. "Actually, there was that real estate woman who wanted to list our house. She was pretty insistent. She wasn't very happy that we didn't want to sell."

Joshua narrowed his eyes. "Did she have a buyer?"

Larry snorted. "She said no, but I didn't believe her. I'm guessing it was another one of these big development outfits. Somebody made an offer on Bill Wicker's down the street. Said they wanted a place where they could keep horses not far from Los Angeles."

"Did he take it?"

"He was thinking about it." Larry shrugged. "I think he was holding out for more money. He's been wanting to move closer to his grandkids back east for a while, but he's not in any hurry. Vultures, they just can't screw this place up fast enough."

Joshua had heard that the developers could be tricky, buying up land under false names or even sending a family to look at a home as though it were for themselves. But poison? That was not only extreme—it was criminal.

The doctors had told Larry that he would continue to feel slightly ill but be able to flush out his system within a few days. What if he'd died? Was someone willing to go that far to build an ugly subdivision? Was there that much money in it that it was worth going to prison to get their hands on this land?

Was there someone out there who would kill for it?

Sheldon's big truck rumbled down the driveway, and Joshua saw the familiar little head bouncing up and down next to him. He smiled as his new friend climbed down from the cab to meet him.

"What are you doing here?" Tyler said as he ran to meet Joshua.

"Well, the Caseys are . . . kind of friends of mine," Joshua explained with a slight hesitation.

"We *are* friends of his," Emily corrected. "And we always will be." She smiled gratefully at him. "Hello, Tyler. Would you like some cookies?"

"Yes, ma'am."

"Then come on in the kitchen, where it's cool."

Joshua accompanied Larry and Sheldon over to the well and was just in time to overhear Sheldon's bitter recrimination. "Bastards. Do you know who did it?"

"Nope," Larry said. "But when I find out, I'll monogram their initials on a shotgun shell and deliver it personally."

Sheldon grinned as though he sincerely enjoyed the

sentiment behind that special delivery. "This isn't the first time this has happened, you know." Sheldon looked around as though he was nervous that prying ears might be somewhere in the deserted shrubbery. "Last time it was right after I made a tank delivery, and I got hauled in by the police." He shook his head.

Joshua felt a chill on his neck like a layer of Tiger Balm over a sunburn, and he shifted closer, pretending to inspect the gush of water coming from the release valve at the bottom of the tank.

"Who was it?"

"Phil Kershner. Had a place on the corner of Mount Gleason and the highway." From the corner of his eye, Joshua watched as Sheldon looked pointedly at Larry.

"You mean, where those condo-looking houses went up?"

"Yep."

With a rush of recognition, Joshua realized that he meant Rowland Hughs's fifteen-house project that he and Simon had been working on. Joshua hadn't lived in the area before their construction had begun.

Sheldon glanced around again, this time flicking his eyes toward Joshua, who pretended he could hear nothing over the flowing water. Then he muttered something about "that developer" and something that Joshua thought was "don't trust him," before raising his voice to a normal level and saying, "Okay, let's check the level. Should be near empty."

Feeling it was safe now to look directly at him, Joshua turned to watch as Sheldon climbed the metal ladder to the top of the water tank. When the fluttering in his chest began, Joshua knew he was about to see one of those somethings that no one else could.

Turning, he saw that Tyler had come back out of the house and was standing behind him watching. And over him was the waiflike child, and she was motioning from Tyler to the water truck and shaking her head firmly.

And Joshua found himself wondering whether it was Rowland Hughs who was not to be trusted, or Sheldon Tucker.

Chapter 34

When Joshua and Greer returned to their house, they noticed Simon sitting on the porch steps. He was on the top step, in the shade, leaning against the thick, square stone pillar, his head at an awkward angle, his mouth open. It was only as their tires crunched the gravel that he startled, and Joshua realized he had fallen asleep in that uncomfortable position. He wondered why Simon hadn't opted for the far-more-inviting porch furniture.

"Hi, Sy. What're you doing here?" Joshua asked as he got out of his mom's car. He kept his voice friendly, but the fact that Simon must have walked over six miles from the closest bus stop in the hottest part of the day was not lost on him.

Greer had come around the car and was standing near the base of the steps. "Hi there," she said to him. "You must be Simon. Why don't you come in?"

"Yeah, uh, okay. Thanks," Simon muttered as he got to his feet.

"So, what brings you by?" Joshua tried again as they went up the steps together. He was also wondering how Simon had found the house. That was cleared up a minute later when Luke came out his front door and said, "Oh, good, you're here. That young man was wandering around, said he was looking for you, and I told him he could wait on the porch. I hope that's okay."

"Sure, that's fine. Thanks," Joshua called to him. Luke grunted a reply and went back into the relative cool of his home.

"You want something to drink?" Greer asked both boys.

"I'll get it," Joshua said, noting Simon's red, over-heated face. He quickly poured two sodas over ice as his mother gave him an understanding look and disappeared upstairs.

Joshua handed over the soda and Simon gulped it down eagerly. "What's up?" he tried for the third time.

This time, after a glance at the stairway up which Greer had disappeared, Simon shrugged, and said, "I wanna talk atcha."

"Sure," Joshua told him. "You want to sit down?"

Simon's eyes cut around the room again. "Can we talk somewhere private?"

"We'll go up to my room," Joshua suggested, and led the way up the stairs to his room in the back. As a matter of habit, he looked across the space between his house and Luke's and into Joy's bedroom window. She was seated at her desk with a textbook open in front of her. He had to smile at the picture; ten months ago she would have set herself on fire before she spent a Sunday afternoon hitting the books.

Simon was standing in the doorway, taking in Joshua's room with an expression of envious disbelief. Joshua wasn't so oblivious that he didn't realize how lucky he was to live in such a nice house, to have a stereo and expensive furniture, but he had grown up privileged enough to feel like what he had was the norm. Looking at it now from Simon's point of view, for the first time it seemed excessive, and for some reason that he didn't really understand, Joshua felt a wash of shame heat his face.

"Have a seat." Joshua gestured to the bed, and he took the chair at the desk.

Carefully, as if he thought he might break it, Simon sat at the very end of the bed, stroking one hand surreptitiously along the faux suede coverlet. Then after another look at the room, he fixed his eyes on Joshua. They were tense and fatigued.

"I think I'm in trouble, and I didn't do shit, I swear."

Simon's hands had landed on his knees, where they clutched at his dirty jeans.

Thrown, Joshua wasn't sure what to say. So he just waited.

"They're gonna think I did it. I didn't like the motherfucker, but I didn't do it."

"Do what?" Joshua asked. A sneaking suspicion that he probably should be very cautious about believing anything that Simon said came forcibly to him; he tried to quell the as-yet-unfounded distrust.

"Shit, you know. The police came and talked to you—they said they did."

"Oh, you mean the fire at the store?"

Simon did not answer him, just watched him with a combination of suspicion and neediness.

"But it wasn't you, right?" Joshua asked, and was surprised by his own calm.

"No fucking way, man. It wasn't me." Simon's pupils were so large they were almost indistinguishable from his dark brown irises. "I'm not retarded; I know they'd come looking for me."

For a long moment, the two young men looked at each other across the room. Though the distance was only a few feet, their backgrounds might have made it a continental divide, but Joshua knew that Simon was reaching out to him and somehow that lessened the gap.

"I believe you," Joshua said, though a section of his brain dropped to its knees, praying he wasn't being a complete sucker.

The three words seemed to release Simon from some kind of brace that had been holding him up, and he crumpled forward, resting his elbows on his thighs and his face in his hands. "I'm so fucking tired, man. I can't sleep."

"Why not?" Joshua asked him automatically.

For a moment it looked as though Simon was going to tell him, his face crumpled the way his body had, and then he seemed to catch himself. But when he spoke, his protective shell had returned and he was evasive.

"Don't know. I have bad dreams sometime. It's stupid, I know."

"No, it's not stupid," Joshua said heatedly. He was almost irrationally pissed off that someone would have spent their life being told they could feel nothing, fear nothing. "Dreams can be scary as shit. I had one the other night that woke me up; I was sweating and, well, hell, I was *scared*."

Simon turned to look up at him, the faintest hint of a smile on his face. He glanced around the well-appointed room in the strong-walled house. "What were you scared of?"

Joshua returned the smile somewhat sheepishly. "Fire. It was a dream about fire, and it was scary."

Simon looked away quickly, but he didn't altogether change the subject as Joshua had suspected he would. Instead he said, "I don't dream about that."

Sensing that to ask what he did dream about would be tantamount to screaming, "Shut up!" at Simon, Joshua waited, and when Simon said nothing more, he tried another tack. "How come you tried to save that dog?"

Simon's eyebrows shot up in bewildered surprise before he could stop himself. He clearly had not been expecting that question. Then his left shoulder twitched forward, and he shrugged as though to cover the involuntary action and said, "I don't know."

"Tell me about the dog you had," Joshua prompted.

A flash of affection crossed Simon's face but was quickly clouded by pain, like a momentary patch of blue sky bullied away on a stormy day. "He died."

A thought came to Joshua. "Did he get hit by a car?"

"No." Simon's mouth had tensed to a thin line. Joshua thought he wasn't going to say any more, but then Simon said, "My old man shot him." Again the unconscious tic, again the masking shrug.

"Wow," Joshua said softly. "That sucks."

Simon looked Joshua briefly in the eyes. It was a questioning, slightly suspicious look, as if to see whether Joshua was mocking him. Seeming reassured, he added, "He was a fucker." Tic, shrug.

"He die too?" Joshua picked up a small stone bear fetish that he kept on his desk and pretended to examine it to move his focus off Simon.

"Yeah," Simon half laughed, half snorted, but Joshua had never heard anything less amused in his life.

"Not a real great dad, huh?"

"You could say that."

Joshua was thinking hard and fast. He was almost sure that the malignant male figure he had seen over Simon was his father, but he was unsure why the image seemed so intent on evil for Simon. His brain was racing to find a way to ask Simon all the things he wanted to know without revealing why.

"Can I ask you something?" Joshua said, still as conversationally as possible.

Simon nodded.

"Why did your father kill your dog?"

Joshua was sure he knew the answer. But when Simon answered in a flat, detached voice, it surprised him.

"He used to beat me up a lot, and one time Spike tried to stop him, so he shot him."

In spite of all his efforts to remain outwardly unaffected, Joshua's mouth fell open and he spat out, "He shot your dog because the dog tried to protect you from him?"

Simon was staring at the floor near his feet. "Yeah," he said as though that kind of thing happened every day. Maybe it did where he came from.

"You know what?" Joshua asked, and waited for Simon to look up at him. "You're right. He *was* a fucker."

Simon couldn't suppress a little laugh, but it didn't last long.

"So what happened to your father?"

Simon's eyes dropped again, his shoulders drooped, and he looked infinitely exhausted. "Somebody killed him."

"Bummer."

Slowly, Simon's eyes came up and met Joshua's again,

and this time, even through the fatigue, Joshua could
see the hatred and the fire. "He had it coming," he said.

Trying to stay cool and at least pretend he could con-
verse offhandedly about what to him were unthinkably
appalling events that were Simon's life, Joshua nodded.
"Sounds like it." And with that small gesture of commis-
eration, it seemed that the last of Simon's energy left
him in a single exhalation. His body slumped farther
forward, like a children's blow-up party jumper that had
been unplugged, and his features sagged as though he
were decades older.

Concerned, Joshua said, "Listen, you look ripped,
man. Why don't you catch some z's? I got some stuff to
do; I'll wake you up in a little while. You want to have
dinner with us?"

The look of relief on Simon's face was intense. He
nodded, mumbled a thank-you, and fell backward onto
the bed, feet still on the floor.

Joshua turned away and pretended to be busy at his
desk. He flipped through the leather-bound notebook in
which he kept his observations and read through a few
of them without absorbing anything. In a few minutes
he stole a look back at Simon and let the book lie open
on the desk. The boy had curled up on the foot of the
bed in a fetal position. He was out.

Joshua turned his chair to face Simon with the utmost
care to not make any noise. Then he took a few deep
breaths, closed his eyes, and concentrated on the sensa-
tions in his body, searching for the warm tingling, trying
to call it up.

And it answered. With a prickling heat this time that
seemed unique to Simon and his visitors. Opening his
eyes, Joshua could see the image of the man hanging
over Simon, glaring down at him with such intense malice that Joshua felt a jolt of fear. "No," Joshua whispered, "you can't have him."

The figure turned his opaque black eyes on Joshua,
and he felt the gaze land on him like the sights of an
Uzi. He imagined the white light around him and forced

danger back away from him. "No," he repeated, "you cannot have him."

The man's face, so devoid of the light and bliss that Joshua had always previously seen around those who had moved on, turned again to Simon with such a dismissive disinterest in Joshua that it filled him with outrage. As the figure fixed its vapid gaze on Simon again, the boy shifted and moaned in his sleep.

"No," Joshua said again, "you cannot have him." But even as he watched, he could see the impressions of darkness that were emanating from the male figure toward Simon. Joshua focused hard on the black ropes of energy, but he could think of no way to sever their connection; they seemed immune to his fledgling efforts to affect them.

A sound from below broke through Joshua's concentration, and as though waking from a deep sleep, he suddenly became aware of the room, of the sleeping Simon, of the absence of the otherworldly figure, and of the fact that he was drenched in sweat.

"Joshua?" he heard his mom call from the bottom of the stairs, and when he didn't answer right away, he heard her start up.

Rousing himself, he moved to pick up a towel he'd dropped on a corner of the bed. He was wiping the perspiration from his face when something arrested his attention. In his uneasy sleep, Simon had shifted onto his stomach and his shirt had separated from the top of his jeans, exposing a strip of skin around his midsection. There, near his waist, Joshua could see the inky stain of a rough homemade tattoo. It looked like some kind of bug—no, a spider. His mother called out again and he went to the door, exiting quietly so as not to wake Simon.

"Yeah?" he answered his mom in a whisper. Noting her raised brows, he explained, "Simon fell asleep. He's really exhausted from walking here in the heat."

Greer narrowed her eyes at him but only said, "I don't blame him. Detective Sheridan is downstairs; he wants to talk to you."

Before he could stop himself, Joshua asked in a raspy whisper, "Does he know Simon is here?"

Greer's brows darted up again, but she shook her head no. "He asked to see you. I told him you'd be right down."

Nodding, Joshua passed his mom, who turned and followed him down the stairs.

The solid detective was standing in the living room near the dark fireplace. His partner was nowhere to be seen.

"How can I help you, Detective Sheridan?" Joshua asked politely as he came into the room and sat down on one of the armchairs. His mother crossed to the sofa.

"I've got a favor to ask you," Detective Sheridan said. "First, I have to tell you both something that is not yet public knowledge, so I'm going to ask you not to repeat it to anyone until I say so."

"Sure," Joshua said, not at all sure if that was the correct answer. He felt like maybe he should raise his right hand or something. Greer nodded solemnly.

"We've got an ID on the body from the fire up by the development. It's a man, a local merchant named Armen Farrad."

The name, though fairly new to Joshua, had become familiar. He was the head of the citizens' committee, the man who owned and ran the little Eastern European grocery on Foothill. "I'm sorry to hear that," Joshua said, and he meant it. "He always seemed like a genuinely nice person whenever I went in there."

"He was also the man who put Simon Gomez in probation camp," Detective Sheridan said grimly.

It took Joshua a full three seconds to put together what Sheridan was suggesting. "You think Simon killed Mr. Farrad?" he asked, shocked. "I can't believe he's capable of *that*."

The corners of Sheridan's mouth flickered upward a fraction in a rare display of either emotion or amusement; it was impossible to distinguish which. Joshua realized that winning an argument with a homicide detective about what people were or were not capable of was like betting on a horse that wasn't even running. "We'll see" was all the detective said in rebuttal. "But I need to talk to Simon Gomez, and I can't find him. I've been to his aunt's, and he didn't come home last night. You said you saw him on Friday?"

"Yes." Joshua shot a look at his mother; she was watching him calmly. To his relief, her expression revealed nothing.

"There was something else." Sheridan took out his notebook and flipped through it, though Joshua was sure he didn't need to. "On the wall of the store, after the fire, someone had spray painted a spider. Does that mean anything to you?"

Through Joshua's head a succession of rapid images passed. The rough spider, carved into the ravaged oak; the spider tattoo that he had just seen on Simon; and a quick flash of something he had never seen before, the painted shape of a spider on a door, the black paint dripping in long, careless streaks. Sterling had showed the spider on the tree to the fire captain. Had the captain forgotten about it, or had he told Detective Sheridan?

From the corner of his eye, he saw his mother move, and so did Detective Sheridan, apparently, because he quickly asked, "Ms. Sands?"

Greer shifted and thought before she answered. "It's just that recently I saw an image that contained a spider's web. I don't know if it has any bearing on that or not."

"You *saw* it?" the detective asked speculatively.

Greer sighed and smiled patiently. "In a vision, yes."

Joshua could see the big man struggling to keep an open mind. He'd had experience with Greer's visions once before and been unable to deny their validity. Still, it hadn't been easy for him. "And in what form?"

"It represented danger," Greer explained. "Being caught in a web of danger."

"And who, if I may ask, is in danger?" Sheridan had stopped even the pretense of examining his pad.

Greer smiled beatifically, first at the detective and then at her son, whose eyes she held as she answered.

"Me," she said, her voice betraying no fear. "It was me."

From the recesses of fabric came the muted sound of a cell phone ring. Detective Sheridan thrust a hand into his pocket. "Excuse me," he said, and extracting the phone, he stood and walked out into the hallway.

"What are you talking about?" Joshua asked his mother, alarmed.

"I'll explain later. Does it mean anything to you?"

Joshua hesitated and then said, "Yes . . . maybe."

Detective Sheridan was back. "I'm sorry, but I had to take that. I'm afraid I have to go. We've located Mr. Farrad's next of kin."

"Oh," Greer said softly, and standing, she laid a hand on Sheridan's arm empathetically. "I'm so sorry. That must be very difficult for you."

For a fraction of a second, the big, granite face looked genuinely shocked. Joshua guessed it was possibly the first time that anyone had ever offered *him* sympathy instead of the family of the victim.

"It's part of the job," he said gruffly.

"Still, it must be very hard. I'm sorry."

Sheridan felt his breath catch. This woman was something rather amazing; it was as though she had sensed his carefully suppressed despondency. He started into the hallway. "I'll be in touch," he said.

And he was out the door before Joshua had to make the choice to betray his new friend's trust in him, or lie to an officer of the law.

Chapter 35

Joshua fixed a plate with a ham sandwich and a pile of Doritos and took it up to his room. Opening the door carefully, he saw that Simon was still unconscious on the bed as he had been throughout the afternoon, though now he was snoring softly. Setting the plate down on the desk in Simon's view if he woke, he stood for a moment wondering how long it had been since Simon had had a decent night's rest. It was unlikely that he'd slept very soundly at the fire camp, and it sounded as though things had not gone too smoothly for him since he'd been released.

Joshua tiptoed out and back down to the kitchen. Sterling had come in and was making a pot of coffee. The heat of the late afternoon made Joshua feel lethargic, and though the sweltering temperature seemed a vote against a hot beverage, the very smell of the brewing caffeine prodded his sluggish brain into activity. His mother was seated at the table, and she gestured to the chair next to her.

Sterling brought the pot to the table and poured for all three of them. Then they each went through their separate yet distinctive rituals of personalizing their coffees. Adding just the right dollop of milk, stirring in half a teaspoon of honey, watching for the perfect shade of caramel, tasting for that slight hint of smoothing sweetness or the tang of strong bitterness.

Without sounding at all judgmental or fatherly, a trick that Sterling had somehow mastered, he said, "So, your

SPEAK OF THE DEVIL

mom told me you're harboring a criminal suspect in your bedroom." There was enough of smile in his eyes to let Joshua know that the words portrayed merely the outward appearance of the situation and not a definition of it.

"We don't know that." Joshua could hear how defensive he sounded.

"No. We don't. But if the police are looking for him, and you're not telling them that he is directly overhead, that could be interpreted as aiding and abetting." Sterling looked completely unconcerned by his own statement as he raised his cup to his lips and took a cautious sip.

Guardedly, Joshua asked, "Mom, what were you saying about seeing a spider?"

"I didn't say that," Greer answered firmly. "I didn't see a spider. But when Detective Sheridan asked if a spider *meant* anything to us, I remembered seeing a web, and one seems to suggest the other." She looked intently at her son. "Have you seen anything like that?"

Sterling answered for him. "We saw a spider carved into the oak tree that burned at the site."

"So it's probably the same person who, at least, set the fires at the site and the store?" Greer asked.

"Could be," Sterling mused. "But if Sheridan thinks that Simon was out for revenge on Mr. Farrad, it doesn't follow that he would start a fire at the development. I mean, why would he?"

"It's not him," Joshua said earnestly, relieved that his mother's vision was only vaguely related. "I just *know* it's not him. He needs to sleep for a little while and then I'll talk to him. I'm sure he'll be glad to answer Detective Sheridan's questions."

Greer had not spoken yet, but now she asked softly, "Why don't you think that Simon has anything to do with this? I mean, I understand having that kind of feeling, but all this does sound a little damning."

"You wouldn't understand," Joshua muttered into his cup, but the lovingly ironic look in his mother's eyes made him realize how banal that was. If his psychic mother couldn't understand a nonverbal impression, then no one could. He sighed and gave it a shot. "Okay, here's the deal," he said. He explained again about seeing the man who he felt sure was Simon's father and shared his new knowledge that his father had killed the dog while it was trying to protect Simon. Both Sterling and Greer shook their heads at the harsh reality of Simon's youth, but other than that, they listened without comment. When he had finished, Joshua waited a moment and then asked, "What do you think?"

"So, you're saying that you think the father is making Simon do bad things, or that he's making bad things happen to Simon?"

"The second," Joshua said. "He wants to hurt him."

Greer had turned to look at Sterling. "Why would the father want to hurt Simon now?"

Sterling shrugged. "Pissed off that the kid is alive and he isn't?" he suggested flatly. "Listen, I know that both of you are tuned into a channel that the rest of us can't hear, and I definitely bow to your expertise in that area. But frankly, in Simon's case, I'm more worried about what's likely to influence him on *this* side of the veil." His eyebrows arched knowingly as he gave each of the other two a pointed look.

"What do you mean?" Joshua asked, but he remembered Simon's tough-looking friends, and he wondered if his primitive tattoo was a rite of passage into a gang. He also knew that being marked with ink was not the only requirement for membership in that kind of club.

"I mean," began Sterling, "that I've been in Simon's situation, maybe not as bad, but my father was a mean drunk, and my mother spent her life chain-smoking and collecting dole. There was nobody to turn to, except the other bad boys my age with nobody to teach them anything either. They were the only ones who were there for me when nobody else was, but the price of having them on my side was huge. When kids have no adult influence that is worth respecting, there are no rules but the ones they make, and let's face it—left to themselves, adolescents and teenagers aren't really known for their exemplary behavioral choices." He nodded at Joshua. "Present company excluded."

Joshua half snorted. "I didn't exactly grow up alone in the inner city."

Greer stroked her son's arm with a smile, then reached out to rest her hand on Sterling's. "How did you get out?" she asked, and couldn't resist adding, "You came out magnificently, if you don't mind my saying."

Sterling lifted her hand to his mouth and kissed the back of it. "No, I don't mind at all. Thank you. The fact is that I lucked into a brutally tough teacher in seventh grade—an ex-rugby player with a lopsided face to prove it named Mr. Norman—who recognized that I had a brain that was being neglected, and with a little, uh, persuasion, he helped me turn my life around. *But,* I still had to make the choice to do that for myself, and that choice involved giving up the protection of the only family I knew. It wasn't easy."

"So what made you?" Joshua asked.

"Fear. My friends started dying, for stupid reasons. Fights, shot by the police, drug overdoses, and I knew my turn would come soon enough." He shrugged again and looked almost embarrassed. "The truth is, I was scared." His face hardened as he added, "And I was right to be. As far as I know, only two of the old gang are still breathing. One's doing life for turning someone's skull inside out with a crowbar, and the other one is me."

Joshua was gazing at Sterling with a newfound admiration. What must it be like to drag yourself up out of a life like that? He found himself thinking that living a decent life was hard enough *with* all the advantages.

"You know, it's interesting how similar those influences are to the kind that Joshua is sensing," Greer was saying. "It can be very helpful to have someone recognize the negative forces, even to put energy into exorcising them, but it cannot be done solely from the outside. The person himself has to make a strong choice that will change the energy." She tilted her head to one side and looked across the room at nothing in particular, trying to find the words to describe it. "It's as though, their whole lives, they've had a melody playing inside them, and it's been discordant, out of tune, but it's what they are—not what they are made of, but what they've been made into—and they have to change the tune, if that makes any sense."

"But you change things sometimes," Joshua said, watching her eagerly, hoping for a clue that would teach him how to help the sleeping boy upstairs, how to dispel Simon's houseguest from hell. "When you make charms and, uh, stuff, you can give energy, right? Like when you made that bracelet for Joy."

But Greer was shaking her head. "No, I can only open a door. The truth is, what other people call magic is only a lending of strength or energy. It can't be created, it has to be taken from somewhere before it can go somewhere else. I couldn't change Joy, I could only connect myself to her." She stopped and laughed slightly. "And anyway, it didn't work the way I intended, did it?" She smiled at her son, who looked self-consciously away.

"No," Joshua agreed. "It connected me to her, so that means that I can do it too?"

"It's very dangerous to take on someone else's darkness, and it's useless if they don't want to let it go." Greer spoke softly but with intensity.

"Why the hell wouldn't they?" Joshua asked, as though that was a no-brainer.

He was surprised to see the sad smiles that his question produced on the faces of his mom and Sterling. They looked at each other, sighed together, and then turned their attention back to him.

"Because," Sterling said, and his eyes went distant and unfocused as he visited a place in the past that was as gray and sad as it was out of his reach, "they don't know they have a choice."

"What the hell does that mean?" Joshua spurted out, frustrated.

"It means that they have always believed that things will go badly, will go wrong. More importantly they have no reason to believe that *they* are anything but bad and wrong; and so they are," Sterling told him.

"Well, that sucks," mumbled Joshua.

Sterling laughed, and the solemnity of the moment was shattered with the almost-tropical feel of his warmth. Then he leaned on his elbows and looked directly at Joshua. "But there are the Mr. Normans in the world. The kick-ass, take-no-shit-from-any-punk-kid teachers are out there. And there are the Joshua Sandses. The kid-out-of-the-blue-who-just-believes-you-can-do-better, who does better himself and so proves that it *must be possible*." He smiled gently; Joshua was speechless.

"But," Sterling went on, "it comes to this: If Simon has anything to do with—or knows anything about—these fires or this murder, he's going to have to pay the piper. *And so will you.* For now, that means you have to convince him to go in and talk to Detective Sheridan on his own steam. That will make a big difference if he's innocent."

Joshua thought of the spider inked into Simon's skin and felt a sting in his own midsection. Very quietly he asked, "And what if he's guilty?"

"Then he has to face that music too."

With a long, hot exhalation, Joshua rose from his seat and left the kitchen without looking back. He went up the stairs and down the hall. Hesitating for only a moment, he turned the knob and went into the room.

But the bed was empty. Glancing frantically around, Joshua could find no sign of Simon. With a rapidly sinking feeling, Joshua went down the hall, checking all the other rooms and ending back in his own room in case he had somehow overlooked a five-foot-eight human being, but he knew it was no use; Simon had snuck away. He crossed to his desk and leaned against it, looking down at the plate he had brought up. The sandwich was gone.

And so was his notebook.

Chapter 36

Loc drove with his head tilted to the left, to catch the wind from the open window. His car was old and the air-conditioning had ceased working long before he had bought it. He ran his hand along the rim of the door, feeling the smoothness of the paint job that he and his brother had done themselves. Unlike so many of his friends, he'd chosen something subtle, white with some flame detailing along the fenders. It wasn't that he hadn't liked the louder colors, but he was smart, and as much as he might have enjoyed the attention, he also knew that drawing it could be a very bad thing.

He could sense Tic's impatience from the seat next to him. The younger man twisted constantly in his seat and lit another cigarette.

"Gimme one," Loc ordered, and pulled one from the offered pack. He lit it and increased his speed. They were past the streetlights, and darkness spilled away on either side of them. One of the headlights, weak and in need of an adjustment, illuminated the road ahead, and the other spilled light crazily off the left. Loc breathed in the nicotine and held it for a moment before letting it slide heavily out his nostrils. The smoke tasted good to his stoned senses, the speed exhilarated him, but he was careful, always careful, not to attract too much attention, not to offer an excuse to any police officers who might be randomly cruising the deserted road.

Suddenly, a figure several feet from the road flashed quickly into view as they passed. Loc sat forward and braked. Without the wayward light, he would have missed him. "Shit, there's that motherfucker," he muttered. Pulling onto a wide section of the shoulder, he made a U-turn and doubled back, coming up alongside the lone pedestrian.

"Yo, Sy, where you been?" Loc's voice was controlled, as always, but he was pressed to keep the anger out of it.

Simon approached the car almost reluctantly and leaned down. "Workin'."

"Get in," Loc told him. He took another long drag on the cigarette and then tossed it out the window. It bounced, sending out tiny coral-colored sparks before it came to rest just past Simon's feet. He absently watched the small, glowing torch, smoking on the dry ground as he waited for Simon to climb into the backseat. Then he turned and fixed his steely brown eyes on the younger boy's shape, silhouetted in red by the taillights. "You ain't been working," he said coldly.

He expected no response and he got none.

Loc pressed the accelerator and felt the gas burn through the engine as the tires spun and then caught. A thrill passed through him, the thrill of motion, of power.

Chapter 37

This was going to be the hottest, driest Columbus Day on record. Jenny got to the coffee shop before six a.m. and started setting up. She had quite a few customers already waiting, mostly parade volunteers who were eager for a refill as their to-go cups from home had proved severely deficient for such an early Monday, and a holiday to boot.

Once the initial rush was over, Jenny started to move her operation outside. The parade would come right down her little section of the high street, and already people had begun to set up lawn chairs or wagons, staking out their view spots. Jenny brought out several large coolers that she had purchased for the occasion and then went to her car to get the bags of ice that she had picked up at the twenty-four-hour grocery store on her way in.

She had bought the smaller size so they wouldn't be too heavy and there would be no danger in her lifting them, even as pregnant as she was, and their chilly plastic exteriors felt good against her shoulder and neck, where she balanced them awkwardly on the trip from the parking lot to the coolers. She looked up at the mercilessly clear sky and shook her head. Six a.m. and it was already hot. It was going to be a brutal day.

"Can I help you with that?"

Jenny turned as quickly as the precariously balanced bags would allow and saw Reading standing outside the door of her café.

"Uh, yeah, actually that would be great. I've got these

two, but there are six more in the trunk of my car." She gestured with a nod of her head to where the trunk stood open.

Reading strode over, heaved out all six bags effortlessly. He came back, three in each hand, and held them up as though they were balloon bouquets. "You want them in here?" he asked.

"Yes, please, two in each cooler," Jenny said. In one swift, continuous movement, he set down the bags, ripped them open, and emptied the frosty, rounded pellets into the coolers. Then he straightened up, wadding the excess plastic into a small ball in his massive hands.

"Anything else?" He waited for her response unblinkingly.

"Well, I could use some help carrying out the sodas. My help seems to be running late. Tell you what, coffee's on me, okay?"

"Good deal." Reading followed her into the shop, and they went behind the counter into the back room.

It wasn't until they were in the small, dark room that Jenny felt the many tiny, scurrying claws of discomfort crawling up her spine. On the street with the open space around them, her proximity to a powerful man had not seemed important, but in the cramped, darkened storeroom, it suddenly alarmed her. She pressed her back against the stacked cases of teas and coffees and avoided making eye contact with him. What was it about this man that gave her the creeps? She ventured a glance up at him and found him watching her intently. That was it, she decided; he just plain looked at her too long.

"It's these against this wall," she said, and turning away she reached for the case on top.

"Not so fast," Reading said in a throaty bass, and Jenny's heart skipped a beat as she felt his hand land heavily on her shoulder. Then Reading's voice rumbled out, "I'll get these. You can open the cases and put them in the coolers."

With a deep, cooling breath, Jenny pulled away from his hand and skittled sideways from the room, mumbling her thanks. She was so flustered that she forgot to ask him what kind of coffee he would like, and it was only after they had successfully transferred several dozen plastic bottles of water and soda that she remembered her offer.

"Reading, thank you so much! What can I get you?" Jenny gushed enthusiastically in an effort to compensate for her unrealized suspicions.

"Plain coffee, large one, please."

"How about a muffin?" she encouraged.

"No thanks. I've got to go."

"Aren't you going to watch the parade?" Jenny asked as she went behind the counter, filled a large paper cup with the fragrant liquid, and slipped a sleeve over it.

Jenny heard Reading give a short, contemptuous laugh. "I prefer real excitement to this Mayberry crap."

As she handed Reading the coffee, Jenny looked up at him, and her newfound warmth cooled a bit.

He was watching her so fixedly that she couldn't help comparing his gaze to a predator's. *This,* she thought to herself, *is what a rabbit sees when it spots the coyote midpounce.* His eyes were somehow attached to her every movement; he seldom blinked, as though to miss something in that fraction of a second would be an unpardonable weakness.

But Jenny was no rabbit, and her trepidation morphed quickly into anger.

"Is something wrong, Reading?" Jenny asked sharply.

He started, his eyes widening in surprise. "I'm sorry, was I staring?"

"Yes, you were."

Disarmingly, Reading looked slightly embarrassed. "Mindy says I do that. I don't notice it. I guess it comes from being trained as a sniper in the army."

Jenny leaned weakly against the counter, which she was very grateful to have separating them. "You were a *sniper*?" she asked weakly.

"Yeah, in Desert Storm, and the whole thing is, focus, and don't blink. Plus"—he leaned down and she saw him consciously look away and then back—"don't tell

Mindy I said this, but I always had a thing for pregnant women, and you're about the prettiest pregnant woman I ever saw."

Jenny waited two beats before saying pointedly, "Except for your wife, of course."

"Goes without saying," Reading said with a wink that was anything but innocent. Before Jenny could whip up some indignant anger, he had turned and was out the door.

"Okay, that was disturbing," Jenny said out loud to herself to dispel the shakiness that felt as though some heavy object had crawled down her throat and was oscillating rapidly inside her.

The door chimes sounded again and she started anxiously. But it was Leah who came in.

Relieved, Jenny sang out, "Morning, girl! What the hell are you doing up this early on a holiday?"

"Hi. Oh, I'm supposed to represent the business sector of the community by sitting in the stands with the councilwoman, mayor, et cetera."

"The parade doesn't start until ten," Jenny noted, glancing at the time.

"I know. I couldn't sleep, and I wanted to talk to you." Leah had reached the counter now, and crossing her arms protectively, she leaned against it and shuffled her feet.

"Oh no. What's wrong? Please don't tell me that nice fireman turned out to be some kind of asshole."

Leah looked shocked. "Weston? No! He's been . . ." Her face reddened quickly with an accompanying smile. "He's been fantastically sweet. And patient," she added. "In fact, he was at the house last night."

"Oh ho!" Jenny said. "And?"

Leah frowned. "And he got called out on a brush fire."

"Oh, was it bad?"

"Yes." Leah's face took on an exaggerated pout. "He didn't get done until it was too late for him to come back. As far as the fire goes, I suppose the good news is that only about a hundred square feet near the road were burned. Somebody tossed a cigarette out a car, they think."

Jenny was shaking her head. "Damn shame on both counts," she said. She'd automatically made Leah a non-fat latte and poured herself a cup of coffee. "Okay, let's go sit down. What is it you want to talk to me about?"

But a customer came in, then another, and Jenny was busy for a few more minutes, during which Leah moved to a table by the window and nervously tapped her manicured nails on the tabletop. She knew that the thoughts she was harboring were serious accusations, and she desperately needed to sound them off someone with sense. In the last few months she had come to realize that the high school graduate who ran the coffee shop had more sense than most of the university-educated community leaders put together.

Finally, there was enough of a lull for Jenny to join her. "Okay, spill," she said. "And you'd better make it brief. I have an idea that today is going to be insane."

"Okay." Leah took a deep breath. "Here goes. Weston took me up in the helicopter and I took the plans for the Golden Door development with me. I just had a sneaky suspicion that something was up."

"Really?" Jenny's attention was fixed on Leah.

"You see, the phase three, which the community is fighting, has basically been approved by the county and city zoning offices, except for one thing."

"Which would be . . ."

"A second exit road. There has to be more than one emergency access for that many homes so residents can vacate in case of a catastrophe, or to let emergency vehicles in if the primary access is blocked."

Jenny nodded. "That makes sense."

"Anyway, here's what I noticed." Leah leaned in and lowered her voice, even though the nearest customer was two tables away. "The Caseys, that nice older couple who had an unexplained fire on their land, are smack-dab in the perfect place for that road to go through."

Leah glanced around and dropped her voice to a whisper. "In fact, there's really no alternative route."

"Wow. Have they refused to sell to the developers?"

Leah shook her head to show her bafflement. "That's the thing! I've spoken with them, and except for a stray real estate agent almost a year ago, no one has made an offer on their land. The neighbors got an offer not long ago, but they're still holding on and there's been no other interest."

"But"—Jenny held up a bright orange acrylic nail— "if it *was* arson, don't forget that the development site was the second victim."

Leah dropped her elbows heavily onto the table. "I know," she moaned. "It doesn't really make any sense. That's why I'm talking to you about it."

"Why don't you bring this up to the city council?"

Leah frowned deeply. "Think, Jenny. The Hughses have gotten this development through in spite of major environmental and community opposition. I'm talking about a massive, organized push to keep them out. I think it's unlikely that there isn't some kind of kickback going on. It might be a legal kickback—politicians are great at writing those into their job descriptions—but even I have to admit that it looks like big money won out against all odds—again."

Jenny was staring knowingly at Leah. "You've left something out," she said.

Leah sighed. "I know. The man heading up this opposition turns up dead. In a fire *at the very development* he was opposing. Is he the one who set the second fire, which would mean it has nothing to do with the first one?"

"Could be. Was he the kind of person who would do that, you think?"

"I have no idea," Leah said with a firm shake of her head. "From what I hear, he was very passionate about his causes, but I never heard about him doing anything illegal." She paused and shrugged. "And just as importantly, do I think the Hughses are capable of murder?

The answer to that is a flat no. I mean, they love money, but they seem decent enough, and the additional homes were already approved, so what would be the sense of that? I mean, as far as Susan Hughs is concerned, this second road is just one more bureaucratic hoop out of hundreds for her to jump through, and trust me, she's a show dog. What do you think?"

"Okay, listen. Every year we have fires. Every year, it seems, some psycho idiot has to go turning the hills into bonfires for their own personal entertainment. So these fires might just be random, unrelated incidents. In fact, that's far more likely than a conspiracy. On the other hand, I trust your instincts. *But* I think you need proof before you make any accusations, especially if these developers have the city council in their pocket."

"I know," Leah groaned. "But if it *is* a possibility and people's lives and homes are being endangered, then I can't just do nothing."

Jenny sat back and grinned wickedly at her friend.

"What?" Leah asked, confused.

"Well, look at you," Leah said, crossing her arms over her chest. "You care."

"Oh, shut up," Leah said, but she couldn't hide the grin that commandeered her own face.

"Okay, here's what you have to do." Jenny leaned in. "You have to get someone at Golden Door to confess something to you. You need inside information."

"How do I . . . Oh." Leah leaned her head back and looked up at the ceiling. "I think I have an idea."

The door chimes rang, and Jenny rose from her chair. "You always were a bright child," she said, and left Leah and her mind to their own machinations.

Chapter 38

Even sitting perfectly still on her porch, Greer could feel beads of sweat forming on her chest and beginning their slow trickle toward one another until they were heavy enough to slide freely down between her breasts. But she ignored the feathery sensation and focused instead on the images inside her head.

But, search as she might, she could find nothing to help her, only a vague crackling energy that was carried to her on the rising, hot wind. Danger hung in dark masses, hovering somewhere over the forest around her, but revealing only its impending presence to her, no hints of where or when it would strike. One word kept repeating itself to her: *soon*.

Beside her on the table was the hiking map on which she had marked the keys that she had seen in R.J.'s paintings. She tried to focus on his energy, but all that came to her was anger, which didn't help much. She sighed impatiently and tried to let go of her frustration as it was only blocking any real indications she might receive. Finally defeated, she opened her eyes. Cupping her chin between fingers and thumb, she ran one hand down her neck, wiping away the perspiration like a squeegee on a windshield.

Joshua stood at the window and watched her come out of her trance. He could see that she was worried, and after her assertion that she had seen herself in danger—in a web—he had not slept well. Moving suddenly, as though motivated by a spasm, he went to the door and opened it.

"Mom?" he called softly.

"Morning, honey." She turned tired but smiling eyes on him, and he could see that her pupils were slightly dilated for so bright a day, a side effect of deep meditation.

"Are you okay?" It felt awkward to ask the question. As though he were the parent, and she the child in need of help or supervision. He twisted the doorknob absentmindedly.

"I'm fine. Well, actually, I'm a bit frustrated. Come sit down." She gestured to a porch swing near her, and Joshua moved to it and sat stock-still, using the tension in his legs to keep the swing from rocking in its pendulum-like motion.

"What's up?" he asked, trying to keep his face relaxed.

Greer's full mouth shaped into an *o,* and she exhaled slowly. "I told you that a key, the old-fashioned kind, has appeared in my visions when I have had a presage of a fire. Does that mean anything to you?" Joshua shook his head. "It showed up over the image of the two fires that have happened. What I haven't told you is that I've seen two more keys—not a fire, just the key—over two more paintings."

Joshua felt his heartbeat quicken and his skin flush as though he'd just been stung by something poisonous. "Two?" he croaked.

His mother nodded.

"And when did you see yourself in the web?"

She placed her hand over his. "Earlier that day, but I don't think that meant I was in danger anytime soon. I don't even think that they are necessarily connected," she finished quickly, trying to erase the panic that had appeared on her son's face like an obscene word on a playground. "I'm far more worried about Jenny. She's the one for whom I sense imminent danger."

"Mom." Joshua's voice felt harsh, as though the dry wind had roughened his throat. "There's something I didn't tell you either. That spider image. I saw it on Simon. He has a tattoo, here." Joshua pointed to the small of his back, on the right side. "I still don't think it's him, and I can't even figure out why I don't, but if it is him, and that has somehow put you in danger . . ."

The back of Greer's fingers brushed his cheek. "Thank you for telling me, but I saw a web of darkness. I think it means that I was caught in some kind of dangerous intrigue. I told Detective Sheridan about it because he asked if we'd seen anything, but a web and a spider are two very different images. Do you understand?"

Joshua's head felt as if it were filled with Cream of Wheat, and though he nodded, the starchy, lumpy mass turned to quicksand that sucked in every negative possibility and spit out self-loathing.

"Perhaps," Greer said softly, her thoughts apparently far away, "Simon's spider signifies that he's trapped as well."

"I should have told Detective Sheridan he was here! I should have stopped him from going! What if it *is* him starting these fires and I could have stopped it?" Joshua blurted out in an anguished voice.

To his surprise, his mother turned to look at him with complete calm. "But you don't think he is," she said as though that settled it.

"I think I should find him."

"No. Remember what we discussed. He has to help himself first. I'm going to go to the coffee shop and watch the parade with Jenny. I'll feel much better about her if she's near me. I don't suppose she can get into too much trouble with the milk steamer." Greer smiled to herself and shared it with Joshua.

"No, I don't suppose you can either. Promise me you won't go anywhere else?" Joshua asked, amazed at the proprietary tone in his own voice.

With an overwhelming sense of love and gratitude, Greer leaned forward and kissed the top of her son's head, vowing silently to love him like this forever.

"I promise," she whispered. "And could you, until this is over, stick to hiking near the house?"

He had to laugh at her barter. "Sure, I can do that."

She gathered her purse and keys, and Joshua waved as she drove off. As he stood to go back into the coolness of the house, he saw a mug of tea sitting on the little side table and moved to pick it up, but halfway there his eye was arrested by the sight of a map.

With his lifelong passion for hiking, he recognized his own map of the local mountains instantly; that was not remarkable. What had attracted his interest were the markings that someone had made on it.

Keys. There were four of them, with dates underneath. Breathing shallowly, Joshua picked up the map and studied it. Two of the keys were at the locations of the fires that had already happened, and the dates below them confirmed to Joshua that that was what they represented. The other two keys were in locations that were, as far as he knew, still unscathed. He held the map closer to his face to read the tiny numbers written underneath them, dates that shouldn't be there because the fires hadn't happened.

At first he thought he was misreading it, and then he had to think for a minute about what his mother had said: She had seen two more keys on different locations, but she hadn't said she knew when the fires might happen.

Both of the dates were the same.

Both of them were today.

With a jolt, Joshua stood bolt upright. "She knows when," he said out loud to nobody. "And she knows *where* they're going to be."

Suddenly, as though it were only a few feet from his face, the little dog was barking at him with silent fury.

"Oh Christ," Joshua moaned, letting the map fall to his side as an acidic bile rose up in him. "Simon."

Chapter 39

Plumes of gray smoke, buffeted by the wind, were just beginning to gather visibly over the farthest ridge when he reached his second chosen spot. The sight of it sent a thrill of accomplishment through him, charging him with power and control. It had caught beautifully, just as he'd planned it, and the hot wind that fed it gusted against his face as he reveled in the ominous reality of what he had created.

But he would have to work more quickly now. He had chosen the first spot because it was in a location that was not likely to be sighted until the fire was large enough to create a huge amount of smoke, and the winds were on his side, breathing life into his monster and erasing the early traces of its presence at the same time.

Leaning down, he gathered an armful of dry brush and took a plastic water bottle filled with lantern oil from his backpack. He soaked the brush liberally and then scattered it around, careful to place it underneath the edges of large swaths of sage so dry that the leaves crumbled at his touch and released their sweet fragrance into the air. He smiled at that. These idiots used burning white sage to cleanse their expensive homes, a Native American ritual they had abominated with their artificial hipness. *Well*, he thought with a furious satisfaction, *this'll be a cleansing they won't soon forget*.

A single spark from his lighter set off the blaze, and he stood upwind, transfixed by the gemlike glow of the sapphire yellow flames that moved in erratic waves across the eager landscape, turning opalescent orange and even bluish green as it consumed everything it touched. Within minutes, the strong arm of the wind had spread the multifaceted fire into a crescent that burned outward and away from him. Still he stood, watching with adoring eyes this child of his rage. It expressed so perfectly, so eloquently everything he felt inside, the destructive, hungry need. As he watched, he felt an absolutely sexual arousal. No, it was better than sex, it was better than drugs—it was power. It was his. He owned it.

Just ahead and to the left a group of deer broke from the burning underbrush and stopped, confused and fearful, just inside the partial ring of flame, sniffing the air.

Burn, you insignificant little fuckers, he thought. *Feel my wrath and my power. You are nothing. I am everything.*

Then slowly, into his trance of power came a realization that he could hear something that he shouldn't over the crackle of the brush and the *swoosh* of the wind. A human voice floated up. Someone was shouting something. Rotating slowly in place, he realized that the someone was along his path back. Still in a dream state, he searched the landscape around him, planning an alternate route back to the road, but in the time he had stood, high on his euphoric rush of endorphins, something had changed, and now a new sensation broke him away from his intoxicating elation, bringing him back to his senses. The wind, which had been pushing firmly at his back, was now whipping his shirt and hair away from his face.

The wind had changed.

Spinning, he saw the fire had begun to close around behind him. Crashing forward, he made for the few open feet of unburned brush and passed through just before, with a rushing *swoosh*, a wall of flame closed in behind him. Coughing from the smoke that was now rushing into his face, he tried to get his bearings and find the trail that would lead him down to safety.

But any recognizable signposts were gone. Ahead of

him, a solid wall of smoke undulated and pulsed like some vast, otherworldly barrier. Whipping around, he faced the fire, swelled now and pressing its cruel weight and heat on his face. Suddenly—and for the very first time—he understood the fear that he had seen in the eyes of the insignificant deer, and his drunken sensation of omnipotence sobered in the space of a single second into a terrifying realization that he was equally mortal, completely vulnerable, and nothing more than another piece of carbon-based fuel to the inferno that he himself had created. The horror of it shut down his logical thought process and he spun, disoriented and lost, gasping and searching for safety. Consumed by a debilitating panic, he plunged blindly into the indiscriminate, choking, black smoke.

Chapter 40

"Simon!" Joshua's voice was rising, growing hysterical as a few hundred yards ahead of him he spotted smoke struggling to form a column in the wind—and below it, waves of heat. "Simon!" he shouted. He would have to go back soon; this wind could shift the as-yet-unseen flames in a few seconds. Joshua knew all too well, and he also knew it was unlikely that anyone else had spotted this fire, and the sooner he could report it, the better chance the firefighters would have.

But still the little dog appeared in front of him, barking in hysterical silence, and Joshua could not give up. He forced himself forward, half running along the steep path through thick shrubbery that grabbed at his pants and tore the bare skin of his arms.

Without warning, the shrubbery fell away and a large, open field of dry, golden grass spread out on either side of him. The path split into three directions, one of them directly toward the rapidly accumulating smoke, one off to the right, and one to the left that appeared to curve back down toward the road. Once again the little dog was yapping insanely over the left-hand path, but this time Joshua did not need him. Ten yards away, like a coffee stain on a pale, wheat gold tablecloth, lay the prone and motionless figure of a young man. Sprinting forward, Joshua closed the distance between them and dropped to his knees next to the figure, who was lying facedown, one arm sprawled out, the other crooked awkwardly underneath his body, as though the boy had fallen in a full-out run. Joshua could see a drying trickle of blood from the left ear and, inches away, the rock that had probably caused the damage.

Joshua felt quickly along the neck for signs of life and was relieved to detect a faint pulse. Pressed for time and alarmed by the small bits of ash that were already landing on the prone figure, he flipped the boy over. It was Simon.

"Wake up! Simon, can you hear me? It's Joshua. We've got to get out of here." But there was no response. He leaned down and put his face close to Simon's mouth, checking for breath. The boy's skin smelled as though he'd been hovering over a barbecue, but he was breathing. Joshua slapped at Simon's face as he glanced furtively back over his shoulder; he could feel the strong wind gusting toward him from the direction of the now thickly rising smoke. It was still two ridges beyond where he crouched next to the unconscious boy, but he knew, with a cold metal hand gripping his heart, that it was coming, and he had only a precious few moments until not only would he smell the smoke but he would be able to taste it.

Chapter 41

Leah deliberately placed herself next to Rowland in the row of folding chairs that had been set up under a sunshade in front of the library. She asked politely after Susan, and Rowland told her that her back was still sore, so she had elected to remain at home, working from her bed. He chuckled proudly at that.

Wondering how in hell to broach the subject of criminal actions, Leah turned her attention to the parade passing in front of them. A convertible car had been covered in red, white, and blue streamers, and perched on the top of the backseat several overheated cheerleaders were waving their like-colored pom-poms and smiling fixedly from their red, sweaty faces. Next came a local precision-riding team, horses and riders alike decked in shiny, royal blue satin. Strong gusts of wind threatened to separate cowboy hats from riders, and most of the faux cowgirls kept one hand on their reins and the other pressed firmly on the crown of their hat.

Just behind the horses, a huge hook-and-ladder fire truck, resplendent in its polished red glory, rolled slowly along, bearing its local heroes and receiving shouts and cheers from the gathered onlookers. The firefighters themselves seemed only grimly pleased, as though to show too much enthusiasm for the adulation would somehow lessen the seriousness of their jobs. Leah couldn't help herself from searching through the faces above the starched, dark blue uniforms for Weston though she knew that he wasn't there. He was flying observation today, and the fire conditions were peaked out at *extreme*. As Leah was buffeted by a hot blast of Santa Anas, she wondered how difficult it was to fly in this unpredictable atmosphere. And worse, how anyone could bear to fight a fire in it.

Rowland rose from his chair and went to speak with the councilwoman, who beamed on him while Leah watched surreptitiously. She waited until they broke apart and Rowland had gone to take a water bottle from a cooler before she joined him.

With no other ideas, she plunged in awkwardly. "So, by the way, the Caseys were in the bank the other day." She glanced pointedly at Rowland, who did not react to the name. "Do you know them? They own about six acres and a little house in the perfect spot for you to build the exit road from phase three."

Rowland turned and watched as a group of children dressed as clowns straggled along with various pets on leashes, drawing indulgent exclamations over their cuteness from the crowd. "No, I don't believe I've met them."

"You don't know *of* them?" Leah asked, suggestively.

"I don't believe so, no."

"Well, I do. And I know that they haven't been willing to sell, and that has been a problem for you."

Rowland turned to look at her. *Good,* she thought, *I've got his attention.*

"And I think I might be able to induce them to sell." She lowered her voice and leaned in close to add, "For a reasonable fee." Rowland said nothing, so she went on. "I told them that you would be willing to sweeten any random offer they may have had, and they seemed to prefer that to the alternative."

Rowland's eyes had narrowed. "And what *alternative* would that be?" he asked her suspiciously.

"Let's just say, other *persuasions*. They're willing to overlook any previous, uh, misunderstandings if the price is right."

Rowland bit his lower lip and appeared to be thinking quickly. After a moment he glanced around to see if anyone could overhear them, and then he drew her away by taking her arm. "Let me get this straight," he said in a rumbling, half-whispered voice. "You're telling me that they've come to think I've tried to *persuade* them to move, or sell out, and that if I offer them the right price now, through you—with a fee for you, of course— they will sell to my company? No questions asked?"

Leah felt a rising excitement and could have kicked herself for not finding a way to record this conversation, but it was too late for that. "Yes, basically, that is what I am saying."

Rowland smiled flatly and nodded. "Well, basically, this is my answer." His hand tightened on her upper arm. "I have a good mind to report you to the better business association, or maybe even the police. What you are talking about is blackmail and bribery, and, young lady, I do not now, nor have I ever used those kinds of criminal behavior in my business dealings. Frankly, I'm appalled and insulted, but I'm going to do you the favor of assuming that this is an isolated case of very bad judgment and that you will not ever pursue this course of action again. Not with me, my business, or any other, and let me tell you why." He released her arm as though it had sprouted contagious skin lesions. "I will be watching you." And with a strong glare that Leah would not have thought possible from those flaccid eyes, he turned and stalked away, glancing in every direction as though checking to see if anyone had overheard her accusations.

Shaken, Leah struggled to catch her breath and regain her composure. Her head was spinning and the heat was suffocating her. She wasn't sure what to think. Was Rowland calling her bluff? Did he think he didn't need her help or was he really on the up and up? Light-headed and unable to take a deep enough breath, Leah slipped through the crowd and headed down the street back to Jenny.

It was tough going on the packed sidewalk where the storefronts met the street, but the way thinned as Leah came onto a parking lot, offering more scope to the swarming observers. The hot wind snatched her breath from her chest, and Leah's vision began to swim. She felt nausea and panic welling up in her, squeezing the air from her lungs. Pausing next to a large tanker truck, she placed her hands on her knees and put her head down, struggling to control the hyperventilation that was overwhelming her, a weakness she thought she had overcome. *What had she done?* Had she just jeopardized her own standing for some insane, imagined wrongdoing? And if Rowland *was* guilty but denying it, would he be willing to blow the whistle on her?

"Are you all right?" The voice came from an older man, dressed in impeccably clean jeans, a plaid shirt, and a high baseball cap emblazoned with the familiar logo of a trucking company. The voice was gruff, but the tone was kind.

"I'll be fine," Leah gasped, but she found she couldn't raise her head without setting the world spinning.

"Come sit down," the man ordered firmly. "Tyler! Get one of those iced teas out of the cooler!"

Leah found herself guided to a folding lawn chair, the kind with the crisscrossed, brightly colored nylon strapping. She sat down and kept her head low as a cold plastic bottle was slipped into her hand.

"What wrong with her, Grampa?" a boy's voice asked with frank curiosity.

"Nothing. She's fine—it's just the heat. Don't stare, boy."

Leah pressed the icy bottle against the back of her neck and ventured a glance up. A young boy was now watching her with furtive glances from the side as he obediently kept his nose pointed toward the street. The effect was so innocently funny that Leah found herself laughing, and with the laugh, she drew a deep breath. After several mercifully spontaneous gulps that filled her lungs, she was able to sit up and speak.

"Thank you. I'm so sorry. It's probably the heat and the crowd. I'm all right now. Thank you." But when she tried to stand, the wooziness in her head won out over the embarrassment that was making her want to flee. She sat back down.

"Are you going to throw up?" the boy asked, watching her unabashedly. "I can get you a bucket."

Leah laughed again at the practical offer. "No, I don't think so. But thanks again." She studied the boy, who was watching her curiously, without any kind of revulsion or distaste. As though, if she did throw up, that would be nothing new to him. "I'm Leah," she said, extending her hand. "What's your name?"

"Tyler Tucker, and this is my grandfather, Sheldon Tucker. Nice to make your acquaintance," he recited.

Utterly charmed, Leah sat back in the chair and opened the iced tea. It was overly sweet, but the cold liquid felt heavenly in her dry throat. "Are you watching the parade from up there?" Leah asked, noticing that there were two more chairs, tied down to a horizontal ladder that ran the length of the tank on the truck.

"Yep, but it's really hot in the sun, and my hat won't stay on, so I came down to sit in the shade."

"Are you enjoying the parade?" Leah asked, still weakly, but feeling closer and closer to normal.

Tyler's eyes lit up. "I like the horses."

"How about the fire trucks?" Leah assumed that would be the favorite of all little boys.

"Oh yeah, I like those too, but I see them every day."

"Is your dad a fireman? Or, uh," Leah amended her sexist question quickly, "mother?"

Tyler shrugged and said, "Nope, I live with my grandfather."

Taken aback, Leah stuttered, "Oh, that, uh, that must be cool."

The small shoulders shrugged. "It's pretty cool. We mostly have to work a lot. We take water to the fires, or to people's houses. That's how come I know the firemen."

"Oh." Leah's voice grew conspiratorial and she was thrilled to feel a surge of pride as she said, "I know a fireman. His name is Weston. He flies the helicopters."

Tyler's eyes had gone large and round. "Wow," he breathed.

"I got to go up in one." Leah nodded as she shared her secret. "It was *really* cool."

"You think I could go?" the small boy asked.

During this exchange, Sheldon had stood slightly to one side as though uncomfortable with small talk, but now he cut in. "Tyler, we don't invite ourselves."

"It's okay," Leah said, squinting and smiling up at the older man; then she turned to Tyler again and gestured for him to come closer. Trustingly, he leaned in so closely that she could smell the sweetness of his skin, the sweetness of a child who has not yet been polluted with the indulgences of adulthood or the unavoidable souring of puberty. It amazed Leah that something that simple could stir up so much longing in her, and she found herself, for a first instant, aching for a child of her own. Remembering herself, she whispered, "I owe you a favor, so I'll ask him, but I can't make any promises." She sat back and winked at the boy. His eyes were shining with expectation.

Will I ever know that purity? With a frisson of panic, Leah wondered if she was ever meant to have a child in her life. Instinctively she knew she wasn't ready, and she had no mate. But she wondered, by the time she had finally found herself and conquered her many fears and healed her many wounds, if it would be too late.

Chapter 42

Joshua struggled to move Simon into a sitting position from which he could try to lift him. The boy was smaller than he was, but it would be a cruel test of Joshua's endurance to carry him all the way back down the steep trail to the road, especially at the speed that he feared they would need to outdistance the approaching blaze.

Simon's arm slipped through Joshua's sweaty hands, and his body slumped heavily back down with a thump like a sack of rice dropped onto a cement floor. The sound made Joshua wince. Frustrated, he stood up for better traction and glanced nervously at the danger that loomed behind him. Even before he turned back to Simon, Joshua could feel the uncomfortable prickling of an unwelcome presence joining them.

The male figure was glaring down at Simon, a hungry hatred written on his cruel features. Joshua had never had much patience for the myths of religion, but if ever he *could* believe in the existence of a satanic entity, a devil, it was in this moment.

The despairing chill of helplessness in Joshua's heart was quickly stomped flat by a rising rage. "No!" shouted Joshua, and he could feel his anger swelling him with strength that overcame and surpassed his reservations and self-doubts. "You cannot have him!" The demonic figure turned its vacuous eyes to him, and Joshua did not flinch or look away; in his righteousness and need for action he felt no fear. Instead he spoke clearly in a strong, even voice without panic or uncertainty. "You have no place here," he said evenly, fortified by an instinctive knowledge that he was speaking an absolute truth. "Move on."

The figure wavered, but remained. As though to illustrate that he could act on the physical plane in a way that the spirit could not, Joshua stooped again, and this time he succeeded in getting Simon hoisted up onto his shoulder. He began, with slow but steady steps, to move toward the path.

But as he turned, Joshua could see the flames clearly, advancing like a marching army toward the open field where he stood. The wind had assigned the direction and the fiery front was moving far more quickly than Joshua would be able to manage with Simon on his back.

Think, Joshua screamed silently at himself. He tried desperately to force his memory backward to a time when he was young and he had listened to his father tell him about the forest and survival. Survival in snow, in floods, and in fire . . .

I remember! Joshua studied his surroundings and realized that he was in the perfect place to *maybe* make it work. The wind was blowing north to south, forcing the fire ahead of it. As gently as possible, he laid Simon down close to the middle of the large field and then, running toward the burning shrubbery at the north side, gathered up a handful of the dried grass and lit one end, creating a makeshift torch. *Please let the wind hold. Don't let it change direction,* he prayed. He knew that if it did, his plan for survival would quickly become a death sentence. Running south back past Simon's unconscious form, he moved from right to left, lighting the grasses, and as the wind fanned his small fires from the same direction as the oncoming front, Joshua's new fire burned away from where Simon was lying, flaring up quickly and running wildly toward the shrubbery on the south side of the field.

They were surrounded by fire now and the heat was brutal. To the north, the gusting wind forced the flames southward and caught on the meadow grass, beginning the fire's rush toward the spot where Joshua was crouch-

ing next to Simon, ready to move. Behind him, the
grasses flared up, burned out quickly, and left a smolder-
ing carpet of sooty black. With a heave, Joshua lifted
Simon again onto his shoulder and hurried onto the
burned-out area he had created as one fire blazed on
ahead of him and the other rushed in behind.

He stomped out a few still-smoldering stalks and put
Simon down on the charred remains of the grass; then
he lay down next to him and covered both their faces
with his arms. The heat was so strong on his exposed
skin that Joshua thought it might burst spontaneously
into flame. With no choice but to endure and wait,
Joshua covered his face with his T-shirt to try to filter
the abrasive air and put his head down. The snapping
bite of the fire as it consumed everything around him
filled his ears and brought to his mind horrible images
of a slavering, insatiable beast whose mouth was a gaping, fiery furnace, its breath a volcanic blast that sucked
instead of repelled.

Then he heard another sound, and his heartbeat leapt
at the *throp-throp* of a helicopter's blades. He twisted to
peer through squinting, streaming eyes up at the sky,
praying the aircraft would see them. He tried to call out,
but his voice was lost in the roaring of the beast and
whine of the rotors, and though he could hear the helicopter, he could see nothing but a thick swirling layer
of smoke that would surely block any view downward
as well, and he had no choice but to bury his face again
in the hot remnants of the grass. The oncoming flames
had burned to within ten feet of them when they met
suddenly with a shortage of fuel at the burn line. Joshua
felt more than heard a pounding of hooves and chanced
a tentative glance up. In this eye of the storm several
deer had taken refuge, and they stared with terrified
eyes at the flames all around them for a moment before
the pursuing flames flickered out, and then they bounded
back toward an open space between the shrubbery, leaping yards at each prance with acrobatic grace. Joshua
watched them disappear into a haze of smoke and felt
an overwhelming sense of relief and gratitude that his

actions may have helped, at least, the deer. And with a strange calm, or perhaps it was a euphoria brought on by smoke inhalation, he felt an overwhelming gratitude for his life, for the beauty he had seen, for those whom he had loved, and he was surprised to find that instead of being afraid to die, he was thankful to have lived. In the fleeting second before he shut his eyes again, the smoke that closed in behind the animals seemed to swirl into the shape of a huge bird, wings outstretched, an owl that rose swiftly toward the darkening sky.

Chapter 43

Greer was standing next to Jenny watching the parade when a leaden heaviness filled her so suddenly that she staggered back a step and sank into the chair that Jenny had set out. For five seconds all animation seemed to have been vacuumed from her body, and then it returned with a rush and a palpitating heart. She knew with absolute certainly that something was wrong with Joshua.

Jenny did not notice her friend's collapse because at the same moment a confrontation had broken out on the street. A group of protesters had moved into the path of the vehicles, effectively blocking their path, and they were shouting angrily, brandishing placards, and a scandalized murmuring rippled over the onlookers.

Jenny went up on tiptoe, trying to see over the teenagers in front of her, and strained to read the words painted on the signs. She could make out COLUMBUS WAS A SLAVE TRADER, and SHAME OF AMERICA. The disrupters seemed to be primarily Native Americans, and many were dressed partially in Native garb, but a few of the two dozen or so protesters were clearly of European decent.

The police moved in quickly, and the protesters sank to the ground and passively resisted arrest. Only one man remained standing, surrounded by the others in a tight group, so that the police had trouble reaching him without stepping on his companions. Now that the crowd's attention was riveted on the confrontation and the confused marching band had stopped playing, Jenny could clearly hear what the lone speaker was shouting.

"Your actions will be your destruction! A country that celebrates a lie is nothing but a lie itself! Columbus killed more people than Hitler, and yet you have a day to honor him! This is an atrocity!" The crowd began to boo and catcall in defensive anger.

The police were forcing their way through the circle of protesters. Though the seated people shuffled together more tightly to hinder their movements, the local authorities seemed intent on removing this discordant note from their carefully planned day of national pride and they struggled on.

Someone in the crowd behind Jenny shouted, "What's going on?"

Without taking her eyes off the spectacle in the street, Jenny called back, "It's R.J. River! He's protesting the fact that we're celebrating a genocidal slave trader that we have mistakenly elevated to godlike status. Is that wrong, you think?" Jenny asked, her voice dripping with sarcasm. She turned to Greer, expecting to find a commiserating expression, and was shocked to see her friend slumped in a chair, her face drained of color and life.

Grasping Greer's arm to help her up, Jenny gasped, "Greer, what's wrong?"

A faint, brave smile fluttered over her friend's face and she whispered, "Joshua. He's in danger," as tears filled her eyes.

"What? How do you know?" Before the question was out, Jenny could have kicked herself. It was unthinkable that Greer would *not* know if someone she loved was in peril.

But before any more words could be spoken, the air was rent with the piercing sound of a siren at close range. Both women raised protective hands to their ears and turned to see the fire trucks, lights spinning, sirens blaring, starting to inch forward. The police officers halted their efforts to move in on R.J. and looked up inquisitively at the firemen on the truck. One of them was leaning from the window, gesturing to his walkie-talkie. The message was clear: They had been called out.

Without another word or effort, the protesters stood and cleared quickly to one side, the police opened the barricades to a cross street, and the crowd parted as cooperatively as though it had been rehearsed that way, and as soon as the huge red engines had cleared the tight spaces, they accelerated powerfully away, leaving a ringing silence and shocked crowd in their wake.

Everyone started talking at once. The police returned to the demonstrators, who stood patiently waiting to receive the recriminations and fines that they had obviously accepted would be the outcome of their actions.

But Jenny was focused only on Greer. She helped her friend into the coolness of the shop and led her to a group of armchairs.

"It's begun," Greer said faintly as she sank into one of the chairs.

"What has?" Jenny asked, confused.

"The fires. There will be two today."

Jenny bit her lip but was unable to repress the question that she was trying to restrain. "Is that why Joshua is in danger?"

Greer closed her eyes and took a deep breath. "I don't know," she said at last. "I only know that he's in danger, and I don't know. . . ." She pressed her hands to her mouth.

"Come on, don't cry," said Jenny with her usual forceful determination. "We've got to focus on what we can do to help."

The door opened and Jenny looked up, annoyed at the interruption, but her irritation vanished when she saw Leah, who had frozen at the sight of the unexpected tableau.

"Bingo!" Jenny said. "Leah, have you got a cell phone number for Weston?"

Leah spoke hesitantly, completely thrown by the possible relevance of the request. "Uh, yeah."

"Call it," Jenny ordered. "You said he was flying observation today, right? We need to know where this fire is, and what's going on."

"I know where it is," Greer said, looking up. "I know where both fires are, though they may have joined together by now."

Both of the other women stared at her without comment, waiting for any further revelations.

When no more were forthcoming, Leah said slowly, "Let me get this straight. You knew that fires were going to be set today—assuming they were set, which seems likely since the fire department just left the parade with their sirens on—and where, and you didn't *tell* anyone?"

Greer smiled mirthlessly at her. "Who would have believed me?" she asked sadly. "And I could have been wrong. I sometimes am, you know. I hoped I was this time. . . ."

Jenny spoke with a falsely cheerful voice. "Then maybe you're wrong about Joshua being in danger."

The look in Greer's eyes as she turned to her smashed any hopes that Jenny might have had into a powdered mass.

Without another word, Jenny spun and headed to the counter, where she snatched up her keys. "I'm locking up," she said. "Let's go."

Chapter 44

•

The big water truck's air brakes hissed like a cornered snake as Sheldon slowed to make the sharp turn onto the shortcut that would bring him out at the holding area set up by the incident commander for the latest brush fire. His window was down, and the hot wind caught him so forcibly in the side of the face that he had to squint and turn away from the brunt of it.

Next to him Tyler sat holding the detailed emergency services map with one finger pressed on their destination so fixedly that his hand seemed to be glued in place. Sheldon smiled at the thought of the boy's efforts to help him; he'd been determined to learn to navigate, and for an eight-year-old, he was catching on fast. Sheldon worked the gearshift and the sound of the engine dropped into a struggling growl as they started up the low incline. They bumped their way along for two miles before they arrived at the spot that Sheldon had known might give him trouble.

Last winter, southern California had seen the heaviest rainfall in a century. The steep, usually dry rocky hills had been inundated with water that had seeped into cracks and swollen the soil, increasing its weight until the simple force of gravity had brought portions of the hillsides down into the dry canyons and riverbeds, sometimes taking huge trees and boulders with it.

One of these minor landslides had landed near the curve of a creek bed, usually dry but now swollen by the rains into a small but raging river. The mass of rock and mud had diverted the torrent into another low area, and the rerouted river had pounded against the base of this road until, at about three a.m. on a black, dripping night, it had given out, dumping a large curving section of the entire road—asphalt, shoulder, double yellow lines, and all—into the cold rush of the storm.

The lone home owner in the area had heard the crash and gone out to investigate, narrowly avoiding tumbling headlong into the liquid void. In the indeterminate blackness, the asphalt and the void were almost impossible to distinguish, which meant that anyone driving along would not have seen the jagged end of the road until they were head down in cold, angry water. He had set up flares and used his trash cans to create a barrier, and because of his efforts, no one had died that night. Not there.

Since then, the county had come and commandeered a portion of the Good Samaritan's land and bulldozed a large, U-shaped temporary road around the bite-shaped loss of pavement. That was nine months ago, and there had been no further effort to repair or improve the shoddily created bypass. Instead, those months had left it pitted and rough, far worse for wear. Sheldon came to a stop and leaned out his window, surveying the ruts and potholes for the landmines that they were to his truck, which was fully loaded with almost four thousand gallons of city water on its way to fight a fire in an area with no services.

"How does it look, Grampa?" Tyler asked anxiously, biting his lower lip.

"Oh, not too bad," Sheldon lied. He was trying to judge the distance between his tires and plot a route that would spare his suspension. One particular rut looked at least the depth of his tires. But just off to one side of the road, the underbrush was fairly flat and he couldn't see any major obstructions. If he could get one line of tires safely on that . . .

Sheldon sighed. It was go for it, or go back and drive over twenty minutes around. He knew what twenty minutes could mean to fighting this kind of fire. He also got paid by the load, unless there was waiting time at the site, and the quicker he dropped this one and went back for another, the more profitable his day would be.

"Okay, we're gonna take it slow. Sit down, boy," Sheldon ordered and stomped the clutch to the floorboard as he jockeyed the lever into low gear.

The big truck rumbled forward, lurched to the right as the wheels hit a large hole, straightened, and then shifted again as the back wheel dropped into the same hole. Sheldon turned hard and lined up the left wheels off the side of the road on the shrubbery. It was about two feet high, and spikes of dried California sunflower wavered in the gusting wind. They had moved almost halfway along and Sheldon was starting the wide turn that would place both axles firmly on the asphalt road up ahead when his left front tires hit an unseen gully in the shrubbery. The truck tilted left, and he tried to adjust by angling the tires to the right, but even as he made the motion, he heard the nauseating crunch of metal on rock and then a thick snap.

The truck ceased to move forward. Sheldon carefully tried to apply the gas, but the grating crunching that met his efforts made him grit his teeth. He set the parking brake, knocked the gearshift into neutral, and with a quick order to Tyler to stay put, climbed down to survey the situation.

It wasn't good. The front axle of the truck was jammed up over a half-buried boulder that he might have cleared if it hadn't been for the foot-and-a-half-deep hole next to it that had been hidden under the tight shrubbery. Sheldon cursed softly as he lay on his back on the burr-ridden shrubs and slid under until he could better make out where the two surfaces that were never meant to meet had done battle.

The boulder had won. The axle was bent, twisted up—not much, just a few inches—but the weight of the water and the engine as the truck wheel had dropped into the hole had been its demise. Backing off it would only do further damage.

Sheldon wiggled his way back out and pulled his cell phone from its case on his belt. No service. Damn.

He looked both up and down the road, though he couldn't see very far in either direction because of the curves. He knew that he wasn't far from the fires as the crow flies; in fact, now that he was immobile, the smoke seemed ominously close. He climbed back up into the cab and cut the engine.

"What's wrong?" Tyler asked.

"Bent an axle. We're gonna have to wait until somebody comes along; then the county will send a tow truck to get us out. We'll use the tow truck's radio to let 'em know we won't be working anymore today."

Tyler's face was taut with concern. "Are we gonna be okay, Grampa?"

Sheldon nodded slightly. "We're gonna be fine. Hot, but fine."

"What about the truck?" In his short time with his grandfather, Tyler had come to understand that it was the truck that provided work, and everything they had. He had come, in his less-than-a-decade's existence, to the conclusion that the truck was a living thing, that they needed it to be somebody, to be safe.

"He'll be out of commission for a few days, but we'll get him fixed, don't worry."

"But, Grampa . . ."

"Tyler, not now," Sheldon snapped at the boy. He was worried enough as it was, and the boy's anxiety was only multiplying his own. Tyler sat back quickly, cowering against the seat. Sheldon stole a glance at him and wondered again if it had been a mistake to take him on.

But what had been the option? His own son, Tyler's father, had died drunk driving at twenty-three, and too many nights Sheldon had stopped by to check on Tyler only to find his mother passed out or not even there, and the boy, alone, hungry, filthy, uncared for. And his sister . . .

Sheldon shuddered, trying to shake loose the huge, steel hook that pierced his heart and yanked ruthlessly every time he was unable to block the memory of the baby girl's face. Better not to think of her.

No, thought Sheldon. *Tyler's only got me, and I'm gonna be here until he can go it alone.*

There is no one else.

Chapter 45

Simon had always suspected he would go to hell, so he was improbably composed when a landscape of colorless destruction swam into a consciousness permeated with pain. He was thirsty beyond anything he could imagine, the ground was ashen gray and hot to the touch, and the hot air scratched his throat as he tried hopelessly to raise his head. A wave of nausea racked his body and he vomited the slight contents of his stomach onto the ground.

Wiping his mouth with the back of his forearm, his head cleared enough to look around, though it pained him to open his eyes or turn his head.

"Simon?"

Confused, Simon rolled agonizingly onto his side and looked up at the figure that had spoken his name. He had always imagined that he would be alone in this eternity of suffering; his head swam thickly as he tried to assess this new concept of a roommate in hell.

"Simon, can you stand?" It looked like Joshua. *Why is he here?* This was wrong, certainly. Nice white guys go to nice white heaven, right? Years of early Catholic dogma slogged through the mud that was Simon's befuddled brain. Was this some kind of trick?

Tentatively, afraid that he would have no voice or that the effort of speaking would cause excruciating pain, Simon managed to croak, "Joshua, is that you?" His voice sounded like an emaciated rat crawling from a dry, dusty hole.

"Yes, it's me," Joshua said. "Listen, we've got to get down to where I left my car. Can you walk?"

Simon's head flopped to one side and moved in a slow circle as he tried to get control of it. "You have a *car*?" he managed to rasp.

"Yes. Come on."

As the taller young man reached down and started to help Simon to his feet, the smoke in the air cleared just enough for Simon to see a few dozen yards. With the glimpse of the war zone, and a massive effort, he began the process of returning to earth. Joshua was here, there had been a fire, somehow they had survived it, so far . . .

"How did you find me?" Simon asked. Each word felt like a razor slicing at his raw throat.

Still holding Simon around the waist with one hand, Joshua slipped a water bottle out of a carrier and held it to Simon's mouth. Simon drank, sputtered, the first of the warm liquid stinging his tortured throat, but then the sensation eased and he gulped greedily until the bottle was empty.

"Better?" Joshua asked.

Simon nodded and repeated his question with a voice still not his own, but human at least. "How did you find me?"

Joshua's face was expressionless as he said, "Your dog showed me the way."

"I read your little book," Simon told him as he swayed and tried to find his balance enough to move forward. "You're a freak."

A blaze of pain shot through Joshua's eyes but he said, "I know."

Simon grasped Joshua's shoulder and forced himself to take a first step. "But right now," he said through gritted teeth, "I'm really glad you're *my* freak."

He couldn't hear much through the banging pain in his head, but Simon felt a vibration go through the other boy's body that he thought might be the spasm of a laugh.

"Okay," Joshua was saying, "one step at a time. I'll

help you. It's only about a quarter of a mile. You can do it."

They struggled forward, progressing only slightly, Joshua pausing often to try to get his bearings in the smoky, hellish environs. The landscape was unrecognizable from his journey up less than an hour ago. He kept checking the line of smoke and fire that was still burning away from them, up across the ridge to their right. On his left, he could also make out a line of smoke, but it was more distant and worried him less.

By guessing from the lay of the land, Joshua chose a route more or less straight down the hillside; he could sometimes make out where the path had been, though there were places that it was obscured by charred shrubbery or fallen, still-steaming limbs of scrub oaks.

Simon seemed to gain a bit more strength as the water rehydrated his system, though he was still leaning heavily on Joshua, and they began to move a bit faster when Joshua could make out the road up ahead. Almost to keep his sanity and to hear something other than the rasp of their breathing, Joshua began to speak. First he told Simon how he had found the map and known that Simon would be there, and that led him to the question he wanted—and hated—to ask.

"Did you do this, Simon?"

Perhaps he hadn't heard, or maybe he was in too much pain to speak, but Simon did not answer.

Then, before he knew it and after an eternity, their feet stopped crunching and slipping on the dry, slack ground and hit solid pavement. Joshua scanned both directions for his car, trying to make a guess in which direction it lay. But even as he came to the conclusion that he had no idea without any remaining landmarks, he heard the sound of a vehicle approaching.

Both he and Simon turned to look, and around the corner came Jenny's jeep, with her at the wheel, Greer in the passenger seat, and someone in the back. In his exhausted state, Joshua couldn't remember her name, but the back of his brain labeled her as "that good-

looking brunette from the bank." The car screeched to
a stop in front of them, and Joshua was glad to hand
over the support of Simon to the other two women and
put his own arm around his mother's neck as she led
him to the car.

She put him in the passenger seat and paused to push
his filthy, damp hair back from his forehead.

He smiled weakly at her. "Hi, Mom," he said. "I
found him."

Greer's eyes shone with love and what he recognized
as unrealized, unbearable fear of loss as she said, "You
did good, honey. You did good."

Leah was wiping Simon's head with a shirt she seemed
to have taken off herself as she was only wearing a very
light silk undershirt. "Verdugo Hospital, I think," she
said with authority.

"No," Simon muttered, seeming to come to life.
"No hospitals."

"We're not giving you a choice," Jenny told him.
"Let's go."

Greer climbed up into the backseat and bit down hard
on her lip to keep from screaming. Every nerve in her
body was drunk with adrenaline, and relief flooded
through her anxiety-ridden brain with such engulfing intensity that it took every ounce of sense and strength
she had not to be reduced to a quivering mass of hysterical
Jell-O. Between watching her son with grateful, almost un-
believing eyes, she stole glances at the destruction on the
hillside above them, and at the evidence of its growing
threat—an unnatural, dirt-colored mushroom that darkened the sky overhead. She bit down harder, until she
could taste blood, trying to distract herself from the horrific
thought that in this gathering inferno, Joshua and his friend
Simon were the lucky ones.

The survivors.

Chapter 46

The helicopters had been flying overhead at regular intervals, but they were so far above and so intent on delivering their loads of soapy water to the fire that Sheldon had been unable to attract their attention. The wind was gusting strongly toward them from the direction of the fire, bringing flakes of ash, some as large as his fist, floating eerily down around them.

It was one of these, a remnant of a sycamore leaf, that landed a few yards from the truck, its edges still rimmed with red lace, living fire that transferred its dangerous mission to the submissive ground cover that had lain for months waiting for this message, this whisper of rebellion on the wind.

It took very little, a gentle nudging, a subtle argument fueled by the breath of the wind, to incite the frenzy of combustion. The thin line of heat pressed against the willing dry grasses, and with an almost silent intake of oxygen, it exhaled words of flame. Then, like a rumor spreads through a small town, the conversation quickened and swelled until a large area just behind the truck was burning steadily.

Sheldon had kept his eyes fixed on the rim of the hill and had seen the flames begin to crest it, so he did not notice the more imminent threat until it was high enough to be seen in the side mirror of his cab.

"Holy shit!" he exclaimed, coming bolt upright in his seat. Without stopping to respond to Tyler's terrified question of what was wrong, he leapt from the truck and

ran to see how close the encircling fire was: only a couple of yards and burning fast. For a moment he considered grabbing Tyler and running, but he knew that was
hopeless. The fire on the ridge would hit the road soon
enough, and this new outburst was only one of many
that could flare up anywhere at any moment.

He ran back to the open cab door, climbed up, and
cranked the key in the ignition to start the engine that
would enable him to access the water. As he did, he said
as calmly as he could to Tyler, "Stay in the truck. We've
got a new fire behind us, and I'm gonna water down
around us."

"Can I help, Grampa?" Tyler asked. His eyes were
huge with fear, but his small face was set with
determination.

Sheldon thought about the amount of gasoline in his
fully loaded truck and caved. "Okay, but you do exactly
what I tell you. If I tell you to run, you do it, boy. You
hear me? You run and you don't look back."

"Yes, sir," Tyler said.

"On the tank," Sheldon ordered. Tyler didn't even
bother to open his door. He just climbed right out the
open window, reached a hand to the metal ladder, and
was up in ten seconds.

Sheldon ran to the back of the truck and unrolled a
short length of fire hose, attaching it to the out spigot
at the base of the tank. Then he fired the generator and
waited for pressure.

But even as he did, the flames were at his feet. He
hopped sideways and slapped at the sparks that landed
on his pants and burned through to his skin. "Run the
hose into the tank, Tyler!" he shouted up. "And get
ready to jump if I say so!" With the fire at his feet and
inches from climbing up under his truck, he ignored the
intense heat at his ankles that he knew meant his jeans
had caught fire, and threw the lever. Water began to
rush from the hose. He sprayed in a tight, controlled
circle around him and then the truck, creating a ten-foot
barrier on one side, but the fire was moving quickly
around him now. Crouching, and willing himself not to

feel the pain on his calves where the material had
burned away and his skin was scalded, he sprayed underneath the truck, saturating the ground beneath it.

The fire had traveled to a group of dry sycamores and
willows that stood at the edge of the dry creek bed,
forty feet from where he stood. The smoke was choking
him now.

We need this water, we need the tank, Sheldon thought.
It's our only chance. "Tyler!" he shouted up. "Open
the hatch!"

Coughing, his eyes streaming from the smoke and unable to see more than a few feet ahead, Sheldon gave
one last spray around him and shut off the valve. Then,
discarding the hose, he started for the ladder on the
tank.

The first movement almost brought him to his knees.
Looking down, he could see the frayed fragments of his
now-wet jeans where they had burned just below his
knees, and the skin on his right shin looked like something that was not his.

"Grampa!" He heard Tyler's terrified cry from somewhere above him in the swirling ash and smoke. Gritting
his teeth to keep from crying out, Sheldon forced himself
to make the agonizing climb, favoring his right leg and
pulling himself up each rung with the strength in his
wiry arms.

"Tyler, get in the tank!" Sheldon shouted when his
head cleared the top of the truck. He could see the trees,
crisp as tinder but rich with combustible sap, burst into
flame with explosive rapidity, and the burning leaves
began to fall, whipped by the wind into willing and eager
virgin patches of bracken and shrubbery.

"Are you all right? Grandpa?" Tyler's voice trembled
with fear as he started toward Sheldon. "I'll help you."

"No!" Sheldon shouted, the pain and the effort of
maintaining making his head swim and his whole body
shake with weakness. "Get in the tank. I'm coming,"

"I'll help you, Grandpa," Tyler repeated, reaching out
a small hand to grasp at the hot metal of the cross
ladder.

Sheldon stopped where he was and focused his streaming eyes on the young boy, who was still ten feet away. The smoke was so thick now that he could hardly breathe, but he commanded himself to speak calmly and clearly. "You promised me you'd do what I told you, Tyler. You get in that tank, and shut the lid. I'm coming. I'll be right behind you."

"But—"

"Do what I'm telling you, boy!" Unable to keep his eyes open any longer, Sheldon put his head down and started to drag himself forward along the length of the tank. Above the crackle of flames, he could hear the creak of the hatch and then the echoing splash as Tyler's thin body dropped into the water.

Sheldon's grasp on his consciousness was growing tenuous, and he was finding it harder not to succumb to the excruciating pain in his leg. Yet even as he slipped farther from reality, he felt an overwhelming new understanding about what it was to love someone more than yourself.

It is a gift. Not to *them, but* from *them.*

Sheldon laid his face against one of the stinging-hot rungs and let his body hang limply as he gathered the last of his strength; then, with a Herculean effort, he lifted his head and looked the last five feet along the ladder to the hatch covering. It was cracked open, and through the two-inch space he could see the eyes of his grandson. But the smoke was moving around them like a predatory thing, seeking out openings and stealing the clean air.

This is my fault, Sheldon thought desperately. *I never should have brought him.* Praying that his voice was loud enough to carry, Sheldon whispered, "Shut the hatch, Tyler. It's gonna be all right. Shut the hatch."

Chapter 47

The visibility was close to nil, and Weston was relying primarily on his instruments. He estimated the distance to the ground, focused on the orange glow in the gray gloom, and pushed the stick forward as he dropped his altitude. Just over the line of fire, he released the load of extinguisher, maneuvering the control stick with experienced finesse to compensate for the sudden weight change and the buffets of unpredictable wind. Sweat was beading and running down his forehead as he lifted away, banking sharply and fighting for altitude.

It was when he cleared the smoke that he saw the new fire. He gestured to the young female firefighter who sat beside him and then spoke into the microphone in his helmet. "Command Center, this is chopper one. We've got a breakout." The woman checked their coordinates and quickly reported the exact location. Weston changed his course to circle the blaze so that they could make a more detailed report.

As he came opposite the windward side, he spotted the truck, lost as an abandoned ship in a flaming sea, and he circled lower. There was something on top of the truck, something he couldn't quite make out in the haze. Urging his craft forward and down, he squinted at what he now realized was one of the water tankers, closer, closer, until he could make out the . . .

"Holy shit," his partner, Jonni, muttered under her breath. "Command Center, we've got a victim down."

"This is Command. Hold for the IC," crackled over the airwaves.

As Weston waited impatiently for the incident commander to get to their frequency, he hovered fifty feet or so above the truck. The wind from his rotors flattened the flames nearest the rig and they danced insanely before leaping up stronger than before.

"Chopper one?" came a gruff voice. "Report."

"We've got a stranded water tanker, and it looks from here like the driver is unconscious on top of it. I can't make it out, but he's definitely injured, possibly dead. Request permission to attempt a rescue." It was Weston who spoke, but he got a quick nod of agreement from Jonni, who turned questioningly to look at a third firefighter.

"You in, Eddie?"

The man, a veteran, nodded grimly. "I'm in." There was no hint of hesitation in his commitment.

"Negative," snapped the IC. "I've got a ground unit on the way."

But even before the IC's directive was out, Weston's partner had gasped and pointed.

"Oh my God, there's a kid in there!"

Weston swung the helicopter to one side so that he could peer down at the top of the tanker. And there, just as Jonni had said, was the torso of a small boy, half-out of the tanker's hatch, waving furiously at them and pointing at the prone figure of the man. From his jump seat, Eddie was craning his neck to look down on the scene.

"There's a child in the truck," Weston spoke into his mike, "and the fire is closing in. It's only a matter of a few minutes until it's up under that truck, and if there's any gas in it, it's a bomb waiting to go off. We've got to drop in." Years of flying in extreme conditions kept Weston's voice calm, but his heart was pounding as he looked from the flames to the boy's flailing arms.

"What do you think, Eddie?" he asked over his shoulder.

"I think the guy sprayed the area around them, but

in this heat and wind, that shrubbery will be dry in no time, maybe already is. And your assessment is accurate. Five minutes, maybe less."

"Command Center, can we get an ETA on the ground unit?" Weston said firmly.

"Estimated to arrive in seventeen minutes," came the dispatcher's voice.

Weston looked at Jonni's face. She looked grimly back at him, then said the two words that decided them. "Too long."

"Command Center," Weston said, "request permission for an immediate evacuation. The situation is extreme. We've got a man down and child surrounded by active fire."

There was a pause, a crackle, and then the merciful response. "Proceed with extreme caution."

Weston switched the stick to his left hand and held up his right, palm toward Jonni. "Let's do it."

She smacked his palm with her own as she unbuckled her belt and got up out of the seat. Eddie was already sliding open the helicopter door. They were both dressed in protective suits, but she quickly donned gloves and a helmet, and strapped on a harness as Eddie hooked a long, wired ladder into two eyebolts riveted to the floor of the helicopter. Jonni kneeled, looking down as Weston positioned the helicopter only a few feet above the stranded vehicle.

"Go!" Eddie ordered, and Jonni dropped the ladder. It unrolled partially and landed with a thud on the top of the tanker, near Tyler. He reached out for it, but Weston's voice boomed out on the PA system.

"Hold on, son. We're coming to get you."

Jonni swung herself out with practiced ease and slipped down the few feet until she was standing on the horizontal ladder. She moved quickly to the prostrate figure of the man and checked for a pulse. Then she moved to the boy and lifted him out of the tank. He struggled to get to the man, but Weston could see Jonni's lips moving fast as she held on, and the boy seemed to wilt. She pulled a second harness from her belt, quickly strapped

him in, and then gave Eddie a thumbs-up. He lowered
down a safety line, which Jonni hooked to the boy's
harness, and then they climbed the ladder together,
Jonni's body behind his like a net. He made it close
enough for Eddie to grab him under the arms and heave
him in.

"Grampa," he shouted. "Help my grampa!"

"We'll get him son, don't worry," Eddie shouted over
the sound of the rotors, but he looked questioningly at
Jonni, who was already positioning the stretcher on its
cords. "Can you lift him?" he asked her.

She gave a second thumbs-up and then was gone
again, and within seconds Eddie was lowering the
stretcher on its winch. Jonni held the wavering stretcher
just to one side of the ladder, securing it quickly at both
ends with hiker's clamps. Then she rolled Sheldon's un-
resisting form onto it, quickly strapped him down, released the clamps, and motioned for them to take him
up. She was right behind it, almost running up the swinging ladder, and Eddie hauled her in before they both
secured the stretcher and gave Weston the all-clear signal. With a stomach-lurching swoop, they took off
toward the hospital. Eddie hovered over the motionless
form of Sheldon; he had strapped an oxygen mask over
Sheldon's nose and mouth. The old man's eyes were
closed, and one arm hung limply off the side of the
stretcher.

Jonni took off her helmet; her thick, short-cropped
blonde hair was plastered to her head with sweat. She
sucked in a deep breath and moved to sit on the bench
next to the child, who was staring with fascinated eyes
at these mythological heroes surrounding him.

In all his eight long years, in all his preadolescent
dreams and fantasies, he had never imagined something
as exciting as this. But before he could succumb to the
awe of relief and amazement, he had to know: "Is my
grampa going to be all right?"

"We're going to get him to a hospital in a few minutes, and they're going to take care of him," she said
with what she hoped was a reassuring smile. But she

couldn't help glancing nervously at Eddie, who had a stethoscope pressed it firmly to the naked skin of Sheldon's chest where he had ripped open the shirt. His face was a picture of concentration, and impossible to read.

In truth, Jonni had worked so fast and under such duress that she had no idea if the boy's grandfather was alive or dead.

Chapter 48

Joshua had been given a once-over in the emergency room and told to go home and expect to spend the next few days coughing up some lovely yellow mucus. That, the intern had informed him and his mother dispassionately, would be a good thing. It would mean that his lungs were cleansing themselves. If it turned green, he should see a doctor.

Simon's lungs were in worse shape, and after an MRI scan of his head for internal bleeding, he was admitted to a room. Joshua insisted on waiting for him and the inevitable appearance of Detectives Sheridan and Wright. After all, he had called them himself.

When they came, Joshua was sitting next to Simon's bed, where the other boy was sleeping fitfully, an oxygen mask fitted tightly over his nose and mouth with an elastic strap, but his breathing was constantly interrupted by a raucous cough that made Joshua's croupy one sound tame by comparison. He rose to greet the two men, who were grim faced and bore their exhaustion like sacks of gravel on both shoulders.

Joshua motioned for them to step into the hall; with a sour look at the figure in the bed, Sheridan turned and went out.

"So, you found him, just by accident, I'm going to assume," Sheridan said by way of letting Joshua know how they were going to play it, "at the source of the most recent arson. Is that right?"

"Well, yes, sir, but . . ."

"And"—Sheridan held up a finger—"he was at your house the day I came looking for him, but you didn't tell me."

"Yes, sir. I'm sorry, but . . ."

"*And* you still think he didn't do it."

"Yes, sir," Joshua said. He couldn't think of anything else to say.

Detective Wright cleared his throat but said nothing, and Joshua wondered if he was trying to keep himself from making a more disdainful noise.

Sheridan's eyes bored into Joshua's. "Go home," he said in a hard voice. "Go home before I arrest you for aiding and abetting."

"I don't think he did it." Joshua could hear the pathetic tone of his own voice. He had no proof, other than his visions, and those were worth nothing in the harsh world in which Sheridan lived.

Sheridan seemed to lose patience. "Okay, that's it. You listen to me, and you listen good. There have been four arson fires that we know of. All of them he"—Sheridan pointed a finger at the ward door behind which Simon lay—"was close to. One of them either killed or covered the death of the man who sent him away to probation camp, and witnesses have testified that Simon Gomez had vowed to pay him back."

"I—I know," stuttered Joshua. "But you don't have any proof that he would do anything so extreme. I know he was in the wrong place at the wrong time, I know it looks suspicious, but I don't think he's capable of murder!"

Both detectives looked at Joshua now with such fixed intensity that it shut him up. Sheridan said in a dangerously soft voice, "Don't you?"

"No!" insisted Joshua, but there was a sinking feeling in the pit of his stomach that told him they knew something he didn't.

"What?" he asked.

Detective Wright glanced at his partner and received a curt nod. He said, "Simon Gomez was originally made a ward of the court and placed in supervised foster homes for three years because of something he did when he was ten years old."

Sheridan's face was glacial. "You have no idea of what this boy is capable of. Go home."

Joshua's mouth had gone dry. He tried to swallow, but it didn't help. When he spoke, it came out as a whisper. "What did he do?" Both men stared at him with closed, icy expressions. "Please tell me," Joshua pleaded. "Please."

Sheridan's barrel chest went up and down with a huge sigh, and though his face did not change, Joshua thought that he detected something in the granite eyes. Something that might have been pity, but he did not know for whom. Then, with the flat intonation of an expert observer who has trained himself to watch but not to feel, not even distantly, he spoke.

"He killed his own father," Sheridan told him. "Shot him."

And Joshua felt that he too had taken a bullet.

Chapter 49

Leah was in the waiting room with Jenny and Greer when Joshua returned to them. He shook his head sadly at his mom, and she stood to put her arms around him.

"He's going to arrest him," Joshua said sadly.

"I'm sorry, honey." Greer rocked him gently.

Jenny and Leah both felt intrusive and had the sensitivity to look away. At that moment, a woman with a determined, scrubbed look and a badge that declared her as a county-employed social worker came in leading a small boy by the hand. His face was white, his clothes were damp, and he was staring blankly as though he'd seen something so horrible that his eyes had refused to see anything more.

With a shock, Leah realized that this was the little boy she had met only that morning. "Tyler?" she asked tentatively. The boy did not respond, but the woman, a tough-looking matron, stopped and looked up sharply.

"Do you know this boy?" she asked, eyes narrowed.

"Yes," Leah said, and immediately dropped to her knees in front of Tyler. "Honey, do you remember me? You helped me this morning. My name is Leah."

The matron pulled him back. "I'm sorry, I can't permit you to speak with him." She turned abruptly away.

"Where's his grandfather?" The question came from Joshua; he had come to stand behind Leah. Tyler did not look up at him.

The matron's eyes wavered with indecision; she

glanced down at Tyler almost fearfully and then said, "I'm not at liberty to answer that."

Joshua leaned forward and put a hand on the boy's shoulder. "Tyler, buddy? You okay?" The boy did not respond. He continued to stare, unseeing, at the air in front of him.

"Where are you going to take him?" Leah asked.

"I'm sorry, but unless you are family, I can't tell you anything," the matron said, and then, not unkindly, she pulled Tyler's arm and he marched forward without seeming to know or care what was happening to him. But as he reached the door, he turned and looked over his shoulder as though the voices that had spoken to him had finally found their way through a thick fog. For just a second his eyes connected with Joshua's. And in that second, all the fear and misery of the world were in the tilt of his head and the fragility of his small hands. Then the glass doors slid shut behind them.

"Oh no. Oh my God," Leah said, pressing her hands to her mouth. In the space of Tyler's single glance back, a need to take that horrible blank look from his face and replace it with the joyful, mischievous smile she had seen that morning overpowered her. It seemed a desecration that she must stand there and do nothing. The emotion was so unfamiliar and so all-consuming that she actually swayed from the impact.

Greer and Jenny had turned to Joshua. "Who is that?" Jenny asked.

"The guy who drives the water truck," Joshua said in a mesmerized voice. "It's his grandson. Joy and I watched him for a few hours the other day." He was staring at the place just above where Tyler had disappeared, staring at the spot where he had seen—for a fleeting instant—the image of the waiflike little girl. She had been reaching a hand out toward and looking earnestly at—could it be?—Leah. In a kind of trance, Joshua turned to look at the career banker. "I thought that he might be in danger from his grandfather. I, uh, saw something." He was squinting at Leah, trying to understand what the ethereally frail phantom child had meant. Why had she been reaching out to this childless executive as though for help? Leah was nice enough, Joshua thought, but she had always struck him as a person who, having been damaged by experience, used all her strength healing herself—and the rest of the world would have to take care of itself.

But Leah too was staring at the place where Tyler had disappeared. There was a look of revelation on her face, as though she had both discovered and lost something precious.

Slowly, she turned to the other three. And to Joshua's utter surprise, instead of cowering away from the child's pain, she spoke with absolute resolve. "We've got to find out where they're taking him. We've got to help him."

As they started out to the car, Joshua found himself thinking. You just never know about people. *You just never know.*

Chapter 50

The next morning, Greer could smell smoke as soon as her mind flickered out of a disturbing dream world and into the worrisome new day. She stood for a long moment at her window surveying a sky hazy with billions of particles, the belched refuse of a not-too-distant inferno. She searched vainly for clouds, moisture, some kind of relief, but she could see none. "If only it would rain." She breathed the words like a prayer offered at the altar of a cruel god. An impartial, pitiless god for whom there was no benevolence without sacrifice.

Then she went downstairs and did something she was usually religious about *not* doing: She turned on the news.

The fires were raging out of control, and firefighters were being called in from other counties to set up a line of defense. As a precaution, some of the fringe neighborhoods had been asked to evacuate, and Joshua's old high school gym was called into service as a temporary shelter. The Red Cross had shown up within half an hour with cots, blankets, and emergency food supplies. Video footage showed families pulling up in trucks and cars loaded down with everything from computers to baby books to sofas. The variety of valued items was fascinating.

Joshua came in wearing nothing but a pair of flannel pajama pants and sat down in front of the TV. Greer noted that his arms and chest were filling out; he had lost his teenaged scrawny look, and it was being replaced by solid musculature. She smiled to herself. Her boy had become a man.

Turning her attention to the news, she was much less impressed. As usual, there was an abundance of trauma-laced sound bites delivered in ill-disguised, hopeful tones, interviews with people predominated by questions of what they would feel if the worst happened, generic shots of burning trees in undisclosed locations, paid experts who expounded on the deadly horrors of fires in general, and an almost complete absence of factual information. As a result, they spent twenty minutes watching before they both threw up their hands in disgust and turned off the TV, and Joshua went to phone the forest service fire station to talk to someone who had no commercial time to sell and an audience that wanted information and not sensationalized entertainment.

After he had told the ranger, a Mr. Layton, where they lived, his response was reassuring, for now.

"You're not in any immediate danger. The fire is burning west of you and expanding north and south. It's the south we're concentrating on putting out at this point."

The second line beeped just as Joshua was thanking the mercifully practical ranger. He clicked over.

"Hi, Joshua. Is your mom there?" It was Jenny.

"Sure, hold on. How's things up at your house?" he asked as he gestured to his mother, who had come into the kitchen and was making coffee.

"Grim, but not on the middle of the grill. Did you hear about Golden Door?"

"No."

"It's toast. Everything is gone, nothing but a bunch of blackened toothpicks sticking up out of slabs on the ground."

Joshua's skin prickled as he thought of the Caseys just a few miles away. "What about the houses nearby?"

"Everybody else seems to have survived so far; they set up a line of defense between the development and the existing neighborhoods. I guess the mowed-down acreage of Golden Door created enough of a dead zone for them to turn it."

"Wow," Joshua said, trying to get his brain around the fact that almost three hundred not-yet-completed, but happily uninhabited, homes were now gone. He wasn't sure how to feel about that. He was very relieved for the Caseys.

Greer had come to stand near him. She was watching his face with a concerned, questioning expression.

"Here's my mom. Let us know if you hear anything more, okay?"

"You betcha."

Greer took the phone from her son as he said, "Golden Door is gone." She felt a swelling of fear for its proximity to the rest of the community, but a chord twanged of justice about the fate of the greedy, land-grabbing development itself.

"Jenny? Hi. Everybody okay?"

"So far." Greer could hear her friend's compassionate sigh. "But you know they've evacuated all of Alpine Village, upper Black Oak, and Vogel Flats, right?"

"Yes, that much I saw on the news. It made for a tragic thirty seconds, though they had to keep cutting away from people who were smiling and waving at the camera to get that much."

"I know. People's spirits are still really good. Only one home has been lost and that was uninhabited, nobody there. But it's been brutal for the people fighting it. The firefighters have been at it all night, and more are coming in from the surrounding counties. They're working in twelve-hour shifts and sleeping in Red Cross tents on the high school playing field. I think we should do something for them."

Greer couldn't have agreed more, and helping would go a long way to alleviating the excruciating helplessness that she was experiencing. "What?" she asked eagerly.

"Well, I'm going to pack up every cake and muffin I've got, plus about a hundred gallons of fresh coffee, and go set up in the cafeteria. That's where they're feeding them—so far cold sandwiches and water, from what I've heard. I've called everybody who has a business or a restaurant I know in the area to enlist them, and now I'm activating the phone tree to see if we can bring in some volunteers and hot meals. Wanna come?"

"I'm on my way. Anything I can do to help, I'll do it." Greer hung up the phone.

"What are you going to do?" Joshua asked her with a tremor of trepidation.

Greer looked at him with firm determination written on her charming face. "I'm going to make a casserole."

Chapter 51

As evening fell, so did the spirits of the people assembled at the high school. The firefighters were coming in, grateful for the huge outlay of food provided by the citizens and for a cool shower in the locker rooms, but then they stumbled to the large tents and collapsed into unconsciousness on the uncomfortable makeshift bedding in the hot, airless shelters.

In the gym, the temporary inhabitants were also rapidly losing their sense of humor. The first night and day had been filled with greeting friends, hopefulness, and cooperation, but as the hours had worn on and the novelty had worn off, patience had worn thin. Arguments were breaking out over sleeping arrangements, noise, supplies, and the lack of news about when they could go home.

Leah stood surveying the mass of humanity and wondered how long it would be before a fistfight, or worse, broke out. She'd been there since she got off work at five, and so far she'd had little to do except help Jenny deliver industrial-sized vats of coffee and hand out bottled water. There were far too many people in the space, and the air-conditioning was insufficient to fight the relentless heat outside. Though NO SMOKING signs were on every door, there were still people standing in groups with lit cigarettes, and she had seen more than one bottle of some god-awful rotgut being passed around, the result being an increase in volume, rage, and indignation from those trying to maintain a respectful decorum.

Leah suspected that a small number of the people weren't evacuees at all, but just lost souls who had found three free meals, beds, and something interesting going on.

There were quite a few children. Most of the kids had grouped up and were playing on the stage end of the auditorium, but a few cowered close to their parents in this unfamiliar and frightening place.

Leah was leaning against the swinging door, half-in and half-out of the now pungently funky atmosphere in the gym, wondering what she could possibly do to help, when she saw him. Tyler was seated on one of the cots at the far end of the room. He was leaning back against the bleacher wall with his knees drawn up under him, his arms wrapped protectively around himself.

At first Leah was uncertain that it was him. Then she saw the large woman, who was wrangling three other children, go and sit next to him. She seemed to be pleading with him, but he shook his head, and the woman, looking not a little frustrated, gathered the rest of her brood around her, and they set off for the long line waiting to be served dinner on paper plates just outside in the parking lot.

As the woman passed her, Leah heard her say to one of the other kids, "He doesn't want to. We'll bring him a plate."

Glancing around as though she might be caught on videotape, Leah started across the room, zigzagging her way between the rows of cots and mats on the floor. When she came level with Tyler's, she stopped and stood shifting her weight from foot to foot as she struggled to think of something to say.

But it was the boy who spoke first, raising his eyes fearfully to see who was hovering over him. He saw her looking, if possible, as terrified as he felt, and he mustered a small smile.

"Hi," he said in a tiny voice. "I remember you. Do you have to stay here too?"

"Uh, no," Leah said falteringly. "I came to try to help, but I don't think I'm making much of a difference, but

I'm okay." She realized with ironic amusement that he was making her feel better. "How about you?" she asked softly as she sat next to him.

Tyler's eyes glazed again and dropped to the blanket he had twisted in his fingers. "I'm fine," he whispered.

Leah knew she wasn't supposed to ask, and she was well aware that she might be crossing a line by doing so, but she couldn't stop herself. "Who is that lady you're here with? Is she an aunt or something?"

For a few seconds Tyler didn't respond, and then he shook his head, almost imperceptibly. "I have to stay with her for a while."

"How do you know her?" Leah asked.

He shrugged, just a tiny up and down of his frail shoulders. "I don't. A lady from the hospital brought me to her house. She's a foster lady. She said I have to stay with her."

Leah felt her heart crack painfully open and the blood that leaked from it saturate her stomach in a queasy, angry rush. She raised one arm instinctively to put it around the boy's shoulder, but her own inhibition as well as a sense of propriety stopped her.

"Tyler," she said softly, hoping beyond hope that she was not asking too much from this fragile child, "where is your grandfather?"

His body went rigid, as if he were trying to refuse it any free will, but she watched the quivering shake his frame, and this time she could not restrain herself from placing a hand on the center of his back and rubbing it softly. "Shhh, it's okay. I'm sorry, I shouldn't have asked you." Leah wanted to sew her own mouth shut.

"He . . . he . . ." Tyler struggled to get it out. "He got burned, and they said he breathed in a whole lot of smoke, and that's really bad, I guess, and he . . ."

"Shhh. It's okay. It'll be okay." Without thinking, Leah drew Tyler's trembling body up against hers and encircled him with her arms. Then she began to move, rocking gently back and forth, and without realizing it, Leah began to hum, a low note that Tyler could feel in his own pain-drenched body, and very slowly, it worked its way inward until, at last, it reverberated against the dense core of his tortured heart, nudging it back to life.

The foster mom returned with her bickering children in tow, bearing a plate for Tyler, but after exchanging a sympathetic glance with Leah, patiently went about feeding the other kids without interrupting the releasing of grief.

Leah kept up the soft, vibrating hum, and after a long while, Tyler's sobs softened, the aching lightened, and still wrapped in a stranger's arms, the broken boy fell asleep.

Chapter 52

Leah was back on the serving line in the cafeteria when Weston came in, his face smeared with black soot and exhaustion. She left her post to greet him.

"Hi there," she said shyly.

He looked at her the way a person does when they spot someone they know in an unlikely place, with that space in their brain that can't quite connect the person with the location. It was a fleeting look, and then he glanced down at the dirty apron she was wearing and smiled.

"Well, well, look who's here being of service," he said, and Leah found she was stunned at the level of pride she felt. It was nice, actually, just being here, one of a hundred faceless people, no glory, no profit, just a group of citizens banding together to help in a bad situation. She had always felt annoyed at the prospect of giving time for "nothing," and now she discovered that she was actually getting something: She felt like she was contributing.

"Oh, I'm being of service, all right," Leah said blandly. "I'm serving up mashed potatoes by the ton. How is it out there?"

She was immediately sorry she had asked when his expression darkened beyond the soot on his face. "Brutal."

She tried to be positive. "Maybe it'll rain. The news said there's a chance, only about ten percent, but a chance," she said, and his shrug told her eloquently that

that would be nothing short of a miracle. "You want something to eat?"

"Anything," Weston replied, and she saw the fatigue that weighed down his movements and seemed to blur the edges of his usually formidable physique.

"Sit down. I'll get you a plate," she said firmly, her newly awakened nurturing gene dialing in like a strong signal on a radio. "You want pork loin or lasagna, or both?"

"Both. Where did all this food come from?" he asked, seeming to notice the long line of tables laden with cakes, salads, and casseroles as well as the steaming plates of food for the first time.

"We brought it," Leah said, and the word *we* seemed to turn her inside out. She felt again that surge of . . . not pride really. More of *belonging*. Her community had done this, had cared, and that made her feel she was a part of something worthwhile. Embarrassed by the wetness that came inexplicably to her eyes, she walked quickly to the buffet line and began to fill a plate with everything she thought Weston might like.

It was nice to have someone to take care of, she thought as she piled tuna salad on top of some greens. Tyler's pale, pinched face kept interrupting her thoughts and bringing with it a rending, suffocating sensation. Who would take care of him? She felt strangely compelled to help him, but she didn't know how. She didn't even know what would happen to him. Fighting back tears, she backed away from the table and ran into something solid.

"Leah, I'm sorry." It was Sterling carrying in a huge box. Behind him, several other men, equally burdened, were trailing through the crowd on their way to the kitchen. Following the train backward, Leah could make out Rowland just outside the double doors, supervising the unloading of a rental truck the size of a moving van.

"What the . . ." Leah exclaimed.

"Who knew opportunistic exploiters could be philanthropists too?" Sterling said with a sly grin. "Rowland called me to ask about the local stores, and we just went and bought out the entire meat and vegetable sections at Vons, and did a run to K-B Toys for the kids." He was smiling incredulously now. "Who knew?" he repeated.

"But, but . . ." Leah stuttered, trying to find the words to express the Taser-stun reaction that was surging through her body. "He lost the development. They let it burn—it's gone. He must be . . . uh, furious."

Sterling raised his eyebrows and nodded. "You would think so, but all I've seen is gratitude for the people who did what they could and are fighting to save the rest of the town. Gotta go." He hoisted the heavy box a little higher and moved on toward the kitchens.

Leah carried the plate to Weston in a stupor. She could not compute Sterling's news. The stocky figure of Rowland in her periphery vision seemed to pulse for attention, try as she might to ignore it. Weston thanked her for the food, and she sat down beside him and stared down at the table.

"I thought it was him," she said.

"Thought what was him?" Weston asked between huge forkfuls of lasagna.

"I thought it was Rowland Hughs who was setting the fires, trying to scare people into selling their land so that he could put in a road that would make phase three permissible." She looked up at Weston, who wasn't really getting her ramble but was getting that he didn't need to, that this smart woman was working something out and he was the sounding board.

"I thought he was the arsonist, or at least that he was paying someone to do it. I even pretty much accused him of it yesterday morning." Weston frowned and Leah went on quickly. "I was trying to get him to confess to me by making him think I could help him. When he denied it, I thought he was bluffing, trying to cover." She stopped and forgot to breathe in for a long beat.

Weston had turned to watch the parade of expensive goods being brought in and the Red Cross supervisor thanking a protesting Rowland Hughs profusely. "Him?" he asked, his eyes still following the procession of donations, and when Leah nodded, he added, "Good cover." But he didn't say it unkindly.

Then, as though the sight of someone being generous had unleashed a new flood of thought, Leah leaned intently toward Weston. "Listen, there's a little boy here. He's with a temporary foster mom. I met him yesterday morning, and his grandfather was hurt in the fire."

Weston's head came up, and he let the fork rest, forgotten, on his plate. "I know—I picked them up. It was bad. How's the old guy?"

Leah realized that she didn't know. "I, uh, I'm not sure. I thought that he was dead." She paused as Weston dropped his head and sighed with obvious feeling. "But I'm not sure now that you mention it," she hastened to add. "I mean, nobody told me that exactly. I just assumed. Can you find out?"

Weston looked up at her and formed his question with his strong mouth very slowly: "Why?"

A spurt of anger flared in Leah. "I'm not being one of those vultures who just want to hear bad news," she retorted hotly. "I want to know if the boy needs help, and what will happen to him."

Weston seemed unruffled by her indignant reaction. "Well, if the grandfather is deceased, or physically incapable of caring for the boy, and he has no other family that's willing to take him—or capable to take him—he'll become a ward of the court and be placed in temporary foster homes."

"You mean he'll be adopted?" Leah asked.

"No," Weston explained. "He'll go into the foster care system. That means he'll be shifted every few months— up to two years max—from foster home to foster home, unless he becomes adoptable *and*—here's the catch— someone wants to adopt him." He looked sad. "Which is unlikely. The number of kids his age out there on the adoption list is pretty staggering, I'm afraid."

"Oh." The tear in Leah's heart separated further. "That poor little boy," she whispered. "That's horrible. And you know this is true *because*?"

"My family was a foster care provider, remember? I

told you on the Ferris wheel." Weston suppressed a yawn and resumed eating, more slowly, as though he were too tired to chew. His eyes were crinkled at the edges. "It used to really bite when the kids had to leave. They'd become like brothers and sisters to me, and then one day, someone from social services would come, and they'd be gone. I never really knew where they went. Sometimes I'd get a letter or two, but they'd fizzle out."

"Why didn't your parents adopt them?" Leah asked incredulously.

Weston smiled. "They did adopt two—both my sisters. But we couldn't adopt all of them, and most of the kids weren't available for adoption. Their parents were still around, maybe in prison or rehab, and they hadn't relinquished legal custody. And so my folks just did what they could within a very flawed system."

Once again Leah found herself regarding Weston as though he were some anomaly, the kind of person you read about in *Time* magazine or see on *Oprah*, the kind who made her cry hopeful, private tears, but whom the cynical part of her could never quite buy. He certainly seemed to be one of those rare, hard-to-find, truly good people. That thought caused her a stab of guilt about someone else. Slowly, she turned to look directly at Rowland. An apology was owed.

"You get some sleep," she said to Weston, and surprising herself yet again, she leaned down and kissed his sweaty, filthy forehead without the slightest hesitation.

He caught her hand as she turned to go and gave it a squeeze when she looked questioningly back at him. "Thank you for helping with all this," he said earnestly, and then he released her and turned back to his meal.

Thinking that her efforts compared to his were like a crayon stick figure next to Monet's haystacks, she crept almost apologetically across the cafeteria and out the door to where Rowland was signing some paperwork with the driver of the truck.

She stood, uncertain of what to say until he noticed her with cold, distasteful recognition; she resisted fleeing only by grabbing her own moxie by the scruff of the neck and hanging on tightly. "Mr. Hughs?" she began. "I'm afraid I owe you an apology."

He had begun to turn away, but he looked back and she sensed again that innate quality of decency in him. The hard expression softened into that of a shrewd person who was willing to listen, but it had better be good.

"Yesterday morning I said some things to you that were misleading. I was operating under a misconception that you and your development might be responsible for these fires, and I was trying to trap you into admitting it. It was wrong. *I* was wrong, and I'm sorry." Leah found that both her voice and her hands were shaking, just like when, as a small girl, she'd been forced to confess something to her unforgiving father. She dropped her eyes to the pavement and muttered again, "I'm sorry. I know you lost the development, and I'm really grateful for all your generosity."

She glanced up, forcing herself to make eye contact before she beat a hasty retreat, but his look of open sadness held her fast.

"I know," he said with a huge sigh. "I can understand why you would have thought that. I asked around about you, and it was pretty obvious that you were not in the bribery game as a rule. You've got a champion reputation as a hard worker and an honest person." He grinned a little. "That must have taken some balls, young lady. I salute you."

Leah was stunned, as much by being told she had balls as by his obviously resentment-free forgiveness. "It, uh, was a little scary," she confessed.

Rowland sighed again, and the despondent expression returned. "I'm insured for the construction. I mean, I'll take a hit, that's for damn sure. The profit margin will plummet. But it's Susan I'm sad for." He was shaking his head. "That woman has worked so hard on this deal, and now the whole thing is gone." Rowland put his fingers against his thumbs and then extended them suddenly. "Poof! Just like that. She won't lose much, but she won't make a penny of profit either, and she's really poured her time and effort into this for over three years."

Leah thought about her meetings with Susan Hughs, her intensity and focus on getting the deals done in spite of any obstacles. She realized now that Susan hadn't just been working for a salary or the enrichment of her husband and their company; she'd seen this deal as "The One" that would put her over into real wealth, guarantee her security, make her somebody—independent of her husband—and a force to be reckoned with. All of those were tangible things that Leah easily grasped.

"I'm so sorry," she told Rowland. "I could see what it meant to her, and I get it. I really do. Believe me," she said. "Where is Susan anyway?"

"She's home, trying to salvage her back and her sanity. She's the one who organized all this, the food, the toys, and transporting it. Hired the drivers, recruited the grocery stores—all that from flat on her back. She's planning on coming in tomorrow to help out."

"Wow." Leah was impressed. "That's pretty amazing of her, of both of you, considering you guys don't even live in this neighborhood."

"No," Rowland said, and they both turned to look at the eerie red glow where the fires beyond the black ridge of hills illuminated the low ceiling of smoke that divided the valley from the sky. "No, we never got that chance."

Chapter 53

Everything about the morning was ashen gray: the sky, the ground, the very air. Joshua stood on the edge of his porch, and his eyes were drawn to the one thin strip of color in the dirty-laundry landscape, a faint carnelian glow at the very edge of the horizon.

Joy came out of her house and came over to stand silently beside him. Neither spoke for a long moment, just watched the ash fall, like lethal, intermittent snow, flurries of death, remnants of living things, environments, habitats.

"It's scary," Joy said in a voice as vulnerable as the fragile, dried buds of flowers that would crumble with the softest of pressure.

"I know," Joshua said. And he was so intent on his sorrow for what was lost and would still be lost that it was a full minute before he realized that she had placed her hand in his and was leaning against him. It was another minute before he worked his arm around her and then pulled her up against his chest. She came gratefully, snuggling her head in by his shoulder and wrapping her arms around the small of his back. The fit was perfect, and for a long time they stood, perfectly still, untouched by anything outside them and glad to have found that something so new could be so familiar.

But soon the sound of movements in the kitchen behind them peeled open the soft opaque walls of their private cocoon, and feeling exposed, they pulled apart.

"I've got to get ready for school," Joy mumbled and

hurried away. Joshua watched her go with furtive, hopeful glances, but she did not look back to confirm or acknowledge the spiking leaps of his heart.

His thoughts spun and in an effort to keep up with them, Joshua turned quickly and went into the kitchen. His mother was making coffee; her smile gave him no clue as to whether she had witnessed the melding on the porch.

"Sterling's on his way over with Jenny. We're going by her shop to pick up some supplies and then back to the high school to help out making breakfast before I go into the salon. You want to come?"

"Yeah," Joshua said. He and Joy had spent several hours the night before washing dishes, and he'd been surprised how quickly the menial job had gone by with Joy doing the time beside him. "But I want to visit Simon at the hospital first." Then, at his mother's half-pitying look, he added, "I know. But I just don't quite get it. I keep thinking about the key image that you saw. That must mean something, and I can't think of anything that would connect Simon to a key. It just doesn't seem to fit."

"And you still don't believe it's him." It wasn't a question.

Joshua took a deep breath of the cool inside air and felt his frustration heat it to a steamy gust as he exhaled. "No, I don't."

The sound of Sterling's car on the gravel distracted them from the conversation until he and Jenny came inside and helped themselves to coffee as Greer inducted them into the conversation.

"Joshua and I were talking about the fact that I've seen an image of a key over each of my premonitions of the fires."

"And that must mean something." Sterling echoed Joshua without knowing it. "But what?"

"Well, that's what we don't know," Greer said. "It could be representative, or it could be literal, part of an expression, like 'all keyed up.' "

"But it must have something to do with the arsonist!" Joshua exclaimed in frustration. "It must."

"Not necessarily." Greer's voice held a cautioning note. "It could just represent something to me. It could mean that, oh I don't know, that I was 'unlocking' the location of the next fire."

Joshua leaned toward her and used some of her own advice back on her. "Does that *feel* right to you?"

Caught, she grimaced into her coffee. "No, it doesn't."

"Okay," Sterling said, and reached a long arm across the counter to pick up the pad and pencil by the phone. "Let's make a list. Who could a key represent?"

"Uh, a locksmith?" Joshua asked.

"Good. Okay." Sterling wrote that down.

"How about a home owner?" Jenny suggested.

"Doesn't help us much," Greer said. "Although, I did think it could have signified Rowland Hughs handing out keys to many people. But based on the fact that his property has been a casualty, I think he's safely out of the running."

"He's out," Jenny chimed in, and in a few succinct sentences, she told them about Leah's aborted attempt to trap him, his denial, and Leah's subsequent apology.

A brief hush followed her story, a moment of respectful silence for the destruction of the eyesore they would have cursed in existence. Then Greer spoke up. "I did have my doubts about R.J."

"Yes." Sterling was nodding. "I was hesitant to put that out there, but he did paint all the locations that have been targeted."

"And the rest of the entire county as well. At least the scenic bits," Jenny reminded him.

"That, and the fact that just outside his door he had a wind chime made with an old-fashioned, heavy, metal key. Just the kind I've seen in the visions."

This announcement was greeted with a contemplative silence until Jenny tossed another horseshoe of common sense onto the stake. "But he was being arrested for obstructing the parade right in front of us when the first fire broke out."

"True," Greer conceded.

"But"—Jenny's face looked thoughtful—"he did have a motive. If you remember, he was shouting something about how our behavior was going to be our destruction, or words to that effect. Could he have preset the fires, you think?"

They all looked at Sterling, who, rather than being insulted, merely nodded and said, "It's definitely possible. Any good arsonist should be able to find a multitude of ways to delay combustion."

"Well, then you'd better put him on the list," Greer said sadly. "Damn it," she added. "I really liked him."

"I know he's a nice guy and it seems unlikely, but every freak lives next door to somebody," Sterling said as he wrote the name and a short list of reasons underneath it.

"Who else?" asked Joshua, deliberately not mentioning Simon.

Jenny squirmed. "What about Reading?"

"Who?" asked Sterling, looking up sharply.

"Mindy's husband. You met him at R.J.'s party," Greer reminded him. "He did seem rather enamored of fire. And he seems to enjoy killing things, if the number of hides nailed to his barn means anything."

"Oh yeah, him." He gave Joshua a knowing glance. "We actually saw him with a dead deer draped over the front of his truck, remember?"

"And he gives me the creeps," Jenny confessed. "Whenever I'm up there riding King, he's always sort of lurking around. I just get the feeling that, I don't know, he's the kind of person who would get off on the power of it."

"But what has he got to do with a key?" Sterling asked.

It was Joshua who answered. He had put it together now, the image of the dead buck across the hood of the king cab and the salacious pleasure on the faces of the men around it still stuck in his mind. He could see the animal's eyes, reflective and without depth, the red-black of the fresh blood as it dripped down over the white paint of the truck, across the black lettering stenciled there. In a voice that cut forcefully through the air like a well-aimed rock, Joshua barked out, "He installs security systems." He squinted, trying to recall the wording on the side of Reading's truck and at the same time forget the blood dripping pathetically down over it. "And his logo, it says, 'The *key* to your peace of mind.' "

"Jesus, you're right," Sterling exclaimed, smacking his hand down on the paper.

They all looked at each other. Finally, Greer cleared her throat and said, "Guys, I don't think that's much to go on. I mean, as far as calling the police to say we suspect somebody."

"At least they could talk to him, find out where he was when the fires were set," Joshua suggested. "Do you think Detective Sheridan will go for that?"

The corners of Greer's eyes crinkled as her mouth twisted into a frown. "I don't know." Joshua's eyes were beseeching, and it physically hurt her to not be able to give him what he wanted.

She knew how much he hoped that these fires had been set by anyone but Simon, for whom he had assumed the role of protector, but she could not in good conscience put suspicion on someone else just to ease his mind. So very gently, she said to him, "And what about Simon? Doesn't Detective Sheridan suspect him?"

It was Sterling who voiced Joshua's doubts. "But a key? What does a key have to do with Simon? The only thing I can think of is that he was in fire camp lockup, but it isn't even real jail. I mean, I'd like to give the kid a break—people certainly gave one to me, which is the only reason I'm sitting here right now—but the fact remains that he was at or near the location of every fire, and that *does* look bad for him." Sterling turned hard eyes on Joshua. "What does he have to say for himself?"

"Nothing," Joshua said bitterly. "He won't say anything. It's almost as if he expects the worst and for everyone to expect the worst of him, so what's the point?"

"Maybe that *is* the point," Greer said, trying to gently lead her son to his own conclusion. "Maybe he needs to expect something different for it to be possible."

Sterling was nodding. "Or maybe," he suggested, "he expects the worst for a different reason: a conclusion to his actions."

Joshua did not want to think about that reason. It would mean that everything he felt was wrong. And as disturbing as it was to have these frightening visions, it would be far worse if he couldn't trust them. He stared out the window at the sky. If he let his eyes go out of focus, he could almost imagine that the sky was actually overcast, not with smoke, but with forgiving clouds and their promise of sweet rain.

Chapter 54

Even the light through the ward window looked thick and dusty from the ash in the atmosphere, blown in from several miles away. Joshua stood at the edge of the curtains pulled around Simon's bed and wondered if Simon was asleep or faking it. He saw the boy's eyelids flutter and cleared his throat.

"Simon?"

Slowly, the head on the pillow turned. Half of Simon's head was bandaged, near the left temple, but both his eyes were open and he regarded Joshua warily—yet, Joshua thought, there was a hint of something more, an almost infantile flash of trust and pleasure that broke fleetingly through Simon's otherwise impenetrable shell. "Yo." Simon's voice was dry and cracking as though his throat had been recently stripped and sanded. "Wha's up?"

"Well, shit," Joshua started self-consciously. "Not you, that's for sure."

"They got cops outside?" Simon asked.

Joshua couldn't think how it would help to lie, so he said, as flippantly as he could manage, "Just the one."

"They let you in though?"

"Yeah, they know I came in with you." It seemed to be paining Simon to turn his head to the side. Joshua took a few hesitant steps in so that Simon could look at him standing at the foot of the bed. "Did he charge you?"

Simon looked away but nodded slightly without any

hesitancy or emotion. Joshua waited, letting his weight bear down so heavily on first one foot and then the other that he thought he could feel the arches of his feet flattening to the floor.

Finally, he asked, "Did you do it?"

He did not think that Simon was going to answer, and was about to succumb to the overwhelming urge to give up when Simon spoke. "It don't matter," he said, so softly that Joshua had to think about the words for a minute before interpreting their meaning.

This was it. He had to try now, or never. "Sy," Joshua said, ignoring the other boy's three-word statement because he knew that to argue or dispute it would be exactly what he was expecting, used to, and skilled at defending, "you know how you said I was a freak?"

That definitely had not been what Simon was expecting. His eyes opened wide and his right hand gripped the sheet. "Ye-ah?" he said cautiously, the word sliding out of his slack mouth a little bit at a time, as though only willing to emerge after checking to be sure it was safe.

"Well, I know I am. I mean, I see stuff. Believe me, this isn't something I picked as a friggin' hobby; it just started to happen to me. You know the first time I saw you, up on the fire road? The first day we spoke?"

"Yeah." Simon wasn't letting anything else out.

"Well, I saw something near you. Two things, actually. One was a little dog, a shaggy little thing, friendly, and he was yapping at me, as though he was trying to protect you."

Simon's mouth had closed rigidly, and his eyes were fixed on a spot somewhere behind Joshua's head.

"And I saw something else. I know you read it in my notebook: I saw a figure of a man." Joshua wanted to pause for breath, but he was afraid that if he so much as hesitated he would lose his nerve, so he bulldozed on. "And this man was definitely the most evil thing I've ever sensed around somebody. I think that man was your father. Am I right?"

Simon's eyes flickered to Joshua's, and then he turned

his face toward the window. Joshua could see a muscle in his jaw twitching. "Could be," he said.

"And if it is," Joshua rushed on, "and I'm right about what I think, then you have to make an effort to cut the tie that he's got on you. You've got to do something, make a gesture, or change the way you think, or . . . something, I don't know, but otherwise, he's going to go on having this influence on you that's . . . that's fucking nasty."

Simon still didn't look at him, but the jaw muscle was working furiously now, and Joshua could make out a wet sheen over Simon's eyes that he seemed to be trying to blink away.

There was a long moment when they both struggled for breath, and then finally Simon said, "That motherfucker won't ever be gone. He's waiting for me."

"Because you shot him?" Joshua could hardly believe he had said it so simply.

Neither could Simon, from the stunned look on his face.

"But you shot him because he was going to kill you, right? I mean, he killed the dog that was trying to protect you, and then he came for you."

Simon's eyes had narrowed and he was looking at Joshua the way someone would look at their fairy godmother if she ever really appeared. It was a look that was equal parts awe and terror. "How do you know that?" he croaked. "Who told you?"

Joshua exhaled; he had been most afraid that Simon would just tell him he was crazy and throw him out. "Listen to me, Sy. I know this is going to sound very weird. Hell, it sounds twisted to me, and it's coming from my head. *But he's not supposed to be here.* Don't ask me how I know this. I just do. Like I just know that you didn't start these fires. You didn't do it."

As though on their own volition, Simon's eyes shot up to Joshua's face and he stared at him, his lower lip quivered, and after a visible struggle for control, he asked, "Can you make him go away?"

This was the crucial part. "No," Joshua said firmly.

"But I can help you do it. At least I'm pretty damn sure I can. But I think that *you* have to do something that will change the energy that's around you, *you* have to change the way *you* are." Joshua paused. Even to himself he sounded inane and unbelievable. "Does that make any sense to you? Can you think of anything?"

Simon shook his head and pretended to be rubbing his eyes, but it was a futile attempt to hide the tears that he could no longer subdue. Joshua forced himself to keep looking at the other boy. He knew if he looked away in embarrassment it would be an admission that he had seen Simon's emotion, and that would be an irredeemable offense.

They seemed to stay in that position for a long moment. Joshua could see the constrictive movement in Simon's throat as he swallowed the sobs that were battling silently to escape him.

The large, swinging ward door behind them suddenly opened with a distinctive vacuuming sound like the muffled popping of a hermetically sealed jar, but Joshua was so intent on Simon that he saw the spasms on his face of first raw fear and then hatred before he grasped that the large form of Detective Sheridan had entered the room and was looming just over his shoulder.

"What are you doing here?" the detective asked Joshua, stepping forward, and the intimation that he thought they had already settled this could not have been more clear.

"I came to see my friend," Joshua said, turning to face the meaty man with more bravery and defiance than he felt.

"Your *friend*," Sheridan said, "is in a whole heap of trouble, and you would do best to distance yourself from that large, steaming pile while I'm still willing to let you."

"Please," Joshua said, but it was unclear whether he was saying please to Detective Sheridan or Simon, because his eyes started on Sheridan but shifted to Simon as he spoke the next words. "Please, give him a chance.

Simon. If there's anything you can do to help what we talked about, then now is the time to do it. I'm not giving up on you."

As he spoke, Joshua's focal point rose up and seemed to Sheridan to fix on thin air about two feet above Simon's head. Sheridan cut back the expletive with which his short patience had been about to relieve itself, and snapped his hard jaw shut. He'd seen this before with Joshua Sands, in this very hospital, and he was a smart enough man not to discount something he'd seen substantially validated.

For a moment, the upright youth stood perfectly still, staring frozen; then his eyes flicked to the boy in the hospital bed, as though to check that he was still with him, then refocused on nothing.

Very quietly, Detective Sheridan said, "What is it? What do you see?"

"He's here," Joshua answered in a somewhat louder tone, which made it clear that he was speaking past Sheridan to Simon. "He's here, and he wants you. You've got to do it now, Simon. I can help you cut this tie. I'm sure I can, but you have to help me. You have to let him know that you are making a different choice in your life. You have to tell Detective Sheridan the truth." Joshua's voice dropped as though he were afraid of losing his target, and he stage-whispered, "One way or the other, it'll release you from him."

Joshua was intently staring down the dark figure of Simon's father, who, Joshua could now clearly see, was connected to Simon with black rope like lines of energy—or the absence of it. He didn't know which, didn't care, but he knew that those lines had to be broken. It was taking all his courage, and a great deal of strength, to keep looking at the darkness; he could feel the negativity and evil from the form like it was radioactivity that was nauseating him and making his limbs tremble.

"Please," Joshua said in a whisper, "you have to do it now." He was gathering all the positive strength that he could find from every recess in himself, visualizing it as light and gathering it together like a weapon that he could use—not to shield this time, but to strike.

Detective Sheridan had no idea what was going on in this unique young man's brain, or even in the room, but he could see that it was real. Trusting his instincts over his violently objecting common sense, he turned to the boy in the bed and said, "How about it, son? Do you have anything to say to me?"

There was a gurgling sound from deep in Simon's throat as the last of his resistance crumbled, and his desperate plea for help broke forth with an implosion that sucked back the sound from his silent scream. His mouth opened and his throat worked furiously though nothing escaped, and through the cry's choking stranglehold, he managed to say, "It was Loc." Then the sobs came full volume, his sorrow and pain at last victorious over his fear and misplaced loyalty. "I thought he was my friend. He killed that man and tried to make it look like I did it. He started the fires. He fucking *liked* them, acted like he was some kind of fucked-up god or something."

In the least present part of Joshua's brain, something clicked. Loc. Lock and key. But, as though he were moving toward a target under fire, his attention was on full alert elsewhere. Joshua could still see the male figure looming over Simon, but it was reeling back, like a mole from bright sunlight. As though he were looking at the black lines through a telescope and seeing nothing else, Joshua stared hard at them and hoped fervently that he would choose the right moment.

"Why were you at the start of the fire?" the detective prompted Simon in a smooth, practiced voice that was meant to be hardly noticed.

"We went up there, me and Loc. He said he had something to tell me. We were drinking, and I told the fucker that I figured it out, that he'd popped that Armenian who nailed me for shoplifting, and he laughed at me." Simon turned his head to one side and his face twisted into a mask of horrified betrayal. "He laughed

at me, motherfucker!" He sucked at the air as though
he couldn't get any oxygen out of it. Sporadic coughing
interrupted his attempts to purge the emotional poison.

"And then what happened?"

Simon hacked up a wad of yellow spew and spit it out
into a kidney-shaped plastic bowl on his lap. He lay back
and sucked in huge gasps of air, fighting for speech. "I
was gonna walk on him, and I guess he hit me, 'cause
next thing I knew, I was so fucking dead. I woke up in
hell, but then I saw Joshua was there, and that's all I
know. Ah, shit." He pressed his hands hard to his face,
crying, and racking coughs sent his body into violent
spasms as the yellow phlegm from the smoke was
churned up in his violated lungs. "He was gonna burn
me up, he was gonna burn me." The statement was delivered on a long, quavering note, sounding Simon's staggering realization of his false friend's treachery.

"All right, all right, calm down now." Sheridan took a
step toward the head of the bed, leaving Joshua standing
behind him. In his life he had seen a great many performances given by con artists, guilty criminals desperate
to save their sorry asses. He'd seen outright lies told
with real tears, protestations of remorse and avowals of
innocence sworn on everything from bibles to babies,
but he'd be a monkey's uncle if this were one of them.
This kid wasn't that good. He doubted if anyone was.

Joshua saw the dark form above the bed twist away
from Simon and aim its malevolent gaze at himself. With
a burst of will and an expulsion of effort, Joshua released the light he had mentally gathered, willing his
strength out of his body and slicing through the blackness of the cords that twisted their prying fingers into
Simon's very soul. He had a brief image of the cords
breaking and floating free as they began to dissolve.
Then a great weakness permeated his bones, sucking the
energy from his body in one quick, gasping breath.

Sheridan waited a few impatient seconds for Simon's
sobs to subside, understanding what the boy was feeling;
the only family he had ever trusted had thrown him
under a truck and watched, unblinking and unfeeling,

while the wheels rolled over him. But Sheridan had to
know, and he had to know now. So he said quietly, "I'll
help you, son. I can protect you, but I need a full name
and an address." Simon nodded without taking his hands
from his face. The coughing was coming in barks now,
jerking his body in repetitious waves.

It was only after he'd written the information and
turned around that the detective realized that Joshua
Sands was lying in a heap on the cold linoleum floor.

Chapter 55

"I told you," Greer whispered as she leaned over Joshua's bloodless face. "I told you not to give your strength away. Now you save it; you sleep and let it build again. It will come back. Rest, let your body rest." She stroked his streaked blond hair back from his forehead and kissed it gently. Then she resumed her encouragements and whispered promises of renewed strength.

She had been with Joshua all afternoon. Detective Sheridan had reached her on her cell phone, and when she met him at the hospital, he had recounted the strange story. The attending physician had explained that her son's vital signs were strong and that there was no discernable injury. It was as though he had collapsed from exhaustion and fallen into an unconscious sleep—not a coma, he had added. His pupils and reflexes were reacting normally. Sheridan had expected her to dissolve into tears, to fold inward as she heard the story of Joshua's collapse and subsequent exhausted state, but once again, this woman had completely surprised him.

As he and then the doctor had spoken, the concerned creases around her stunning green eyes had lessened, smoothed as her face relaxed, and then deepened again as a smile he could only define as proud had slowly spread from her full mouth to her entire face.

"He's going to be all right," Greer had said, patting the detective's arm as though he were the one who needed comforting. "He gave Simon a gift of his own strength. I warned him not to because I thought—and obviously I was right—that he didn't know yet how to gauge it. He couldn't control it, and it took its toll. But he didn't go too far. He'll sleep for a day or so, and then, he'll wake up, and I'll give him hell." She had chuckled and patted Sheridan's arm again. "This is all very strange to you, and you have really taken it well. Thank you."

Sheridan often had the disorienting sensation that he'd missed a step when he was talking to Greer Sands, but at that moment he had had the distinct impression that he'd skipped an entire flight of stairs. Struggling for equilibrium, he had said, "Well, I don't know about that, but if this kid, Loc, whose real name is Lamont Martinez, is the arsonist and murderer, and we can pick him up, we'll all sleep a whole lot easier."

Then he had allowed himself a rare relaxing of his guard. "Your son really went out on a limb for a kid he didn't even know very well."

"You have no idea," Greer had said with a glow in those remarkably green eyes.

Hours later, Joshua was still in a motionless sleep. Sterling had come and sat with her for a long time, until she had sent him away because of his questions and fretful efforts to be helpful. She needed quiet and privacy for Joshua.

Without really caring what time it was, Greer glanced at her watch. Almost midnight. The curtains to the outside world were open, but the darkness revealed nothing more than a reflection of herself bending over her son's sleeping form, softly lit by a solitary light near the bed. Greer studied the picture for a moment and was struck by the continuance of her life caring for Joshua. One day, she knew, he would lean over her bed, and she hoped that he would have learned to be accepting and at peace with that time. If there were a measure of her success as a mother, it would be to prepare him for a peaceful and happy life in a world without her in it.

But her prayerful thoughts were interrupted when the image in the glass changed. Everything except her face faded into black, and she saw herself once again with the black wings hovering above her, a dark web wrapping itself around her startled face.

She exhaled hard and broke her eyes away with an effort, bringing the rest of the room back into her field of vision. Breathing in strained gasps, she grasped Joshua's hand as much to take strength as to give support. Then she sat down hard on the chair next to the bed and whispered with a ragged breath, "It isn't over."

Feeling shaky and overcome with fatigue, she propped her feet up on the side of the bed, laid her head back, still holding Joshua's hand, and gave herself up to thinking about the meaning of her visions.

A short time later, she was flying over a forest, and the forest turned from darkest green to a glowing, undulating red. She swooped and tried to avoid the tendrils of flame that shot out, grasping at her. And then she was no longer flying but sitting in front of an old woman with the silent gray wings of an owl. She stood with her back to Greer, her wings wrapped around her like a cloak of hushed softness, watching the distant fire as it flickered untamed and seemed to dance rhythmically to its own final and terrible tattoo.

Then, slowly, and with an awesome sensation of importance, the woman turned, and Greer could feel her connection to the crone. She could feel it without question or explanation because she knew that the connection between her and the owl woman was the connection of the earth to all living things.

Without words, the woman communicated her need to Greer. And then the crone's eyes filled with tears, and as her tears fell, the fire's rhythm sputtered and changed as rain began to fall onto the tormented earth.

Greer groaned slightly and twisted in her chair, seeking a more solid position in which to sleep without falling to the floor. Next to her, Joshua opened his eyes. He took in the dark hospital room, his immense fatigue, and his mother passed out in an uncomfortable chair, still holding his hand.

With an effort, he squeezed her fingers gently, smiled, and drifted gratefully back into the restoring comfort of slumber.

Chapter 56

This is what the weather in hell is like, Jenny was thinking as she drove through a dawn crusty with ash, breathing air that stung the nose with its acrid scent. She turned on the radio and listened for updates on the fire. She was almost to Foothill Boulevard when the local news got its turn. The fire was still burning out of control, though the courageous efforts of the firefighters had turned it away from the populated suburbs of Tujunga, Sunland, and Shadow Hills. They had one outbreak almost sixty percent contained, but the bulk of the fire had turned into the Angeles National Forest and was moving east, where there were several small pockets of homes and ranches.

It was difficult, sitting in her car with the air conditioner on full blast at five thirty a.m., to imagine the hellish conditions under which those firefighters were operating. The temperature was one hundred degrees nowhere near the fire, unpredictable gusting winds causing new flareups in impossible-to-plan-for directions. She was shaking her head with amazement when a word from the announcer broke through her thoughts. The word was *cherry*, and it was that word in conjunction with *canyon* that ripped her from her musings and caused her to give the volume switch a hard upward twist.

". . . to recap, then," the announcer was saying, "the fire is now moving east toward the Cherry Canyon, Vogel Flats areas. All the roads through to Palmdale and Lancaster have been closed. No traffic is allowed through at this time, to permit free access to emergency personnel and to facilitate evacuations. . . ." He went on for a few more moments in a serious tone before switching to a more cheerful note. "Now let's go to Bob Edmund to find out if the weather is going to let up. Bob, we sure could use some rain!"

A new voice, nasal and tremulous, entered the car. "Not too much chance of that, I'm afraid. There are some thunderclouds gathering offshore out over the Pacific, but while these Santa Anas keep blowing from the opposite direction—" Jenny had heard enough; she switched off the radio and pulled over, tapping at the wheel with one hand while she fumbled for her cell phone with the other. She pressed a single digit and waited while it speed dialed.

"Hey there! This is Mindy, Reading, David, and Amy. We're not home right now, so leave a message." The voice on the machine seemed to be mocking her.

Jenny waited for the beep and then said, "Hi, it's me, Jenny. Are you guys all right? I heard the fire is headed toward Cherry Canyon. Are you going to be able to get the horses out of there? Hello? Is anyone there?" She paused, but there was no response. "Call me if you need help."

Cursing, she disconnected and kept hearing the word *evacuation* over and over in her head. Was it possible that the police had forced them to leave without letting them get the horses out? Jenny's head was swimming. She knew the plan. If there was a fire, the horses would be evacuated to ranches farther down in the flats. Friends and neighbors with horse trailers would get out as many of the animals as possible, and the rest would be walked down, if possible, and released if all else failed. She also knew that many of the people in the high school gym had been forced to evacuate; many of them were very worried about animals they had unwillingly left behind. Reassurances had been given that animal rescue teams had been deployed, but who knew? Besides, Mindy and Reading housed far more horses than they had trailers; it would take several trips to get them all out. Maybe she had called between trips or they were just too preoccupied to answer the phone.

King. Jenny had a brief, horrible vision of him trapped in his stall as the fire closed in around the barn before she shut the image from her mind, made her decision, and pulled out, whipping a U-turn in the deserted residential street. She would go and offer what help she could. She pressed the accelerator and urged her SUV toward the ranch.

Detective Sheridan knocked on the door to the Sunland apartment and listened hard. Not twenty feet behind him, the Five freeway was already noisy with constant traffic, much of it diverted by the fire to the east. There was no answer, no discernable movement on the other side of the hollow, thin door. Sheridan lifted his chin in a gesture to the two officers on the far side of the door and stood back. Both of them were dressed in vests and helmets with face masks, holding shotguns. One of them called out loudly, "Police! Open up!"

They waited for ten seconds before Sheridan said, "Let's go." And the second officer moved in front of the first with a crowbar, handed off his shotgun to Sheridan, and with two sharp jerks fueled by rampaging adrenaline, popped open the door. The first officer dropped to one knee with his shotgun raised as the second took his back from Sheridan, then stepped in ahead of the kneeling officer. "Police!" he shouted. "If anyone is in here, you need to come out with your hands on your head!"

But except for the artificial ocean sounds of the early morning traffic, there was no response. They checked the apartment quickly, Sheridan noting empty tequila bottles, drug paraphernalia, and filthy, unmade beds. Once certain that no one was hiding there, they went to work, and it was less than three minutes before one of the officers was calling for Sheridan. He had flipped up a stained mattress, and inside a tear in the box springs beneath was a large stash of cash. Sheridan flipped through a pile of hundred-dollar bills held together with a rubber band and estimated quickly.

"About ten grand here," he said. "Keep looking." Sheridan had been around too long to think that that money had been honestly earned. For Lamont Martinez to have that kind of cash lying around meant one of two things: Either he was dealing drugs, which was highly likely, or—and it was this thought that twisted his gut until it felt like a tangled mass of squirming worms—someone had paid him to set those fires.

Jenny ran into the roadblock about a mile from the cutoff that would take her to Mindy's ranch and King. The highway patrol officer was adamant. Nobody got through. She argued, she pleaded, she lied, but it was to no avail. The officer on duty kept a calm voice and a level tone, but he glanced meaningfully at her swelled stomach and raised his eyebrows at her as if to say, *Are you fucking nuts? You want to endanger that baby for a horse?*

What he didn't understand was that Jenny's maternal instincts were raging more out of control than the fire, and that meant saving a living thing that she cared about was paramount. She felt the instinct to protect burgeon up in her and take control of her emotions, overwhelming her with determination. Unable to sway the officer, she turned around and backtracked. When she came level to the dirt fire road down which she had ridden King many times from the barn on the way to a trail along the dry creek bed, she pulled over and sat with her heart beating in her throat so hard that she thought it might gag her. She turned on the radio and listened. The fire seemed to have turned north. She looked up, and though she could see the deepest mushroom of smoke spreading out in every direction, it did not appear to be imminently near. Surely it could not cover that much space in less than an hour. She estimated how much time she would take in the worst-case scenario. Ten minutes' rough ride up the fire road if she kicked it. The same amount back down if they were already gone. Otherwise, add ten minutes to do whatever she had to do to help, even if it was just releasing the horses. She thought of those faithful, affectionate creatures, possibly stamping in their stalls, smelling smoke, desperately trying to obey their instincts to run, to flee, but trapped. She reached for her cell phone with scant hope of reception. There was none.

Her hands went protectively to her stomach, but she remembered something her doctor had told her. "Your baby is very well cushioned and protected," he had said. "As long as you don't do anything that would hurt yourself, your baby will be fine." Jenny was nodding to herself, talking herself into this brash course of action. Her nerves were running around her body like a couple hundred kindergarten kids hopped up on Oreos and Jolt cola all simultaneously having meltdowns in the same room. She also remembered her doctor saying, "So be careful, and don't take any chances at this stage that might injure you!" but she selectively edited that part out. Nothing she was planning on doing would endanger her child.

Grasping the wheel tightly with her left hand, she patted her stomach once, said, "Okay, baby, let's go for a little ride," and shifted into low gear.

Greer had presided over making two hundred gallons of coffee at the high school cafeteria and was preparing to leave for the salon when she saw Susan Hughs, immaculately dressed for helping out in pressed khaki slacks and a white, sleeveless button-down shirt, supervising a group of people setting up a huge barbecue grill that had been towed in behind a pickup truck. It was a professional unit, the kind designed for large-scale outdoor events, and it was brand spanking new.

Greer paused to watch Susan. Her sleek, well-groomed black hair was pulled into a tidy bun at the nape of her neck, but a few tendrils had worked their way out, and they blew into Susan's face. She had to keep brushing them away with her long, manicured fingers as she walked to the back of the pickup truck, which was filled with boxes, and began to give instructions to the three workers who were with her.

In spite of all the confusion and tension around her, Greer felt the same fear and concern for Susan that she had the first time she'd met her. The woman was in danger, and suddenly Greer was overcome with the need to warn her. How could she leave this woman to face some unknown threat without at least attempting to give her some chance at averting it? Yet it would be difficult. It was very important that she not place the seed of possible illness or risk where it might not have been. This was why Greer had always downplayed her gift, sharing it only with people she knew, why she had never promoted it as a career or a life choice: It was too much responsibility.

But that was a double-edged sword. Telling someone of her premonitions of imminent danger might seem too great a responsibility to take on, but it had proven to be an even greater—and more tragic—responsibility when she had ignored it. Still unsure of how to begin, or what to say, Greer crossed to where Susan was now standing with one hand shading her sunglass-covered eyes from the direct morning sun.

"Susan? Hi, Greer Sands. Wow, thanks for doing this. I'm sure everyone will be so grateful."

"Hello, Greer. Nice to see you." Susan shook hands with her customary firm, confident grip, and Greer had to consciously block the vision of blackness in Susan's chest.

"Listen, uh," Greer began, "could you spare a moment to talk?"

The only indication that she found this a surprising request was that Susan's head tilted slightly to one side and there was a half-second hesitation before she answered in her brisk, businesslike tone, "Of course. Shall we go in and get some coffee?"

They went together past the line in the cafeteria and directly into the kitchen, where Greer poured some of the freshly brewed coffee into a plastic mug for Susan. "The cream is out there," she said.

"Don't need it," Susan said curtly, taking a cautious

sip and visibly squelching an expression of distaste. "What can I do for you?" she asked, every pore exuding efficient readiness and attention.

"I'm not sure," Greer said. "I think first I should explain that, as crazy as it sounds, I get premonitions."

Susan's eye glazed only for a second before she recovered her outward poise and she said factually, "You're psychic."

"Yes. I know that's hard to believe, and I don't blame you for doubting me. But for instance, I've known the location and even the dates of some of these fires."

Real interest sparked in Susan's black, almond eyes. "Really?" she said with feeling and leaned forward, just a little, wrapping both her hands around the cup. "Do you know who is setting them?" She was whispering, and Greer found herself answering in a like tone.

"No. I mean, I've been getting indications, but that's not what I want to talk to you—"

"What kind of indications?" Susan looked eager, and it occurred to Greer that with her practical, problem-solving mind, she might think that she could solve the puzzle that had so far eluded Greer, and catch the bastard who had destroyed her housing project.

Greer wondered if she could. "Well, I've seen a key—that's been the main image. Also there's been an owl and indications of death and danger—"

"A key?" Susan interrupted. "Does that mean anything to you?"

"No, I'm sorry to say that it doesn't. I mean, I have a couple of ideas, but I'm still working on it."

"Really?" Susan said again, and her eyes looked thoughtfully away as she took another sip of the coffee without seeming to taste it this time. Greer could almost see the wheels of her brain working.

"Does it mean anything to you?" Greer asked, suddenly inspired at the notion. The Hughses had obviously been a target of one of the fires; maybe it was related to them.

But Susan was shaking her head. "Not that I can think of right off. Have you asked many other people?"

Greer had to laugh. "No. Well, I did tell the detective on the case. There's some history there, but I know he'd still much rather think I'm just delusional. Once again, I really can't blame him." Susan was still staring thoughtfully at a spot on the stainless steel counter; she reached out a lacquered nail and scratched distractedly at it. Greer took a deep breath. "Listen, Susan, the reason I'm telling you this is that, I, well, I've gotten a sense about you as well."

Susan's eyes shot up to Greer as her sculpted brows came down in concern. "Me?" she asked, surprised. "What do you mean?"

"I mean that I sense something dark around you, inside of you actually, and it's probably nothing, but if it is an indication of something going on inside of you that shouldn't be, I would hate myself for not telling you and giving you the chance to have it checked out."

Susan was staring with open surprise at Greer now, and Greer braced herself for the onslaught of indignant outrage at her presumption, but Susan's attention was still with her, focused on the information, as though she were assessing not just the possibility but the source of the data. Finally she said, "Something inside of me? Do you mean an illness?"

Greer let out a frustrated sound. "I don't know. All I know is that I saw something dark, in the vicinity of your chest, that shouldn't be there. Usually when I see darkness or blackness, it means danger, something is not right. Normally I see it striking or looming on the outside of a person, which would signify some endangering event, but this time . . . I'm just not sure. It's probably nothing, like I said, but I thought you should know. Please don't take my very shaky observation as proof. I've been wrong in my interpretations, many times."

"I see," Susan said thoughtfully and slowly. She opened her mouth as if to ask another question, but she was cut off by Leah's sudden appearance behind her.

"There you are!" Leah called out to Greer. "I've been looking for you." She crossed to Greer quickly and barely seemed to notice Susan or her intensity. "I heard on the radio that Cherry Canyon is threatened. That's where Mindy's ranch is."

"And Jenny's horse," Greer added, alarmed.

"Yes. And then I went to the coffee shop, but Jenny never opened. I've been trying to call her cell phone, but it doesn't even ring, goes straight to message. Reading and Mindy are not responding either. And Jenny's not at her house. I drove by there; her car is gone."

Greer's stomach felt like it had been set on agitate. It flip-flopped and churned its contents into a frothy, tangled wad. "Oh no, do you think she's gone up there?"

Leah narrowed her eyes and shook her head slightly before she said knowingly, "What do you think? It's *Jenny*," and Greer understood that she meant Jenny, fearless Jenny, would consider no other option.

Susan had caught up with the conversation. "The road up into the canyons is blocked; state patrols are up there. She can't get in."

Both Greer and Leah looked at her while they considered this; then Greer thought about her last ride with Jenny and the route they had taken down to the creek bed trail, the route along the fire road. "She knows an alternate route," Greer said, and the thought of the black wings hovering over Jenny's image sent an electric shock through her nervous system. "Oh my God, we've got to stop her!"

Leah's face went white. "What? Shouldn't we just call someone?"

But Susan had straightened up, discarded her coffee with a slosh onto the counter, and grabbed Greer's arm. "You stay here and keep trying to reach her," she told Leah, whipping a card from her pocket and handing it to her. "Call us if you hear anything."

"But there's only very spotty cell service in the canyons," Leah objected.

"Then leave a message and we'll check it when we get back down the hill. We'll call the state troopers on our way, but they've probably got their hands full." Dismissing Leah, she pulled at Greer and nailed her right in the eyes as she said, "Let's go get her."

Greer remembered the account of Susan's ramming her Range Rover into the side of the burning trailer and pulling out the unconscious guard. It took her only a moment to assess that this was a woman of action, with the gumption to do what they needed to do to help Jenny, if she was truly in mortal danger.

Slowly, then with increasing decisiveness, Greer nodded her head. "Yes, let's go get her," she echoed.

When Jenny drove right up to the entrance of the barn, the place had the smell of desertion about it. Looking down the aisle she could see that about half of the stalls were empty, a couple of the doors left swinging open, and Jenny could venture a guess as to how many were gone: eight, the size of Mindy's horse trailer. So she had left and taken as many as she could.

The remaining horses paced their small enclosures outside the barn or moved nervously back and forth from there to their stalls inside. Each of them was streaked with yellow; at first Jenny's jacked-up brain thought it might be some kind of flame retardant, but she realized that it was numbers. Someone had spray painted a phone number on the flank of each horse. So, they had been intending to come back and release them if the fire came too near. But Jenny knew that no one would be allowed to come back up the main road. Even as she got out of the car, Jenny could hear the twitchy neighing of the trapped animals as they scented the increasing smoke in the air.

Twelve horses. She had no idea what to do. Even if she could get halters and lead ropes on all of them, they would never follow her calmly down the hill. At the first opportunity or sudden movement, they would bolt. She stood for a moment and considered the situation, understanding why Mindy had chosen to leave the horses she couldn't take in their stalls instead of releasing them. There was still a good chance that the fire would turn, and the horses on their own might be trapped by the fire, or injure themselves by panicking.

Still frantically debating a course of action, Jenny

started down the aisle, calling out to King to bring him in from his outside pen, but as she drew level with his stall, a chill train of stupidity ran up a frozen metal track on her spine. He was gone. Mindy had taken him with the others.

"Shit," she swore under her breath, but in the same moment, she turned and saw the doe-eyed mare that occupied the stall next to King's. Softening her tone, she reached out a hand and stroked the mare's head with a firm touch, trying to calm the skittish horse. "It's okay, Buttermilk. I'm going to get you out of here." Deciding to act made Jenny feel infinitely better. She reached for the halter and lead outside Buttermilk's stall and went in. After a small chase, she managed to corner the nervous mare and slip on the halter. Then, keeping a strong pressure on the lead, she led her out, fastened her quickly in the cross ties and ran to the tack room.

As she saddled the mare, she glanced repeatedly over her shoulder toward the open end of the barn. The smoke seemed to be climbing, slate gray and bulbous, from much closer now. The view from the front of the ranch was across the road to a lower ridge of hill, and beyond that was a second, more imposing range of mountainous landscape, and it looked to Jenny like the base of the fire had reached the far side of that higher ridge, and the wind was blowing hard toward her.

She was slipping the bridle on when something at the edge of her vision arrested her attention: a movement halfway up the near ridge, just across the road, maybe a football field's length away. She paused and squinted in the hazy brightness. Her common sense was telling her it must be an animal, a deer or a coyote, but her brain was saying, "Coyotes don't wear plaid."

It was a man, making his way through the brush; he seemed to have something in both hands. His right arm was rising and falling in great swaths, and Jenny realized that he must be cutting a path. In his other hand he was carrying something more substantial. It looked like a tank. Could it be a firefighter? Her brain gave her the same answer: "Firefighters don't wear plaid either."

Careful to keep her car between her and the figure, Jenny crept up to the vehicle and opened the barn-side door. She rummaged in the pocket behind the front seat and came up with a pair of binoculars that Lewis had given her for her last birthday. Bracing her arms against the side of the car window, she focused on the figure.

It took only a second to identify him as Reading. Muttering to herself about what that psycho could be up to, she honed in on what he was doing. He had obviously been forging a path with a machete, which he had now shoved back through his belt. He was fumbling with whatever the other apparatus was that he had been carrying. She could see now that it was a tank of some kind attached to a long tubing, and with a shock of alarm, Jenny saw flame burst from the end of the tubing.

"Oh God, oh no," she breathed. "It's a flame thrower. He's starting the fires." She was speaking out loud, trying to make sense of this. "Oh Christ, Joshua was right, it is him. Okay, okay, think. It's okay. I've got to get out of here. But . . . Jesus!" she exclaimed as she saw the brush in front of Reading leap into flame. He started to scramble away, cutting sideways across the ridge, setting the hill behind him alight as he went.

There seemed to be only one choice now. Indifferent to whether Reading saw her or not, Jenny ran down the length of the barn, opening the stall doors as she went. Most of the horses were reluctant to leave and paced or reared in fear as she tried to shoo them out into the open. "Hiyah!" she shouted. "Go! Get out!" In seven minutes, all the horses but one were stamping in a group near the ring. The last horse, a huge three-year-old stallion only recently saddle broken, was facing off with Jenny in his stall, nostrils flaring. She moved hesitantly to one side, trying to suggest he choose going through the open door instead of her own body. Instead, he turned his tail and threw a kick, which Jenny only just avoided by jumping backward.

She hit against something solid, but the something gave and then caught her as she started to fall. She twisted violently and looked up into a face so completely smeared with black that, for one disoriented minute, Jenny thought the man was wearing combat makeup. But even before she had regained her balance, she realized that it was Reading, and he was staring at her with frighteningly angry eyes.

"What," he said slowly, his voice chillingly level, "the fuck are you doing here?"

She couldn't speak. She backed away into the corner of the stall, wrapping her hands protectively around her swollen abdomen.

Reading's eyes stayed on her as though they'd been glued there. "Are you insane?" he asked.

"Probably," Jenny answered, her voice coming out in a squeak. Behind Reading, the hill was spewing flame and ash. Blackened as he was by the soot, he looked like a denizen of hell.

"Please," Jenny said, "let me go. I never did anything to hurt you. I won't tell anyone it was you, I promise."

Reading's angry mouth tightened and he took two steps closer to her. An un-pregnant Jenny would have fought him to unconsciousness, but now she curled inward, trying to protect her stomach and her unborn child. "Please," she repeated.

He grabbed roughly at her arm and yanked her forward, hard. "Come on," he said. "You've wasted too much time; we've got to get out of here."

Baffled, Jenny peered up at him, her eyes stinging from the new drifts of smoke from the nearby hills. "Wha-what?" she asked.

"I set the fires nearby to try to create a firebreak. I keep a hundred feet around the house and the barn cleared all the time, but this fire is a mother, and I don't know if it will be enough, so I'm stealing its fuel before it gets to us."

Still pulling Jenny, he watched the fire he had set burn down to the road. "We're not going that way: The fire is moving toward our route out." He pointed with the hand that wasn't fixed on Jenny's arm to the flames licking the top of the ridge near the base of the valley. "We're cut off from that exit."

Jenny's brain was kicking into gear, but as though the shift were set in fifth and she was starting out from a dead stop, the wheels were having a hell of a time catching up to the rotations. "What about the fire road?" she asked.

"Same thing, few more minutes. We've got to go up, above the fire road. And for that, we need horses." He glared at her meaningfully again and Jenny ventured a tentative smile.

"Whoops," she said. "But if the fires you set will turn it, won't it be safer to stay here?"

Reading released her arm and went quickly to get the stallion's halter from its place near the stall door as he answered her. "It might save the house and the barn, but the buildings can survive searing heat and insufficient oxygen. Can you?"

"Is that a trick question?" Jenny had never in her entire life felt so incredibly stupid.

"We have two choices, get in the water tank and hope we don't get poached, or ride like hell. Which do you vote for?"

Without another word, Jenny ran for the tack room. She was back in thirty seconds with the bridle marked with the stallion's name. It took both of them to steady the ton of living tension and get him saddled.

"One more thing," Reading said, and before Jenny could wonder what it was, he had grasped her by the shoulders and shoved her backward against a hundred-gallon horse trough. It caught her in the backs of her knees and she went in with a splash, going completely under. She surfaced again and stood, sputtering and dripping after Reading pulled her out and plunged himself in. "That's to keep you and the baby cool, and sparks from catching your clothes on fire," he told her.

Then Reading mounted and offered a hand to Jenny, but she shook her head, pointing to where Buttermilk was dancing frantically in her cross ties.

"I'll ride her."

Reading leaned down, holding the impatient stallion

back with nothing but sheer force on the leather reins. "Are you that good?" he asked.

All of her survival savvy surged forward, swelling Jenny with a familiar raw courage. She sensed the same refusal to fail, to lie down and accept weakness, that had kept her alive and sane against all odds in a life marked by brutality and poverty, and it seemed now as though every unthinkable trial had all been a preparation for this moment. Fixing him with shining eyes and a knowing smile, she said clearly, "Watch me."

She moved rapidly to unhook the cross ties and then mounted Buttermilk even as the horse began moving rapidly away from the approaching fire. By the time they reached the end of the barn aisle and hit the open, she was cantering, and Jenny slowed her to a walk next to Reading, who was struggling to restrain the stallion. "What about the other horses?" she asked.

All his attention and efforts were apparently on handling his own mount, but she could have sworn she detected a note of sarcasm as he said, "Watch me." He shot her an appraising glance, then said, "They'll stay together if we can break them together, that's their instinct, but we've got to force them onto the high trail. The fire road will lead them back down into the direction of the fire. You take the right."

Jenny had never done any wrangling, but the principle seemed relatively simple. Use your horse to block any routes you don't want the other horses to take. Crossing the yard at a canter, she worked her way along the ring side of the jittery horses. She could hear the crackle of the flames behind her now, and the only way she could endure the heat was to ignore it, pretend that it would end in a minute. When she was positioned, she looked back to Reading.

With a cowboy whoop and a kick, he released the stallion, which broke instantly into a full run straight toward the group of horses. For a terrifying minute, Jenny was sure they were going to scatter and stampede toward her, but just before colliding with the group,

Reading pulled hard on the reins with his left hand while waving furiously with his right at the flank of the horses in back. The stallion turned sharply and bolted away from the other horses, toward the trail across the pasture and under the oaks. Remembering her role, Jenny kicked hard at Buttermilk. As one, the small herd started, and then began to run, away from Jenny, following the lead of the young stallion. Soon they were all in a full run across the crispy dry pasture and Jenny was muttering through forceful exhales, "Please don't be any holes, please don't be any holes."

As the trail narrowed under the oaks, Reading slowed the stallion and let the group of horses go on ahead of him.

"They're on their own now!" he shouted as Jenny came up near him. "Follow me, and stay as close as you can," and then he took off under the trees. She followed, but just as she was about to make the curve that would block the view back to the ranch, she slowed up and glanced back.

She could see nothing but angry, billowing waves of solid smoke. She cradled one hand under her baby's cocoon, gave her willing horse free rein, and rode for all three of their lives.

Chapter 57

It was Susan who called the sheriff's office to let them know that it was possible that Jenny had circumnavigated the roadblock up to the Cherry Canyon ranch. She knew someone in the office, and she told Greer that she hoped that might help keep the information from being lost in the confusing barrage of calls from worried home owners, concerned relatives, and reporters hoping for scoops.

As they came near the turnoff, they could see that the roadblock had been moved even farther down the hill and the smoke was belching from behind the crest of the nearby hills. "Holy shit," Susan swore openly. "We're not getting anywhere close to there." She pulled out and continued along the access road, saying, "Maybe we can find a route in behind it. At least we can find a police officer or someone who can tell us what's happening."

Greer nodded dumbly as she watched the black smoke; it seemed to her to keep splitting and surging outward in two directions, like giant black wings that had stolen the sky. "We've got to try to find her," she whispered. "She's in terrible danger."

"So"—Susan sounded as though she were trying to distract Greer from her murky thoughts—"tell me more about these visions. You were going to tell me, before we started out on this little search and rescue, if you suspect anyone."

"I had a couple of notions, but nothing very solid."

"Really, nothing concrete. The key thing doesn't connect it to anyone?"

"Not that I know of." Greer sighed and stared out the window at the ghoulish scene. Her cell phone ringing startled her, and she jumped in her seat so abruptly that Susan swore again and swerved slightly. Greer fumbled for the phone and managed to get it out of her pocket. Praying that it was news that Jenny was safe, she flipped it open. "Yes?"

"Ms. Sands?" It was the gravelly voice of Detective Sheridan.

"Yes?" Greer's stomach felt flattened, as though she'd been punched from the front. She didn't know what he wanted with her, but it couldn't be good news.

There was a pause, and she wondered if he was hesitating before giving bad news, or gathering himself to say something he found even more difficult. It was the latter.

"We've found some evidence that the information we received from Simon Gomez is accurate. It appears that a friend of his, one Lamont Martinez, may have been setting the fires." He paused, and Greer wondered, other than the fact that Joshua had been instrumental in getting Simon to talk to the detective, what this had to do with her. Sheridan went on, "The young man's tagging ID was Loc. Like lock and key."

"Oh," Greer breathed.

Susan was watching Greer as much as the road and she mouthed, "What? Is it your friend?"

Greer put one finger over the phone's microphone and said softly, "No. They think they found out who's starting the fires. It's a kid who's called *Lock*." Susan's face blanched and she shook her head disbelievingly as her eyes opened wide, as though seeing Greer in an entirely new light and with—yes, there it was—fear. Greer was not surprised by Susan's reaction. She hadn't expected Susan to believe her, and even if, as she suspected, Susan was busy writing this off mentally as a coincidence, it would take a minute to convince herself of that. To Sheridan she said, "And you think that's why I was seeing the key?"

Another pause, and then he said with a resigned, exasperated exhale, "Could be, I guess. But here's the thing: We can't find him, but we went to his residence and came up with a bundle of cash. He might have started the fires, but I'm willing to bet my badge that somebody paid him to do it. So . . ." His voice seemed to trickle off before he got enough force behind it to say the next words, "Is there anything else you can tell me?"

"No, not right now. But listen, I have a friend who I think might have driven around a roadblock to try to rescue her horse, and I'm with Susan Hughs right now, and we're headed up to try to find her—"

Detective Sheridan cut her off. "You're with Susan Hughs?"

"Yes, she's been very kind. She's driving me up toward there so that we can see if we can—"

"Get out of the car," Sheridan said sharply. He sounded as though he'd been struck in the face by a bright light of recognition. "Make up an excuse and *get out* of her car."

"What?" Greer's eyes cut sharply to Susan, who seemed to be watching her without regard for the road. Susan's eyes were narrowed and wary.

"I was looking into the arson fire at Golden Door to see if there was any possibility the owners had set it for insurance purposes. That's standard procedure, that was before you told me about your vision, and I just remembered a detail that didn't seem important at the time. Something that didn't register until right now."

Susan had reached behind her seat and pulled her purse into her lap. She had one hand inside of it as she said quietly to Greer, "Hang up the phone." Her graceful, manicured hand emerged from her Prada bag and it was holding a gun. "Now," she mouthed.

As Greer jumped and started to slowly lower the phone from her ear, she heard Sheridan's voice, small and unreachably distant, saying, "Susan Hughs's maiden name is *Keyes*."

Chapter 58

Joshua's roommate was recovering from knee surgery and his leg had been hooked into a contraption that bent it slowly up and then back down again. He wasn't yet conscious, so the only sound was the *whoosh* and *click* of the machine in its repetitive function.

Joshua stared at the wall and wondered what time his mom would come to get him today. The wall was white, devoid of interest or stimulation. *Whoosh, click,* white. *Whoosh, click,* white.

The sound continued until it was softly reminiscent of a train on a track. Joshua listened to it and let his eyes slide out of focus. Between the sound, the lack of color or interest, and his fatigue, he almost didn't notice when the scene around him began to fade until he was seeing another place altogether.

He was seeing through his mother's eyes: He could feel her presence; he could see her hands. She was in a car, one he did not recognize, and it was driving very near the fire. He could see the smoke filling the sky outside the windows, and then he could see a woman at the wheel, a dark-haired woman with Asian features, and he could feel his mother's fear. And then he saw the gun.

Joshua shot up in his bed, gasping, and fumbled for the side-rail supports. He forced himself to banish the vision so that he could struggle out of bed to stand and dress.

He had to rest for a few seconds after he got his shoes

on, and then shuffled determinedly to the door, cracking it and peering down the hall. The nurses' station was empty, and he forced himself to stand upright and walk out of the hospital with every appearance of health and vigor. Just another visitor.

When he got to his car, he collapsed into the driver's seat and leaned his head against the steering wheel while he gathered his strength and his thoughts. "Sterling." He reached into the glove compartment for his cell phone, but he had left it on the day before and its battery had run down. He punched a single number, and even as it rang, the phone beeped repeatedly, warning him that it was about to go dead. When the deep voice answered, Joshua spoke urgently. "Sterling, I'm about to lose my battery. Listen, Mom's in danger. Can you meet me at home?"

"What? Joshua, are you out of the hospital?"

"Please, I need your help. I'm on my way home. Can you meet me there?"

And then the phone went dead.

Joshua's impulse was to drive like a maniac, but he was still woozy and so he forced himself to concentrate on driving safely. It seemed an eternity before he pulled into his own street. He came around the corner of his small, unpaved road into the nook of homes in the forest and almost fainted with relief when he saw Sterling's pickup truck.

Sterling himself was on the front porch, and he came down the steps to Joshua's car as he pulled up. Joshua opened his door and reached out to grasp Sterling by the shoulder. "She's in danger. Mom's in danger. She's with a woman, an Asian woman. She's got a gun, and she's driving Mom toward the fire."

Sterling's face was a mask of incredulity and surprise that morphed quickly into concern. His strong hand fastened firmly around Joshua's wrist. "Do you know where?" he demanded.

"No, God no, only near the fire. Maybe someone at the school will know where she went."

Joshua heard a screen door creak and slam, and in

the back of his mind he knew that someone had come out of the Whitehorses' house.

Sterling didn't even glance up. "The woman, did she look in her forties? Pretty, but in a very overly groomed way?"

"Uh," Joshua thought, trying to hang on to the image that had flown from his immediate vision as the hospital surroundings had come back into view. "Yes, that sounds right. She looked, uh, wealthy. Her hair was straight, black, and pulled back."

Whitney came up beside them. "What's going on? Are you all right?" she asked Joshua.

Sterling's eyes had gone hard and mean. "Whitney, do you have any idea where Susan Hughs could be taking Greer?"

"Yes, they went to try to stop that fool Jenny from driving around a roadblock on Cherry Canyon to save her horse." Whitney was shaking her head. "Jenny. Damn Latino genes. She's the toughest chick I know and I love her, but the woman is *seven months* pregnant, for God's sake. I've been beside myself since Leah called."

Joshua was listening, but his eyes had just fallen on something in his car. He let go of Sterling and lunged for it. It was the map on which his mother had marked the locations of the fires with the miniature keys. The map that had led him to Simon. He held it up to his face and studied it furiously, checking dates and locations against the reports he had heard only this morning.

And then he found it. Not a key, but a mark, a definite mark, penciled in very lightly. It looked almost like a bird—no, wings. "I found her," Joshua said abruptly, cutting off Sterling's explanation of Joshua's call to him. "I think I know where she is—and it isn't Cherry Canyon."

Both the others were looking at him with faces that held equal parts hope and horror.

"Where?" Sterling demanded.

Joshua pointed at the map, swayed slightly, and said, "Phase three."

Chapter 59

Susan took the turn into the development so fast the Range Rover skidded sideways and Greer had to grasp at the armrest to remain upright. They sped past the charred remains of the phase-one houses, which looked like a dinosaur graveyard, their bones left blackening in long rows without tombstones. They flew through the desiccation that had been the intended building pad for phase two, passing the twisted frame of the mobile home as they went. Susan didn't even slow down as they neared the end of the cleared area, and Greer's body, already overloaded with adrenaline, tensed into a solid mass as Susan drove right off the edge of the flattened land, leaving the ground for a few feet before bouncing onto a rough-cut road that was nothing more than a track made by a bulldozer—and that dropped off steeply.

"Susan, please. Think about what you're doing!" Greer pleaded, trying to keep her voice calm. "You're not a murderer. I know you're not. If you were, you would have let that security guard die."

"Drunken bastard," mumbled Susan through pursed lips as she negotiated the rough ruts at an unsafe speed. "That stupid punk kid was supposed to make that a small fire, just enough to make us look like the victims. If I hadn't come up here to pay him off, he would have killed that useless alcoholic."

"He did kill *somebody*," Greer said, trying to verbally slap Susan back to sanity.

"Not on my dime, he didn't," Susan spat vehemently. "*That* had nothing to do with me." She pulled up so abruptly that the seat belt cut painfully into the tender skin where Greer's neck met her shoulder. She recovered and looked up into the barrel of the gun.

It was a ladylike gun, if there was such a thing, carefully chosen for its style, no doubt, yet it still seemed to Greer so wrong in Susan's hand, as though she had picked up a particularly slimy piece of trash, something rotted and putrid. Something deadly poisonous.

"Get out," Susan ordered.

"What if I don't?" Greer tested.

"Then I'll have to shoot you in the car and drag you out. It'll be a little more trouble, but not much."

"Detective Sheridan knows I'm with you," Greer said though a haze of panic. "If you hurt me, he'll know it was you."

Susan smiled cruelly. "Are you having one of your psychic moments?"

"No," Greer said flatly, her anger beginning to mobilize her in spite of her fear, "just stating a fact."

"Because he's going to be amazed to hear how your son and his gang buddy set all these fires and you tried to kill me when I found out and confronted you."

"But Simon already told the detective that his friend was responsible." The thought of Joshua and the pain he would feel at her loss sent a ripple of rage through Greer. She could not, would not, allow it.

Susan gestured with the gun. "Get out and walk away from the car."

"Susan, please."

"Get out!" Susan screamed. She was sweating and her eyes bulged. Greer moved slowly, opening the door when Susan hit the unlock button and moving a few yards away from the vehicle, scanning the bleak, burned-out landscape as she searched for an escape route. There didn't seem to be any cover, or hope.

Susan got out as well, and as she came around the front of the car, she said, "Do you imagine I didn't think of this? Who do you think they'll believe, an upstanding, philanthropic community leader or a couple of kids with juvenile rap sheets longer than the paperwork I had to file to get this fucking place started—" She stopped herself and waved a hand as though to dismiss this waste of time and breath. "Yes, if you need to know, I hired that kid to set the fires, and just my luck he turns out to be some psycho-pyromaniac who gets off on fire instead of just doing the job I paid him to do. If you want something done, you have to do it yourself, which is why I put the poison in those people's tank. They needed to move out, and they needed to go without anyone knowing why. I need the road there, and they have to go. I have been working on this deal for over *three* years; I *earned* this. It's my turn. I thought of everything except . . ." Susan paused, threw her head back, and shouted at the sky, "Except that some ex-hippie psychic would come fuck things up for me! *What* is that about?"

But the sky didn't answer. Not Susan anyway, though Greer was sure she heard something, a soft whisper of huge, silent wings, and as she looked up, she was almost certain that, in the forming clouds mixing with the smoke, she could see the outline of gray wings, beating with a gigantic but utterly soundless force.

When she looked down again, it was at the gun's gaping muzzle and, behind it, the swelling blackness in Susan's chest, and she was struck by the similarity of the two.

"Now I know," Greer said in a soft but steady voice.

She could see Susan's fingers tightening on the trigger, but she seemed to hesitate at Greer's prophetic statement. "Now you know what?" she asked, confused.

Greer was filled with an overwhelming sorrow that she had not had a chance to say good-bye to anyone, and yet there was something else, a calm—a relief really—that she was about to return to the place from which she had come. She smiled through her tears and said, "You'll have to wait and see."

That's when she heard the thunder, a low, rolling rumble. And she looked up at the sky again, expectant. Susan followed her gaze.

But the thunder wasn't coming from the sky. It was coming from just under the spot where the ridge sloped steeply down from them, and as both women searched frantically for some reason or logic that would explain the noise, a herd of horses broke over the crest a few yards away and galloped wildly toward them.

Susan screamed and pulled both hands up in front of her face. Greer leapt forward, ignoring the stampeding animals bearing down on them, and launched herself onto Susan, grasping and twisting the other woman's gun arm tightly in both hands and knocking her to the ground.

The next few seconds were a confusion of dust, soot, hooves, and eternal struggling as time slowed to a denser dimension where the seconds ticked through space as thick as tar. The very air was filled with pain and exertion. Greer breathed it in and was choked with dust churned from the chaos of the hooves and the desperate flight born of inbred fear. She felt a sharp pain in her shoulder the same instant she heard a sharp, hot blast, muffled and infused into the confusing cacophony all around them. She felt Susan's body heave violently against her and then just as suddenly surrender the tension and anger, so that with a barely detectable gasp or sob, she seemed to melt, easing almost gracefully onto the ground. The warm skin of her bare arm under Greer's hand was smooth, in sharp contrast to the coarse and gritty surface on which they both now lay.

And then it was quiet. Very slowly, as though it had only paused to sense a glimpse of the physical world and now it was eager to go on its way again, time picked up its pace, resuming its brisk, inattentive walk on earth. The sound of rushing hoofbeats fading away and the sensation of the ground, still hot from the fire, returned Greer to her senses enough to force herself up onto her knees. Clutching at her shoulder with one hand and Susan's limp arm with the other, she grappled with reason, trying to make sense of what she saw before her.

The gun lay, gleaming and man-made, discordant in a pile of twisted, organic sticks; the horses were disappearing in a cloud of dust and soot that their sharp hooves had churned up; her shoulder was bleeding where one of those hooves had clipped it as the horse jumped over her—all these things came wandering warily into Greer's field of awareness. But there was something else, something that would not show itself. Greer shook her head and forced herself to call the truth into her sluggish mind.

Susan was lying perfectly still. Her white skin on the black earth gave her the artsy look of a black-and-white photograph. Except that there was one color. From the hole in the side of Susan's face, dark red blood was oozing onto the scorched ground.

And Greer rocked back from the realization when it hit her with its harsh and undeniable finality: Susan was dead. The blackness that she had seen inside of Susan had been there not because she was ill, but because the mortal danger that Greer had seen in her future would come from inside of her; she had been the danger to herself. Susan had nurtured it, fed it, and refused any warning about it.

And she had paid the price.

Chapter 60

Reading and Jenny had lost sight of the other horses. When they came to the highest open point on the trail, Reading pulled up hard in front of Jenny and pointed. Off to their far right, on the fire road leading to the south, they could see the forms of the running horses and the telltale clouds of their path.

"They've headed for the already burned-out area," Reading said through gritted teeth. "Smart animals. Now, if they don't get hit by a car, they should be all right."

"Where are we going?" Jenny asked, ignoring the slight cramping in her stomach. It was so hot and arid that her clothes had already dried on her body.

"Down," Reading said, his face unreadable as he scanned hers, possibly looking for signs of weakness. "Here." From a deep pocket in the hunting vest he was wearing, he pulled a full bottle of water and handed it over. "Drink half and pour the other half over your head. I left my truck off the road this morning and hiked back in. In case, well, in case of this." He scanned the dry chaparral below them. And then pointed again, in the other direction. Jenny followed his finger and saw that up to the left, yet another insidious orange line had formed on the crest. "Let's go," Reading ordered. "We've got to beat that fire to the road. If it cuts us off, our only choice will be to go back, and you know what's waiting for us that way."

Revived by the water, Jenny nodded and took the

lead. The trail was steep, and there was nothing for it but to give the horses their lead and let them find their footing at their own pace on the way down.

Jenny tried not to keep looking at the threat that was bearing down on them from the left, but it was mesmerizing and constantly pulled her gaze until she could rip it away again, urging Buttermilk to increase her slipping pace just that little bit more.

After what seemed several endless days, they came to more level ground and she was able to press her lathered horse into a trot. They passed into a deep canyon, working their way as cautiously as they dared around the broken ground and rocks of the dry creek bed, and then the canyon walls fell away, and they could see the road, several hundred feet in front of and slightly above them, and they could see the fire traveling down on the left.

Jenny gasped, estimated the distance, and threw one look back at Reading, who had done the same.

She tightened up both reins in one hand and wrapped the other in Buttermilk's mane, and leaning forward, she shouted as she kicked at the horse, "Run, run like the wind."

The horse took off, her nostrils flaring, her hooves punishing the rough gravel of the dry bed, the hot wind hitting Jenny's face as though she had opened an oven and leaned down into it as the heat escaped, except that in this case, the heat kept on coming.

And so did the fire. With all her willpower and strength, Jenny focused on the road ahead, and only the road. She did not look left or right, though she could see the flames approaching on her left, moving faster than she was, leaping from submissive ground cover to trees weakened with drought. She urged Buttermilk on, giving a kick when the horse needed to jump a bush or a rift in the ground, and still she kept her eyes forward. She was almost there, just a few more yards, when suddenly, a low row of sage in her path burst into flame. Buttermilk began to hold back, but Jenny kept her weight thrown forward. Signaling the horse to go forward with a hard kick and a thrust of her whole body, Jenny let loose a loud, adrenaline-fueled howl, and Buttermilk, sensing the futility of any other course, gathered her great body and leapt, sliding blindly into the air. For a few seconds there existed only the swirl of wind in Jenny's ears, the opaque screen of smoke that blocked her vision, and that curious, lovely weightlessness of flight, and then the ground hit them, and with a crash, Buttermilk's hooves slammed into the sandy soil on the far side of the burning shrubbery. She stumbled and then righted herself and continued on. But they were at the road.

Behind her, Jenny heard the impact of the stallion's great bulk and the continuation of his run; without looking back, she brought the horse up a small, steep incline and then turned to continue on the shoulder of the road. A quarter mile down, they came to where Reading had left his four-wheel drive. They both dismounted, and Reading quickly pulled the saddles from the steaming horses and then slapped them firmly on the rumps to send them running on down the road ahead of them.

"Get in," he barked unnecessarily. He started the engine, and even as he pulled out, he cranked the air-conditioning on high, pointing the vents toward Jenny. "You need to get your body temperature down," he ordered.

Leaning gratefully into the mercifully cold air, Jenny asked weakly, "What now?"

"Now, we go find the horses." He drove very fast, and soon they had distanced themselves from the danger zone behind them. They passed two hook-and-ladder trucks, sirens screaming, heading to fight the fire, and two helicopters buzzed over them, very low, on their way in with their loads of water. In less than two minutes, both helicopters passed over them again, on their way back for more.

"Where are we going to look for them?" Jenny asked.

"Best guess? The ones we just rode will head to a friend of mine's barn nearby. It should be safe. That's where the stallion was born. I'll call them later. The others were heading out over Oak Springs fire road, so

I've got a general idea that we head to the Golden Door development and try to find them as they come out the back side. But you'll stay in the AC. Baby needs your temperature somewhere below uncomfortable."

"I'm feeling fine now," Jenny told him. She closed her eyes and ran a quick physical check. The cramping was gone; her body was cooling. She breathed a sigh of relief and said a prayer of thanks that she had been strong enough, that the baby was okay.

Then she opened her eyes and said it out loud to Reading. "Thank you."

It took about fifteen minutes to maneuver their way through the tangle of back roads, which cut off a huge portion of driving time compared with taking the paved streets. Finally they came to the development entrance and the edge of the desolation, and Reading stopped to look around.

There was another truck already there, a black pick-up, and Jenny almost shouted when she saw who was in it.

"It's Joshua! Greer's son and Sterling too. What are they doing here?"

Reading had already started rolling toward the other pickup. Neither of the men in the truck looked up at first; they seemed engrossed in examining a map of some kind. Jenny actually had to lean out the window to get their attention as she and Reading pulled up beside them.

When Sterling recognized her, his face was a plethora of emotions that seemed to be competing for dominance on his handsome dark face. He got out of the truck and ran over to her.

"Jenny. Thank God you're all right. Did Greer find you?"

"Greer?" Jenny was confused. "What do you mean?"

"I mean that she went after you, she and Susan Hughs, and I think she might be in big trouble now. We're trying to figure out where they might have gone."

"Why would she come looking for me here?" Jenny asked.

Sterling's green eyes darkened. "She didn't. Listen to me, we need to find her."

From the pickup, Joshua called out, "I think I know!" He clambered out and ran to where Sterling was standing next to the four-wheel drive. "Look, I think it's past the phase-three section. I think it's where Susan wanted the new road." He looked in that direction frantically. "But we can't get through there; there's no access. We'll have to hike in as best we can."

"Bullshit," growled a voice from behind Jenny. "Get in."

The huge wheels on Reading's off-road vehicle ate the dirt as they sped toward the far end of the cleared land, and then rolled onto the rough-cut track. They bounced along, jolting and jerking for a few hundred feet until they rounded a curve, and then Reading hit the brakes hard and all of them reached out to save themselves, slamming hands into seat backs and dashboards. Reading's right arm was rigid across Jenny's chest to keep her put.

In the track, just ahead of them, were two figures, one kneeling and the other lying flat on her back.

Joshua fumbled for the door latch, but his relief and his last night's experience rendered him weak and slow, so it was Sterling who was first from the truck, who ran stumbling toward them, heedless of the rough surroundings. Sterling who reached down to encircle Greer in his arms when she turned and looked at him with absolute expectation. It was Sterling who saw the sad picture of Susan Hughs on the ground and who lifted Greer into his arms and who cradled her against his chest as she leaned her head back as though she were a drowning woman craning for a breath of air above an invisible surface and let go of a rending sob.

When Joshua reached them, she was able to touch his face and smile with infinite sadness. "I couldn't help her," she said.

Joshua caught up his mother's hand and looked searchingly into her eyes. "No one said you could," he told her. "She had to make the choice."

Greer let her head fall against Sterling's chest as they started back for the car. "My wise teenage son," Greer muttered through her dry, cracked lips. "How did you get to be so smart?"

Joshua had to fight down the swelling in his throat as a figure flickered into his view over Sterling's shoulder. He looked up into the face of his father, smiling his benevolence down on Greer in the safety of loving arms. "Oh," he said, "I've got a few *really* good teachers."

Chapter 61

It had taken Sheridan only a short time to reach the edge of the cleared land. Leaving his dark blue sedan there, he picked his way across the steeply canted, broken earth in his rubber-soled loafers with patient stealth and gazed down at Susan's inert body with what seemed an almost premeditated disinterest. As she watched him, Greer thought of Susan's husband, Rowland, and felt a submerged ache. How would he feel when he discovered that the woman he thought he had married had been an illusion? She had cheated him.

Greer tried to make it clear to Detective Sheridan that Susan had been acting without her husband's knowledge, though she knew that he would have to investigate all possibilities. She wondered if Susan ever had any honest love for her far simpler, gullible husband at all, or if she had only been using him, like every other resource at her disposal. With a spongy sadness, Greer realized that she would never know, but she hoped—with an inexplicable fervency—that Susan had really loved Rowland, though she didn't know if that made the situation better or worse.

It was still so unbearably hot that after only a few questions Sheridan told them he would meet them at the high school gym to finish his questioning, and insisted that they go there immediately to get first aid for both Jenny and Greer.

Back in Reading's truck Greer had downed a large bottle of water when she got a look at Jenny in the side-view mirror. Her friend's aura was clear, and there was not even the faintest outline of dark wings. Catching in her breath, she reached up and folded down the sun visor, then flipped open the mirror. She exhaled with a grateful, audible noise. The space above her was clear as well.

Sterling reached up a hand from the backseat and placed it on her shoulder. "Don't worry, you look beautiful."

Greer glanced again in the small vanity mirror, this time at her physical reflection, and laughed out loud. Her face was scratched and smeared with soot, her hair a tangled, dry mass, but she turned and looked over the seat back at first Sterling's glowing eyes and then at Jenny's clear aura and said, "Yes, I do, and so does Jenny."

Next to her in the front, Joshua squeezed her hand, understanding her deeper meaning. The dark wings of danger looming over Jenny and his mother were gone.

"The weather's looking better too," Reading contributed from the driver's seat. "The wind's died down, and look." He jerked his chin forward. They all leaned to look through the windshield up at the sky, and there they were—clouds. Gray clouds, promising in their pale pewter tint and downy thickness, not dark with rain, not yet.

"Oh God. Please let it rain," Jenny murmured.

When they reached Sterling's truck, everyone but Reading transferred over. Jenny wanted to go help find the horses, but Reading forbade it as he had already recruited several of his hunting buddies to help out.

The first person they saw when they walked through the doors of the huge gym was Rowland. He was sitting on a bench at one of the long tables with his cell phone in his hand, a look of concern on his face.

Greer looked to Sterling, hoping to find a sense of direction in the dizziness that had grabbed hold of her. He shook his head slowly. "No, it's not for you. Let Detective Sheridan explain it. That's only fair. If Rowland wants to speak to you afterward, and we think it's safe for him to do so, then you can. And I'll be with you." There was such knowing conviction in Sterling's voice and face that Greer trusted his judgment without question. Turning away to hide her tears, she hurried into the kitchen to find Leah.

Jenny was already with her, and the two were locked in a hug, but instead of Leah looking relieved, it was clear at a glance that Jenny was comforting Leah.

"What is it?" Greer asked as she came level with the two of them.

Jenny pulled back and said, "There's a helicopter down, and they won't tell anyone yet which one, or if anyone was hurt, or . . ." She let the word remain silent in her throat, as though saying it would make it real.

Greer moved quickly to Leah and wrapped her in a hug. "Oh, honey, I'm sorry. But let's not make any assumptions, okay?"

Her body still rigid from the unaccustomed familiarity, Leah looked desperately into Greer's face. "Is he dead?" she demanded.

Startled by the question, Greer stepped backward. "I . . . I don't know. It doesn't work that way. I can tell you that I didn't see any danger around him. But I don't read men well and—" The exhaustion and emotion of what she had endured already today welled up inside of her like too much pressure in a waterspout, and the injustice of being expected to know someone else's fate filled her with anger. "You can't ask me to know that! I don't know!" Greer could hear that her voice had a hysterical edge to it.

Leah looked as though Greer had punched her so hard it had knocked the wind out of her. "I'm sorry," she whispered. "Of course you can't. I'm sorry. I'm just so worried." Leah reached one hand in Greer's direction and then let it hang in the space between them for a second before losing her nerve and letting it drop back into a tight fist across her chest. "I don't even know Weston very well. I feel like I don't have any right to feel this strongly about him. I mean, we had, what, two dates? But somehow I . . . I do." She looked searchingly from face to face.

Sterling was the one who responded. "Sometimes it happens that way." Greer felt his arm encircle her waist.

Leah's eyes had fixed on his; her pupils were large, black circles in her rich brown irises, dilated with fear. The rest of her face looked ashen, soft with vulnerability, but as they watched, it twisted into a grimace of pain. "This is why!" she sobbed as her hands flew to hide the nakedness of her emotion. "This is why I was right not to let anyone else in. Even if he doesn't hurt me on purpose, what if something happens to him?"

Excruciatingly conscious of Leah's mortification of letting her guard down, no one moved for a moment, afraid to respond in any way that would make it worse. Then Jenny waved the others away and draped one arm over her friend's shoulders. "Oh shit, girl," she said in an almost humorous voice, "the rest of us love and lose and get kicked and get back up again. Why should you get to go through life all safe and numb and stupid?"

"It's not stupid to protect yourself!" Leah insisted as she looked up at Jenny through her fingers.

"Yeah, it is stupid. What are you going to do? Lock yourself in a padded cell and watch old *Brady Bunch* episodes, where everything comes out fine, until your brain molds? Or come on out into the real world? And fuck, yeah, you might get hurt. In fact, we both know I'd be lying if I didn't say that you *will* hurt sometimes. But you *can't* hurt unless you care, and when you care, you love, and when you love, you get to be alive." Jenny's voice had dropped to a hoarse, imploring whisper, and she knew somehow that she was fighting for her friend's life. "Please, Leah, I'm begging you. Take a chance. Don't seal up again and shut yourself off. Nobody blames you for doing it once, but if something *has* happened to Weston—and we don't know that yet—" she added quickly, "but if it did, you'll hurt, yes, but you'll get through it, and you'll open yourself up again next time. Because, girl, *that's all we've got.* Everything in life is temporary! Everything. So instead of being afraid of losing it, you can choose to be grateful for *having* it. Whatever it is, a pretty day, a lover, a house, *anything*. Am I making any sense?"

Leah looked almost catatonically introspective. Jenny sighed with frustration and went back in for a second round. "Listen. Sometimes—I believe—the world, the universe, God, whatever you call it, puts things or people or experiences in our path and it's up to us to decide what to do about it. We can either embrace it and make it—or them—a part of our lives and see what happens, or we pass by it and then, well . . . we never know. And to me, that would be the saddest thing. It's killing me to watch you close yourself off. It's like you're encased in glass and I want to grab a hammer and smash it."

Leah was staring at Jenny with her mouth open now. She looked absolutely horrified, and for just a moment, Jenny thought that she had pushed her too far. But then, Leah smacked both her hands to her face and said, "I've been so stupid! Oh my God, Jenny." She grabbed her friend's shoulders and shook her, almost violently, a bizarrely radiant smile dawning on her face. "I've been so stupid!" She released Jenny and spun on her heels. "Oh God, you've got to help me."

"What do you want me to do?"

Leah was already halfway across the industrial kitchen when she turned back and raised an imperious hand as though issuing a royal decree. She threw her head back and shouted, "Get me a lawyer!"

Chapter 62

Throughout the afternoon, they had waited anxiously for news about the fate and identity of those in the helicopter, but the authorities had remained adamant: No details would be released to the public until families had been notified and the facts were clear. Sterling was able to corner one fire captain into telling him that so far there were no reports of fatalities, but they were expecting the official report to include injuries. He would not say how serious.

Leah thought about Weston frequently and hoped with all her heart that he, and everyone else, would be all right, but she was mercifully distracted by her new purpose. With a paralegal friend's help, she had located a family lawyer and, after explaining the urgency of the situation to the older woman, had spent three hours in the Glendale law office filling out paperwork and having the complicated legal system explained to her. Leah was painfully aware that even with all her best intentions her move was a gamble and would take time, and the outcome was uncertain.

She returned to the school at about seven, looking exhausted and exasperated, but determined.

Jenny met her with a questioning look. "Well?" she demanded.

"Well, I started the triathlon of paperwork, and I have to wait to be approved, but if I get permission from the family, it could go ahead immediately." Though her words were positive, Jenny could read her friend's uncertainty in the anxious, repetitive tucking of her hair behind one ear.

"Well, you've done what you can do for now, and—" Jenny broke off and squinted over Leah's shoulder.

Following Jenny's look, Leah turned slowly and searched the faces of a group of firefighters who had just come in from their shift, and there was no mistaking him. Weston, tall, handsome, face smeared with dirt and sweat, had spotted her and was crossing to them with a wide, white smile.

As though she were an abandoned accordion, Leah crumpled forward with one huge, exhaled sob of relief. "Oh my God. He's all right, thank God." She covered her face with her hands and spun quickly back toward Jenny, afraid that Weston might have seen her unguarded response. "I've got to get ahold of myself. What's he going to think?" she asked Jenny, wiping her tears away with quick, angry swipes.

But Jenny smiled, and like a child's turn at a piñata, she took Leah by the shoulders and spun her back to face Weston, who was only a few steps away. She leaned down and spoke quietly into Leah's ear. "He's going to think you care about him. Now go." With a not-so-gentle push, she launched Leah forward.

Greer was emptying a large trash bag, but a flicker of light in the corner of her eye caused her to look up. She watched as Weston stopped in front of Leah, took her hands down from her face, wiped away a tear, and then folded her into his arms. The light returned, stronger and brighter. There were wings over Weston, but not the black, terrifying wings that she had seen over Jenny's image. These were made of gold, shining and joyful to see. As Greer watched, the wings opened magnificently and then folded down, wrapping forward around Leah and Weston, and as they did, Greer heard Joshua gasp beside her.

She spun toward him. "Did you see it?" she asked him.

"I saw *her*," Joshua said, confused.

"Who?"

"It's Tyler's little sister. She died when she was very little, abuse I think, but she's there with . . . Weston and Leah." His head moved from side to side as he scanned the room for Tyler, and sure enough, he saw him, but he was sitting at a table on the far side of the cafeteria. "But why is she with them?" he mused slowly.

With all the courage she had left, Leah looked up into Weston's smiling eyes and said, "I'm so glad you're okay. I was so worried all day."

"I know," he said. "And I'm sorry I couldn't get a message to you, but with only four helicopters up we were flying more frantically than usual."

"Are they all right?" Leah asked.

"Yes, one of the guys dislocated a shoulder, and two of the others were pretty badly bruised, but everybody's going be all right. The pilot was Harrison Grafton. He's good under pressure, flew in Desert Storm, and this wasn't his first emergency landing. So they all basically walked away." He let go of her with one arm and touched her face again. "This sure is a nice welcome home. How'd you spend your day?"

"Well," Leah said, taking in a huge, bracing breath, "I'll tell you, but first, there's someone I'd like you to meet. Or, I should say, meet again." Leah took Weston's huge hand in her own small one and led him to where Tyler sat with his temporary family, staring at an untouched plate of food. "Tyler?" she called out softly.

He turned and looked up, way up, at Weston. Slowly a look of recognition dawned across his face. "You're the guy who picked up me and Grampa," he said slowly, as though testing out the words to see if they would work all right.

"Hey there." Weston immediately sat down on the bench across from Tyler, to minimize the height disparity between them. "How's your grandfather doing?" he asked softly.

Tyler shrugged and his mouth tightened. "Not so good. I have to stay with, I mean . . ." He darted a look at the frazzled mother to see if she had caught the impoliteness, but she was busy with a two-year-old who was throwing spaghetti on the floor and she wasn't listening, though she threw a harried hello to Weston when Leah introduced her as Debbie. "I mean, I can't go home until he gets out of the hospital, and they told me that might be a long time."

Weston exchanged a glance with Leah, who shook her head helplessly; she had been unable to get any information about Sheldon from anyone.

"But," Tyler looked up at Leah hopefully, "I might get to go and stay with Leah if he says it's all right."

Weston's smile changed from friendly to perceptive as his eyes moved to Leah, and he watched her face color before returning his attention to the boy. "Really?" he asked. "And would you like that?"

Tyler's eyes darted to Debbie, who was now cursing softly as she tried to wipe the objecting toddler's face with a dry, thin paper napkin. "I think so," he said, almost inaudibly.

Weston watched the boy's sloped shoulders and hopeless expression. "I'd like to come and visit you there," he said. "Maybe we could play some ball. You like baseball?"

The subject seemed to perk up the small boy. His head came up and there was a light in his eye. "Yeah. I don't get to play too much 'cause Grampa has to work all the time, so I'm not very good."

"Looks like you got a good throwing arm to me." Weston appeared to be appraising Tyler's thin arm and finding it impressive. "I could show you a few things. I used to pitch on a team, you know."

Shyly, Tyler nodded, and then in a hesitating voice, untrusting of the possibility, he said, "I'd like that very much, sir."

"Tell you what. You finish eating your dinner. I've got to go get cleaned up and eat something myself; then, if it's still light out and Debbie says it's okay, we can throw a ball in the parking lot." Tyler nodded his assent with cautious excitement. "Okay, I'll see you later."

When Leah and Weston were far enough away to be out of earshot, Weston spoke. "All right. I'll find out what's happening with the grandfather, but I have to ask you something." He stopped and brought her up short, peering with blue intensity down at her. Leah looked back up at him. "Do you really want to do this? Or is it just a moment of temporary insanity?"

The laugh escaped Leah from deep inside of her. "Both!" she told him, and then she sobered and looked over to where Tyler was now eating and watching them surreptitiously. "I don't know why, but I just know that I'm supposed to help him. I remember you saying that sometimes we have to get over ourselves and be of service, and that really intimidated me. I mean, I thought 'being of service' meant feeding all the hungry people in the world, or helping cure a disease, or supporting an entire hospital or a community, or something else that seemed so dauntingly impossible, but now I think . . ." She paused to sort through her thoughts. "I think," she resumed carefully, "that sometimes being of service can mean helping just one other person. Maybe that won't make much difference in the scope of things, but it's what I can do—what I *want* to do—now. I want to make that little boy safe. He needs somebody, and . . ." Leah's throat tightened, and she had to consciously relax it before she could speak. "And I do too." She had meant that she needed to help Tyler, but when she met Weston's eyes, she realized that her confession had been far more encompassing.

Very softly he said, "I'm so glad to hear you say that. I was starting to think I was the only one." And then, right there in front of God and everybody, he kissed her.

Chapter 63

Sterling followed Greer home. He knew that she, like him, was watching the sky eagerly, scanning it to differentiate the smoke from the actual clouds that had been forming all day. It was very hard to tell, especially in the failing light, which of the two were holding sway, or if the clouds themselves were dark enough to promise rain. Sterling listened hopefully to the news station. The brief, unsatisfactory weather report predicted a forty percent chance of rain over the upcoming weekend, but forecast only "partly cloudy in the Los Angeles area with a twenty percent chance of isolated showers, especially in the beach communities for tonight and tomorrow, with temperatures cooling slightly to the low nineties." With a disgusted grimace he punched off the radio and scanned the narrow range of sky above him between the canyons. Twenty percent—not much, but still, a chance.

As they pulled off the paved road onto the rutted dirt track that snaked around the canyon shoulder to the small group of houses where Greer's stood out from the other four nearby by virtue of its larger size and grander mission style, he reflected how lucky she had been that the fire had turned away from this portion of the national forest. "It's so random," he muttered to himself before he remembered that they hadn't been random at all until they took on a life of their own, but were in fact completely planned and premeditated.

He was so lost in his contemplation that it took him quite by surprise to see that the porch of Greer's house, which encircled the raised ground floor, was occupied by quite a few people. He saw Dario, Jenny, Leah, Whitney and her husband, Luke, Joy, and Joshua. Greer had parked and was greeting everyone.

"I didn't know you were having a party," Sterling remonstrated her when he got to the top of the porch steps. "You know the paramedic said that you need to rest tonight. You already spent the day helping out. Don't you think maybe you could let me fix you some dinner and get a good night's sleep?" Then he turned to Jenny. "And what about you?"

"Oh, I'm much more hardheaded than she is," Jenny quipped, straight-faced. "Plus, I went to the doctor and he said we're both absolutely fine."

"I asked everyone here because I need a favor," Greer said by way of explanation. Everyone turned to her as though they had expected something but had no idea what.

As Greer looked around at all their friendly, open faces, she gained the courage to say out loud what she had never thought she could.

"There is another aspect to the gift that I was born with. It's a gift that's been in one woman in every generation for as long as anyone can remember. It's true that Joshua seems to have inherited a different version of the sight, because there are no other women in the line. I was an only child and so is he, but that's not what I'm talking about."

Greer felt a trembling in her chest, and she cast around in her mind for a way to continue. She ran her tongue over her ample lips; her mouth had gone suddenly dry. "Basically, it comes to this." Greer took a deep breath, and what she knew might be a last look at friends who thought her sane, and dove in. "I believe I can effect changes in the natural world, subtle usually, and I've never tried anything like what I want to do tonight. I know I can't do it alone, but if anyone wants to help me, I'm willing to try."

There was a hushed, uncertain intake of breath around the circle of friends.

Finally it was Luke who spoke. "Are you saying you can do magic?"

"I wouldn't call it that. It's more like tuning in to energies that are already out there and turning up their volume, but for lack of a better word . . . yes," Greer said, and the word had a finality to it, like the sound of a sealing casket.

"And what is it you want to do?" Whitney asked, looking nonplussed and fearless as usual.

"I want to try to bring the rain," Greer said.

Another energized hush ensued, this one so long that Greer thought she should go in her house and close the door and lock herself in a closet where she belonged.

Then, after a long, slow intake of breath and a dramatic nod, Luke said in his firm, rumbling voice, "I *like* it."

Greer's head shot up in surprise. "What?"

"I think it's a fucking stellar idea," Dario added. "What do we have to lose? Nothing."

"Wait." Luke held up a hand and narrowed his eyes at Greer. "Were you afraid to tell us this? You were, weren't you?"

Greer nodded shyly.

"Damn, woman," Luke said with a laugh and a shake of his head. "We're *Indians*. Our people have been working with the elements since way before that Middle Eastern guy got nailed to a cross for doing pretty much the same thing."

Jenny was on her feet. "I'm in. What do we do?"

There was only one face that was twisted in concerned distraction. Joshua was watching his mother suspiciously. "What are you doing?" he asked very quietly.

She knew why he was asking. If it would rain, it would give the brave people who were risking their lives a chance to beat this holocaust of a fire. And it wasn't only the people and the property that Greer knew she had to try to help—it was the animals, the habitat, the very land itself. But Joshua knew that using her gift this way would cost her.

"It's all right," she said to him. "I understand how much strength this might take. That's why I'm asking for help, so that it won't all come from just me." She kept her eyes fixed reassuringly on his until he looked away, resigned.

"Okay, I'll help you," he muttered.

"Thank you."

"Let's get going," Leah said. "I would like to say, for the record, that this is probably the most bizarre thing I've ever done."

Joshua looked at the banker for a moment, and then turning to the rest of the assembled, he asked, "Did anyone here *not* know that?"

Their part, apparently, was to sit around her in a circle.

"Everyone take hands," Greer said, "and see if you can hum this same note that I'm making."

They all began, and soon the room was filled with a rich vibration that emanated from their chests, and without thinking or trying, they fell into a pattern of breathing in rotation so that there was no break in the chant.

Though most everyone had closed their eyes and fallen into a kind of meditation, Joshua kept his open and on his mother. She had stopped chanting with them, and he watched her body sway and he knew she was searching for the energies around them and the colors that represented them.

And then she began to chant again, but with a different note, leading them all to change their tone, to slide into a different kind of harmony, and he remembered something she had said: "It's as though, their whole lives, they've had a melody playing inside them, and it's been discordant, out of tune, but it's what they are—not what they are made of, but what they've been made into—and they have to change the tune, if that makes any sense." And he wondered if she was trying to change this melody. Then suddenly she tensed, her body went rigid, and with a cry she sliced at the air in front of her as though separating herself from something, from them.

And then she was falling, slumping forward as though all the life had left her body, and Joshua felt as if he were watching her from a distance, while she slid, deeper and deeper into a fathomless, indigo sky.

Chapter 64

"Mom!" Joshua called out. "You promised you wouldn't!"

Sterling and Luke were next to him before he realized they had moved. Together, they lifted Greer and carried her to a heavily cushioned daybed in the corner.

Whitney's face was white. "What's happened to her?"

"I think that at the last minute she took all the energy from herself," Joshua said. "I think she was trying to protect us."

"But what's wrong with her?" Joy's voice was tremulous.

"I'm not sure." Joshua tried to think about what had happened to him. "It's kind of like, when you give too much energy, your body pays the price. When I helped Simon, I felt like I'd run a marathon with no water and I was just exhausted. But that was nothing compared to this. Mom!" he shouted, grasping her shoulders and giving her a little shake. "Wake up!"

Joshua was beginning to feel a desperation rise up inside of him, but Sterling derailed it immediately.

"She knows what she's doing, Joshua. And one thing I know for sure: She wouldn't willingly leave you, no matter what. So let's think, let's stay focused. We all just felt something happen that we couldn't see, but we helped do it, so we can help now."

"But I don't know how!" Joshua cried. "I need her to tell me!"

Luke was on his feet, starting for the stairway, but

Whitney stopped him with a question. "Where are you going?"

He turned back and said simply, "To bail R.J. out of prison."

He disappeared, and as they listened to his boots on the stairs, everyone turned to look at Whitney for some explanation. She realized that they were waiting for her to enlighten them, so she said, "R.J. is a fully indoctrinated medicine man. He'll know what to do."

It took Luke almost all night to get back with R.J. During that time, there had been many arguments about whether or not to take Greer to the hospital. On the pro side were Leah, Joy, and sometimes Jenny; on the other were Joshua, who knew that there was nothing they could do for her there, Whitney and Dario, who both trusted in Greer's ability, and Sterling, who fluctuated between the two.

Throughout this time, Greer lay as if she were dead and nothing they could do would rouse her, but she was breathing deeply and slowly, and her heartbeat seemed strong. They all moved in and out of the room, nervously making coffee, speaking in quiet voices about the many things that Greer had done, to reassure themselves that this too would come out all right.

Occasionally one of them would go outside and peer up at the sky. Though it remained heavy with clouds, no raindrops fell.

When R.J. came through the door, he walked quickly to where Greer lay, and kneeling down, he put his ear against her chest. Then he closed his eyes and took a slow, steady breath. "She's in the sleep of death," he said. "She's gone beyond waking; she's given too much strength."

"What does that mean?" Joshua demanded.

R.J. fixed his onyx eyes on Joshua, and they glowed with both anger and compassion. "It means that she used her energy to protect us all, and now we have to give her some of our energy back. Call everyone in."

Joshua went to gather everyone, and when he returned, he was annoyed to see that Luke and R.J. had moved his mother's inert form onto a pile of blankets in the center of the room. But she looked so drained of life that he couldn't find it in himself to refuse anything that might help her.

"Everyone join in a circle around her. Sit down," R.J. instructed. As they did, he opened a leather bag draped over one shoulder and took out two objects. "I brought with me the wing of an owl because it is grandmother owl who protects all the creatures, and I know that much of Greer's efforts are on behalf of those creatures. The rattle is for snake energy, which is powerful medicine; it represents overcoming death, dying, and living again."

"What do we have to do?" Joy asked softly.

R.J. never took his eyes from Greer's face. "You're already doing it."

As they watched, and hoped, and prayed, the gray light of dawn began to change the mood of the room, lending it an ethereal quality in the place between what was and the infinite possibilities of what could be. Joshua sensed, as he had many times before, the unnerving knowledge of every potential reality meeting at this place.

R.J. began to chant, and Luke and Whitney picked it up. Watching with his heart chilled by fear, Joshua felt Joy take his hand and squeeze it gently. Gratefully, he held on tight. R.J. was waving the wing slowly back and forth over Greer, and the wind from it was moving the hair around her otherwise motionless face.

For a long while, there were only the quiet dawning light, thick with gray, heavily filtered by the smoke and clouds; the intoning of voices; and the measured breathing of the group of loving friends. Then, from far away, a new sound levered its way into Joshua's awareness: a thin, pattering sound. And with the vague sense that he recognized the sound from long ago, he turned slowly and looked at the window.

When he spoke, it was with a croaking amazement. "It's raining."

Everyone turned quickly to see, registering the sound themselves, smiling and laughing.

But R.J. stayed focused on Greer, and as the rain increased in volume and healing relief, he leaned down and whispered in her ear, "The rain has come to wake you. Come out and see the rain."

And Greer opened her eyes. They fluttered once, looked around at all her friends and their varied expressions of relief and joy, and then closed again as she listened luxuriously to the patter of raindrops dripping from the pines that sheltered her home. A hint of a smile graced her exhausted face.

"I saw her," she whispered weakly to R.J. "Grandmother owl. She thanked me."

R.J. smiled down at her. "I knew she would. Rest now."

As though those words were all the permission she needed, Greer turned her head to one side and slipped into a deep, healing sleep as the rain came down.

Chapter 65

It rained for three days. It rained with a firm thumping as comforting as chicken potpie. It rained tears of relief for the families of the firefighters who saw their loved ones safely home. It rained until the ground squelched joyfully underfoot and the fires were slowed and then silenced, until all that was left was a sooty, black mud punctuated by groping stumps of trees and remnants of shrubs, bare and textured.

While it rained, Greer slept, waking only to take a light meal of soup or toast as she smiled at her friends with sleepy eyes.

While it rained, Leah went to visit Sheldon in the hospital. She found the courage to look at his heavily bandaged legs without wincing, to meet his frightened eyes with conviction and honesty. Some of the courage she borrowed from Weston, who went with her. She offered her help and her home, though she would have been surprised to know that it was her heart that convinced the old man to let her take his grandson into her care. His lungs had been scorched and he could only speak a few words, but those were these: "Love him like he is your own." And Leah cried tears of gratefulness and then stayed close as Tyler visited his grampa, and she was there to comfort and reassure him afterward, pulling him into her lap and kissing his head as she rocked him slowly and told him that everything was going to be all right. He believed her because she was telling the truth. Giving away so much strength was making Leah stronger than she had ever felt before. Her segmented heart was fusing back together.

While it rained, Joy stayed with Joshua. They watched over Greer, or they spent time together in the kitchen, talking softly of everything. Their hands met often and clasped, and soon their lips found each other too. At last the intimacy they had felt for so long was released from the shadows of past violence and stepped out into the dappled, silvery light filtering through the streaks of rain on the windows of the kitchen, where a young couple embraced with tender affection and no regrets.

While it rained, Simon found the courage to talk to his aunt, to tell her that he was sorry, and to thank her for standing by him and caring. He did not use those words—he did not have them yet—but he did his best, something that was new to him. And each time he tried and was accepted, he grew braver until, on the day he left the hospital, he was able to embrace his eight-year-old cousin with the affection of a young man unfettered by self-doubt or a view of the world through cold bars of fear. He had come into the hospital a soul lost and isolated; he went home with a family.

While it rained, Detective Sheridan identified the remains of a body found in the fire as those of Lamont Martinez. There would be no trial, no further investigation, no need of proof and evidence. Nature had delivered her own inevitable justice.

On the fourth day Greer got up just as dawn was breaking and felt life singing through her body. The rain had stopped, and she went out onto the patio and breathed in the moist, vibrant air around her. Brimming with gratitude, she stood for a few moments and felt the bliss of being alive and a part of the whole.

Later that morning Joshua hiked up past the ridges beyond his house, past the waterfall that was trickling slowly for the first time in months, past the oak forest that had been spared deep in the canyon, and came at last over the highest ridge onto a grisly sight.

Before him stretched miles of destruction and acres of blackness. The lovely hillsides had been scorched and scarred. Yet, as he looked more closely, he began to see small spots of white on the earth; they were everywhere. At first he thought they were the white dust of charcoal, but as he walked forward and stooped to investigate, he saw to his amazement that the ground was decorated with thousands of tiny spiderwebs, and even as he watched, he could see more spiders floating in on long silver wisps. They had been the first to come back.

The sound of something heavy in the brush behind him made Joshua spin around. There, only a few yards away, was a buck. The magnificent animal stood and studied him with that wary mixture of distrust and regal detachment. Joshua caught his breath and remained motionless. They regarded each other for a full minute until the buck turned his head, surveying the blackened landscape before him, and then he walked with measured calm back into the regenerating green.

"Wow," whispered Joshua, and all the chill emptiness that he had felt as he took in the devastation flew out of him and his chest felt as though it had been struck by a strong shaft of sunlight on a summer afternoon. Turning again to the miniscule life of the spiders, it came to him why the web and the spider image had been important. The spiders were the first to return, spinning their nets and catching the insects and starting again the cycle of life from the ground up. Their tiny, white-lace creations on their backgrounds of black velvet were the first visible steps in the rebuilding of a community. Beneath them the seeds released by the fire and nurtured by the ash and rain would regenerate, the small animals that had survived would return, and working together, they would re-create the balance. It would take the whole community, all connected by the vast, unseen web, to grow again into a healthy forest. And as Joshua watched, he understood that the people who shared this environment were just another fragile strand of the huge, precarious, magnificent web.

Turning back toward home, he knew that he, like all people, had a choice: to strengthen that web, or to tear it down.

Joshua knew his choice, and now he also felt a new direction for his life. He had been given a gift, and he would not throw it away or deny it. He would use it to help others to recognize the strands of the web that they could not see but that to him shone like silver bands of light. He would share his vision of the connections between people and the earth, and he would help them see the filaments of love that bind us to others, whether they stand before us, or somewhere near yet just beyond our sight.

From *USA Today* bestselling author
KATE PEPPER

HERE SHE LIES

When she discovers evidence of her husband's infidelity,
Annie Goodman's life is thrown asunder and she flees
with her young daughter to the one person she has
always trusted—her twin sister, Julie. In this safe harbor,
the sisters quickly become as close as they were as
children. But when Annie tries to get a job, her safe
harbor turns rocky—she's arrested, her credit cards are
stolen, and her very identity is in question. Seeking
solace with Julie, she finds her twin sister gone—
along with her daughter.

It soon becomes clear that nothing Annie previously
believed is certain—and that she is the only one who
can find her child, and reclaim the life that someone has
stolen from her...